AVALANCHE OF TROUBLE

CINDI MYERS

ARMED RESPONSE

JANIE CROUCH

MIX
Paper from
responsible sources
FSC C007454

This book is produced from independently certified FSC™
paper to ensure responsible forest management.

For more information visit: www.harpercollins.co.uk/green

Printed and bound in Spain
by CPI, Barcelona

MILLS & BOON

First Published in Great Britain 2018
by Mills & Boon, an imprint of HarperCollins*Publishers*
1 London Bridge Street, London, SE1 9GF

Avalanche of Trouble © 2018 Cynthia Myers
Armed Response © 2018 Janie Crouch

ISBN: 978-0-263-26587-3

0818

AVALANCHE OF TROUBLE

CINDI MYERS

For my nieces, Morgan and Kelli

Chapter One

Gage Walker wouldn't have said he was a superstitious man, but he didn't believe in tempting fate. Don't brag about your bank account being full or a big bill will surely show up in the mail that will tap you out. Don't plan a fishing trip in April and leave the rain gear at home just because it was sunny when you left the house. Don't complain about being bored at work or you'll get a call that will have you working overtime for the next week.

When your work was as a sheriff's deputy in a small, rural county, boring was good, or so he always reminded the rookies and reserve cops. Boring meant crime was down and people were happy. The adrenaline rush of a real crime might make your day go faster, but it also meant someone was hurt, or had lost something valuable to them, or, worst of all, someone was dead.

The man and the woman in this camp up near Dakota Ridge were definitely dead, each shot in the back of the head, execution-style. They were both in their early thirties and had probably been a nice-looking couple before someone had tied their hands behind their backs and sent a bullet through each of their brains. The driver's license in the man's wallet identified him as Greg Hood, from Denver.

Judging by the matching gold wedding bands they

wore, Gage guessed the woman was Greg's wife. The couple hadn't been killed for money. The man's wallet still had cash and credit cards in it, and in addition to the wedding rings, they both wore expensive-looking watches. They had been left lying on the forested floor between their tent and the cold remains of a campfire, eight miles from the nearest paved road, about a hundred yards from the late-model SUV registered in their name.

"Creepy." Gage's fellow deputy, Dwight Prentice, came to stand next to Gage, staring down at the bodies. Dwight looked around them, at the still forest, lodgepole pine and aspen so thick in places a man could scarcely walk between the trunks, the evergreen-scented air now tainted with the stench of death.

"Yeah, it's creepy," Gage said. "If someone had it in for these two, why not kill them in Denver?" To his way of thinking, murder belonged in the city, not in the peaceful mountains where he had been born and raised and made his home.

Though he had been a member of the Rayford County Sheriff's Department for four years now, Gage hadn't seen death like this before. People in Eagle Mountain—the county's only town—died peacefully of old age, of diseases or a heart attack, or maybe after a fall while climbing or hiking in the surrounding mountains. A little over three years ago, a young lawyer in town had been murdered. People still talked about that case; it had been so unusual for the quiet community that primarily made its living from tourists.

This case was going to give everyone something more to talk about. "I'll drive down in a few minutes and call this in," Gage said. No company had thought it worthwhile to build cell towers on Dakota Ridge, so this corner of the sheriff's department jurisdiction had no coverage, and the radio wasn't much more reliable. Besides, talking about something like this over the radio pretty much guaranteed that half the town would know about it, since so many of them made a hobby out of listening to police scanners. They would be out here to sightsee before the crime scene techs had even finished pulling on their Tyvek suits.

"I want to have another quick look around first." This was his last chance to size up the scene for himself, before the techs and photographers, ambulance personnel and reporters trampled everything into dust. Oh, they'd do all the right things—cordon off the scene and establish an entry corridor—but never again would the scene look like this, unmarred by tape and markers and footsteps.

Moving carefully, Gage stepped around the tent and bent down to look inside. "Who called this in, do you know?" Dwight asked. He remained standing near the bodies.

"Milo Werth called it in," Gage said. "Said he saw the car parked here two days ago when he delivered propane to Windy Peak Ranch, at the end of the road. He came by this morning to pick up a heeler pup Jim Trotter at Windy Peak had for sale and said the car looked like it hadn't moved. With the pup and his little boy in the truck, he didn't want to stop and look, but thought we should check it out." He unhooked the collapsible baton from his utility belt and extended it, then used it to pull back the tent flap.

Inside was a jumble of sleeping bags, a plastic tote with a lid, and a scattering of clothes. A battery-operated lantern hung from a hook at the center of the tent's dome, and a backpack sat propped to the left of the door. Then he spotted a woman's purse next to the backpack. He pulled out a camera and took a picture of it in place, then pulled on latex gloves and, using the baton, hooked the straps of the purse and carefully lifted it out.

"Looking for ID?" Dwight asked.

"I'm looking for anything that tells me why they were up here."

"That's easy enough to figure out," Dwight said. "They came up here to camp. A nice break from city life."

"Except this isn't National Forest or BLM land," Gage said as he pulled a red leather wallet from the purse. "This is private property. This whole area is patented mining claims."

"Maybe they didn't know that," Dwight said. "Maybe they thought they could pull over anywhere and camp. Nobody bothered them, so they thought it was all right."

"Maybe." The sheriff's department had been called in before to explain to clueless campers that even if the land they were on wasn't occupied, it wasn't free for them to set up camp. Gage opened the wallet and studied the driver's license in the little plastic window opposite the checkbook. Angela Hood had been a pretty brunette with long, straight hair, green eyes and a wide smile. She was thirty-two years old, five feet five inches tall. Gage flipped through the credit cards and store loyalty cards in their clear plastic sleeves next to the license and stopped when he came to a bright yellow card. *In Case of Emergency, Contact Maya Renfro, (sister).* A phone number and address were neatly printed in the space below.

Gage made note of the number, then dropped the wallet back into the purse and replaced the purse inside the tent. "I got a number for her emergency contact," he said. "Looks like it's her sister."

"You could let Travis contact her." Travis Walker was the Rayford County sheriff—and Gage's older brother.

"No, I'll do it," Gage said. Not that he looked forward

to telling a woman her sister had been murdered, but he hoped Maya Renfro could lend some insight into what Angela and Greg had been up to that might have gotten them killed.

He made his way back around the tent to the rough track that led into the clearing. "I'll be back as soon as I make the call," he told Dwight.

"I'll be here."

Gage took another look at the SUV parked at the road—a dirty white, late-model Chevy with a cooler and a black plastic garbage bag in the rear compartment. The couple had probably stashed the food and garbage there as a precaution against bears, which showed they were savvy campers. The techs would go over the vehicle, but to Gage, it looked as if it hadn't been touched. And he spotted no other shoe or tire impressions in the soft soil on the verge of the road. So how had the killers gotten to the site?

He went over the details of the crime scene in his head as he drove the eight miles back to the highway. Once he had a strong phone signal, he parked on the shoulder and called the sheriff's department. "Gage, I've been calling you for the last half hour. Where have you been?" Adelaide Kinkaid, the police department's office manager, or, as she liked to refer to herself, "the woman who keeps everything going around here," addressed Gage as if he was a sixteen-year-old delinquent instead of a twenty-five-year-old cop. But Adelaide talked to everyone that way. It was part of her dubious charm.

Gage ignored her question. "Is Travis in?"

"No, he is not. When I couldn't get hold of you, he had to go over to the high school to take a theft report."

"Fine. I'll call his cell."

"But where—"

Gage ended the call. Later, he would no doubt get a lecture from Adelaide about it being his responsibility to keep her informed of his whereabouts, but annoying her now was worth a little aggravation later.

Travis answered Gage's call on the second ring. "What's up?" the sheriff asked. Two years older than Gage, he had won a hotly contested election two years previously to become the youngest county sheriff in Colorado. Since then, even the detractors who had tried to hold his youth against him had admitted to being impressed with his performance. Gage hadn't been surprised at all—Travis had always been the more serious and determined of the three Walker siblings. Gage, though equally smart and athletic, preferred a more laid-back approach to life.

But there was nothing laid-back about his current situation. "We've got a mess on our hands," he said. "That abandoned car Milo Werth called in belongs to a young couple who got themselves killed up on Dakota Ridge."

"Killed?" A sound like Travis closing a door. "How?"

"Shot in the back of the head. Execution-style—hands tied behind their backs. Greg and Angela Hood, from Denver. They were camping on land up there—probably a mining claim."

"Who owns the claim?" Travis asked.

"I haven't got that far yet. We need to call in the crime scene techs. And depending on what they find, we may need to get some help from the state. Everything about this feels bad to me."

"I'll call CSI as soon as we get off the phone," Travis said. "You head back up there and guard the crime scene."

"Dwight's up there now. I found a next of kin notification card in the woman's wallet. I figure I'll make that call before I head back up. Says it's her sister."

"Hard," Travis said.

"Yeah, but it needs to be done. And if it was our sister, I'd want to know right away."

"Agreed," Travis said. "Fortunately, I talked to Emily this morning. She was on her way to class." Their baby sister was working on her MBA in economics at Colorado State University.

"Good to know. Tell the forensics team there's a pull-off just after mile marker eight. I want it checked for any tire impressions or other evidence. There aren't any signs near the Hoods' car, so I'm wondering if the killers parked there and walked up."

"Will do."

The call ended, Gage pulled up the number for Angela Hood's sister. A woman answered the phone. "Hello?" Her voice was raised to be heard over what sounded like a crowd.

"This is Deputy Gage Walker with the Rayford County Sheriff's Department," Gage said. "Is this Maya Renfro?"

"Speaking." A cheer rose up behind her, momentarily drowning her out.

"I can hardly hear you," Gage said. "Where are you?"

"High school gym. Hang on a minute." The crowd noise rose again, then was abruptly cut off. "I ducked into the locker room," Maya said. "This should be better."

"You're in high school?" Cold sweat beaded on the back of Gage's neck. It was hard enough giving bad news to an adult, but to hurt a teenager that way? "Maybe you should get a teacher in there with you. I can wait."

"*I'm* a teacher," Maya said. "Who did you say you were again? I didn't catch it."

"Deputy Gage Walker with the Rayford County Sheriff's Department."

Silence. He tried to picture her—probably dark-haired, like her sister, with the same green eyes and open face. "Ms. Renfro?" he prompted.

"What's happened?" she asked, her voice strained. "Why are you calling me?"

"You have a sister—Angela Hood?"

"Has something happened to Angie? What's happened to her?"

Better to get this over with. There was no way to cushion the blow. "I'm sorry to tell you your sister is dead."

More silence. No screaming or crying. Gage waited. He could hear her breathing, hard, on the other end of the line. "What happened?" she asked finally, her voice hoarse with unshed tears.

"She and her husband, Greg Hood, were shot and killed at their campsite near here."

"Shot? I don't understand? Was it hunters? Some kind of accident?"

"It wasn't an accident. Did your sister and her husband have any enemies? Anyone who would have wanted to kill them?"

"No! Are you saying they were murdered? While camping?"

"That's what it looks like. Do you know why they were here?"

"They bought the land a few weeks ago and wanted to spend some time on it. They said it was really beautiful up there. Who killed them?"

"We don't know yet. Did either of them mention having an argument or disagreement with anyone? Did they mention arranging to meet someone up here?"

"No. It was just a quick trip to get the lay of the land and make plans."

"What kind of plans?"

"Casey!" She choked out the word. "What about Casey? Is she all right?"

"Who is Casey?" Gage asked.

"Their daughter. My niece. She was with them. Is she all right? Did whoever do this kill her, too?"

Gage felt as if someone had reached into his chest and grabbed his heart and squeezed. "You're sure she was with them? How old is Casey?"

"She's five. And yes, I'm sure she was with them. You didn't see her?"

"No." He squeezed his eyes shut, trying to bring his memory of the scene at the camp into focus. No child's toys scattered about. Sleeping bags and tote box in the tent. Some clothing—maybe something pink, but at the time he had assumed it belonged to the woman. Women wore pink. But now that he thought about it again, the T-shirt had been a little on the small side for Angela Hood. "You're sure your niece was with her parents on this trip? Maybe they left her with friends or a relative."

"They wouldn't do that. Or if they did, I would know about it. If they needed someone to watch Casey, I would do it." Her voice rose, pinched with agitation. "What's happened to her?"

"I promise I'll find out. I have to go now, but I'll call you back as soon as I know something."

Fighting a sick feeling in his stomach, he hit the speed dial for Travis again, even as he started the SUV. "Those two murder victims up here?" he said as soon as Travis answered. "They had a kid with them. We've got a missing little girl."

Chapter Two

Maya Renfro gripped the steering wheel of her Volkswagen Beetle so hard her fingers ached, and depressed the accelerator until she was doing eighty. The roads were dry and clear and if highway patrol stopped her, she'd give them Deputy Gage Walker's number and tell them to take it up with him. Her sister was dead and her niece was missing, and every movement felt as if Maya were swimming through quicksand.

This had to be a bad dream. Real life couldn't be this horrible, could it?

But of course it could. You didn't teach high school for four years without seeing a little of that awfulness—kids kicked out of the house while they were still in their teens, colleagues who died of cancer, budget cuts that sliced into the most meaningful programs.

But life that bad had never happened to Maya before. It shouldn't happen to Angela—or to Casey.

She fought back tears and gripped the steering wheel even harder. She had to keep it together. When she got to Eagle Mountain, she had to be there for Casey.

The cop on the other end of the line—Gage Walker—hadn't even known Casey existed. How was that possible? Angela and Greg never traveled anywhere without a whole carload of kid gear. Not to mention both their phones were full of pictures of Casey, from newborn right up through her fifth birthday party two months ago.

Maya had been at that party. She had brought a tiara for Casey to wear and the little girl had been thrilled. The screen saver on Maya's phone was a picture taken at the party, of her and Maya grinning for the camera.

Casey had to be okay. She had to be.

As soon as the news of Angela's death really began to hit her, Maya had tried to call the cop—Gage—again. The call had gone straight to voice mail. Instead of leaving what would probably have been a hysterical message, she left an aide in charge of her sixth period class, let her principal know she was leaving and why, and rushed home to throw a few things in her car and head for Eagle Mountain.

By the time Deputy Walker had called her back to tell her Casey was missing and they were making every effort to find her, Maya was already speeding toward Eagle Mountain. She didn't know much about the town—it was in western Colorado, apparently located in a beautiful area that attracted lots of tourists. Angela and Greg had raved about the place, both so excited over the mining claims they had bought and their plans for the property. "If this works out, we're thinking of moving to Eagle Mountain," Angela had said at dinner the night before their trip.

"You should come with us," Greg said as he passed Maya a bowl of steamed broccoli. "You could get a teaching job there, I bet."

"You really want to live in a small town?" Maya was incredulous. "Why?" Small towns, by definition, were small, which to her meant limited opportunities, limited entertainment options and maybe even limited thinking. "You have everything you could ever want here in Denver."

"Eagle Mountain is the perfect place to raise kids," Angela said. "If we're going to relocate, now's a good time, before Casey has really settled into school."

Maya wasn't so sure about that. Wouldn't kids get bored way out here in the middle of so much *nature*? Everywhere she looked she saw endless fields, soaring mountains, colorful rocks, rushing streams and vast blue sky—but not many people or buildings. What did people out here do for excitement and entertainment?

How was a five-year-old girl going to survive alone out in all this emptiness?

By the time she turned onto Eagle Mountain's main street, she was exhausted from grief and strain, her stomach in knots with worry over Casey, and in no mood to deal with any slow-talking, easygoing backwater cop, which was the only kind she expected to encounter here. After all, if a man had any real talent and ambition, wouldn't he opt to go someplace with a little more action?

The first person to acknowledge her when she walked through the door of the Rayford County Sheriff's Department was a white-haired woman who wore purple-framed glasses and earrings shaped like pink flamingos. "May I help you?" she asked, eyes sharp, expression all business.

"My name is Maya Renfro. I'm looking for a Deputy Walker."

Any hardness melted from the woman's face. She jumped up and moved toward Maya, hand extended. "You're the sister. We've been expecting you. I'm so sorry for your loss. Such a tragedy." She ushered Maya to a small office down a short hallway. "You must be worn out. Everyone is out looking for your niece, but I'll call and let Gage know you're here. I'm Adelaide, by the way. I'll get you some tea. Or would you rather have coffee?"

"I just want to speak to Deputy Walker."

"Of course. I'll get him here as soon as I can."

Then Maya was alone in the office, a claustrophobic cube of a room with barely enough space for a desk and one visitor's chair. She sat and studied the walls, which were filled with several framed commendations and half a dozen photographs, all featuring a tall, good-looking man with thick brown hair and the weathered face of an outdoorsman. In one picture, he knelt beside a mountain stream, cradling a colorful fish and grinning at the camera. In another, he supported the head of a trophy elk, golden aspens in the background. In a third photograph, he posed with another officer, both of them in uniform and holding rifles.

"That's Gage and his brother, Travis." Adelaide spoke from behind Maya. She set a cup on the edge of the desk. "I brought you some tea," she said. "I know you said you didn't want anything, but after such a long drive, you look like you could use something."

"Tea is fine." Maya picked up the cup and sat stiffly upright in the chair. "So Gage and Travis are both law enforcement officers?"

"Travis is the county sheriff," Adelaide said. "He's out with the others. We're all just sick about this. Things like this just don't happen in Eagle Mountain."

"They happen everywhere, Addie. You know that. We're not special."

The man who moved into the room past Addie was tall and rangy, his khaki uniform streaked with dirt, his face creased with exhaustion. "Gage Walker," he said, extending his hand to Maya. "I'm sorry I wasn't here to meet you."

"I told her you were out looking for her niece," Adelaide said.

"We've got everybody in the county with any kind

of experience in the woods out there looking for her," Gage said. The chair behind the desk creaked under his weight as he settled into it, and the office seemed more claustrophobic than ever with his oversized, very masculine presence. Adelaide returned to the front office, leaving them alone.

Gage didn't say anything for a moment, his eyes fixed on Maya, his expression unreadable. "Why are you looking at me that way?" she asked, setting the teacup on the desk.

He shook his head, as if coming out of a daze. "You said you're a teacher?"

"Yes. I teach high school English at Centennial High School."

Gage shook his head again. "None of my teachers ever looked like you."

She stiffened. "What is that supposed to mean?"

"Well, for one thing, none of them had blue hair."

She touched the ends of her hair, which she had dip-dyed blue only two weeks before. "I made a deal with my students. If they brought up their achievement test scores, I would dye my hair blue."

"Just not what I expected."

He wasn't what she had expected, either. He wasn't slow and dumb, but he definitely looked right at home in this rugged country.

"What happened to my sister?" she asked.

"We're still trying to get a complete picture, but it looks like your sister and her husband were in their camp when someone—probably more than one person—came up, tied their hands behind their backs and shot them."

The picture his words created in her mind was almost too horrible to bear. She forced the image away and bit the inside of her cheek to stave off tears. She couldn't break down now. She had to be strong. "They just shot them?"

"I'm sorry, yes."

"Why? And what happened to Casey?"

"We're trying to find the answers to both those questions. It's possible whoever shot your sister and brother-in-law took Casey with them. But it's also possible she ran away." He leaned toward her. "Tell me about your niece. Is she a shy child—the type who would hide from strangers?"

"Casey isn't really shy, no. But if she saw someone hurt her mother and father, of course she'd be afraid. And having a bunch of people she didn't know stomping around the woods looking for her would probably frighten her even more." She had a clear picture of the little girl, hiding behind a big rock or tree, watching all the commotion around her and too afraid to come out. "I want to go look for her. She knows me. She won't hide from me."

He nodded. "That makes sense. I'll take you up to the camp, but I can't allow you to go wandering around in the woods on your own. The terrain is rough and it's getting dark. Even the trained searchers will have to pack it in soon and wait until morning."

"Maybe she's close to the camp and she'll see me and come to me." Maya stood. "Let's go now. I don't want to waste another minute."

Gage rose also and motioned toward the door. "After you. My cruiser is parked out front."

The black-and-white SUV sported the requisite light bar on top and the legend, Rayford County Sheriff's Department, on the door. Gage walked around and opened the passenger door, then leaned in and scooped an armful of papers, file folders, gloves, a flashlight and who knew

what else off the front seat. "Welcome to my mobile office," he said, holding the door wide for her.

She climbed in, studying the tablet computer mounted
to face the driver, the radio and the shotgun in a holder
beside her seat. Gage buckled his seat belt and started the
engine. "You said your sister and her husband had just
bought the property they were camping on?" he asked
as he pulled out into the street.

"Yes. They closed on the purchase last week and
wanted to spend some time up there, enjoying the scenery." She choked on the last word. Angela wouldn't be
enjoying anything anymore.

"So they bought the property to have a place to camp?
Or did they plan to build a house up there?"

"Not a house, no. They bought up a bunch of old mining claims, with plans to reopen the mines."

"Interesting choice." He turned onto the highway, leaving the town behind. "Most of those old mines haven't
been worked in fifty or sixty years or more. Even then,
most of them never earned much. Though I guess some
people do still dig around in them as a hobby."

"This wasn't a hobby. Greg is—was—an engineer.
He's developed new techniques he thinks will make those
old mines profitable again. He wanted to do a demonstration project here, and use that to sell his equipment
to others."

"That sounds like it could end up being pretty lucra-
tive," Gage said. "Did he have competitors? Anyone who
might have killed him to get his ideas or to stop him from
implementing them?"

"No! That's crazy. He doesn't know people like that.
And he had patents on all the equipment he had designed.
People don't kill other people over things like that. If they

wanted his ideas, they could have bought him out—or tried to."

"So he never mentioned having been threatened by anyone?" Gage asked.

"No. And Angela would have told me if he had. She wasn't one to hide her emotions from me. And if either one of them had thought they were in any danger at all, they never would have brought Casey up here."

"Can you think of any reason someone would have killed them?" Gage asked. "Something in their pasts, maybe?"

"No." She shook her head, fresh tears flowing in spite of her efforts to hold them back. "They were quiet, ordinary people." She blotted the tears with her fingers and angled toward him. "Maybe they stumbled on drug activity—a meth lab or something like that—and were murdered because of it."

"It's possible," Gage said. "And we'll look into it. But most of the meth labs have moved to Mexico these days." He slowed as they approached a bank of lights—headlights, work lights, even flashlights bobbed about in the woods on either side of the road.

"This is where they were killed?" Maya asked, staring at the confusion of lights and people—and lots and lots of trees and rocks and dirt. This was the place Angela had gushed about as being so beautiful?

"Yes." Gage shut off the engine. "Stay with me," he said. "If you go wandering off around here, you could end up falling down an abandoned mine shaft or stepping off a cliff."

"Those things could have happened to Casey," she said, climbing out of the SUV and following him down the side of the road.

"Hey, Gage."

"Hi, Gage."

"Thought you'd packed it in for the night?"

Various people greeted the deputy as they passed. An older man with a crooked nose and bushy eyebrows approached. "Deputy Walker, what are you doing about the press?" he asked.

"I'm not really concerned about the press right now, Larry," Gage said. He turned to Maya. "Maya Renfro, this is Eagle Mountain's mayor, Larry Rowe."

"Ms. Renfro." The mayor nodded solemnly. "I'm very sorry for your loss." He turned to Gage. "Now, about the press. Something like this could reflect very badly on the town if it isn't handled properly."

"Not now, mayor." Gage pushed past him, only to be waylaid a few yards farther on by a petite woman with a large red hound on a leash. "Did you get anything?" Gage asked her.

"I'm sorry, no." The woman stopped and leaned down to pat the dog. "Daisy picked up the scent from the shirt you gave me, but after about a hundred yards, she lost it. I marked the path for you. And we can try again tomorrow if you like. Right now, Daisy is just tired and frustrated."

Daisy stared up at them with mournful brown eyes, then let out a low moan and scratched at one floppy ear with her hind foot.

"Thanks for trying, Lorna," Gage said. He patted Daisy. "Give her a biscuit from me."

Maya spotted Greg and Angela's SUV and faltered. The vehicle was surrounded by a cordon of yellow-and-black tape, and more tape marked a path from the vehicle into the woods. "Is that your sister and her husband's car?" Gage asked.

"Yes."

He took her arm. "Come on. I'm going to take you into their camp, ask you to identify some things. Their bodies have already been taken away. Can you do that for me?"

"Yes." They were just things. She wouldn't think about them in relation to death.

"Step where I step," Gage said. "Don't get off the path or touch anything." He led the way through a section of tape.

"That's their tent," she said as they approached the blue dome tent. "They bought it a couple of years ago, to replace an old one our parents gave them."

"All right." Gage led her to the tent and pulled back the flap. "Take a look inside and tell me if you see anything unusual—anything that doesn't belong to your sister, her husband or Casey."

He swept the beam of the flashlight over the contents of the tent—sleeping bags, backpack, clothing, Angela's purse. Maya covered her mouth with her hand when she spotted the purse and shook her head, swallowing hard against the sob that threatened to escape.

Gage dropped the tent flap and straightened, playing the beam of the light around and behind the tent. Pink tape fluttered from a slender metal stake behind the tent. "This is where Lorna and her dog picked up the scent," he said, guiding Maya over to the stake. "Don't walk in the path, but walk beside it. Call your niece. If she's near enough, she might recognize your voice and come to you."

Maya stared at him, still numb. "Calling her isn't going to help," she said. "We have to look for her."

"Call her. She might hear you. Identify yourself and if she's hiding, she might come out."

Maya shook her head, the tears flowing freely now. "You don't understand," she said. "I could call all night and it wouldn't make any difference. Casey wouldn't hear me. She's deaf."

Chapter Three

Gage stared at Maya. "Your niece is deaf and you're just now telling me?" he asked.

"I'm sorry! I was in shock. And it's not like I think of Casey as my deaf niece. She's just my niece. Being deaf is part of her, the way having brown hair is part of her."

"This is a little more significant than her hair color."

"I said I'm sorry." She stared into the surrounding darkness, looking, he was sure, for the little girl. Gage stared, too, his stomach knotting as the difficulty of their task sank in. Simply getting within earshot of Casey Hood wasn't going to be enough. They were going to have to get her in their sights, and then somehow persuade her that they were friendly and wanted to help her. All of that required light, which meant waiting until tomorrow to continue the search.

He touched Maya's shoulder. "Come on," he said. "Let's go."

She stared at him, eyes wide, red rimmed from crying. She didn't look quite as young as she had when she had first walked into his office. The blue-tipped hair and dangling earrings had him thinking she was a teenager then. He saw the maturity in her eyes now, and the desperate struggle to keep hope alive. "We can't just leave her out there all night—alone," she said.

"We're going to have someone here all night," he said. "I'll have them build a fire and keep it going. Maybe Casey will see it."

"I should be the one waiting," she said.

"No. You should go back to your hotel room and try to get some sleep." She started to argue, but he cut her off. "We're going to need you in the morning. Once it's light out here and we can see, we're going to need you close in case someone spots Casey. She'll recognize you and want to come to you."

She looked out into the darkness again. "Do you really think she's all right?"

"We haven't found evidence to the contrary," he said. "No signs of struggle, no other signs of blood at the scene. I think she got away from the killers." Whoever shot Angela and Greg Hood might have taken the child with them, but that didn't make sense to him. The parents' deaths had been cold and efficient—for whatever reason, someone had wanted them eliminated. Why then burden yourself with a five-year-old child? "I think Casey saw what was happening, became frightened and ran away. Tomorrow, we're going to find her." He touched her shoulder again. "Come on. I'll take you back to your hotel."

"I don't have a hotel room. I mean, I didn't call and make a reservation. I didn't even think of it."

"Then we'll find you one. Come on."

She made one last glance into the darkness beyond the camp, then followed Gage to his SUV. "I'm going to speak to the sheriff," he said. "I'll be right back."

He found Travis with a group of search and rescue volunteers who were packing up to head back to town. "I got some more information about the little girl we're looking for," Gage told them. "Seems she's deaf. So shouting her name isn't going to do any good. We'll need to make eye contact."

"I know a little American Sign Language," one of the SAR volunteers, a middle-aged woman, said.

"That might come in handy," Gage said. "Can you come back to help with the search tomorrow?"

"I'll be here."

They said good-night. Travis waited until he and Gage were alone before he spoke. "Does the sister have any idea what the Hoods were doing up here that got them killed?" he asked.

Gage glanced back toward his SUV. He could see the shadowed figure of Maya as she sat in the passenger seat. "Greg Hood was an engineer who had developed some new equipment he thought could make these old mines profitable. He purchased these old claims to create a kind of demonstration project. He and his wife and the kid were camping up here, checking out their new acquisition."

"Any enemies, threats, anything like that?" Travis asked.

"She says no, and she thinks she would know. Sounds like she and the sister were close."

"All right. Maybe we'll turn up something when we have a chance to go over the evidence from the scene. And I'm going to talk to Ed Roberts."

Gage thought of the old man who was as close as Eagle Mountain came to a hermit. He lived in an apartment above the hardware store, but spent most of his time working an old gold mining claim in the area. "Is his claim around here?" he asked.

"Behind this property." Travis gestured toward the north.

"You think he might have seen or heard something?"

Travis's expression grew more grim. "And he's a registered sex offender."

Gage stared. He knew the department received regular updates from the sex offender registry, but he didn't remember Roberts's name being on there. Maybe it dated from before his time with the department. Now he felt a little sick to his stomach. "Did he molest some kid or something?"

"He was convicted of exposing himself to women—flashing them. It happened years ago, in another state, but still…"

"Yeah," Gage said. "Still worth questioning him."

"In the meantime," Travis said, "we'll have someone up here overnight and we'll start the search again at first light."

"That little kid must be scared to death, out there in the dark by herself," Gage said.

"At least if she's scared, it means she's still alive," Travis said. He clapped his brother on the shoulder. "Go home. Try to get some rest. Pray that in the morning we get lucky."

"I'm going to find a place for Maya to stay. I'll probably pick her up in the morning and bring her up here with me. She's the person the kid is most liable to run to on sight."

"Good idea."

Maya sat hunched in the front seat, hugging herself. "I should have started the engine so you could get warm," he said, turning the key in the ignition. "Even in summer, it can get chilly up here at night."

"I keep thinking about Casey, cold and alone out there in the dark," she said.

"Most of the time, with little kids like this, they get tired and lie down somewhere," Gage said. "We're hoping she'll see the fire at camp and come back there. A husband-and-wife team with the search and rescue squad have volunteered to stay there. They've got kids of their own, so they shouldn't be too scary to Casey."

"If she comes to them, you'll call me." It wasn't a question.

"Of course," Gage said. "As soon as we hear anything."

They drove back toward town in silence. Full darkness had descended like a cloak, the sky a sweep of black in the windshield. When he had a cell signal, Gage pulled out his phone and made a call. "Hello?" The woman on the other end of the line sounded cautious, and maybe a little annoyed.

"Paige, this is Gage Walker. Sorry to bother you so late, but I've got a lady here who needs a room for the night—probably several nights. She's the aunt of the little girl we're searching for."

"I heard about that," Paige said. "Poor thing. And I do have a room. It's my smallest one, but I doubt she'll care about that."

"Great. I'm going to take her to get something to eat, then we'll stop by."

"Sure thing, Deputy."

"When was the last time you ate?" he asked Maya as they neared town.

"I had a sandwich at lunch," she said. "That seems like days ago."

"And now it's almost ten. I know you probably don't feel like eating, but you should. And I'm starving. Let me buy you dinner, then I'll take you over to the Bear's Den."

"The Bear's Den?"

"It's a bed-and-breakfast. You should get along great with the woman who runs it."

"Why do you say that?"

He glanced at her, but it was too dark for him to read her expression. "The hair, the VW bug, the English degree—trust me, the two of you will get along great."

"Why do I get the feeling that's not exactly a compliment?"

"It's not an insult," he said.

"Then what is it?"

He searched for the right words—words that weren't going to offend her, that would convey what he really meant. "You stand out from the crowd around here," he said. "That's not a bad thing."

"You mean the blue hair," she said.

"The blue hair. The attitude."

"You think I have an attitude?" Her voice rose and she leaned toward him.

Gage bit back a groan. Yes, she had an attitude—a "don't mess with me" vibe that shone through the grief and fatigue. "I didn't say it was a bad attitude," he said. "And hey, maybe I'm full of it. Ignore everything I said."

"You're not the kind of man a woman ignores, Deputy."

The words jolted him. Was she flirting with him? But when he glanced her way, she was facing forward again, what he could see of her expression betraying nothing.

Mo's Pub was the only place open this late, so Gage drove there. When they walked in the waitress showed them to a booth. "Any word on that lost little girl?" she asked as she distributed menus.

"Not yet," Gage said.

"Tony was up there all afternoon with the search and rescue crew, and we're all praying y'all find her soon. Poor little baby. She must be scared to death up there on her own."

"This is Casey's aunt, Maya Renfro," Gage said. "This is Sasha Simpson."

"You poor thing." Sasha patted Maya's shoulder. "You must be worried sick. They're gonna find her, I'm sure of it. They won't stop looking until they do."

"Thanks." Maya looked a little dazed as Sasha hurried away to wait on another table. "She sounded really worried—and she doesn't even know me or Casey."

"She has two little girls of her own," Gage said. "And that's the way people are around here. Everybody knows everybody and while it's not exactly family, it's something like it."

"I can see how that would be appealing," she said. "But a little claustrophobic at times, too. Sometimes I like not knowing anything about my neighbors."

Sasha returned and took their orders. Maya ordered a salad, which he expected she wouldn't eat, but she was drinking her soft drink, so that was something. "So what do you do in Denver besides teach English?" he asked.

"I do poetry slams."

Again, not what he would have expected. "That's where people get up and perform poetry they've written, right?"

"Exactly." She didn't even try to hide her surprise.

"We may be a little out of the way here in Eagle Mountain, but we're not completely backward," he said.

"Have you ever been to a poetry slam?" she asked.

"No. But then, I can't say I've ever cared much for poetry. Probably comes from having to memorize 'O Captain! My Captain!' when I was in fourth grade."

"My poetry isn't like that."

"I kind of figured."

She fell silent and Gage focused on his food as soon as Sasha had placed the dishes on the table. When he looked up again, Maya was staring at him. "I'd like to see Angela," she said softly.

He should have seen that coming. "I can arrange that. Maybe late tomorrow." He leaned toward her. "Is there someone else you should call to be here with you? Another sibling? Your parents?"

"I spoke to my parents after I talked to you," she said. "They live in Arizona. My mom isn't in good health and traveling is hard for her. And there's nothing they can do. I told them they should stay put until we know more. And there aren't any other siblings."

"Okay." So she had to bear this all by herself. He would do what he could to ease the burden for her.

"What about you?" she asked. "I know you have a brother—the sheriff. Any other brothers and sisters?"

"I have a sister. She's a graduate student at CSU. Our parents have a ranch just outside of town."

She speared a cherry tomato on her fork. "A ranch as in cows?"

"And horses. The Walking W Ranch has been in operation since 1942. My great-grandparents started it."

"So do you, like, ride and rope and all that stuff?" she asked.

He suppressed a grin. "All that stuff."

"That explains the belt buckle."

He glanced down at the large silver-and-gold buckle, which he had won as State Junior Champion Bronc Rider in high school. "I was riding horses years before I learned to ride a bicycle," he said. "And I still help out with fall roundup."

She shook her head. "Our lives are so different we could be from two different countries."

"We're probably not that different," he said. "I've

found that people behave pretty much the same wherever they're from."

"Well, I'm from the city and I have no desire to ride a horse. And I hope you won't take this wrong, but I thought my sister was crazy when she said she and Greg were thinking about moving here."

"You told me they bought the mining claims for a demonstration project, not to live on."

"That's right. But they were talking about finding a place here in town. They had fallen in love with Eagle Mountain. I don't know why."

"You might be surprised," Gage said. "I've heard from other people that the place has a way of growing on you."

"I just want to find my niece and go home." She looked all in, her eyes still red and puffy from crying, her shoulders slumped.

Gage pushed aside his plate. "You must be exhausted," he said. "Let's get out of here. I'll take you to your car at the sheriff's office and you can follow me to the B and B."

Fifteen minutes later, they parked at the curb in front of the Victorian home Paige Riddell had converted into a bed-and-breakfast. The light over the front door came on and Paige stepped out. "I'm Paige," she said, coming forward to take Maya's bag. "You've had a pretty miserable day, I imagine, so I won't prolong it, but I will say how sorry I am for your loss."

"Thank you." Maya gave Paige a long look. "Gage said I would like you—that he thought we'd have a lot in common."

"That depends," Paige said. "Some folks around here think of me as the local tree-hugging rabble-rouser, but I don't take that as an insult."

"Then yeah, I think we'll get along fine," Maya said.

"Let me show you to your room." Paige put an arm

around Maya and ushered her into the house. In the doorway, she stopped and glanced over her shoulder at Gage. "Don't leave yet," she mouthed, then went into the house with Maya.

Gage moved to the porch swing to the right of the door and sat, letting the calm of the night seep into him. Only one or two lights shone in the houses that lined the street, not enough to dim the stars overhead. He thought of the little girl in the woods and hoped she was where she could see those stars, and that maybe, seeing them, she wouldn't feel so alone.

The door opened and Paige stepped out. "I got her settled in," she said. "Grief can be so exhausting. I hope she's able to get some sleep."

"I'll come by and pick her up in the morning and take her up to the campsite," he said. "We're hoping her niece will see her and come to her. I found out tonight that the little girl is deaf, so she wouldn't hear us calling for her."

Paige sat in a wicker armchair adjacent to the swing. "I can't even imagine how worried Maya is. I don't even know this kid and it upsets me to think of her out there."

Gage stifled a yawn. "Is there something you wanted to talk to me about?" he asked.

"Yes. I wanted to tell you I saw that couple—Maya's sister and her husband—the day before yesterday. And the little girl. She was with them. Adorable child."

Gage sat up straight, fatigue receding. "Where was this?"

"Some of us from Eagle Mountain Conservation went up to Eagle Mountain Resort—you know, those mining claims Henry Hake wanted to develop?"

Gage nodded. Eagle Mountain Conservation had succeeded in getting an injunction to stop the development three years ago. "You saw the Hood family up there?"

"They were unloading camping gear from a white SUV parked on the side of the road. I guess they were camping on one of the claims near Hake's property."

"They bought the claim and I guess a few others in the area," Gage said. "But what were you doing on Henry Hake's land? It's private property."

Paige frowned at him, a scowl that had intimidated more than one overzealous logger, trash-throwing tourist or anyone else who attracted the wrath of the EMC. "We weren't on his land. There's a public easement along the edge of the property. It's a historic trail that's been in use since the 1920s. We established that in court, and Hake and his partners had to take down a fence they had erected blocking access. It was part of the injunction order that stopped the development."

"So you went up there to hike the trail?"

"We had heard complaints that the fence was back up, so we went to check," she said.

"And was it up?"

"Yes. With a big iron gate across it. Our lawyers have already filed a complaint with the county commissioners. We tried getting in touch with Hake, but didn't have any luck."

"He's been missing for almost a month now," Gage said. "No one has heard anything from him, and every trail we've followed up on has gone cold."

"A man like that probably has plenty of enemies," Paige said. "And he hung around with some nasty people. Maybe that former bodyguard of his did him in."

"Maybe so, though we haven't found evidence of that." Hake's one-time bodyguard had died in a struggle with

Travis when he had kidnapped the woman who was now Travis's fiancée. Three years previously, the same man had murdered Andy Stenson, a young lawyer in town who had also worked for Hake.

Paige leaned toward Gage. "It looked to me like work has been done up there on Hake's property," she said. "There's a lot of tire tracks, and maybe even a new building or two."

"I'll see if I can find out anything," Gage said. "Maybe someone working up there saw or heard something related to the Hoods' killing." He stood. "Thanks for letting me know. I'll see you and Maya in the morning."

"I'm hoping she'll get a good night's sleep," Paige said. "And that tomorrow we find her niece safe."

"We all hope that." He returned to his SUV and headed toward the house he rented on the edge of town, but he had traveled less than a block when his cell phone rang. "Gage, this is Al Dawson, over at the high school."

"Sure, Al." Gage glanced at the clock on his dash. Ten minutes until midnight. "What's up?"

"I came in to do the floors here in the gym, but found the lock on the door is broken. Somebody bashed it in."

"Did you go inside?" Gage asked, looking for a place to turn around.

"No. When I saw the damage to the door, I figured I'd better call you. It looks like we've got another break-in."

"I'll be right there, Al. Don't go in."

"I won't. What's going on, Gage?" Al asked. "Travis was out here just this morning to take a report on some items that were stolen from the chemistry lab. This used to be such a peaceful town—now we've got crime all over the place."

"I don't know, Al," Gage said. "But I'll be right there."

Ordinarily, a random burglary wouldn't seem that unusual, but two burglaries in one week was enough to rate a headline in the local paper. Add in a double murder and Gage had to ask what the heck was going on.

Chapter Four

On his way to the high school, Gage called Travis. "Didn't you respond to the high school this morning about a break-in?" he asked when his brother answered the phone.

"Yesterday morning," Travis said. "It's already this morning."

"Sorry to wake you," Gage said. "But I just got a call from Al Dawson, the janitor over there. He says the gym door has been tampered with."

"All the doors were fine when I was out there," Travis said. "The thief got into the lab through a broken window."

"Al thinks somebody broke into the gym. I'm on my way out there."

"I'll meet you."

Al was waiting by his truck when Gage pulled into the lot at the high school. Security lights cast a jaundiced glow over the scene. Whoever had attacked the door to the gymnasium hadn't bothered with subtlety. They had bashed in the area around the lock with a sledgehammer or iron bar. "Is this the only door that's been damaged?" Gage asked.

"I think so," Al, a thin man in his sixties, said. "I took

a look around while I was waiting for you and I didn't see anything else."

"You don't have any security cameras focused on this area, do you?" Gage asked.

Al frowned. "We're a rural school district. Our budget doesn't run to security cameras."

"All right." Gage took out a pair of gloves and pulled them on. "I'll check things inside. You wait here."

But before he could open the door, Travis pulled up. Gage waited for his brother to join them. Travis greeted them, then surveyed the door. "They obviously didn't care about hiding the damage," he said. "Same thing with the science lab yesterday—smash and grab."

"What did they take from the lab?" Gage asked.

"Science equipment—some test tubes and flasks, reagents and a Bunsen burner," Travis said.

"You think it was kids making drugs?" Al asked.

"Kids or adults," Travis said. "We're keeping our eyes open."

"I was just about to take a look inside," Gage said.

"I'll come with you." Travis pulled on a pair of gloves and followed Gage inside, both men careful to keep to one side, out of what they judged was the direct path of entry. Later, a crime scene team would investigate and gather what evidence they could. "I don't hold out much hope of getting good prints," Gage said as he flipped the light switch. Banks of floodlights lit up the wood-floored space. Basketball hoops hung from the ceiling at either end of the gym, and metal bleachers lined the far wall.

"Doesn't look like they did any damage in here," Gage said, surveying the empty room.

"Let's get Al in here and see if he sees anything out of place." Travis walked back the way he and Gage had come. A minute later, he returned with the janitor. "Do you see anything missing, Al?"

The janitor scratched his head. "I don't see anything— then again, I wouldn't necessarily know. You need to get one of the coaches over here for that."

Gage checked the time. Almost one in the morning. "For now, we'll seal off the area and get one of the reserve officers over here to babysit the scene until the crime scene guys can make it over. What time do the coaches show up?"

"Seven thirty or so, usually," Al said. He frowned across the silent gym. "I guess this means I won't be doing the floors in here tonight."

"No one comes in here without an escort from the sheriff's department," Gage said.

They went outside again and while Travis pulled crime scene tape from his SUV, Gage called in a reserve officer to stand guard and made notes about Al's statement. "I'll swing back here early to talk to the coaches," he said.

Thirty minutes later, he and Travis walked back to their cars, prepared to leave. "Did you get Ms. Renfro taken care of?" Travis asked.

"She's over at the Bear's Den," Gage said. "I told her I would pick her up and take her back to the camp in the morning. She wants to help search for her niece, and I think it's probably a good idea. The little girl will recognize her, plus Maya can communicate with her in sign language." He glanced over his shoulder at the high school. "I guess I'll swing by here first, see if I can get anything useful from the coach."

Travis clapped him on the shoulder. "Let me know what you find. I'll see you later at camp."

Gage opened the driver's-side door of his SUV. "And

to think just yesterday I was complaining about being bored," he said. "That's what I get for opening my big mouth."

MAYA LAY AWAKE much of the night, alternately weeping and praying, terrified of what might be happening to Casey, unable to accept she would never see her sister again.

When the clock showed 6:00 a.m., she got out of bed and took a shower, then did her makeup and ventured downstairs. When she walked into the dining room, which was painted a cheery apple green, Paige gestured toward a buffet, on which sat a large coffee urn and plates of muffins. "Help yourself," she said. "The other guests haven't come down yet, but I knew you'd want an early start."

Maya filled a coffee cup and stirred in cream and sugar. "I don't guess you've heard anything from Gage?" she asked.

"I'm sorry, no," Paige said. "I'm sure he would have called you if they had found anything."

Maya dropped into one of the chairs at the dining table. Paige sat opposite her. "I know it's hard," Paige said. "But don't give up hope. Everyone available is looking for your niece—and we've done this before. Two summers ago, a little boy got lost when his family was hiking and they found him the next day, a little cold and scared, but safe."

Maya wrapped both hands around the sky-blue mug decorated with little fleurs-de-lis. "I keep telling myself that we'll find Casey today. I wish I was up there right now, helping to look for her."

"It's still too dark out to see much," Paige said. "And do you even know how to get there?"

"Gage took me there last night." She sipped her coffee. "And I can follow directions, if someone tells me which way to go."

"You might as well wait for Gage," Paige said. "He should be here soon."

"He probably has plenty to do besides babysitting me," Maya said.

"He probably does," Paige said. "But that's the kind of guy he is—a real gentleman. I know it's an old-fashioned word, but it's true. He really cares about people. It's what makes him good at his job."

Maya shifted in her chair, curiosity warring with embarrassment. Curiosity won. "Are you and Gage involved?" she asked.

Paige laughed. "Oh my goodness, no. What made you think that?"

"I know you went down to talk to him after you showed me to my room. I just thought…" She shrugged.

"No. Gage and I are not involved." Paige pinched off a bite of muffin. "Neither one of us is interested in getting serious," she said. "It's easier."

"I know what you mean," Maya said. "I'm not seeing anyone right now, either." Though she couldn't help thinking how nice it would be to have someone she could lean on. She pushed the thought away. She had been standing on her own two feet for plenty of years—no reason to stop now. "How did you end up in Eagle Mountain?" she asked.

"I came here on vacation and fell in love with the place," Paige said.

"Where did you live before?" Maya asked.

"Portland, Oregon."

"This is certainly different from Portland," Maya said.

"Different was what I needed at the time. I was coming off a painful divorce, and both my parents had died in the three years prior to that. I had a little money my aunt had left me, so I used it to buy this place and fix it up." She shrugged. "At the time, I thought maybe I would stay a few years then move on, but I got involved in life here and I love running the B and B. It's a good fit all around."

"I think small-town life would bore me after a while," Maya said.

"There's plenty to do here if you know where to look," Paige said. "Maybe not as many choices as in the city and we're low on anything resembling the club scene, but I've made a lot of friends here. I care about this place and it feels like home."

The doorbell chimed and Paige scraped back her chair. "That's probably Gage."

Maya told herself her heart beat faster because she was hoping for news from Gage about her niece, but she had to admit to the thrill of attraction that ran through her when the sheriff's deputy stepped into the dining room. "Good morning," he said, and nodded and touched the brim of his hat.

The courtliness of the gesture moved her. He looked tired, and there was a heaviness about his eyes that heightened her own sadness. "Did you get any sleep last night?" she asked.

"A little." He accepted a cup of coffee from Paige, and pulled out the chair next to Maya. "I had a late call. Break-in at the high school."

"Kids?" Paige asked.

"Maybe." Gage sipped his coffee.

Maya thought of the students in her classes—a mixed bunch of good and bad. "I guess even little towns like this aren't immune to that kind of thing," she said.

"Kids get bored and in trouble everywhere," he said.

"Though we like to think in Eagle Mountain there's a little less trouble for them to find. No gangs, anyway. Drugs are always a concern, but there's not as much of it here. And people in smaller communities get involved—if they see a kid up to something, they don't hesitate to call it in."

"I guess being nosy has its upside," Maya said.

"It can." He helped himself to a muffin. "We can go whenever you're ready."

"Let me grab my backpack."

She waited until they were on their way before she asked the question that had been foremost in her mind all morning. "Have you heard anything from the other searchers?" she asked.

"I'm sorry. No." He glanced at her, then back at the road. "Have you thought about where Casey might have gone if she ran away? Let's go with the theory that she saw what happened to her parents and ran, scared. Is there anything in particular that she's attracted to? Is she drawn to water? Would she hide in a cave, or would she avoid that?"

"I think a cave would frighten her. I don't think she cares about water, one way or another." She frowned, trying to think past her exhaustion and fear. "I mean, she's five years old. She's a sweet, innocent girl who's never known danger for a minute in her life. Seeing her parents killed—" She shook her head. "She must be terrified."

"We haven't found any indication that the people who killed your sister and her husband harmed Casey," Gage said. "Hold on to that hope."

She nodded. "I will. I'm hoping Casey spent the night hiding, and once she sees me, she'll come out."

"That's what we're hoping, too."

"You were right—I do like Paige. And she vouched for you as a good guy."

"Were you worried I was otherwise?"

"No, but it's always good to have someone verify my first impression."

"Glad I passed the test. Though I can't say I'm all that comfortable knowing you two have been discussing my merits and flaws."

"Ha! As if men don't do the same with women."

"I promise, I haven't discussed you with anyone."

Under other circumstances, that admission might have disappointed her, Maya told herself. But there were bigger things at stake right now. "What's the plan for this morning?" she asked.

"I think you should hang around the main camp. If any of the search team spot Casey, or any signs of her, they can contact the base and we'll get you to that location."

That sounded like a lot of sitting around and waiting for other people to find Casey—not what she had in mind. "What are you going to do?" she asked.

"I want to take a look at the property adjacent to the place your sister and her husband owned. A few years back, a developer bought it and had plans to build a big resort, but he ran afoul of local environmentalists. The property is supposed to be vacant, but Paige told me last night she was up there a few days ago and it looked as if someone had been working there. If I can find whoever that was, maybe they saw something that will lead us to your sister's killer. Or maybe someone there has seen Casey."

"Or maybe this mysterious person *is* the killer." Maya wrapped her arms across her stomach to ward off a chill.

"Maybe." Gage looked grim. "It's something I need to find out."

"I want to come with you," Maya said. "If there are other people working there, it makes sense that Casey would have headed in that direction."

"I don't know what I'm going to walk into," Gage said. "I can't risk putting you in danger."

"I don't care about that." When he gave her a questioning look, she set her jaw. "No offense, Deputy, but I'll do almost anything to save my niece. That's more important to me than anything else right now."

"And if I order you to stay away?" he asked.

"Then you would have a fight on your hands," she said. "And when it comes to people I love, I'm not afraid to fight dirty."

"The scary thing about that," Gage said, "is that I absolutely believe you."

"Why is that scary?"

"Let's just say, I never met a teacher like you. I'm still making up my mind whether I like that or not."

"You don't have to like it. Just don't stand in the way of me taking care of my niece."

"I won't stand in your way," he said. "Unless you're in mine. But I think we're on the same side in this matter. Just respect that I have a job to do. I want to find your niece as much as you do, but I also need to find your sister's killer. I think we can do both."

"Are you going to take me with you this morning or not?"

She waited a long, tense moment for him to answer. If she had to, she would go to his brother, the sheriff. Or she would get the press on her side—there was bound to be a reporter at the site, surely.

"All right, you can come with me," he said. "But if I sense anything dangerous, I'm taking you right back to camp—no arguments."

"All right." That would have to do—for now. Maya had meant it when she told Gage she would do anything to protect her niece. Anything at all.

Chapter Five

Gage wasn't used to people pushing back against decisions he made as an officer of the law, and his first instinct with Maya had been to shut her down. But he had heard the determination in her voice and seen the grief in her eyes, and recognized a fight he couldn't win. He didn't really expect to run into any danger on Henry Hake's land, and if they did, he was confident he could protect them both.

He parked behind Travis's SUV and the sheriff walked out to meet them. "The first group of searchers just went out," he reported. "Lorna has her dog with her, and a couple of other people say they know a little sign language, so if they see Casey, they can try to communicate with her."

"Thank you," Maya said. She looked pale in the early morning light, and Gage read the disappointment in her eyes. She had been hoping for word of her niece when they arrived—she wanted to hear that the little girl had already been found.

Gage put a hand on her shoulder. "Wait over by the fire for me. I need to talk to the sheriff for a minute."

She nodded and moved toward the fire, a sad but determined woman. Gage didn't know if he would be as strong if he were in her position.

"What did you find out at the high school?" Travis asked, bringing Gage's attention back to work.

"I talked to the head coach. He says they're missing three gym mats, a climbing rope and some weights."

Travis's brow furrowed. "Nothing anyone could really sell, and I don't see how any of those things could be used to manufacture drugs."

"Right," Gage said. "So maybe it's just kids?"

"Maybe," Travis said. "Though when kids vandalize a school, they do it to make a mess—graffiti, tearing things up. This doesn't feel like that."

"Yeah," Gage agreed. "It feels like someone went in there looking for some specific items, grabbed them and got out."

"More than one person, probably," Travis said. "That's a lot to carry. Those mats are bulky and the weights are heavy."

"The mats are bright blue," Gage said. "We'll keep our eyes open around town—maybe we'll spot them."

"In the meantime, we'll put extra patrols around the school," Travis said.

"I want to take a look on Henry Hake's property this morning," Gage said. "It's close enough Casey might have wandered over there. She might be hiding out in one of the buildings."

"It's a long way for a kid that little to walk," Travis said.

"Only about a mile cross-country," Gage said. "That little boy who was lost last year was over three miles away from the place his folks had last seen him."

"Give it a go then. Has the mayor talked to you yet?"

Gage frowned. "He stopped me last night, blathering something about the press and the town looking bad."

Travis nodded. "He called me first thing this morning. He's worried Eagle Mountain is getting a reputation as an unsafe town."

"What did you tell him?"

"I told him we were doing our best to find the person responsible for these murders and I didn't think anyone else was in danger."

"What did he expect?" Gage asked. "That you could wave a magic wand and make all the bad things disappear?"

"He's just doing his job, looking out for the town's reputation," Travis said.

"Then he needs to leave us alone to do our jobs."

"If he bothers you again, send him to me," Travis said. "Do you have anything new on this case?"

"Paige told me she was up here with members of her environmental group two days ago and she saw the Hoods unloading their car," Gage said. "The group had heard a report that the public trail that runs alongside Hake's property had been blocked and they came to check it out. Paige said someone had put up a gate and the addition was recent. You haven't heard anything about any new activity at the resort, have you?"

"No," Travis said. "Henry Hake is still missing, and as far as I know, the injunction against his development is still in effect."

"I'll check it out. I'm taking Maya with me." Gage didn't mention she had insisted on coming with him.

"I got a preliminary report this morning on the Hood murders," Travis said. "They were both shot with a nine millimeter. Close range, one bullet each. Killer took the spent shells with him."

"So they weren't killed during a struggle," Gage said.

"I don't think they had a chance. I think they were

jumped, tied up and shot. Two, but I'm guessing three people to do the job."

"And where was the little girl while all this was going on?" Gage asked.

"The coroner puts the time of death around 9:00 p.m., so maybe she was in the tent, asleep."

"The killers would have gone in looking for her."

"Not if they didn't know she existed. Or maybe she woke up when her parents were attacked and crawled out of the tent and ran."

"Tents don't have back doors," Gage pointed out.

"No, but this one had a good-sized tear in the back window screen. A frightened little kid could have gotten out that way."

"And the killers didn't hear her?"

"Not if they were busy with the parents."

Gage nodded. The scenario made sense. "We need to find her today," he said. "She's got to be cold and hungry and scared." If she wasn't lying at the bottom of a ravine or drowned in a creek. He didn't have to say those things out loud—he knew Travis was thinking them, too.

"Check out Hake's. Take others with you if you need to."

"I think Maya and I will have a look by ourselves first," he said. "As it is, if word gets out we were over there, we're liable to hear from Hake's lawyers. They've got the place fenced off like a fortress."

"Let them complain about us searching for a missing child and see what kind of PR that gets them," Travis said.

Gage found Maya standing by the campfire with Mellie Sanger, half of the couple who had stayed at the site overnight. Maya turned toward Gage as he approached, the hope in her eyes like a stab to his heart. "Mellie was telling me they stayed up most of the night and didn't hear or see anything," she said. "I don't see how Casey could have just vanished."

"She's probably afraid and hiding," Gage said. "As she gets hungrier, she'll want to come out." That was all the hope he had to give her right now.

"Good luck." Mellie took both Maya's hands in hers. "George and I will come back tonight if we need to, but we really hope we don't need to."

"Thank you both, so much."

"Are you ready to go?" Gage asked.

"Yes." She hitched her backpack up on her shoulder. "Which way?"

He led the way east, toward the land Henry Hake had wanted to develop. There was no defined trail, and the going was rough, over uneven ground littered with fallen tree branches and small boulders. They crossed a small stream, and then another, then descended into a steep ravine. Gage could hear Maya breathing hard as they climbed back out of the ravine, but she kept up with him and didn't complain. A few hundred yards on, they stopped to drink some water. "How could a little girl have crossed all that?" Maya asked.

"People lost in the wilderness do incredible things," he said. "The little boy we found last year—the one who had wandered away from his parents while the family was out for a hike—ended up three miles away from the trail, in a place he would have had to cross three streams and climbed a small mountain to get to."

"How did they ever find him?" she asked.

"Persistence and luck," Gage said. "Lorna's dog, Daisy, found the trail initially, then a group of volunteers spread out to search a hundred yards on either side of the trail. They found him asleep in the hollow made by an uprooted tree trunk. If they hadn't been looking for him, they might have walked right by and never seen him."

"I don't know if that story makes me more hopeful or more horrified," she said. She stuffed her water bottle back in her pack. "I've been staring at the ground all morning, hoping to see a little footprint or some pink thread—Casey loves pink, and almost all her clothes are pink. I want so badly to see some sign of her that I'm half-afraid I'll start imagining things."

"I'm watching, too," Gage said. "Maybe we'll spot something soon." Or maybe they wouldn't. He kept talking about the little boy they had found last summer to encourage her, but he didn't mention the three or four other people over the years who had become lost and were never found—or whose bodies were found months or years later.

After a half hour of walking, they came to an eight-foot-tall chain-link fence topped with razor wire, hedge roses poking through the wire and blocking the view beyond. "Whoa!" Maya stopped and stared up at the barrier. "What is this doing out here? It looks like something the government would build around an airport—or a prison."

"The landowner, Henry Hake, doesn't like trespassers." Gage wrapped his fingers around the chain link and tugged. Still taut and solid as the day it had been built four years ago, and the thorny roses added to the barrier. "He planned to build an exclusive—expensive—resort community up here. I guess this fence was supposed to keep out the riffraff."

"Casey couldn't have gotten over this," Maya said.

"No, but it's possible she found a break in the fence, or a place where an animal had dug under. Plus, a public trail crosses one corner of the property and it's not supposed to be fenced off." He scanned the terrain on either side of the fence. "Come on," he said, pointing north. "Let's see if we can find a way in."

MAYA TRUDGED ALONG behind Gage, trying hard not to freak out over the idea of Casey being lost out here. Everywhere she looked, she faced another hazard: tree stumps to trip over, holes to fall into, rocks to stumble on. And what about wild animals? Surely there were bears and mountain lions and no telling what else out here that might view a five-year-old girl as a tasty snack. She shuddered and pushed the thought aside. A child couldn't just vanish this way. She had to be somewhere.

"Look here."

Her heart jumped in her chest at Gage's words, and she hurried to catch up to him. He stood alongside the fence, pointing to a depression in the ground. "This looks like a place some animal has been going under the wire," he said.

Maya frowned at the muddy hole. "You think Casey went under there?"

"She might have. She would fit, wouldn't she?"

"Yes, but why would she get down in the mud like that?"

"If she saw people or saw a building on the other side, she might risk it," he said.

She turned to look through the fence. The rose hedge was less dense here, but she didn't see anything but trees at first. Then she spotted what looked like the corner of a building. "If she did go in there, how are we going to follow?" she asked. "I can't fit through that hole, and I know you can't."

"We should be getting to the public trail soon."

Another ten minutes of walking took them to the end of the fence—and to a large iron gate blocking a well-worn trail. "That looks new," Maya said, studying the fresh-looking concrete around the gateposts.

"It is new," Gage said. "And it's against the law to

block a public trail." He looked around, as if searching for something.

"What are you looking for?" Maya asked.

"Something to break that padlock."

The padlock was large and heavy. "I don't think a rock is going to do it," she said.

"No." He drew the gun from the holster at his hip. "Stand back."

"You're not going to sho—" But apparently, he was. The blast echoed through the woods and Maya covered her ears and closed her eyes. When she opened them again, the lock lay shattered on the ground.

Gage pushed open the gate. "Stay behind me, and if we meet anyone, I'll do the talking."

She resisted the urge to roll her eyes at him. She got that he was used to being in charge, but he ought to have figured out by now that she didn't like being ordered around. She forgot her annoyance as she moved farther away from the gate into what looked like a long-abandoned ghost town. The remains of paved streets showed between patches of grass and even small trees that grew up through the asphalt. A few windowless concrete buildings crouched alongside crumbling concrete foundations or stakes topped with faded plastic ribbons that fluttered in the breeze.

Maya moved up alongside Gage. "What is this place?" she asked, keeping her voice low. "It's creepy."

"It was going to be an exclusive resort, with luxury homes, a country club and a golf course."

"Why wasn't it built?"

"Paige and a group of like-minded citizens got together and filed a lawsuit to stop the building. They convinced a judge that this was a fragile environmental zone that wouldn't support that kind of development. The judge agreed."

"Do you agree?" she asked.

He glanced at her. "I do. But I can't say leaving it like this is much better. It's an eyesore." He led the way across one of the crumbling streets, toward a row of three curved ducts jutting up from the ground.

"What are those?" she asked.

"Probably air vents for underground storage, or possibly machinery—a power plant or something. They could even be venting gasses from an old mine."

"I don't think Casey could climb down in them, and I don't see a door."

"No." He walked on, to a windowless building made of concrete blocks. The single steel door was fastened with a heavy bolt, with a lock through the bolt.

Maya put her ear to the door and listened, but heard only the thump of her own pulse. She stepped back and looked at Gage. "Are you going to shoot this lock off, too?"

"No reason to," he said.

They moved on, the only sound the crunch of their shoes on gravel. No birds sang; no machinery hummed. She rubbed her arms against a sudden chill. "I don't like it here," she said. "I think we should leave."

"Something feels off to me, too," he said. "But I'd like to stay long enough to figure out what that is."

"What do you think—"

But before she could complete the question, gunfire exploded from their left and something slammed her down hard into the dirt.

Chapter Six

Gage threw himself onto Maya, forcing her down into the dirt, as bullets cut the air around them. He wrapped his arms around her and rolled with her, into the shadow of the concrete building, on the side away from the shooting. He strained to listen for sounds of movement, but heard nothing but his own and Maya's labored breathing. Slowly, he eased off her, but kept one hand on her back. "Stay down," he said, his mouth close to her ear.

"Did someone just shoot at us?" she whispered, and he heard the terror behind the words.

He didn't answer her question, but instead rose to a crouching position and drew his gun. "I'm going to take a look," he said. "Stay down."

"I'm not moving."

He moved to the corner of the building, staying low, and hazarded a look around the side. No bullets came his way. But in the distance, an engine roared to life, and a car door slammed. He glanced back at Maya, who still lay huddled against the building. "Don't move," he ordered. Then, keeping to the cover of trees and rocks, he started toward what he estimated had been the shooter's location. The spot, in a growth of scrubby bushes on a rise above where he and Maya had been standing, offered cover and a good view of much of the proposed resort development. Whoever had shot at them could have been up here watching them since they had stepped through the gate. Gage shooting off the lock had given them plenty of notice that they had visitors.

He examined the ground around the area. A few scuff marks indicated someone might have been there recently, but he couldn't see any distinct shoe prints. He moved a few feet away from the bushes, to a wide, flat area with the faint indentation of tire tracks. These were probably from the vehicle he had heard. There was only one way they could have driven from here, and it led toward the road. They were probably out there and long gone by now—but he would make sure.

He hurried back down the slope, where he found Maya seated, her back against the door of the building. She looked up at his approach. "Did you find anything?"

He shook his head and held his hand out to her. "Let's head back by the road," he said.

"Can you call for help?" she asked.

"No cell signal up here," he said. He pulled her to her feet. She straightened and brushed dirt from her shirt and jeans.

"Why would someone shoot at us?" she asked. "Is it the same person who shot Angela and Greg? Do you think they have Casey?"

"I don't know. Maybe whoever put that gate up doesn't like trespassers."

They reached the front entrance to the property. Maya stuck close to him, tensed and looking around her. But Gage didn't see a sign of anyone. They set out walking down the road and five minutes later, he recognized Travis's SUV headed toward them.

The vehicle slowed and stopped as it pulled alongside them. "I heard gunshots," Travis said.

"The first shot you heard was me, shooting the lock off an illegal gate across the public trail that runs along one side of Henry Hake's property," Gage said. "The second set of blasts was somebody shooting at us. Did you pass any other vehicles on your way up here?"

"No." Travis jerked his head toward the passenger side of the SUV. "Get in."

Gage held the door for Maya as she climbed into the back seat. "There's some bottled water back there if you want some," Travis said.

Maya took a bottle of water from the box on the back floorboard and handed another to Gage. "Have you heard anything about Casey?" she asked.

"I'm sorry, no," Travis said. He turned the SUV around. "I'm going to take you back to camp and you can talk to the searchers, hear from them what they've seen. Then Gage and I will come back up here."

"I looked around, but whoever took the shots at us didn't leave much behind," Gage said. "Some faint tire tracks. No bullet casings or shoe prints."

"Maybe you missed something," Travis said. "What were you doing when they shot at you?"

"We were walking around," Gage said. "Looking for anywhere a little kid might hide or might be drawn to."

"Did you find anything?" Travis asked.

"No." He glanced back at Maya. "She's out there. I know it," he said. "We're going to keep looking."

She nodded, but the sadness in her eyes was a weight on his heart.

CASEY'S CHEST HURT. Every breath felt like something was cutting her on the inside. But she was too afraid to stop running—too afraid of the men with the guns. The men who had hurt Mommy and Daddy.

Her eyes filled with tears, making the world look blurry. She tripped on something and fell hard. Pain shot up her knee and she cried out. She had fallen so often since she had run from the camp the night before last. Was it really that long ago?

She crawled to the base of a big tree and huddled there, tears streaming, nose running. She wiped at it with her sleeve. *Stop crying!* she ordered herself. Crying didn't help anything. She closed her eyes and tried to think.

Aunt Maya was here. Casey had seen her, with the big policeman. Or maybe not a policeman. What did you call them when they wore brown instead of blue? A sheriff? A sheriff's deputy had come to their school once. He was Alexa Steiner's dad, and he had told them when they were in trouble, they should find a law officer to tell.

Was Aunt Maya in trouble? Was that why she was with the deputy? Or maybe he was protecting her from the men with guns. He had pushed her down when the men began firing.

And Casey had run. She had to run. She was so afraid of the men—more afraid than she had ever been. So afraid it made her shake, just to remember what had happened. She didn't want to remember. She drew her knees up to her chest and rested her head on them and shut her eyes. If only she could go to sleep and wake up to find this was all just a nightmare.

But she had slept last night—curled on the ground under a tree that looked a lot like this one—and when she woke in the morning, she had been scared all over again, not knowing where she was. Everything here looked so different from home—so many rocks and trees, and the big open sky and no buildings or streets or people she knew.

"Mommy," she whispered.

But her mommy wasn't going to come back again. Neither was her daddy. She had seen them lying on the ground, bleeding, and the bad men looking in the tent—the tent that Casey had crawled out of when the men had grabbed Mommy and Daddy and tied them up. Then she had run again, as long and as far as she could. She had to stay away from those bad men.

Her tummy growled and she raised her head again. She was so hungry. She had drank water from a stream last night and again this morning, but she didn't have anything to eat. When she saw those buildings, she thought she might find some food, but instead, the bad men had come and scared her away.

A bird screeched overhead. She looked up and followed its flight, into some bushes with red things on them. She stood and went over to the bushes. The red things were berries—raspberries. She picked one and popped it into her mouth. It was little but so sweet! Hurrying, she picked more, stuffing the berries into her mouth until her hands were covered with the bright red juice and her arms were covered in scratches from the prickly bushes. She moved from bush to bush, eating as many of the berries as she could find. They tasted so good—better even than candy.

When she had eaten all the berries she could hold, she walked until she came to another stream. She crouched down beside it and washed her hands and face, then scooped up water and drank. Now that she had eaten, she was so tired. But she couldn't just lie down out here in the open—the bad men might see her.

She looked around and saw a hole in the middle of a clump of bushes—like the door to a little cave. She went over to it and looked inside, at the smooth carpet of leaves. It was just big enough for her to curl up. She crawled in and did so, and thought of a storybook Aunt Maya had read to her and the picture in the book of the little squirrel curled up in its nest. She was like that squirrel, safe in this nest. She closed her eyes and thought of the squirrel, and of Aunt Maya. Maybe she would come soon and take her away—far away from the bad men.

DOZENS OF PEOPLE were swarming around Angela and Greg's camp when Maya returned with Gage and Travis. The blue tent still stood to one side of the fire pit, with the clothing and sleeping bags inside. Maya wondered if they had left everything in place as a landmark for Casey to hone in on. She was surprised to see Paige there, standing with a pretty brunette. Gage's brother, Travis, moved ahead of Gage and Maya and kissed the brunette on the cheek and she smiled up at him—the kind of smile only people in love exchange.

"Lacy and I brought some food up for the volunteers," Paige said. "And we thought we would help with the search if we could."

"I saw the gate over the trail, over by Hake's place," Gage told her. "I shot the lock off, so it's open now."

"The county says they'll order Henry Hake to take it down," Paige said. "As soon as they find him. I tried calling his office, but nobody answers."

"Somebody must be running the business in his absence," Gage said.

"Where is he?" Maya asked. "Why can't you get in touch with him?"

"No one knows where he is," Paige said. "He's been missing about a month now." She held out her hands, palms up. "He just disappeared."

"We've been looking for him," Travis said. "But if someone doesn't want to be found, it can be tough."

Paige took Maya's hand and squeezed it gently. "How are you doing?" she asked.

"I'm hanging in there." Later, when this was all over and Casey was safe, she would probably collapse, but so far, she was managing to stay strong thanks in part to all of these people—none of whom she had known before yesterday—who were helping to search for Casey.

"We're going to find her," Paige said. "You can't give up hope."

Maya nodded. Hope was the only thing keeping her upright.

"We need to warn everyone to stay away from Hake's place," Travis said.

"Why is that?" Lacy asked.

"Somebody took a shot at Maya and Gage when they were over there just now," Travis said. "As soon as I spread the word here, he and I are headed back over there to investigate."

"Be careful," Lacy said, then bit her lip, as if wishing she could take back the words, but Travis only squeezed her hand.

"I always am," he said.

"Someone shot at you?" Paige stared at Maya, open-mouthed. "Who?"

"That's what we're going to find out." Gage turned to Maya. "You'll be okay here while I'm gone? If you want to go back to town, I can find someone to take you."

"No. I want to stay here. I can't leave until we find Casey."

"And here come more recruits," Paige said, looking over Maya's shoulder.

She turned to see two men approaching. The shorter of the two was also the more muscular, with bulging biceps and a shaved head. His companion was tall and lean, with a weathered face and short blond hair.

"We closed up early and came to see what we could do to help," the blond said.

"Maya Renfro, this is Brock Ryan." Gage indicated the blond. "And Wade Tomlinson. They own Eagle Mountain Outdoors."

"We brought our climbing gear in the truck," Brock said. "Just in case."

"Speaking of climbing gear," Gage said. "Somebody stole a climbing rope from the high school last night. Any ideas who would take something like that?"

"Maybe some kid who was into climbing?" Wade answered. "Good gear is expensive—more than most high schoolers can manage without help from Mom and Dad."

"Can you think of anybody we should question?" Travis asked. "Maybe a kid who's been hanging around your shop?"

The two men exchanged looks. "I can't think of anyone," Wade said.

"Me, neither," Brock agreed.

"Go talk to Tony with search and rescue," Travis said. "He's coordinating the volunteers." He turned to Maya. "I think you should stay here in camp, so people know where to find you if they have any sightings. Casey is probably afraid, and she might not readily come to anyone but you."

She nodded. "Of course I'll stay. I—"

"What's the reason for all this commotion? I've had people tramping all over my land all day and I want it stopped now!"

They all swiveled to see a big, hawk-nosed man with a striking cascade of snow-white hair past his shoulders stalking toward them. He halted in front of Travis, though he practically vibrated with rage. "These people don't have any right to come on my property. What are you going to do to stop them?"

"Hello, Ed," Travis said. "I went over to your place yesterday to talk to you, but you weren't home. Or at least, you didn't answer the door."

"Just because somebody comes to my door doesn't mean I have to talk to them," Ed said. "What are you going to do about all these people invading my privacy?"

"We're looking for a little girl." Travis took one of the flyers that had been distributed to all the volunteers from his pocket and unfolded it. "Have you seen her?"

The flyer featured a picture of Casey—the one from her birthday party that Maya had given to Gage to use. She watched the old man's face as he studied the picture. After a few seconds, he thrust the flyer at Travis. "I don't have anything to do with kids," he said.

"Except that young woman in the park in Pennsylvania," Travis said.

Ed's face flushed a dark red. "That was fifteen years ago. I leave everybody alone and I ask that they do the same for me."

"So you didn't see a young couple—this little girl's parents—over here next to your property and wonder what they were up to?" Gage asked.

Ed glanced around at the crowd. Everyone within earshot had stopped to listen to the exchange. "I saw some people over there," he said. "But I didn't talk to them. I keep to my property and they kept to theirs."

"Did you see anyone else over here?" Travis asked. "Any strangers? Or did you hear anything? Any shouting or gunfire?"

"No."

"Would you have called us if you had?" Gage asked.

Ed just scowled at them.

"Do you own a gun?" Travis asked.

"A man has a right to protect himself."

"We're going to want to search your place," Travis said. "The one in town and the one up here."

"You can't do that without a warrant."

"Then we'll get one."

"You have no right! I'll—"

But a shout and the sound of running feet interrupted him. A young man and woman raced up, breathless. "We found this," the man said, and held up a small pink sock.

Maya swayed, fighting dizziness, her gaze fixed on the bright pink sock—so tiny in the man's hand. A strong arm came around her shoulders, and she looked up into Gage's concerned face. "Do you recognize it?" he asked.

"I… I don't know. I mean, it's so small. But Casey loves pink. She always wears it."

"Where did you find it?" Travis asked.

"It was caught in some bushes, beside a creek down there." He pointed to the north. "I marked the spot with my bandanna."

Gage's hand tightened on Maya's shoulder. "That's on your land, isn't it, Ed?"

Chapter Seven

Gage's arm around Maya's shoulders was warm and strong, holding her up and silently encouraging her to hang on. "I'm all right," she said, her eyes fixed on the sock. As long as she looked at it, she didn't have to look at the old man. Had he hurt Casey? But then, why come into camp and call attention to himself this way?

"I'm going to get someone to take you back to town," Gage said. "I know the waiting is hard, but we want to do this right, get the warrant, make sure we don't overlook anything."

She nodded, and her shoulders straightened. "All right."

"We'll take her back with us," Paige said.

"We'll do our best to distract you," Lacy said.

"Is that okay with you?" Gage looked her in the eye. That steady gaze made her feel stronger—calmer.

She nodded. "Just call me as soon as you know anything."

"I promise I will."

Paige drove the three women back to the Bear's Den. "Make yourselves comfortable," she said, showing them into a sun-filled room on the top floor of the three-story house. "I'm going to open a bottle of wine."

Lacy settled on the end of the sofa, legs curled beneath

her. "One thing you should know about the Walker men," she said. "They don't give up. They'll find your niece."

Maya sat at the opposite end of the sofa. "I know they're trying," she said.

Paige joined them, a bottle of white wine in one hand, three glasses in another. She handed them each a glass and poured the wine. "What we really want to know is all about you," she said. "Who is Maya Renfro?" She sat in an armchair across from the sofa. "You're not just Casey's aunt or Angela's sister. It's too easy to put people in those little boxes."

"Paige doesn't like boxes." Lacy sipped her wine and smiled.

"I'm guessing someone with blue hair doesn't like boxes, either," Paige said.

Maya sipped the wine, buying time to think. "Maybe I just haven't found the box I fit in yet," she said. "I'm single. I'm from Denver, and I teach school."

"I'm studying to be a teacher," Lacy said. "I'm hoping to go into elementary education."

"I teach high school. Teenagers are practically a different species. Challenging, but I think that's why I like them." She fingered the blue ends of her hair. "I never would have done this if my students hadn't challenged me. I told them if they improved their test scores, I'd dye my hair. They did, so here I am. But I'm thinking of keeping it. It unsettles some people and I'm enough of a rebel I like it." She shrugged.

"What else?" Paige prompted. "Any hobbies? What do you do for fun?"

"I perform at poetry slams."

"One of the women I knew in prison did that," Lacy said. "Not slams, really—but she wrote poetry and performed it for the rest of us. She was really good."

Maya stared at the pretty brunette over the rim of her wineglass. "Prison? Did you work there?"

Lacy laughed. "No, I was in prison for three years. I was wrongfully convicted of killing my boss."

"Travis Walker got her out," Paige said. "He proved she was innocent, then found the real killer."

"I take it you and the sheriff are involved?" Maya asked.

Lacy's smile made her seem to glow from within. "We are. And believe me, I'm the last person I'd ever expect to fall for a lawman."

"The Walker brothers are both easy on the eyes," Paige observed. "And even though Gage says he's not interested in a relationship, I'll bet he would change his mind for the right woman."

Maya felt both women's eyes on her, even as she studied the contents of her glass. "He's been very kind," she said, determined not to betray the flutter in her stomach when she thought of Gage.

"They come from one of the town's founding families." Paige leaned over to tip more wine into Maya's glass. "You should see if Gage will take you to visit the Walking W Ranch some time."

"It's pretty spectacular," Lacy said. "Like something out of a Ralph Lauren ad—big log ranch house, rolling pastures right up to the base of the mountains."

"Why did they go into law enforcement instead of running the family ranch?" Maya asked.

"Oh, they're still involved with the ranch," Lacy said.

"Their dad is only in his early fifties, and he's one of those men who seem like he could still be going strong for another thirty years," Paige said.

"Travis has never come right out and said so, but he

really wants to help people," Lacy said. "It's important to him to make a difference in his hometown."

"He could make a difference in a city, too," Maya said.

"Sure he could. But this is home."

"Don't take this the wrong way," Maya said. "But I never understood that—feeling so tied to a place. I mean, isn't it kind of, well, limiting to live in the same place all your life, with the same people who know everything about you?"

"I know what you mean," Lacy said. "And I used to feel the same way—especially when I was a teenager, dying to get away." She shrugged. "But then I went away, and I couldn't wait to get back. There's something special about this place. It kind of gets under your skin."

"But you're from here," Maya said. "I've never lived anywhere but the city."

"That was me, before I came here," Paige said. "I always thought a small place would limit me, but it's the opposite. I've really grown here and been able to try new things. In the city, there is always someone who has done what you're thinking about doing and they've done it better. That can be inspiring, but it can also be paralyzing. Here, if you want to do something, you may be the first to try it—like starting an environmental group, which is what I did."

"Or a poetry slam." Lacy nudged Maya with her toe. "We don't have that here."

"I'm not sure Eagle Mountain is ready for poetry slams," Maya said. She didn't bother to point out that she wouldn't be staying in town long enough to get involved in anything. As soon as Casey was safe, Maya would need to take her back home. They would need time to heal in the place that was familiar to them both.

"How long do you think it will take them to get the

warrant to search that man's place?" she asked, unable to tear her thoughts away from that topic for long.

"I don't know," Lacy said. "Probably not long. The judges know Travis and he has a good reputation. They trust his judgment, and he wouldn't ask for the warrant without proof."

"I had no idea old Ed had a record," Paige said. "I just thought he was a grouchy old hermit—another town character."

"Maybe that's all he is," Lacy said. "He may not have anything to do with any of this."

"If he does, Travis and Gage will find out," Paige said.

Lacy set her empty wineglass on a side table. "I wish there was more we could do to help," she said.

"You're doing a lot," Maya said. "Being with me like this now—it helps so much." It struck her that back home, she didn't have friends like this. She was on good terms with the other teachers she worked with, but for so many years, Angela had been her best friend. Paige and Lacy couldn't replace her sister, but being with them helped her feel less alone.

As soon as Maya was safely away, Gage rejoined Travis, who was just ending a phone call. "I've got the request for the warrant started," he said. "While we wait, we can go back to Hake's place and have a better look around."

They rode together, in Travis's vehicle. "Do you really think Ed had anything to do with the Hoods' deaths?" Gage asked as Travis drove.

"He never struck me as the particularly violent type, but who knows? Maybe he thought Greg Hood was a threat to his own mining operation. Or maybe he's a sicko who wanted the little girl."

"Yeah." You didn't have to be in law enforcement for

very long, or in a big city, to learn that people did horrible things to each other all the time—even people you would never suspect.

When they reached the fence that marked the boundary of Henry Hake's land, Travis parked at the road and he and Gage walked into the development, past the fading sign announcing the resort, with its rendering of soaring log chalets and cobblestone drives set amidst golf greens, swimming pools and stables. The picture bore little resemblance to the crumbling concrete and weeds around them. "Where were you when the shots were fired?" Travis asked.

"Over here." Gage led the way to the cinder block building. Travis tried the door, which was still padlocked. "The shots came from over there." Gage indicated the slope that rose up from the building. "That little bunch of trees in there."

The two brothers walked up the slope, and Travis knelt to study the rocky ground beneath the scrub oaks. Then he examined the faint tire tracks Gage pointed out. "We'll take a casting, but I'm not holding out hope we'll find anything," Travis said. He looked around the empty landscape. "Whoever this is, they know how to clean up after themselves, not leave any trace." He stood. "I want to take a look around at the rest of the place."

The afternoon sun beat down on what was left of the streets, and a breeze that carried a hint of a chill fluttered the flags on the wooden stakes that marked lot lines and building sites that had long been abandoned. "This place gives me the creeps on a normal day," Gage said as he and Travis walked past rusting rebar jutting up from half-finished foundations. "But this afternoon, even before the shots were fired, it felt like someone was watching us. Maya felt it, too."

"I don't sense that now," Travis said.

"No. I think whoever was here earlier is long gone."

"I need to take a look at the official plat of this place and see if these air vents are on there," Travis said, as he and Gage drew alongside the arching metal structures.

"That's a good idea," Gage said. "I don't hear any fans or machinery or anything."

They walked around the side of the structure, down a steep slope and around to the back. Travis walked slowly, studying the ground, then pushed aside the arching branches of a stunted juniper to reveal a metal door. Unlike the other structures around them, the door looked new, the dark green paint—the same shade as the juniper branches—bright and fresh.

Travis tried the door. It didn't budge. He straightened and let the branch fall back into place. "Without a warrant, we can't get in."

Gage scratched his ear. "If we said we heard something, and we thought Casey might be trapped in there..."

Travis sent him a look. The *don't be an idiot, little brother* look that Gage had known all his life. Then he led the way back up the incline, to the mouth of the air vents. He cupped his hands around his mouth and shouted down one of the tubes. "Hello! Casey, are you in there?"

Gage held his breath, straining to make out any noise coming from the vents, but the only sound was the wind flapping the plastic flags on a row of survey stakes. "She can't hear us," he said, remembering.

"I know," Travis said. "But I was hoping maybe vibrations..." He let the words trail off and the two walked on, to the highest point of the property, overlooking Dakota Ridge and the valley below. Gage squinted against a glare from something downslope that was reflecting light back into his eyes. "What's that down there?" he asked, pointing toward the brightness. He squinted more, focusing in, gaze traveling from the starburst of glare along a dark shadow, and something smooth like glass. Honed in and fully alert, he touched Travis's arm. "Is that a car down there?"

Travis stared also. "Maybe. Let me get my binoculars from the cruiser."

While Gage waited for Travis to return, he studied the slope above what he was now sure was a car. The terrain was mostly bare rock, though maybe that was a broken branch there and a dislodged boulder a little farther up—evidence that the vehicle had careened down that slope before coming to rest in a knot of trees. There was an old mining road up there, used now by hikers and a few of the more daredevil four-wheelers. He couldn't imagine who would be fool enough to drive a full-sized automobile up there.

Travis returned at a trot, panting a little as he stopped and lifted the binoculars to his eyes. "It's a car," he said. "Or rather, some kind of SUV. Black. I can't see anyone in it, but we'll have EMS on standby just in case."

"Can you read the plate?" Gage asked.

Travis's boot scraped on rock as he shifted his weight. "Yeah. And I know that number." He lowered the binoculars, a frown deepening the *V* between his eyebrows. "That car is registered to Henry Hake. We may have finally found him after all."

Chapter Eight

By the time Gage and Travis made it back to the camp, Deputy Dwight Prentice had arrived with the warrant to search Ed Roberts's property. "Call Gracy's Wreckers in Junction and tell them we've got a vehicle we need to bring up out of the canyon below Dakota Ridge," Travis told Dwight as he accepted the warrant paperwork. "And we'll need to send search and rescue over there to see if there's anyone in the vehicle."

"Off Dakota Ridge?" Dwight frowned. "Where? Who drove off there?"

"Gage and I saw the vehicle from over at Henry Hake's place," Travis said. "It's an SUV with tags registered to Hake."

"He's been missing almost a month now," Dwight said. "If he's in that vehicle, he isn't alive."

"We're not sure he's in there," Gage said. "But we have to check."

"If there's nobody alive in the wreck, we can wait until morning to retrieve it," Gage said. "But we need to find out. I want you to go over there with the search and rescue crew."

"Will do," Dwight said.

Travis was reviewing the paperwork when Lorna Munroe approached, the bloodhound, Daisy, straining at the leash. "I wanted to let you know we found a match for that little girl's sock the searchers found earlier," Lorna said. "I gave the second sock to Daisy and she followed the scent for half a mile or so along the creek before she lost it. So many people have tramped through these hills recently looking for that child that I think it's getting tough to pick out one trail from all the others."

Gage bent to scratch behind one of Daisy's long ears and she rolled her eyes up at him in a mournful look.

"We appreciate you trying," Travis said. He folded the papers and tucked them into his shirt pocket. "Come on, Gage," he said. "We'd better get going."

The brothers didn't speak on the short drive to Ed Roberts's place. Ed met them in front of what could only generously be termed a shack. The tin-roofed building was the size of a backyard storage shed, constructed of scrap lumber salvaged from old mining structures, with a single window and a door that had started as a green slab of wood and warped as it dried so that it no longer closed all the way. "We got the warrant," Travis said, and handed Ed the papers.

Ed adjusted a pair of wire-framed glasses on his nose and studied the documents. Gage had been prepared to have to argue with the old man—maybe even physically restrain him. But Ed only took off the glasses and said. "You'd better come in and get it over with."

Inside, the floor of the one-room building sloped toward the back, and the small space was crammed with an old leather recliner patched with tape, a wooden trunk that doubled as a table, a battery-operated camping lantern and packing boxes full of books, mining equipment and ore specimens. "You can look all you want," Ed said. "There's no place to hide anything here."

Gage met his brother's eyes. Ed was right—with all

three of them inside, there was hardly enough room in the shack to turn around.

Travis peered into a box of books. From where Gage stood by the door, most of the titles appeared to have to do with mining or history. "Did you have any arguments with Greg Hood?" he asked.

"Who?" Ed asked.

"He's the father of the little girl who's missing," Travis said. "He and his wife own the property to the south of your place. Somebody shot them and killed them."

Ed blinked. "Was he a young man, sandy hair and expensive clothes?"

"That would be a pretty good description," Travis said. "Did you and he argue?"

"No! I talked to the man exactly once. I met up with him when I was walking my property line. Just him. We got to talking. He went on about some invention he had that was going to make all these old mines profitable again."

"So you lied earlier, when you told us you didn't have anything to do with Greg Hood," Gage said.

"We exchanged a few words, that's all. They minded their business and I minded mine."

"So the two of you didn't disagree about anything?" Gage asked. "Maybe you thought his invention was going to cut into your own profits from your mine?"

"I didn't take him seriously," Ed said. "I've met plenty of folks in my time who think they're going to buy a claim and get rich. Then they find out what hard work mining really is, and how tough it is to make it pay off, and they give up and go home. I figured this guy would be the same."

"So the two of you had a nice, pleasant conversation," Travis said.

Ed glared. "I told him the last thing I wanted was a bunch of folks with dollar signs in their eyes traipsing around up here."

"What did he say to that?" Gage asked.

"He laughed. He thought I was colorful. A character."

"That didn't make you angry, when he laughed?" Travis asked.

"I told you, he didn't matter one whit to me. I've seen his kind before. Big thinkers—not such big doers. If he wanted to play around out here with his invention, it wasn't any skin off my nose—as long as he stayed off my property."

"Did he?" Travis asked.

"As far as I know, he did."

"When was this, that you saw him?" Gage asked.

Ed considered the question. "Day before yesterday, in the afternoon."

"What about Henry Hake?" Travis asked. "Did you ever run into him?"

"He's that developer who wanted to put in that big fancy resort, right?" Ed asked.

"Yes," Travis said. "Did you ever have any conversations with him?"

"Never met the man. Never cared to. I saw him on television a couple of times, talking up the place, and I drove over there one day to look around. They had built a big fence around the land, and had No Trespassing signs every few feet. I thought they were crazy if they thought they would ever get rich people to pay a fortune to live up here. Even I don't come up here after the snow starts. The only way in is on skis or snowshoes or on a snow machine. And the first time an avalanche comes down on one of those fancy homes he wanted to build, he'd lose his shirt in the lawsuits that would follow."

"So you haven't been over to look at the property recently?" Travis asked.

"I drive by it all the time," Ed said. "It's an eyesore now. The county ought to make them clean it up. They cut down all those trees and poured all that concrete and now it's all sitting there, a blight on the land."

"So you haven't been over there, just to look around?" Gage asked.

"I already told you, no. Those places attract the wrong kind of people."

"Who is that?" Gage asked.

"The folks who want to build the fancy houses and the environmentalists who protest against them. I got no use for any of them."

"You don't have much use for most people," Gage said.

Ed lifted his chin. "That's right. But I didn't kill anybody, and I didn't hurt that little girl."

"We're going to take a look outside now," Travis said.

Ed followed them outside. "You want to look in my outhouse?" he asked. "Go ahead."

"Gage will take care of that," Travis said.

Gage sent his brother a look that told Travis payback was in his future. But the outhouse—a portable toilet rented from a local company—wasn't as bad as Gage might have feared, and it was definitely empty.

Next, they visited the mine adit, a timber-framed hut extending from the side of the hill. "It's a hundred feet to the main shaft," Ed said. "There aren't any lights, so if you're going to look around, I hope you brought your own illumination."

Travis unclipped a heavy-duty flashlight from his belt. "We'll be fine."

He led the way into the tunnel, Gage reluctantly following. Ed remained outside. "Let's hope the old man doesn't decide to wall us up in here," Gage grumbled.

"What made you think of that?" Travis asked.

"Just my dark imagination."

The tunnel sloped upward, rock pressing in on all sides. Before they had gone more than half the distance, they both had to hunch over to avoid scraping against the ceiling. Water ran down the center of the tunnel, making footing slippery. "I hope we don't run into any bats," Gage said. "I hear bats like these old mine tunnels."

"Shut up," Travis said, and played his light over the walls and ceiling, the light glinting on bright flecks in the gray granite.

"Is that gold?" Gage asked.

"Probably pyrite or quartz," Travis said. "Fool's gold."

Eventually, they reached the first shaft—a round hole at their feet scarcely wide enough to accommodate a man. Travis shone the light on a wooden ladder fastened to the wall of the shaft. "I think I should wait up here while you check this out," Gage said, eyeing the narrow opening. "If something goes wrong with you, I can run for help."

Travis glared at him, but pocketed his flashlight and knelt beside the shaft. "Light my way down," he said.

Gage knelt beside the shaft and shone the light into the opening. Travis climbed down, the soles of his boots ringing hollow against the wooden rungs of the ladder. Within a few minutes, he landed at the bottom of the shaft. Less than a minute later, he started back up. "There's nothing down there," he said.

Gage reached down to give him a hand up. "I'm sure Ed got a charge out of knowing that."

Travis wiped his hands on his pants. "We had to look, but I don't think that little girl is here."

The two trudged back to the cruiser. Ed was nowhere in sight, but that was fine with Gage, who had no desire to speak with the grouchy old man. He climbed into the cruiser and stared out at the lengthening shadows. "I don't like the thought of that little kid out here another night," he said.

"No." Travis started the engine. "And the longer she's missing, the lower the odds we'll find her okay."

"Maya wants to spend the night out here, in case Casey shows up. I think I should stay with her."

"All right." He turned onto the road. "Though I don't think she's going to fall for your charms as easily as some of the local women."

Gage scowled at him. "I'm not trying to charm anyone here. Maya is a nice person in a horrible situation."

"But as you have said so often before, you like women. And for some reason I can't fathom, they like you. Don't complicate an already complicated situation."

"I'm not trying to complicate anything." And he wasn't setting out to seduce Maya. Yes, he had dated a number of women in town, and maybe that had given him a certain reputation. But it wasn't a bad reputation—all the women he had dated knew he would show them a good time and keep things fun. They all enjoyed themselves and nobody got hurt.

He didn't see Maya the same way. There was nothing fun about what she was going through. He just wanted to be there to help if she needed it. He stared at the blur of scenery rolling past. "Maya is only going to be in town a little while," he said. "I'll do what I can to make that time easier on her."

And if he had regrets when it came time to say goodbye, no one had to know that except himself.

THE THREE WOMEN were starting on a second bottle of wine when the wail of a siren cut off their conversation. Maya didn't pay much attention—she was used to hearing sirens at all hours of the day and night, but apparently the sound was cause for alarm here in Eagle Mountain. "That sounds like an ambulance," Paige said, setting aside the wine.

She moved to the front window and Lacy followed. "It is an ambulance," Lacy said. "Do you think it's an accident? Or maybe someone had a heart attack?"

"Maybe."

The other two women were so concerned, Maya began to be nervous also. "Do you think they found Casey?" She stood on shaky legs. "Why didn't someone contact me? If she's hurt—"

"We don't know that yet." Paige hurried over to put her arm around Maya, even as she pulled her phone from her pocket and punched in a number. "Hello, Adelaide? This is Paige Riddell. We just heard the ambulance and wondered if you know where it's going?"

She listened for a moment, then said, "Wait a minute. I'm going to put you on speaker so Lacy and Maya can hear. They're with me. Would you mind repeating that?"

Adelaide's voice was loud and clear on the phone's speaker. "I said, Travis and Gage found Henry Hake's car in the ravine below Dakota Ridge."

"Was Henry Hake in the car?" Lacy asked.

"They don't know," Adelaide said. "They've got search and rescue out there trying to figure that out—the ambulance is headed out there on standby. Though if poor Henry's been in that car as long as he's been missing, he's past any help the EMTs can give him."

Maya sank onto the sofa once more, too shaky to

stand. "We thought maybe they had found little Casey," Paige said.

"Not yet," Adelaide said. "Travis did say there was no sign of her out at Ed's place."

"Thanks, Adelaide," Paige said. "You'll let us know if you hear anything?"

"You'll probably hear from Travis or Gage before I do."

Paige ended the call and sat next to Maya. "I'm sorry it wasn't better news," she said.

Maya nodded. She was fighting hard to keep it together and not break down. She had to hold on to the hope that Casey was alive and okay, but the more time dragged on, the tougher that was to do.

The doorbell rang. Paige patted Maya's shoulder and stood. "I have to get that."

"Of course."

She left and Maya listened to her footsteps retreating down the stairs. "Would you like more wine?" Lacy asked.

Maya shook her head. "I think I've had enough." She didn't think she could drink enough to forget for one second about her lost niece or her dead sister, so why bother trying?

Then a man's voice drifted upstairs, and every nerve in her body leaped to attention. She stood and walked toward the door to the hallway, even as the man's footsteps started up the steps. "Hello, Maya," Gage said.

She studied his face, trying to read the emotion there—was he coming to bring bad news, good news or no news at all?

"We don't have any word about Casey yet. I'm sorry," he said. "But we didn't find any sign of her at Ed Roberts's place. We checked his apartment in town, too, but I really don't think she's been there."

"Thanks for letting me know." She marveled at how calm the words sounded, even as her stomach churned.

"Do you still want to go out to the camp tonight?" he asked.

"Yes."

"Then I'll take you," he said.

"You don't have to do that," she said. "I know where it is now. And I'm sure you have work to do. I'm not your full-time job."

"The sheriff wants an officer out there overnight, so I volunteered," he said.

"All right. I'll just pack a few things."

When she left, Paige and Lacy were questioning him about Henry Hake's car. In her room, Maya stuffed a backpack with a fleece pullover, hat and gloves, and another pullover that would be way too large for Casey, but would keep the girl warm if she was cold. She looked around the room but could think of nothing else useful to bring, so she hurried back upstairs. Gage met her in the hall. He didn't say anything until they were in his SUV.

"If you want to see your sister and her husband, the coroner has the bodies ready for viewing," he said quietly.

The meaning behind his words hit her like a bucket of ice water. She had kept all her energy focused on Casey, not allowing herself to think about Angela and Greg, and the fact that they had been murdered.

Gage must have read the emotions on her face. "I know it's a lot to ask," he said. "But we need you to confirm the identification."

She clenched her hands, nails biting into her palms. "I won't believe they're gone until I see." Even then, she wasn't sure the reality would ever sink in. Angela and

Greg were so young. They weren't supposed to die. Not this way.

"I'll let him know we're on our way."

He made the call while she sat, numb, staring out the windows but not seeing anything. Gage touched her arm. "You need to fasten your seat belt," he said.

"Oh, sure."

He drove across town, to a white Georgian building with columns across the front and a circular drive. A low sign by the drive read McCasklin's Funeral Home. Gage drove around to the back and led the way to a side door, which was opened by a middle-aged man in a dark suit. "I'm Ronald McCasklin," he said, offering his hand. "I know this is a difficult time for you, Ms. Renfro. Please let me know if there's anything I can do to help."

Given his profession, he had probably said words similar to this many times before, but they struck Maya as sincere. "Thank you," she whispered.

"They're in viewing room one," McCasklin said to Gage.

"This way." Gage put a hand on her back and guided her down the hallway, their footsteps silent on the thick burgundy carpet.

"I thought we'd be going to a hospital or a morgue," she said, keeping her voice soft.

"We don't have either of those here," Gage said. "When the coroner needs facilities for an autopsy, he uses this place." He opened the door with the gold numeral one affixed to its center. The overhead light cast a soft golden glow over the figures lying side by side on rolling steel tables, sheets pulled up to their chins, as if they had merely stretched out for a nap.

But no one napping would be this pale or this still. Maya stopped halfway across the room, rooted in place by the sight of her sister and brother-in-law's cold, impassive faces. Whoever had worked to make them presentable had combed their hair over the worst of their injuries, but couldn't completely hide the wound over Angela's forehead. Maya put a hand over her mouth, trying—and failing—to stifle a sob.

Gage turned her into his chest and she surrendered to that calm strength. He held her while she sobbed, not saying anything—not trying to quiet her or uttering any of the awful empty platitudes people turned to in such times. He simply stood there and held her, and let her soak his uniform shirt with her tears.

Chapter Nine

Maya didn't know how long she cried, but after a while she managed to stem the tide of tears. Gage stuffed a handkerchief into her hand—not a paper tissue, but a white cotton handkerchief that smelled of starch. "Are you ready to leave?" he asked.

She nodded. "Yes." She had seen more than enough. The people lying on those tables bore a resemblance to Angela and Greg, but they weren't them. The personalities who had given life to those waxen shells were gone from this place. That was the loss she was mourning, the deaths she might never come to terms with.

Ronald met them at the door and silently pressed a plastic cup of water into Maya's hand. She nodded her thanks and let Gage lead her to the SUV. He helped her into the passenger seat and buckled her seat belt, as if she were a little child.

He said nothing, and she appreciated the silence. After a while, some of the shock began to recede. She sipped the water and stared out at the houses they drove past. "Where are we going?" she asked after a while.

"Nowhere in particular," he said. "Just driving. Checking on the town. It's part of the job to keep an eye on things."

"So you're looking for crime?" She studied a bungalow they passed, the front yard filled with blooming flowers. "Is there a lot of that here?"

"Not really. But I'm not really looking for crime. Or not only looking for crime. I'm looking for signs of anyone in trouble. It might be a kid out after dark by himself, or a man who's locked himself out of his car. It might be papers or mail piling up at a house where I know an elderly person lives alone."

She shifted toward him. "It's like you're watching over the whole town."

"I guess you could think of it like that."

She drank the rest of the water and set the empty cup on the floorboard. "Seeing Angela and Greg that way—it was so horrible, and yet, I think I had to do it. To accept that they're really gone."

"If you hadn't done it, would you regret it?" Gage asked.

"Probably, yes."

"Then you probably made the right decision."

"Maybe. Do you have any idea who killed them?"

"Not yet. We've got someone going through the items in the tent and their SUV, hoping for a clue. And we have their phones and are looking at those records."

"What are you looking for?"

"Someone they might have talked to or arranged to meet. Anyone they might have had an argument with."

"You don't think it was an accident—a hunter's stray bullets or something like that?"

"No. Whoever killed them did so deliberately." He glanced at her. "I'm sorry. That's hard to hear."

Yes, it was. But she would rather know the truth than try to soothe herself with lies. "I can't imagine what either of them could have done to upset anyone," she said. "They both had so many friends in Denver. And they were so happy." She bit her lip, dangerously close to another flood of tears.

Gage swung the SUV back onto the town's main street. "I thought maybe we'd get some food to go and take it up to the camp," he said.

"All right." She didn't feel like eating, but he was probably hungry. He had been working most of the past two days. "You must be exhausted," she said.

"It hasn't caught up to me yet, but it will. Then I'll sleep twelve hours and be good to go again. It's like this when something big is going down."

He stopped by a café and she waited in the cruiser while he went inside. She pulled out her phone and pretended to focus on it, aware of curious eyes on her as people walked by on the sidewalk or came to the doors of adjacent businesses. Maybe some of those people felt sympathy for her, or maybe they were only curious about the woman with blue hair who was riding with the deputy, wondering if she was his latest conquest.

Gage returned to the cruiser, a large brown sack in his hand, which he stowed in the back seat. "Anything else you need before we head out of town?" he asked.

"I don't think so."

As he drove toward the highway, she angled toward him, searching for anything to distract her from her grief and worry. "Paige told me you have a reputation as the town Casanova," she said.

He glanced at her, then shifted his gaze back to the road. "Don't believe everything you hear."

"But you have dated a lot of women."

"I'm friends with a lot of women. We go out and have a good time. I don't go around being a jerk and breaking hearts."

"Okay." What had Paige said… *Gage says he's not interested in a relationship.*

"So what is it—you just don't want to be tied down, or you're afraid of getting hurt, or what?" she asked.

"You think a guy needs a reason to be single? That if he is, it means he's hurt or damaged or something?" No mistaking the annoyance in his voice.

"No. I was just curious." And it was interesting that he got so defensive.

"What about you?" he asked. "Are you seriously dating anyone?"

"No." She wasn't dating anyone at all.

"So are you afraid or hurt or something?"

"Or something." She faced forward once more.

"I'm all ears," he said.

She sighed. She had asked for this, hadn't she? And what difference did it make if she shared her sorry dating history with Gage? In another day or two, she would probably be leaving town and would never see him again. "I dated a guy for three years," she said. "About the time I was expecting him to pop the question, he told me he wanted to break up. And yeah, it hurt. And maybe it made me a little gun-shy. So I'm not blaming you for not wanting to get serious with anyone—I was just curious."

He didn't say anything, his hands rubbing up and down the steering wheel as if he were debating between polishing it and ripping it off the steering column. "I dated a woman right after I started with the department," he said. "I wasn't thinking about marrying her or anything like that, but I was really into her. She told me she didn't see a future with a law enforcement officer—the job is too hard on long-term relationships. I decided she was right."

"Just like that, you let one woman decide your future?"

She half expected a growl to accompany the glare he sent her way. "You let one guy who dumped you decided *your* future."

Touché. "Isn't that great?" she said. "We have something in common."

A heavy silence stretched between them as the road wound up above town. It narrowed and the growth of trees became thicker, the houses fewer.

"Being a deputy in a rural county like this isn't as dangerous as being a cop in the inner city, maybe," he said. "But there are risks. I know my mother worries every day about Travis and me. Lacy worries about Travis. I don't see any reason to put that burden on anyone else."

"The right woman wouldn't see it as a burden."

"Then I guess I haven't found the right woman."

He pulled onto the shoulder in front of Angela and Greg's property. A Rayford County Sheriff's Department cruiser sat in the space where their SUV had once been parked. Maya supposed the vehicle was at some sheriff's department facility now, being examined for evidence.

A tall, rangy deputy walked out to meet them. "Maya Renfro, this is Deputy Dwight Prentice," Gage introduced him.

Dwight shook her hand. "I'm sorry I don't have any new information about your niece," he said. He turned to Gage. "Search and rescue confirmed there's nobody in that car, so the wrecker will be out tomorrow midmorning to haul it out."

Maya left the two men discussing this and moved to the fire ring, where a few coals still smoldered. Angela and Greg's tent sat to the side. Maya glanced in the door, then looked away. Empty of the clothing and sleeping bags and other things that had belonged to her sister and Greg, the tent was just another object cluttering up the landscape.

Gage joined her, carrying two camp chairs and the brown paper sack. He handed her the sack and set up the chairs, then began adding wood to the fire. "When the sun goes down up here, it gets pretty cool," he said. "We'll be glad of the fire."

Casey would be cold, she thought. Maybe she would see the fire and come to them.

She sat in one of the chairs and Gage took the other and began unpacking their dinner. He passed her a barbecue sandwich. "Try to eat something," he said. "There's chocolate pie for dessert."

Maya started to cry. The burst of tears shocked her—she had thought she had pulled herself together. But his mention of the pie undid her.

Gage set aside the food and took her hand. "What is it?" he asked.

"Chocolate pie," she sobbed. "It was Angela's favorite."

"I'm sorry," he said. "I didn't mean to upset you."

"It's not your fault." She grabbed a paper napkin and blotted her eyes. "How could you know? And I've got to learn to cope with this. I can't fall apart every time something reminds me of her."

Gage released her hand and sat back once more. "That will take time."

She nodded and picked up the sandwich. "I'll be fine. I promise I'm not going to do this all night."

"Would it help to talk about her?" he asked. "Tell me a good memory you have."

She had so many memories of Angela—she searched for one that would give him a good picture of their relationship. "When we were in middle school, she had most of our classmates convinced that she and I were twins—our story was that she was smarter, so she had managed to skip a grade, which explained why she was ahead of me in school."

"Sounds like she was pretty persuasive."

"I thought being twins would be cool, but I was annoyed that she insisted she was smarter—even though it was probably true."

"When Travis and I were in middle school, *he* told everyone that I wasn't his real brother—that our parents adopted me when the circus came to town," Gage said.

"That wasn't very nice."

"When my mother found out, she grounded him and made him spend the first month of summer vacation scraping and painting one of our barns. By the second week, we both complained so much she made me go out and help him." He tossed another branch on the campfire. "I guess in the end, it made us closer."

"I was always grateful to have a sister who could be my friend, too," she said. She had been lucky, even if her luck had run out too soon. She wrapped her half-eaten sandwich in a napkin and set it aside. "I think I'll have some of that pie now."

The pie was excellent—densely chocolate and smooth as silk, whipped cream mounding the top. "Angela would have loved that," she said when she was done, her voice only a little shaky.

Gage leaned forward and wiped a smear of chocolate from her mouth. Such a simple gesture, yet it struck Maya as one of the sexiest things anyone had ever done for her. Was there something wrong with her, that she could feel aroused at a time like this? Or was it only a testament to how much life fought to win out over death every time? Was this just a way for her body to remind her that for all the bad things going on right now, she had to hold on to the promise of good in the future?

Their eyes met and she realized Gage was feeling it, too. She leaned closer and put her hand on his shoulders and kissed him. A gentle brush of her lips, then a harder caress, then a fierce, openmouthed kiss. A thrill raced through her and she leaned in to it, exulting in this feeling that somehow cut through the smothering blanket of grief.

He returned the kiss with a fierceness that matched her own, his hand gripping her shoulder as if to steady them both.

He pulled away first. "Whoa," he said, his voice a little hoarse.

"Yeah, whoa." She looked away, her cheeks warm, wondering what had come over her.

He leaned over to poke the fire, she suspected to give them both time to recover. But then he froze. "Did you hear that?" he whispered.

"Hear what?" She couldn't hear anything over the pounding of her heart.

He held up one hand, head cocked, staring into the darkness past the fire.

Then she heard it. A small, thin wail.

She was on her feet and racing toward the sound before she even realized what she was doing. Gage pounded after her, the beam of his flashlight cutting a path through the darkness ahead of them.

And then they saw her—the tiny, stumbling figure. Casey wailed and held out her arms. Maya scooped her up, then sank to her knees, her tears mingling with those of her niece as they clung together.

Chapter Ten

It seemed to Gage as if half the town was waiting in front of the sheriff's office when he pulled up with Maya and Casey. As soon as he had found a good cell signal, he had phoned Travis to give him the news and asked him to have the EMTs meet them. Though Casey appeared to be in good shape, considering she had spent the last forty-eight hours wandering around in the woods, he thought it would be a good idea to have her checked out, just to be sure.

The EMTs—or possibly Adelaide—must have spread the word, because despite it being after nine o'clock on a weeknight, cars crowded the street for three blocks on either side of the station, and a broadcast van from a Junction television news program was set up in the middle of the street.

"How are we going to get Casey through all those people?" Maya asked from the back seat, where she held the little girl on her lap. At camp, Casey had accepted some water and a few bites of pie, but had refused anything else and had clung fiercely to Maya, spending most of the ride to town with her face buried in Maya's shoulder. Sometime soon, Gage would have to interview her about what had happened to her parents, but that could wait.

"They'll let us through," he said. "The EMTs will meet

us inside." He flipped on his lights and eased around the TV van, aware of a cameraman filming their arrival. He parked as close to the front door as he could. When he stepped out of the SUV, a cheer rose from the crowd. He opened the passenger door, and leaned in to help Maya and Casey out.

But when he reached in to take Casey, the little girl shrank back and shook her head. "No," she signed—a communication that was clear even to Gage.

"It's okay, honey." Maya spoke as she signed to the child. "Gage is our friend. He's just going to hold you for a little bit while I get out of the car."

Casey turned her head to look at him. The courage shining behind her fear gave rise to a fierce protectiveness in him. Some person or persons had destroyed her world with a couple of bullets, but Gage would do everything in his power to see that she wasn't hurt again.

Maya had said her niece was learning to read lips, so he looked directly at her and tried to enunciate carefully. "Will you let me hold you for just a bit while your Aunt Maya gets out of the car?" he asked. "Or you could stand here beside me?"

Casey's gaze shifted to the people who were crowding around the SUV, including the cameraman who had moved in close. "Back off and give her some room," Gage growled.

The cameraman and the others moved back, and Gage returned his attention to Casey. "Go to Gage," Maya urged. "I'll be right here."

Casey nodded, took her arms from around Maya's neck and reached out to Gage. He picked her up and held her with as much tenderness as he could muster, as if she was made of spun sugar.

Maya climbed out of the cruiser and the reporter

stepped forward, but Gage blocked him. "How did you find her?" the reporter asked.

"She came to her aunt," Gage said, as Maya took Casey once more. He put an arm around her and escorted her into the station, ignoring the reporter's follow-up questions. There would be time enough later to share the story with the rest of the world. Now, he had to take care of the child and her aunt.

Inside the station, most of the force and Adelaide waited to greet them. "We're all really happy to see you, Casey," Travis said, speaking carefully to the little girl. "How are you feeling?"

In answer, Casey buried her head in Maya's shoulder once more. "I think she's a little overwhelmed," Maya said.

"And who wouldn't be?" Adelaide stepped forward. "Let's get you both into the conference room, where it's quieter. The EMTs can check her out there. Do you think she'd like something to eat? I can make her a peanut butter sandwich with the crusts cut off. My grandchildren always liked that."

"That would be great," Maya said. She let Adelaide usher her toward the conference room, trailed by two EMTs. Gage started to follow, but Travis put a hand on his shoulder. "Tell me what happened," he said. "Then you'll need to make a statement for the press."

"We were sitting by the fire at the camp and she came out of the woods toward us, crying for Maya," Gage said. No point mentioning that seconds before, he and Maya had been kissing like reunited lovers. Even the memory of that kiss scorched him, the heat so intense and unexpected. All that talk on the drive from town about his plan to avoid getting too deeply involved with anyone, and one kiss from her had pulled him under like a riptide.

"Did she say anything about what happened to her parents?"

Travis's question pulled Gage away from his memory of that moment by the fire, back to the present. "No. She hasn't said much of anything at all," he answered.

"We need to find out what she knows," Travis said.

Gage looked toward the conference room. The door was open and he could see Casey sitting in one of the chairs, half a sandwich in one hand, a child-sized blood pressure cuff around her other arm. Maya sat to one side, her profile to the door. "Should we have a counselor or someone with us when we question her?" he asked. "If she did see her parents get shot, I don't want to traumatize her more."

Travis nodded. "Good idea. I'll contact the victim advocate program in the morning and ask them to send someone over. I'm sure they have advocates who specialize in working with children." He glanced toward the conference room. "We won't push for anything until then, but if Casey volunteers any information, we'll make note of it."

"If she wants to talk, we'll listen," Gage agreed.

The brothers went into the conference room and found the EMTs packing up their gear. "How is she?" Gage asked.

"A few bug bites and some bruises," the female EMT, Merrily Anderson, said. "She told us she drank creek water, which kept her hydrated, but it also means she was probably exposed to giardia. If any symptoms show up, she'll need to see her pediatrician. Other than that, as soon as she has a good night's sleep and a couple of good meals in her, she should be fine."

Casey laid aside the half-eaten sandwich and signed something.

"She says she lost her socks," Maya translated. She signed to the girl, speaking for the benefit of the others in the room. "We found them. We wondered why they weren't on your feet."

The girl's fingers moved rapidly in answer. "She says they got muddy, so she took them off to wash in the creek," Maya said. "She hung them on a bush to dry. Then she forgot which bush."

"Did she stay near the camp the whole time?" Gage asked. "Did she see the people looking for her?"

Maya passed on the questions and waited for the girl's answer. "She says she was afraid to go with them. And then she walked away and didn't see them anymore. When she came back, she saw me and you sitting by the fire."

"I'm so glad you saw me," Maya said as she signed, tears sliding down her cheeks. "So glad."

"Has she mentioned anything about what happened to her parents?" Travis asked.

"No." Maya gave the girl a look filled with worry. Casey had gone back to eating her sandwich. "Do you want me to ask her? I'm afraid it will upset her."

"You don't have to ask her now," Travis said. "But we'll need to know what she knows to help us find the killers."

"I know," Maya said. "I just hate to put her through that. She's been through so much already."

"We're going to bring in a victim advocate who specializes in working with children," Gage said. "She'll help us get the information we need with as little trauma as possible."

"That would definitely help." Maya stifled a yawn. "Right now, I think we're all exhausted."

"Let me take you back to the Bear's Den," Gage said. "You and Casey can both get a good night's sleep."

She glanced toward the door. "I really don't want to face that crowd again."

"I'll talk to them." Travis dug his keys from his pocket. "My Toyota is parked out back," he said, handing the keys to Gage. "Go out that way."

No one had thought to stake out the back entrance to the station, so Gage, Maya and Casey were able to leave quickly and quietly. By the time they reached the B and B, Casey had fallen asleep. She didn't wake when Gage took her in his arms. He carried her up the walkway and Paige opened the door for them.

"You must all be worn out," Paige said. "Take her straight back to Maya's room and we'll talk in the morning."

In the room, Maya folded back the covers on the big four-poster bed and Gage settled the little girl with her head on the pillow. Casey sighed as Maya pulled the covers around her and turned onto her side.

Maya looked down on her for a moment, then turned toward Gage and rested her head on his shoulder. "I'm so exhausted and relieved and grateful and sad," she said. "Thank you—for everything."

"I haven't really done anything," he said, but he tightened his arms around her and she made no protests when he pulled her close.

"You were there," she said. "I knew I could count on you. That helped. You've made me feel less alone." She rested the palm of her hand on his chest, over his heart. "When I kissed you earlier, I wasn't really planning on that. It caught me off guard." Her eyes met his and he felt a fresh jolt of heat. "But I'm not sorry it happened."

"No," he said. "I'm not sorry, either."

"Everything about the past two days is a little unreal," she said. "Including you."

She was offering him an easy out—a safe way to dismiss what had passed between them and make it about the heat of the moment. But for once, he didn't want that. He kissed her—just a brief brush of his lips across hers, then he stepped back. "Oh, I'm real all right." He took another step back. "I'll see you in the morning." He had no idea where these feelings between them were headed, but he was willing to stick around to find out.

Though Maya was exhausted, she lay awake a long time, Casey's little body curled next to her in the bed. Intense relief that her niece had been found safe warred with worry about their future. What did she know about raising a child—especially one who had been through such a traumatic experience? Casey was counting on her and the responsibility weighed heavily.

She finally drifted to sleep and woke with a start to find Casey watching her. "Where are we?" Casey signed.

"We're in Eagle Mountain," Maya answered. "In a house owned by a nice woman named Paige. Would you like to take a bubble bath?" The little girl was filthy, but Maya hadn't had the heart to wake her the night before to make her take a bath.

Casey nodded and sat up and swung her legs over the side of the bed, still dressed in the clothes she had worn for days. "You can wear one of my T-shirts until we get your clothes," Maya told her. She would have to ask Gage what had been done with them.

Ordinarily, a bubble bath was sure to coax a grin from

the little girl, but though Casey seemed to enjoy the pampering and even played with the bubbles, mounding them in her hands and forming them into fanciful shapes, she remained solemn, her normally constantly dancing hands mostly still.

Maya had just helped her from the tub when a knock sounded on the bedroom door. Paige stood on the other side, a plastic bag in her hand. "An officer dropped these off earlier this morning," she said. "Adelaide realized Casey would need clean clothes, so she talked the sheriff into releasing them."

"Bless her." Maya took the bag. "And thank you."

Paige glanced toward the open bathroom door. "I heard the water running and thought it was probably safe to come up. I wanted to let you sleep as long as possible. I know you're both exhausted."

"Once I finally got to sleep, I pretty much passed out," Maya said.

Paige lowered her voice. "How is she?"

"Quiet. Quieter than usual. And serious. More serious than a five-year-old should be."

Paige reached out and squeezed Maya's shoulder. "I imagine it will take time. But being with you is going to help her. Clearly, she trusts you."

Casey trusted Maya to do the right thing, but Maya had no clue what that might be. She felt a tug on her shirt and looked down to find Casey, wrapped in the oversized bath towel. "Paige brought your clothes." Maya spoke and signed, then held up the plastic bag.

Casey took the bag and stood staring at Paige.

Paige squatted down so that she was at Casey's level. "Do you like waffles?" she asked.

Casey looked up at Maya and Maya translated the

words into American Sign Language. "She's still learning lipreading," she told Paige. "And yes, she loves waffles."

"Then as soon as you're dressed and come downstairs, I'll make you one—with whipped cream and strawberries, if you like."

Casey nodded and trotted back to the bathroom with the bag containing her clothes. When the door had closed behind her, Maya turned back to Paige. "Gage said the sheriff's office will have a victim advocate who specializes in children present when they question her."

"And you'll be there, too, I imagine," Paige said. "Are you her guardian now?"

She didn't say *now that your sister is dead*—Maya appreciated that. "Yes. When Angela and Greg talked to me about it when they made their will, I never expected it was something I would really have to do. It's such a big responsibility and I haven't a clue."

"You love her and that will go a long way toward leading you in the right direction, I believe," Paige said. "And there are a lot of people you can ask for help."

"When we get back to Denver, I want to find a counselor for Casey to see—someone who can help her deal with everything she's been through."

"That's a great idea. Has she said anything about her parents?"

"No. And I can't decide if that's bad or not."

"I think it's probably normal." Paige stepped back. "Come down when you're ready. I'll have fresh coffee and those waffles."

Casey emerged from the bathroom a few moments later, dressed in a denim skirt and a pink tee, a hairbrush in her hand. "I need help with my hair," she signed.

"Come sit on the bed and I'll fix it for you."

Calm settled over Maya as she went through the familiar, soothing motions of brushing her niece's hair and fastening it into a ponytail. The two had spent many happy afternoons playing hairdresser, taking turns combing and styling each other's hair, laughing at some of the crazy results they had achieved.

At last, she laid aside the brush. "How about some breakfast?" she asked Casey.

The little girl nodded.

Downstairs, Maya was relieved to see that they would be alone with Paige. "Where are your other guests?" she asked as Paige set a mug of steaming coffee in front of her.

"I just have two other couples here right now. They left early this morning to go climbing." She set plates in front of them filled with golden waffles drizzled with strawberry syrup, more berries and mounds of whipped cream on top. Casey's eyes widened, and her expression held more life than Maya had seen since she and her niece had been reunited.

"I think she approves," she said, and picked up her own fork.

They were just finishing the waffles when the doorbell rang. A few seconds later, Paige returned to the room, followed by Gage—a Gage who wore a starched uniform and smelled of a woodsy aftershave. Maya's heart thudded wildly as he filled the doorway to the dining room, and she struggled to maintain her composure. Memory of the incendiary kiss they had shared by the campfire rushed back.

A tug on her shirt allowed her to tear her gaze away from him and focus on her niece. "Why are your cheeks so red?" the little girl signed.

The question only made Maya blush more. "I must have eaten too fast," she answered—a completely ridiculous reply, but all she could think of at the moment. "You remember Gage, don't you?" she added.

Casey nodded. She began signing, fingers moving rapidly.

"What's she saying?" Gage asked.

"She says she saw you with me. By that little building. And the man was shooting at you." Maya's voice caught. "She says she ran away because she was afraid the man would hurt us, the way he hurt her mommy and daddy." As Maya finished speaking, Casey put her face in her hands and began to sob.

Maya slid out of her chair and gathered Casey to her. "It's all right, honey," she murmured, rocking the child against her and smoothing her hair. "I'm not hurt. I'm okay." Even though she knew Casey couldn't hear her, she needed to say the words.

Gage squatted down beside the chair. "Ask her if the man who was shooting at you and me was the same one who hurt her parents," he said.

"I can't do that," Maya said. "Can't you see how upset she is? We need to wait for the victim advocate."

Gage's jaw tightened, and she could almost hear his teeth grinding together, but he stood. "She's supposed to be here at ten, so I thought I could give you a ride to the station."

"I can drive over in my car," Maya said.

"You could. But it will be easier to get through the reporters if you're with me."

"Reporters?" Maya glanced over at Paige.

"I hadn't mentioned them yet," Paige said. "They've been gathered outside since dawn. And the crowd is growing. I had three calls this morning from national networks. I finally had to take the phone off the hook."

She frowned at Gage. "Can't you do something about them? They're interfering with my business."

"As long as they're not trespassing on your property, there's not a lot we can do," Gage said. He returned his attention to Maya. "Travis thinks we should have a press conference this morning, and let them take some pictures. It's up to you whether you want to grant any other interviews, or allow Casey to speak to them."

"Absolutely not." She stood, one hand still on Casey's shoulder. "I'll do the press conference, but I won't allow them to talk to Casey. Fortunately, she won't be able to hear their questions."

"Let's schedule the conference for one. That will give us time to meet with the victim advocate first." He stepped back. "We'll leave when you're finished with your breakfast."

Maya looked down at Casey's mostly empty plate. "I think we're done." She put her hand on the girl's cheek, capturing her attention. "Let's go wash your face and you can brush your teeth, then we're going to go with Deputy Walker for a while," she signed and spoke.

Casey sniffed and scrubbed at her eyes, then climbed out of her chair and carefully pushed it back into the table. "I'll wait by the door," Gage said.

Maya nodded, breakfast sitting like a rock in her stomach. She knew Gage needed the information Casey could give them in order to find Angela and Greg's murderers, but seeing the little girl upset tore her apart. She trusted Gage, but she didn't think she could keep quiet if he did anything to hurt her niece.

Chapter Eleven

The three of them braved the gauntlet of reporters, Casey hiding her face against Maya's shoulder and Gage walking with his arm around them both. He ignored the shouted questions and kept his focus forward. He realized they had jobs to do, but behind the feel-good story of a lost child who had been found lay a double murder and a lot of pain. He saw no need to put that suffering on display for the public.

Nobody said much of anything on the ride to the station. Though Gage hadn't spent a lot of time around children, Casey struck him as too quiet for a five-year-old. She sat in the booster seat he'd borrowed from the department and stared listlessly out the window. Maya was quiet, too. He could feel tension radiating off her—and more than a little resentment at him, that he had brought the little girl to tears. Couldn't she see he had a job to do? A job that required him to do ugly and yes, sometimes hurtful, things? He didn't want to hurt a little girl, but the longer they waited to find out the information she could give him, the more time a killer or killers had to get away—and maybe even to kill again.

When the three of them entered the sheriff's office—through the back door again—a silver-haired woman in a dark purple suit stepped forward to meet them. "I'm

Darla Rivers," she said, offering her hand. "I'm the victim advocate." She shook hands with Maya, then smiled down at Casey. "Hello, Casey," she signed as she spoke. "My name is Darla, and I hope we're going to be friends."

"You know ASL," Maya said.

"Yes. Casey isn't the first deaf child I've worked with." She moved to the sofa in a small waiting area and sat down. "Casey, would you and your aunt come sit with me?" she asked.

Maya led Casey to the sofa, where the little girl settled between the two women. Talking and signing, Darla explained that her job as a victim advocate was to be Casey's friend and to look after her interests and what was best for her—no matter what anyone else in the room thought. Casey listened intently, but Gage wondered how much a child that young could understand.

"Deputy Walker and the sheriff need to ask you some questions about what happened in the woods," Darla continued, signing as she spoke. "I know it might be hard to answer some of their questions, but anything you can remember will help them to catch the bad people who did this. Are you ready to try to help us?"

Casey hesitated, then took Maya's hand and nodded. Gage glanced at Travis.

Travis sat and pulled his chair closer to the sofa. Gage did the same. "We're videotaping this interview," Travis explained. "That allows us to capture all the sign language—Casey's language—and we also may be able to use the tape as evidence in court, so that Casey doesn't have to testify in person."

"That's good," Maya said.

Travis turned to Casey. The little girl stared back at him. She didn't look intimidated, but determined. In fact, her expression mirrored that of her aunt. Maya gripped the child with one hand and kept the other hand in a fist resting on her thigh.

Darla opened a large satchel and took out a drawing pad and some colored markers. She handed these to Casey. "I thought we would start by having you draw us a picture," she explained. "Draw a picture of what happened in the woods, when the bad people came."

Casey looked doubtful, and turned a purple marker over and over in her hand. "Go ahead," Maya urged. "You're very good at drawing."

After a moment, Casey put aside the purple marker and chose a black one. She began to make marks on the paper—a tent. Trees. The campfire. She put a little stick figure in the tent, lying down. That would be Casey, Gage guessed. Then two stick figures by the fire, one with long hair—her mother and father? The marker hovered over the page, then Casey bent low, shielding her work with her body, the marker squeaking against the pad. A tear fell on the page, making the marker run, and then another. Casey dropped the marker and turned her head away.

Darla handed the child a tissue and rubbed her shoulder, then slipped the pad from her lap. She studied the drawing a moment, then handed it to Travis. Gage leaned over to look at the drawing. Casey had added two figures in black—larger than the others. One of the figures held what was clearly a gun, and the little girl had drawn dashed lines from the gun to both her parents. The starkness of the scene made Gage feel a little sick—and angry that a child had had to witness such a thing.

"This is good," Travis said, addressing Casey, even though she wasn't looking at him. He turned to Darla. "Ask her if she can describe the shooters—were they male or female, tall, short, fat, thin? Did they have beards or wear glasses? Did they say anything? Did they argue with her parents and if so, what about? Did she see what kind of vehicle they were in?"

Darla nodded and began signing. Casey stared, wide-eyed, then began shaking her head back and forth, hair flying. Then she whimpered and turned away, and crawled into Maya's lap, her sobbing the only sound.

Maya wrapped her arms around the child. "We have to stop," she said. "This is too upsetting."

Travis looked grim. "We need more information if we're going to catch these two."

"Let's take a break and calm down," Darla said. "Then we can try again." She touched Maya's shoulder. "Let me take her for a little bit. You go outside and get some fresh air."

She nodded and left. Gage stared after her. "Maybe I should go talk to her," he said.

"It's your funeral," Travis said.

Outside, Gage found Maya leaning against the brick of the building, arms folded across her chest. She glanced at him when he came to stand beside her, but quickly looked away. "If you came out here to try to talk me into letting you bully Casey with your questions, you're wasting your breath," she said.

"I'm not bullying her and you know it." He leaned against the brick also, so close their shoulders were almost touching. "Did you ever think that it might be good for her to talk about what happened? That talking might make it less scary for her?"

"So you're a child psychologist now?" She turned on him. "A couple of nutcases destroyed her world and you want her to keep reliving that moment?"

"I want to find those two nutcases and stop them." He took hold of her arm, as much because he wanted that physical contact as to stop her from storming away from him. "Did it occur to you that if the people who did this find out Casey saw them, they could come after her? We need to find them before they do that."

All the color left her face and if not for his hand steadying her, he thought she might have fallen. "Come after her?" she whispered. "Gage, no—you can't let that happen."

"I don't intend to. But I need to know what she knows. Every little thing she can tell us is more than we have to go on right now. I don't want to hurt her, but more than that, I don't want them to hurt her."

She nodded and pulled away. He let her go. "If Darla thinks it's okay, you can question Casey some more," she said. "I'll try not to let my own anxieties influence her."

"I know it's not easy for you," he said. "But think of it this way—Casey survived two nights in the woods on her own. She's a very tough little girl. A very brave one."

"She is, isn't she?" She no longer looked so pale, and some of the bleakness had receded from her eyes. "Thanks for reminding me of that."

"Let's give her a little more time to recover," he said. "In the meantime, I need you to do something."

"Oh?" She eyed him warily.

"I need you to look at Angela and Greg's belongings and see if there's anything out of place," he said. "It can be disturbing, seeing things that belonged to someone you loved, laid out this way, tagged as evidence in a crime. But I need you to try to put aside the emotion and be as objective as possible. We can study these items all day and not see what you can see in a few minutes. We need to know if anything strikes you as out of place or not right or not characteristic of your sister and her husband."

"All right," Maya said. "If you think it will help."

"I don't know if it will help, but I'm determined to do

everything I can to find their killers. They deserve that much." He put his hand on her shoulder and looked her in the eye, hoping she would see the emotion behind his words. "You and Casey deserve that, too."

GAGE'S WORDS—AND the look in his eyes—touched Maya. But the thought of doing what he asked, looking through objects that had been so close to Angela and Greg, hurt. She took a deep breath, fighting for a calm she didn't feel. This was important. She couldn't bring Angela back to life, but she could do this one thing to help Gage and his fellow officers find Angela and Greg's killers. "I'm ready," she said.

He led her back inside and into a standard conference room of beige walls and gray tile floor. Banks of fluorescent lighting cast a harsh white light over the items laid out on long tables in the center of the room. Maya scanned the collection and recognized a blue-and-white cooler that had held drinks at countless backyard barbecues and two blue plastic storage containers of the kind her sister used for storing everything from Christmas decorations to out-of-season clothing. Next to the storage containers, someone had arranged what she assumed was the contents of the containers—canned food, paper plates and plastic utensils, a blue tarp, first aid kit and rain gear. A camping stove, lantern, two camp chairs, a backpack, some books and Angela's purse completed the collection of evidence.

Seeing the purse here hurt the most. The bag was light blue leather, with a silver butterfly charm dangling from the strap. Maya had been with Angela when she purchased the bag, both women crowing over the fact that it had been marked down 40 percent off at an end-of-season clearance sale. She approached the bag warily, cringing at the bright yellow Evidence tag attached next to the butterfly charm. "You can touch anything you want," Gage said. He waited by the door, as if giving her room to process all of this.

She picked up the wallet—a red leather one their mother had sent for Christmas last year. Maya had one just like it. "Angela used to say she kept her whole life in her purse," she said. She opened her wallet to reveal a driver's license and half a dozen loyalty cards for grocery stores and a pharmacy, a single credit card and a library card. The money compartment held nine dollar bills and the change compartment was empty. "She never kept much cash. She preferred to use her credit card for everything."

She set aside the wallet and considered the assortment of tissues, lipsticks, bandages, pens, makeup and a cell phone that made up the rest of the contents of the purse. She picked up the phone and debated turning it on. "We checked out the phone," Gage said. "No calls after the one she made to you the day they arrived in Eagle Mountain."

"She wanted to let me know she got here all right." Her voice broke and she set the phone back on the table, fighting for composure. She couldn't break down now—not yet. She had to keep it together, for Angela and Greg. Gage remained by the door, though she sensed him poised to spring into action, perhaps even to pull her out of the room if she started to go over the edge.

The idea strengthened her and she moved on to the backpack and its contents. Here was her brother-in-law, Greg—the always-prepared scientist, with his first aid kit, ordinance maps, binoculars, granola bars and books. She picked up the top volume on the small stack of reading material. *"A History of Mines and Mining in Rayford County,"* she read aloud. "That sounds like Greg."

She set the book aside and stared at the rest of the items laid out on the table. Grief dragged at her, like one of those lead aprons the dental assistant draped over her before she took X-rays. She shook her head. "I don't see anything unusual or out of place," she said. "They were just two ordinary people. There was no reason for this to happen." The last word came out in a sob she was unable to hold back. She bowed her head, then felt strong arms come around her. She turned into Gage and rested her head against the hard wall of his chest and sobbed, giving in to the grief and the opportunity to let someone else hold her up for a few moments.

By the time her tears were spent, his shirt was soaked and she was embarrassed, but still she kept her eyes closed and didn't move. Here in his arms was so safe and warm, and as she rested there, she became aware of other sensations—his clean, masculine smell and the steady, strong rhythm of his heartbeat, the solid bulge of muscles in his arms, and the way her own body warmed to his appealing masculinity. Here was a reminder, in the midst of the worst time of her life, that she was still very much alive and grateful for all that entailed.

Gage eased her away from him, though he kept his hands on her upper arms. "Better?" he asked.

She nodded. "But your shirt…"

"I have another one in my locker." He glanced toward the items on the table. "Thanks for taking a look. I know it was difficult."

"I wish I had seen something that could help you. I feel so helpless."

"You can't see what isn't there. And you are helping. You're a living, breathing reminder of what we're working for. Not that we wouldn't give our best, regardless. But sometimes, seeing how what we do impacts real lives is the incentive we need to put in another hour or dig a little deeper. We won't give up."

Watching him as he spoke, the intensity in his eyes and the emotion behind his words, she believed him. She trusted him. She had known Gage Walker less than two days, yet already she believed she could trust him with her life.

WHEN GAGE AND Maya rejoined Casey and Darla, they found the two coloring. They were working on a drawing that depicted all kinds of flowers—a much happier drawing than the all-black picture Casey had drawn for them. Gage took his seat across from them once more, and Maya perched on the end of the sofa. Travis joined them. "Did you see any flowers while you were in the woods?" Travis asked.

They waited while Darla conveyed his question in sign language. As the conversation continued, she served as translator.

Casey focused on filling in the petals of a large daisy with a pink marker, setting aside the color to sign. "I saw some yellow ones and purple ones," she signed. She replaced the cap on the pink marker and chose a yellow one. "I ate some raspberries. They were really good."

"That was smart of you, to find and eat the raspberries," Gage said.

She shrugged. "I was hungry."

"You said you saw me and your Aunt Maya by the little building," Gage said. "What were you doing when you saw us?"

"I saw the buildings and thought there might be food there, or someplace warm to sleep. But all the doors I tried were locked, but then I saw you and Aunt Maya."

"What happened then?" Travis asked.

"I was going to go to you, but then I saw the men talking. So I hid and watched. Then I saw it was one of the men—one of the bad men." She pressed her lips tightly together.

"So you ran away," Gage said, very gently.

She nodded and made a sign that Gage could clearly understand as going away—one finger drawn from one side to the other across her body. Then she began to sign more rapidly, and he was grateful for Darla's translation.

"I saw them shooting, and I was so afraid they had hurt Aunt Maya. I ran and ran until I couldn't run anymore. And then I didn't know where I was."

"You said one man," Travis said. "There was only one man who shot at your aunt and Deputy Walker?"

Casey nodded.

"And there were two men who shot your mom and dad?" Travis asked. "And the man who shot at your aunt and Deputy Walker was one of them?"

Another nod.

"Was he a big man?" Travis asked. "Was he bigger than Deputy Walker?"

She studied Gage, sizing him up, then made a sign that clearly conveyed the man she'd seen was shorter, but broader, a fact Darla confirmed.

"What color was his hair?" Travis asked.

Casey shook her head and continued to sign.

"She says he was wearing a hat," Darla said. "A knit cap, I think. It was black. All his clothes were black."

"What about the second man?" Travis asked. "The one who was with this one at camp?"

Casey took a deep breath, the struggle to remember—or maybe all the sadness that went with remembering—playing out across her face. Then she began a series of rapid signs—too rapid for Gage to follow. "The other man was about as tall as Deputy Walker," Darla said. "But...thicker. I think she means bulkier. He had a gun, too. She doesn't know which one shot her mother and father. Maybe both of them."

Casey leaned against Maya and closed her eyes. "I think she's had enough questions for today," Darla said.

"Just one more question," Travis said. "Is there anything else she wants us to know?"

Darla tapped Casey's arm to get her attention, then relayed the question. Casey looked at Gage, eyes big and bright with unshed tears. She made a series of signs he tried hard to understand, but could not. Darla gasped.

"What is it?" Gage asked. "What did she say?"

"She says the tall, bulky man saw her peeking out of the tent. He looked right at her and she thinks he shouted," Darla said. "He may have tried to follow her but she got away. But she's very afraid he will try to come after her and hurt her, too."

Chapter Twelve

Darla's words sent a cold shard of fear through Maya. Her first instinct was to grab Casey and pull her close, but she didn't want to alarm the little girl. Casey was counting on the adults around her to keep her safe, so Maya couldn't let her niece see her fear. She put a hand on Casey's head. The little girl looked at her, her eyes intent. "I'll protect you," Maya signed, though she had no idea how to do that.

"We should go back to Denver," she said out loud. "We'll be safer there."

Gage took her arm. "Darla, you and Travis stay with Casey while Maya and I talk."

Maya started to protest that she didn't want to leave Casey right now, but the look in Gage's eyes warned her he wasn't going to take no for an answer. Arguing in front of the child didn't seem like the best choice, so she reluctantly followed Gage into his office.

He shut the door and faced her. "Running away to Denver is a bad idea," he said.

"I'm not running away," she said. "Denver is my home. It's Casey's home."

"I don't think it's safe," he said. "The killers could follow you there."

"It will be harder to find us in a big city."

"How hard will it be for them to find out where you work—where you live?" he asked. "Once they know that, they can watch you and learn where Casey goes to school." He moved closer, until his chest was almost touching hers. The move could have been threatening, but it only reminded her of how close they had been around that campfire. The memory flashed across her mind at the feel of his arms around her, his body pressed against hers. She pushed it away. She didn't want to remember that moment—she couldn't remember it right now.

"Eagle Mountain is a small town," he continued. "Strangers and suspicious people stand out. You'll have the whole town watching out for you here."

Everything he said made sense, but it didn't lessen her urge to run and hide. "I need time to think," she said.

"I don't want you to go," he said.

She stared at him, her heart racing painfully. "I'm not sure what you mean."

"Yes, you do." He moved closer still, their bodies touching now. "You knew it when you kissed me there by the campfire. I never intended for it to happen, but I care about you. And I care about Casey. I want to help you protect her. I want to protect both of you."

She tried to swallow, her mouth dry as she remembered the ferocity of that kiss, how that moment with him had cut through all the fear and uncertainty. And she remembered afterward, too, when he had been so gentle with Casey. The little girl had trusted him, at a time when she had every reason not to trust a stranger. She spread her palms on his chest, not pushing him away, but giving herself a little space. "This isn't a good time for this," she said. "For us."

"You're right—it isn't. And it would be an easy out

for me to use bad timing as an excuse to step back from this, but I won't. I can't."

"I need time to think," she said again.

He must have heard the desperation behind the words. He stepped back. "Think all you want," he said. "But do it here, where I can help you and Casey."

"I'd better go to her," she said. "She'll be wondering where I am."

Casey was so engrossed in conversation with Darla that she scarcely looked up when Maya and Gage returned. "I was telling her about my cats," Darla said. "One of them is a real goofball."

"Thanks for distracting her," Maya said. "And thank you for all your help today."

"That's my job, but it's also something I enjoy a great deal." Darla pressed a business card into Maya's hand. "I'm officially Casey's advocate now, so call me if you need anything at all. And I'll be checking in with you again soon."

"Let's go back to the B and B and see about lunch," Maya signed to Casey.

They said goodbye to Darla, and started across the lobby with Gage when Adelaide called to them. "Come over here a minute," she said. "There's something I want to show you."

The three of them moved to Adelaide's desk. "All of this is for you," she said, pulling out a plastic box filled with cards and several stuffed animals. "People have been dropping them off since yesterday."

Maya translated this news to Casey, whose eyes widened. The little girl plucked a pink rabbit from the box and squeezed it to her chest. Maya blinked back sudden tears. "I don't know what to say," she said.

"The whole town is so glad to know that Casey is

safe." Adelaide handed her one of the cards. "You should read a few."

Maya slid the card from the envelope and opened it. *I helped with the search and stayed up nights worrying about that little girl. I cried tears of joy when I heard the news she was safe. I'm so sorry you both have had to go through such sorrow, but remember you are really a part of all of us now. Best wishes for a happy future. Barbara.*

Maya stared at the mound of cards in the box. "This is amazing."

"You take them home and read through them." Adelaide handed over the box. "We opened them all, just to make sure there were no nasty-grams. I'm sorry it has to be that way, but you can't be too careful."

"I understand," she said.

While Maya and Casey looked through more of the cards, Maya was dimly aware of the front door to the station opening. She glanced back at the stocky man in a red T-shirt who entered. "Hey, Gage, you're just the man I wanted to see," the newcomer said. "I might have a lead on those thefts from the high school."

"Would you mind waiting just a minute?" Gage asked her.

"Go ahead. We'll be fine waiting here." Casey hadn't even looked up from the cards. A stuffed animal under each arm, she traced one finger over a colorful photograph of wildflowers on the front of one card. Later, when they were alone, Maya would ask her niece what she thought of this outpouring of support. For Maya, it helped ease her pain a little to know they weren't alone.

GAGE LED WADE Tomlinson into his office and shut the door behind them. "What can I do for you?" Gage asked.

"Is that little Casey out there?" Wade asked. "She

looks like she's doing pretty good for a kid who was lost in the woods for two nights."

"She's a remarkable little girl." And her aunt was a remarkable woman—one who had turned Gage's easy-going life upside down. "What did you want to talk to me about?"

Wade lowered his stocky frame into the chair across from Gage's desk. "You said you wanted to know any-thing that might help you track down the school robbers. I might have something, though I don't know if it will really be any help to you."

The high school case seemed to have happened weeks ago, though Gage realized it had only been two days since the second break-in. He sat behind his desk and picked up a pen, prepared to make notes. "What have you got?"

"Brock and I were climbing over in Shakes Canyon yesterday afternoon and we ran into two guys we haven't seen around here before. Young skinhead types—you know the kind—shaved heads and Nazi tattoos. Bad atti-tudes. I talked to them a little—they said they're camped out in the woods south of town. I'm not saying they're the ones behind the vandalism, but something about them struck me as wrong, you know?"

It wasn't much to go on, but it wouldn't hurt to give these two a closer look. "Thanks," Gage said. "We'll check them out."

Wade stood. "Something about them wasn't right," he said. "And I don't mean just the Nazi stuff. Maybe they had something to do with the shooting of that little girl's parents."

"We aren't ruling out anyone at this point." He stood also, and moved toward the door.

"Has Casey been able to give you a description of the killer or anything?" Wade asked.

"She's told us some. We're still working with her on that."

"Yeah. I guess little kids aren't the most reliable witnesses."

"Casey is reliable," Gage said. "She's going to be a big help to us."

He escorted Wade out, then joined Maya and Casey at Adelaide's desk. "Look at all this," Maya said, indicating the bin full of cards and toys. "I still can't believe people brought them for Casey. It's amazing."

"Everybody was concerned about her," he said. "We're all glad she's safe." He squeezed her shoulder, hoping she would understand that he would do everything in his power to keep her that way.

He picked up the bin and she and Casey followed him out to his cruiser. "Did that man know who took those items from the high school?" Maya asked, as she fastened Casey into the booster seat in the back of the SUV.

"He had an idea about a couple of people he thought I should check out—I'll follow up on them."

Casey, still clutching the pink bunny, tugged on Maya's sleeve. When she had her aunt's attention, she signed. Maya smiled. "She says she's going to name the bunny Bitty Bunny."

"Cute name," Gage said.

When they were all buckled in, Gage started the cruiser and headed out onto Eagle Mountain's main street. "Is sign language hard to learn?" he asked.

"American Sign Language isn't any more difficult than any other language," Maya said. "Easier than most, I imagine. We all started learning it as soon as Casey was born and it didn't seem like it took that long. I guess the main difference is that it's a physical language instead of a spoken one. The movements of your fingers and hands are important, but so is your expression."

"I've been watching you and Casey talk," he said. "It's like you're communicating with your whole bodies."

"In a way, we are. I think it's a very beautiful language."

"I'd like to learn," he said. "It would probably help me in my work."

Maya turned to face Casey. *"I'm telling her you want to learn sign language,"* she said. "She says you should—then the two of you could talk."

He pulled the cruiser to the curb in front of the Bear's Den. "I'll stop by when I get off shift this evening," he said.

"You don't—" She stopped and shook her head. "That would be great," she said, and turned to help Casey.

He watched them make their way up the walk and into the B and B. She had been about to tell him that he didn't need to stop by—that they would be fine without him. He wondered what had changed her mind. Was she beginning to see him as an important part of her life?

He pulled away from the curb, thoughts churning. Maybe he should let Maya do what she wanted and take Casey back to Denver. He could talk to the police there and arrange for them to keep an eye on her. That would be the easiest solution. Without them here, he would be freer to focus on his work and go back to the no-hassles, stress-free personal life he had worked hard to put together these last few years.

His head told him that was the right thing to do—but he wasn't so sure his heart was down with that plan.

MAYA SET THE box of cards and toys on the table in the hall. Paige had left a note, her writing a cramped scrawl on a piece of torn notebook paper. *Out running errands*, it read. *The other guests are out as well. I have a new couple checking in this afternoon. I should be home before they arrive, but if they show up early, their check-in packet is on my desk in my office, next to the dining room.*

"I'm hungry," Casey signed.

"I'll see if there's anything in the kitchen for lunch." Maya set the note aside. "You take the stuffed animals upstairs to our room. We can look through the cards together after we eat."

Casey grabbed a blue bear and a purple hippo out of the bin and raced up the stairs with them and the pink bunny. Maya felt a little lighter as she listened to the girl's feet pound up the stairs. It was such a normal kid noise—and maybe a sign that the trauma she had endured hadn't permanently damaged her.

In the kitchen, she found tuna, mayonnaise, pickles and bread. She decided to make tuna sandwiches. Later, she would go shopping and replace the supplies, but she didn't think Paige would begrudge them to her now. She would look for something special as a gift for their hostess as well—maybe some good chocolates or fancy cookies.

She was assembling the sandwiches when she thought she heard the front door open. "Paige, I'm in here," she called.

But Paige didn't answer. Maya finished making lunch and washed her hands, but she couldn't shake the certainty that she had heard the front door. "Paige?" she called again, and moved into the front room.

No one was there, and a glance out the front window showed Paige's car wasn't parked at the curb or in the driveway. Maybe Maya had imagined the noise. Her nerves had certainly been on edge the past few days.

Maybe what she had heard had just been the normal settling of a place this old. She started up the stairs to tell Casey lunch was ready.

Halfway up, a strangled scream broke the afternoon silence. "Casey!" Maya shouted, and ran up the remaining stairs. She raced toward the closed door to the bedroom she and Casey shared and was struggling with the knob when pain exploded at the back of her head and everything went black.

Chapter Thirteen

"We are still interviewing Casey about what happened to her," Travis told the assembled reporters. "We're working with specialists to make sure we get everything she can tell us about the killer or killers, without causing her any more pain than necessary. In the meantime, we are investigating other angles of this case. I'm confident we are going to track down these people and stop them."

Some of the crowd gathered in the conference room at the Rayford County Sheriff's Department applauded as Travis completed his prepared statement to the press, while other hands flew into the air and reporters began firing questions. Gage stood next to and slightly behind his brother, studying the crowd. The mayor was here, impatiently shifting from foot to foot and glowering at the crowd, as the sheriff responded to six variations of the same question, which was asked first by a reporter from the Denver paper. "Who do you think did this and why?"

"Our investigation is ongoing." Travis repeated this and variations of the phrase for the next ten minutes until Gage, on a prearranged signal, stepped forward and took the microphone. "Thank you all for coming today," he said. "That's all the questions we have time for."

Mayor Larry Rowe moved to the microphone. "I'd just like to say that the town of Eagle Mountain is shocked and horrified by these recent events," he said. "And that this is not at all in keeping with the character of our town and its citizens." He glared out at the room, as if expecting questions, but another officer was already ushering the press out of the room.

Gage waited until the mayor had also left, then turned to Travis. "Want to ride out and look for these two skinheads Wade reported?"

"Where do you plan to start looking?" Travis asked.

"They were climbing in Shakes Canyon. We'll start there."

The two brothers left the conference room. Adelaide hurried toward them. "Dispatch just requested a unit report to 192 Elm Court," she said. "They got a 911 call from that address, but no response."

It took half a second for the address to register. "That's the Bear's Den," he said. "Who made the call?"

"The dispatcher says the line is still open, but she's not getting any response."

Gage was running now, Travis right behind him, already on the line to dispatch. "Put out a call for backup," he ordered.

Gage raced to his SUV. He had dropped off Maya and Casey less than twenty minutes ago and they had been fine. He should have gone into the house with them. What if the killer had discovered where they were staying and had been in there waiting for them? Gage should have thought of that.

He pulled the cruiser to the curb and cut the engine. Travis pulled in behind him. A quick glance showed nothing untoward about the house's appearance. The front door was closed and everything on the outside looked in order. One hand on the weapon at his side, he hurried up the walk, Travis at his side.

The front door, which should have been locked, opened easily when he turned the knob. He shoved it open and waited a second before he peered carefully around the frame. No sign of a disturbance in the front hall. "Maya!" he shouted. "Paige! It's me, Gage."

No answer.

"Paige's car isn't out front," Travis said.

Struggling to control his racing heart, Gage drew his weapon and started for the stairs. Halfway up, he heard what might have been crying and ran the rest of the way, to the hallway, where he spotted Maya, slumped on the floor in front of the door to one of the bedrooms.

He dropped to his knees beside her, relief leaving him weak when he realized she was alive and breathing. Blood seeped around a lump at the back of her head, but the pulse in her neck beat steadily beneath his fingers and as he carefully rolled her over, her eyes fluttered and she groaned.

"It's okay. You're going to be okay." He gently rubbed her hand between his palms and she opened her eyes and stared up at him, gradually bringing him into focus.

"Gage," she said softly. And then louder. "Gage!" She tried to sit up, but he pushed her back.

"Take it easy," he said. "You've got a knot the size of a hen egg on the back of your head. What happened?"

"Someone hit me, I think." She fought against his hold and this time, he let her sit up. "Casey!" she said. "We have to find Casey."

Gage helped Maya to her feet. She swayed and held on to him, then steadied herself. "Did you call 911?" Travis asked.

"No. Is that why you're here?"

"Dispatch said they received a call from this address, but no one said anything."

"Casey knows to call 911 in an emergency," Maya said. "Angie and Greg taught her that." She groped for the knob on the bedroom door. "I heard a scream and was on my way in here when someone hit me."

The door opened to reveal an attractively furnished bedroom with a neatly made four-poster bed, antique dresser and slipper chair. A purple stuffed hippo lay on the floor in front of a closed door. Maya, Gage close behind her, hurried to the door. She tried to turn the knob, but it wouldn't budge. "It's locked," she said, and began pounding on the door.

"If Casey's in there, she may have locked herself in to get away from whoever hit you," Gage said. He glanced around the room and spotted an empty phone cradle. "Was there a phone in there?" he asked.

Maya frowned at the base unit, which sat on the bedside table. "I guess so. I hadn't really paid attention. I always make calls on my cell phone." She pounded on the door. "Casey!" Her face twisted in anguish. "I know she can't hear me, but I don't know what else to do. What if she's in there and hurt?"

"Let me see." Gage gently moved her aside and examined the doorknob. "Do you have a paper clip?" he asked.

"Maybe in my purse."

"Get it. I think I can insert it in this hole here and pop the lock." He indicated the small hole at the base of the doorknob.

She moved away and returned a few moments later with a paper clip. He straightened one end and inserted it into the hole. Something clicked and he was able to turn the knob.

Maya rushed in ahead of him. She pulled back the shower curtain to reveal Casey huddled in a small ball at one end of the tub, the pink stuffed rabbit clutched in one hand, the phone in the other. Maya lifted the sobbing girl from the tub and Gage took the phone. "This is Deputy Walker," he told the dispatcher. "Everything's under control here. You can cancel that call for backup."

"Ten-four."

"I'll search the rest of the house," Travis said, and left them.

Gage ended the call and laid the phone on the bathroom vanity. Maya had set the little girl on the side of the tub and was signing to her. Casey didn't answer at first, but then her fingers began to move, with small gestures at first, then with more assurance.

"She says she was in the bedroom, playing with her new stuffed animals," Maya said. "She got the phone and was pretending they were calling her friend Sophie to invite her to a tea party. Then the door opened and a man was there. She's pretty sure it was one of the men from the woods—one of the men who hurt her mom and dad. She screamed and ran into the bathroom and locked the door."

"Smart girl. Tell her she did the right thing."

"I told her. She says the man tried to get in, and she dialed 911 and hid in the bathtub. The man stopped trying to get in and she waited for me to come get her."

"He may have heard the sirens approaching and decided not to stick around," Gage said. He pulled his phone out of his pocket. "I'll get a team out here to dust for prints. Maybe we'll get lucky." Luck hadn't been on their side much in this case, although the killer hadn't succeeded in getting hold of Casey. He studied the blood clotted in Maya's hair. "Do you want me to get someone out here to look at your head?"

She touched the back of her head and winced. "No, I'll clean up the blood and take a couple of aspirin and

I'll be fine." Her eyes met his. "Except now I'm terrified that this guy is going to come back."

"He won't find you here," Gage said. "I want you to come back to my place with me. At least until we can find you a spot in a safe house."

He expected her to argue, but instead, she looked relieved. "That sounds like a good idea."

"What's going on here?" Paige stood in the door of the bedroom, Travis behind her.

"I didn't find anyone in the other rooms," Travis said.

"Someone came into the house, hit Maya over the head and tried to grab Casey," Gage said. He looked at the little girl, who was focused on the pink rabbit. "Casey was smart enough to lock herself in the bathroom and call 911. She says the guy who was after her was one of the men who killed her parents."

"They know Casey can identify them," Maya said. "As long as they're out there, she's not safe."

"We weren't able to get much of a description from her earlier," Gage said. "It's more difficult with children anyway, and with Casey being deaf, well, I guess you could say the language barrier gets in the way."

"Let's get her with a police sketch artist," Travis said. "Maya can translate. With patience, we might be able to coax a good image from her."

"Only if Casey agrees," Maya said. "I don't want to upset her any more."

"Let's find the artist, first," Travis said.

"Are you saying someone broke into my house?" Paige asked. "How?"

"Let's take a look."

"We're coming with you." Maya picked up Casey and followed the others down the stairs.

Gage examined the front door. "This was closed, but unlocked when I got here," he said.

"I know I locked it when I left," Paige said. "I always do."

"It was locked when Casey and I got here," Maya said. "I opened it with my key, and I know I locked it back." She had a clear memory of turning the dead bolt after she closed the door.

"It doesn't look as if anyone has tampered with the lock," Gage said. He closed the door again and turned to Paige. "Who has the key?"

"Guests are given a key when they check in," Paige said. "And I have one, of course. But that's all."

"Let me see your key," Gage said.

She handed over a silver key ring with what was obviously the key to a vehicle and a silver house key. "It would be pretty easy for someone to take this to a locksmith and have a copy made," he said. "Where do you keep the keys?"

Paige led them to a desk in a small office just off the dining room. She took a key from the top drawer of the filing cabinet and unlocked the center drawer of the desk, and took out a small plastic tray with half a dozen keys inside. "They're all here," she said after a quick scan of the tray's contents.

"But it wouldn't be that tough for someone—a guest or someone else who was in here—to get a hold of one of these and have a copy made," Gage said. "I'll ask the local locksmiths, but depending on when the key was made, they might not remember. Meanwhile, you should probably have the locks changed."

"I certainly will," she said.

"I'm taking Maya and Casey to my place, until we can

find them a spot at a safe house," Gage said. "They'll be safer there."

"What am I supposed to do if this creep comes back?" Paige asked.

"We'll run extra patrols by here," Travis said. "Get the locks changed."

"And if anyone asks, tell them Maya took Casey back to Denver," Gage said. "That might throw the killer off the track."

"We'll have Adelaide spread the word," Travis said. "She's more effective than the newspaper for distributing news."

"I'll help you with your things," Paige said and took Maya's arm.

The two women and Casey headed back upstairs. Travis turned to Gage. "I can call the Montrose sheriff and he can probably get you a spot in one of their safe houses this afternoon," he said.

"I think Maya and Casey will be more comfortable here for now," Gage said.

"You mean *you'll* be more comfortable," Travis said.

Gage didn't bother trying to deny it. "I don't trust anyone else to look after them the way I will," he said. "The killer or killers are here in this town—our town. I'm not going to rest easy until we stop them, and until we do, I'm going to have a twenty-four-hour guard on Casey and her aunt."

"I've never known you to take the job quite so personally before," Travis observed.

Gage met his brother's eyes with a hard look of his own. "Don't fight me on this," he said.

"I'm not fighting," Travis said. "And who knows— maybe spending more time around Casey will help you gain her trust. The more comfortable she is, the more she'll be able to tell us about the killers."

That would be good, but Gage was really hoping that spending more time with Maya would help him to gain *her* trust.

WHILE CASEY GATHERED up her stuffed animals, Paige helped Maya collect scattered clothes and toiletries and stash them in her suitcase and backpack. "Are you okay with going to stay with Gage?" Paige asked.

"I feel safer with him than I do anywhere else right now," Maya said. She added a sweater to the clothes in her suitcase. "No offense—I don't blame you at all for that guy getting in here."

"I know you don't." She handed Maya a pair of shoes. "Gage seems very serious about wanting to protect you. No one has ever questioned his dedication to his job, but I'd say there's a little more than that at play here."

Maya tugged on the zipper of the suitcase, glad to have something to focus on besides Paige. "He's probably just angry that the killer was here in town, practically right under his nose, evading all his efforts to find him."

"I don't think that's it—or not all of it."

"I don't care why Gage is taking us in, just that he is. At least with a cop watching over us, I won't be afraid to let Casey so much as go to the bathroom by herself."

"I think you should care," Paige said. "And before you pretend you don't know what I'm talking about, I'll be blunt—I think our commitment-phobic cop has fallen in love with you."

Maya fumbled the suitcase. "That's crazy. We hardly know each other." People didn't fall in love that fast— especially a man who had sworn relationships weren't for him. Yes, Gage had said he "cared" about her—but that didn't mean love, did it?

She hefted the suitcase off the bed. "Casey needs all my energy and attention right now," she said. "Gage knows that."

"While you're devoting yourself to Casey, it wouldn't be the worst thing in the world to have a man like Gage devoted to you," Paige said.

"You're reading too much into this," Maya said. "I need help and Gage is chivalrous enough to want to help, but he hasn't known me long enough to get attached. A week after I've left town, he won't even remember me."

"Hey." Paige grabbed her arm. "Don't say that. I haven't known you long, either, but you're my friend now. If you need anything, I'm here to help. Me and a lot of other people."

What had she done to deserve people like Paige—and yes, Gage—in her life? And what would she have done without them to help her through the past few days? She put her hand over Paige's. "Thanks. That means a lot."

Casey, her arms full of stuffed animals, joined them. She carefully set the toys on the bed and turned to Maya. "Don't forget the cards," she signed. "I want to look at all of them."

In all the commotion, Maya had forgotten about the box of cards townspeople had sent. "Thanks for the reminder," she signed. "We'll get them right now."

Gage and Travis met them at the bottom of the stairs. "We're going out the back door," Gage said.

She flashed him a worried look. "Why? Do you think the killer might be watching the house?"

"I'm just being cautious." He took the suitcase from her hand while Travis picked up the box of cards and Casey's bag.

"Where are we going?" Casey asked.

"We're going to stay with Gage for a few days," Maya said, signing as well as speaking for the others' benefit.

Casey turned and studied Gage. "You mean, like a sleepover?" she asked.

"Not exactly," Maya answered. "We're just going to stay at his house."

"What did she say?" Gage asked.

"I was just explaining that we're going to your house for a few days," Maya said.

"But what did she say to make you blush?"

She debated making up a lie, but why bother? "She asked if we were going for a sleepover."

Everyone around them laughed, and there was no mistaking the glint in Gage's eyes. "Tell her I'm going to keep you both safe," he said.

Maya hesitated. "I don't want her to think there's anything she needs to be afraid of."

"She's a smart kid. Smart enough to know that if the killer broke in here to try to get her, he's liable to come back. I want her to know she doesn't have to worry about facing him alone."

"You're right. I'll tell her. And thank you."

While Maya relayed Gage's message to Casey, he turned to Paige. "Do me a favor and take a look around outside," he said. "I want to make sure no one's keeping an eye on the back door."

The idea that the killer might even now be watching them made Maya's skin crawl. She was grateful Casey wasn't able to hear Gage's words, and she hoped the little girl hadn't picked up on his concern. Paige went outside and returned several moments later. "There's nobody out there," she said. "I even walked all the way around the house."

Gage had moved his cruiser into the alley behind the B and B. He and Travis stowed Maya and Casey's belongings in the back, then bundled them into the vehicle. "I'll check in with you tomorrow," Paige said. "Try not to worry. And remember—if you need anything, you call."

"I will."

On the drive to Gage's place, Casey was cheerful, playing with her new stuffed toys, signing to them and moving the paws of the bear as if he was signing in answer. Her resilience amazed Maya. But was it really healthy? Maybe she was in denial about what had happened and it would all come back to haunt her later.

Gage slowed and pulled into the driveway of a cedar-sided cottage set against a backdrop of tall pines. "Here we are—home sweet home."

The house reminded Maya of a cabin that might have been home to a miner or a rugged outdoorsman a century before, with heavy stone pillars framing a cozy front porch and a rusty metal roof sloping steeply from a high peak. Inside, the rooms featured honeyed wood floors and lots of natural light from an abundance of windows. "Your room is back here," Gage said, leading them down a hallway to a bedroom furnished with a queen-sized bed with a black iron frame and a small dresser. "You don't mind sharing, do you?" he asked. "Casey could bed down on the sofa, but I thought she'd be more comfortable with you."

"This is perfect," Maya said. "I'll feel better having her close."

Casey tugged on his sleeve and began signing. He looked down at her, raising his eyebrows in question.

"She wants to know if you're going to catch the man who hit me and tried to hurt her," Maya translated. So the little girl hadn't forgotten what had happened.

Gage squatted down so that he was eye level with her. "I'm going to do my best to catch them," he said, enunciating carefully. He glanced up at Maya. "Tell her that—and tell her she was very brave and very smart this afternoon. She did exactly the right thing, locking herself in the bathroom and calling the police. I'm really proud of her. And I know her parents would be proud, too."

Casey's gaze fixed on Maya as she translated, then she turned to Gage and put her arms around him, buried her face in his chest and began to sob. He looked startled for a moment, then gently returned her embrace. "Go ahead and cry, honey," he said softly, rubbing her back. "Maybe that's what you need, after all you've been through."

His eyes met Maya's over the top of the child's head, and something expanded inside of her, a warmth and lightness that made her catch her breath. Here was a man she could depend on—the kind of man who wouldn't lie or expect too much or do anything but be there for her. Was this what love felt like?

And if it was, what in the world was she going to do about it?

Chapter Fourteen

Casey's sobs subsided after a few minutes and she pulled out of Gage's arms and went into the bathroom. Maya was still looking at Gage with that mix of awe and compassion that made his heart stumble in its rhythm. "Your shirt is wet," she said, nodding to the place on his shoulder where Casey's tears had soaked through the fabric.

"It'll dry." He went to the window and checked the locks. "I don't think anyone saw us driving over here, and we can trust Paige and Travis not to spread the word. We're putting an extra officer on duty to keep an eye on the B and B, in case the man who attacked you comes back."

"This is crazy," she said. "Casey is just a little girl. Why would anyone want to hurt her? But why would anyone want to kill Angela and Greg? None of this makes sense."

He turned away from the window and saw that she had wrapped her arms around herself, as if trying to ward off a chill. "Come here," he said.

"Why?"

So I can try to kiss that frown off your face. What would she do if he said that? But with Casey liable to walk back in the room any second, he reined in his desire. "I want to take a look at your head," he said.

She came to stand by him and he examined the wound on the back of her head. Blood had crusted in the roots of her hair, and she flinched when he touched the swollen lump. "Sorry," he said. "Do you want to take a shower and clean that up?"

"Yes." She glanced at Casey, who came out of the bathroom and began arranging the trio of stuffed animals on the bed.

"Don't worry about Casey," he said. "I'll watch her while you're in the shower."

"Have you had much experience with five-year-olds?"

"Pretty much none, but I think I can manage for twenty minutes or so, while you clean up."

She got Casey's attention and signed to her—Gage assumed she was explaining the situation. Casey sent him a look he couldn't interpret, then nodded, apparently agreeing with the plan. Maya gathered her things and went into the bathroom. Casey watched after her, a worried look on her face.

Gage tapped the little girl's arm and motioned for her to follow him into the other room. Now what? He looked around the room for something to entertain a child. There was television, but that struck him as a cop-out. And would she really enjoy the show if she couldn't hear it?

Inspiration struck. He picked up a pillow and pointed to it, eyebrows raised in a questioning look. Casey looked doubtful, then made a sign with her hands. He tried to imitate it, which elicited a fit of giggles. She made the sign again, more slowly. A gesture like someone cradling a pillow to her head. That made sense. He copied the gesture and she nodded and gave him a thumbs-up.

Gage set aside the pillow and picked up a book. Casey put her palms together, then opened them, as if she was opening a book. All right! That was easy. He copied her and they were off. For the next fifteen minutes, he would pick an object, Casey would demonstrate the sign for that object and Gage would do his best to copy her, his efforts rewarded with a mixture of giggles, frowns and encouraging nods.

Maya, hair still damp and smelling of a floral soap, appeared in the doorway. "What are you two doing?" she asked.

"Casey is teaching me sign language," Gage said.

Casey signed to Maya, her fingers moving too rapidly for Gage to follow. Obviously, he still had a lot to learn.

"I asked her if you're a good student," Maya said.

"What's the verdict?" he asked.

"She says you're pretty good."

"Tell her I have a good teacher." His sheriff's department phone rang. "I have to answer this," he said, and went into his home office.

"Hey," Travis said when Gage answered. "How are things going?"

"They're going good. Casey's teaching me sign language."

"That's good. I called to update you on the report from the Bear's Den. The techs didn't find anything to point to our killer."

"I wasn't holding out much hope that they would."

"No," Travis agreed. "The attacker knew enough to wear gloves, and none of the neighbors noticed him entering the B and B. People go in and out of there all the time, so one more person would be pretty much invisible—especially if he had a key."

"We'll try the local locksmiths," Gage said. "But I'm not holding out much hope."

"Also, I got the report on Henry Hake's car," Travis said. "Thought you'd want to hear it."

"Sure. What did they find?" He leaned back against the desk. Casey's laughter drifted from the other room. Amazing how she could laugh, after all she had been through.

"Hake wasn't in the car and neither were his prints," Travis said. "It had been wiped clean."

"Any idea how long the car had been down there?" Gage asked.

"Nothing certain, but long enough for the leaves on the tree branches it broke on the way down to turn brown."

"So it could have been down there since shortly after he disappeared."

"That would be my guess. I'm going to try again to get in touch with the men who invested in the resort. According to Hake's assistant, they called a lot of the shots from behind the scenes. Maybe he had a dispute with one of them that went wrong."

"They're refusing to talk to you?"

"So far, they've avoided me altogether. The numbers I have go to phones that aren't answered, and there's no way to leave a message. I haven't been pressing it, but now I will."

"I still need to make it out to check on those two guys Wade told us about," Gage said.

"I sent Dwight out to look for them this afternoon, but he hasn't come up with anything yet," Travis said. "Not that Wade gave us much to go on. And we have plenty of other things to keep us busy. We can't afford to be a man short anytime, but especially right now."

If Travis was trying to make Gage feel guilty, it was working. "Tomorrow, Maya and Casey can hang out at the station while I get some work done," he said. "They'll be safe there."

"I've located a police artist who has a lot of experience working with children," Travis said. "His schedule is open tomorrow. If we can get Darla back over to serve as interpreter, maybe they could meet tomorrow. But that only takes care of one day."

"I know. Just give me until tomorrow, at least, to figure something out. Maya was talking earlier about going back to Denver."

"She'll need to go back sometime," Travis said. "She has a job. And Casey is probably in school."

"Yeah." The idea of Maya leaving—and of Casey leaving, too—tore at him. "I'd feel better about them in Denver if I knew they were safe."

"If this guy—or guys, since Casey said there were two of them—are still hanging around town, we're going to catch them," Travis said. "They're going to make a mistake. Though it would help if we knew if this was a random killing, or if it had a connection with something Angela and Greg Hood were involved in."

"We're going to have to dig deeper into their backgrounds," Gage said. "That's something else I can start working on here."

"Good idea."

They ended the call and Gage returned to the living room. Maya was brushing Casey's hair as the little girl played with her stuffed animals. "Everything okay?" she asked.

"The technicians didn't find any evidence at Paige's place." He sank into the recliner opposite them. "The man who attacked you probably wore gloves."

"I wish I had seen him." She shook her head. "He came up behind me so fast."

"Travis is looking for an artist to work with Casey. In the meantime, it would help if we knew if your sister and her husband had a previous connection with the killers."

"I've been wracking my brain, but I can't think of anyone who would have wanted to kill them."

"Who did they purchase that mining claim from?" he asked.

"It belonged to an elderly couple in Boulder—a professor, I think. He had owned the land for a long time, since he was young. It wasn't listed for sale. Greg researched land around here and thought this was exactly the kind of place he wanted, so he visited the man and persuaded him to sell."

"How old was he?"

"In his late eighties—almost ninety, I think."

Then he probably hadn't decided to go after the Hoods. "Did he have children or grandchildren who might have objected to the sale?"

"No. That was one of the reasons Greg was able to persuade him to let it go. He planned to leave most of his estate to charity, and he agreed that cash would be a better gift to leave than these mining claims that couldn't even be built on." She laid aside the brush and patted Casey's shoulder. The girl sat back on the sofa, stuffed toys hugged to her chest, watching the adults.

"I'm starting to feel bad, keeping you away from your job."

"Don't. And what about your job? When do you have to be back?"

"I talked to my principal yesterday and let him know what's going on. Right now I'm on bereavement leave, then I'm entitled to parental leave to get settled in with Casey. That will bring me almost to the end of the semester. We agreed I should probably wait and start again with the new semester in January. It will mean I have to dig into my savings, but I'll be okay. I'm grateful I'm able to take the time."

"What about Casey's schooling?" he asked.

"She's in kindergarten, but I'm not worried about her falling behind." She smiled down at the little girl. "She's already reading simple books and counting. She loves learning and is very smart."

"I can tell."

Casey began signing. "She wants to know if we can have pizza," Maya translated. She put a hand on her stomach. "I just realized we never had lunch. I was making it when all the commotion happened."

Gage stood. "We can definitely have pizza. We even have a good place that delivers." He turned to Casey. "What kind do you like?"

He couldn't interpret her signing and looked to Maya for answers. "Some words don't have a symbol in American Sign Language," Maya explained. "So you do what's called finger spelling—spelling out each letter. She just told you she likes pepperoni."

"I'm impressed," he said. "That's a pretty big word for a five-year-old."

"Well, she misspelled it, but she was close enough I understood," Maya said. "I have this theory that ASL makes kids—and probably their parents, too—better spellers. But I could be wrong. Anyway, if you really want to learn ASL, start memorizing the alphabet. If you don't know the sign for something, you can always finger-spell. It's awkward, but you'll get your point across."

"Good to know. Any other requests for the pizza?"

"Just pepperoni. It's my favorite, too."

"One pepperoni pizza coming up."

BY THE TIME the pizza arrived, Maya was beginning to feel more relaxed than she had since coming to Eagle Mountain. Yes, there was still too much unsettled in her life, and she could never forget that Casey was still in danger. But for whole minutes at a time, she was able to put aside her grief and fear and simply be with Gage and Casey.

Though Casey stayed close, the child seemed less sad and silent than she had been earlier. She continued to sign to Gage and laugh at his awkward responses. Those giggles were like a balm to all the ragged edges in Maya's spirit.

They followed up pizza with more signing lessons, and then Maya noticed Casey's eyelids beginning to droop. No wonder, considering the past couple of days she had had. "I think it's time for a bath and then bed," she signed.

Predictably, Casey tried to argue. When Maya wouldn't budge, she tried a different gambit. "I'm supposed to have a story at bedtime," she signed.

"What did she say?" Gage asked. "Why are you frowning like that?"

"She's asking for a bedtime story," Maya said. "I don't suppose you have any children's books around here."

He actually turned and studied his bookcase, as if someone might have stashed a copy of *The Poky Little Puppy* there when he wasn't looking. "I'm not seeing anything," he said. "But go ahead and give her a bath and I'll see what I can come up with."

She hauled a reluctant Casey to the bathroom, the little girl's spirits improving when Maya added a generous dollop of bath gel to the water, creating satisfying bubbles, with which Casey amused herself until her fingers and toes were well wrinkled. Maya toweled her off and helped her into pink pajamas.

In the bedroom, they found Gage waiting, a hardbound book in his hand. "What have you got there?" Maya asked.

"It's a photo album my mom gave me a couple of Christmases ago." He sat on the edge of the bed and opened the book. "She made one for each of us kids."

Casey slid under the covers, then leaned forward to study the first pictures. Maya sat on Casey's other side and leaned over her. The picture was of three children—two boys and a girl—each on horseback. "Is that you?" Maya asked, pointing to the middle child, who clearly had Gage's eyes.

"That's me and Travis and our sister, Emily. I thought I'd tell a story about growing up on the ranch, and you can translate."

Casey clapped her hands at this news, and her fingers began flying. "She wants to know what your horse's name was and if you had cows," Maya asked.

"The horse was named Rusty. I got him when he was three and I was ten. He still lives on the ranch. And we had plenty of cows. Hundreds of them."

Maya listened, as enthralled as Casey, as Gage told about growing up on a cattle and horse ranch near Eagle Mountain, doing chores around the ranch, riding horses, exploring old mines and having what sounded like an idyllic childhood. As Gage flipped through the album, pausing over pictures of him and his siblings and parents and a series of orphaned calves, stray dogs and injured birds Gage had nursed back to health, she got a sense of a fun-loving but intensely compassionate kid who had grown into a man determined to right wrongs and defend the defenseless.

By the end of the album, Casey's eyes were closed, and she only murmured sleepily when Maya and Gage each kissed her good-night. Leaving the light in the adjacent bathroom on as a night-light, Maya switched off the lamp and she and Gage tiptoed from the room. He put his arm around her and she leaned into him. *I could get used to this*, she thought. Another voice warned her that this wasn't her real life—not the one she belonged in, where she lived in the city and taught school and did her best to raise her niece without the help and protection of this small-town lawman. Gage was a wonderful man, but she didn't really belong in his world, or he in hers.

"Can I get you anything?" Gage asked. "A glass of wine or some tea?"

"No, I'm fine." They sat next to each other on the sofa. "I can't thank you enough for all you've done for us," she said. "I know part of it's your job, but—"

He put his hand over hers, silencing her. "You know this isn't just about the job," he said. "I wanted to help. I only wish I could do more."

Her eyes met his and the pull of something deep inside of her drew her to him. She tilted her head up and his lips found hers, and a tension she hadn't even acknowledged eased, like a flower bud breaking open. He pulled her close, his heat enveloping her, his heartbeat a strong, steady rhythm against her chest. Desire burned off the last remnants of inhibition and suddenly all she wanted—all she *needed*—was to be close to him, to love and be loved and to let that love obliterate all the worry and fear and uncertainty that had come to define her life.

He pulled her over into his lap, one hand cradling her hip, the other caressing her breast. She arched to him, the evidence of his desire hard against her thigh. He trailed kisses along her jaw, then pressed his lips to the pulse at the base of her throat. She slid one hand between the buttons of his shirt, fingers brushing across the hair on his chest, a thrill piercing her.

"You know I want you." He spoke the words against her throat, his voice a low growl.

"Yes." It was all the speech she could manage, her senses overwhelmed. He brushed his hand across the tip of her breast and she moaned and shifted against him, aching to be closer still.

His hand stilled, and he rested his forehead on her shoulder. "Maybe we should go into the bedroom," he said. "We don't want Casey coming out and finding us like this."

Casey! Guilt doused all passion like a bucket of icy water. How could she have forgotten about Casey? She pushed away from Gage. "If she wakes up and comes looking for me, I can't risk her not finding me," she said.

The lines around the corners of his eyes deepened and he looked pained, but he nodded. "You're right." He eased her off his lap. "Sorry. Lousy timing."

"It's not your fault," she said, chilled already without his warmth. She had a sudden flash of a future full of moments like this—of passion cooled by the weight of her responsibilities. Not that she had ever had a very active love life up until now, but being responsible for a small child seemed to limit her opportunities even more. Not every man was likely to be as understanding as Gage.

"I don't know whether to be flattered or concerned that you look so sad," he said.

She shook her head, trying to banish the sorrow that threatened to overwhelm her. "I was just thinking about all the things that are going to change in my life now," she said. "I mean, I've known things would be different since I got your call about Angie and Greg. But I think the reality of that is only just now beginning to sink in. And I'm also realizing how much I don't know—how much I can't anticipate."

"My dad always told me, 'Don't borrow trouble,'" Gage said. "Don't worry about things that haven't happened yet." He caressed her shoulder, and she fought the urge to lean into him again. "You're a smart woman. When the time comes, you'll make the right decisions."

"I'll make the decisions," she said. "And hope they're right." But what was the right decision with Gage? If she only had herself to think about, she might risk a relationship with this cop who had a reputation for never being serious—the small-town guy who didn't fit with her big-city life.

But this wasn't all about her anymore. She had to make the right choices for Casey, too. And the little girl needed stability more than anything right now. She didn't need new situations and new people in her life. Maya stood. "I think I'd better say good-night."

"Good night." Gage didn't reach for her hand or try to pull her back. Instead, he let her walk away, into the bedroom, where she closed the door behind her. Did it cost him anything to let her go so easily? Earlier, she had sensed he was struggling, but maybe she had only been projecting what she wanted. After all, in a few days when she went back to Denver, he would return to the life he had always known, while her life would never be the same again.

Chapter Fifteen

The next morning, Maya and Casey accompanied Gage to the sheriff's department, where someone had converted one of the conference rooms into a kind of playroom, with art supplies, games and toys. Adelaide met them at the door with a little girl about Casey's age. "This is my granddaughter, Rhea," Adelaide said. "She wanted to come play with Casey today." Adelaide leaned closer to Maya and lowered her voice. "I explained to her that Casey can't hear, but you know children—they'll find a way to get along."

"Thank you for bringing her," Maya said. She made introductions and the girls headed for the piles of art supplies. Maya settled into a chair at the conference table while Adelaide sat across from her.

"How did it go at Gage's place last night?" Adelaide asked.

"It went fine."

"He seems to think a lot of you and Casey." The older woman studied her, like a bird watching a juicy bug. What did she expect Maya to say—that she and Gage had enjoyed a night of torrid lovemaking? Was she hoping for gossip about Gage's prowess in bed?

"He's been a big help to us," Maya said. "It was kind of him to open his home to us." Certainly, she had felt physically safer with Gage than she would have at the B and B—though the man unsettled her emotionally like no one she could remember.

"He and his brother are two of the finest men you'll ever meet," Adelaide said. "I can't tell you the young women in this town who have set their caps for Gage, but the best of them haven't managed to hold his attention for more than a few months."

"Gage doesn't think a long relationship is a good idea with his job." Maya repeated the words Gage had told her. Had he been trying to warn her off, even then? What had happened to change his mind—or had she been misreading those signals, too?

"A man in Gage's position needs a wife and family to ground him," Adelaide said. "To give him a reason to come home at night and to remind him that being careful is a good thing. It doesn't mean he can't do a good job. Family is the best reason in the world to do their job."

Obviously, the older woman had a lot of opinions about what Gage—and probably Maya, too—needed. Time to steer the conversation in another direction. "How long have you worked for the sheriff's department?" she asked.

"Seven years. My husband was an officer here for almost thirty years. He retired and a year later, he died of a heart attack. I was about half-crazy, sitting around our house all alone with nothing to do, so when I heard the woman who had this job was quitting and moving out of state, I came down and told the sheriff at the time that he ought to hire me."

"Wasn't it hard, being married to a man who might be killed every time he went to work?" Maya couldn't believe she had asked the question—she hadn't even been aware of the thought until she blurted it out.

Adelaide shifted, crossing her legs. "It was if I let myself think about it too much," she said. "But look at how he did end up dying—that could have happened if he was a baker or an accountant or anything."

"I guess you're right," Maya said. "I hope Gage finds the right woman." That was the appropriate thing to say, wasn't it? The timing was all wrong for the two of them, so she should wish he would find happiness with someone else—though the thought made her stomach tighten and her fists clench.

"What about you?"

Maya stared. Was Adelaide suggesting *she* was the right woman for Gage?

"You've got that girl to raise now. Do you have a man back in Denver you could see yourself settling down with?"

"Oh. No, I'm not seeing anyone."

"I'm not saying you couldn't do a fine job raising her on your own," Adelaide said. "Plenty of women—and men, too, I imagine—do a fine job by themselves. But if you can find someone to love and share the burden, it's a help and a comfort."

"Casey needs all my attention right now. I don't have time."

"So you're going to wait until she's grown before you look twice at a man? Haven't you heard of multitasking? I'll bet you do it all the time already. You're a teacher, right?"

"Yes." What did that have to do with anything?

"If you can handle a class full of kids, some of whom don't even want to be there, I think you've got plenty of energy to deal with a little girl and a man."

The phone sounded and Adelaide stood. "I'd better answer that. If you or the girls need anything, let me know."

The two little girls, giggling, worked together on a

poster-sized drawing of what might have been a zoo full of animals. A curly-haired woman with a bucket in one hand and what might have been a carrot stood in front of the giraffe, a big smile stretched across her face. A monkey swung from a tree behind her and a big-eared elephant arched his trunk over her head. That was the woman Maya wanted to be—serene and happy in the face of chaos.

She wanted to be a size four with perfect hair, too. Life didn't always give people what they wanted. Right now, she wanted Gage to find the killer who had murdered Angie and Greg, who was threatening Casey. She wanted Casey to be safe and maybe, one day sooner rather than later, to be happy. Then she could start to think about her own happiness.

HENRY HAKE'S HOME was the sort of stone and cedar chalet favored by wealthy second-home owners—a combination ski lodge and mini-mansion, with soaring beams, antler chandeliers and expanses of double-paned glass that looked out on the aspen-studded slopes of Mount Rayford. Travis drove his SUV past the open black iron gate and parked on a paved driveway, the concrete scored to look like cobblestones.

"The place looks deserted," Gage said when he stood beside his brother in front of the oak double doors at the front of the house. Dried leaves had collected in front of the door and old pollen dusted the windowsills.

"My guess is, Hake hasn't been back since he disappeared," Travis said. He pulled on a pair of latex gloves and took a key from his pocket. "State patrol sent a couple of officers out here after Hake's office manager reported him missing, but they didn't find anything suspicious."

Gage, also gloved, followed his brother into the house.

A stone-floored entry opened into a great room with a double-sided fireplace and oversized log furniture with thick leather cushions, red-and-green wool throws draped artfully here and there. What looked to be a genuine grizzly bear rug stretched in front of one side of the fireplace, and bookshelves soared almost to the ceiling between the massive windows. Gage gave a low whistle. "Hake lived here by himself?"

"His assistant said he entertained a lot—clients and investors." He moved across the room to a door on the other side and opened it.

"What are we looking for?" Gage asked.

"Any information about those investors or the silent partners he had in the Eagle Mountain Resort project," Travis said. "Hake's assistant swears she doesn't know their names and she never met them."

"Do you believe her?"

"She hasn't given me any reason not to. She seemed genuinely distressed by Hake's disappearance and has been cooperative." He crossed the room to a dust-covered desk.

"I take it you've already searched his office," Gage said.

"I would have, but the assistant told me Hake moved all the business files here to his home office, about a week before he disappeared. The plan was to shut down the other office space and run everything out of here. He paid her a generous severance package. She was packing up the last of the office furniture and supplies when she called to report him missing."

"What is she doing now?" Gage asked.

"She moved to Colorado Springs and has a new job." Travis tried the top drawer of the filing cabinet that sat behind the desk, but it wouldn't budge.

"Is there a key in the desk?" Gage asked.

Travis opened the middle drawer of the desk and rifled through the contents. Gage turned to study the open shelving along the opposite wall. Not much of interest there—some copy paper, a paper cutter, box of envelopes, half a dozen books. He walked over and pulled one of the books from the shelf. "*The Deadliest Game—Chemical Warfare in World War II.* Looks like Hake was interested in military history," he said, seeing that the other titles on the shelf also dealt with different aspects of the war.

"I found the key." Travis held up a pair of small gold keys held together with a loop of wire. He turned and fit one of the keys into the top drawer of the filing cabinet. The drawer slid open easily.

Too easily. The two brothers stared at the empty drawer. Travis opened the other three drawers—all just as vacant. "Why bother locking an empty filing cabinet?" Gage asked.

"According to the Colorado State Patrol investigator's report, made the day after Hake's disappearance was reported, this cabinet was full of files pertaining to Hake's businesses," Travis said. "At the time, they didn't think anything in here was relevant to what they were considering a case of a man who had left town of his own accord for a while, but the report definitely mentions them."

"And now they're gone," Gage said. "Who took them?"

Travis's eyes met his. "Maybe the person who put Hake's car in that ravine."

At ELEVEN THIRTY, Darla joined Casey and Maya in the conference room-turned-playroom. "The sheriff told me what happened after you left here yesterday," she said. "How are you doing?"

"I think I'm more shaken up by the whole thing than

Casey is." Both women turned to watch Casey, who, after greeting Darla, had gone back to coloring with Rhea. "She had the presence of mind to lock herself in the bathroom and call 911. Gage thinks the attacker heard the sirens approaching and fled."

"The police artist Sheriff Walker found to work with Casey will be here shortly," Darla said. "I'll translate her descriptions to him and we're hoping together we can come up with a picture to help us identify the culprit. Once he's captured, you'll both feel better."

The door opened and Gage walked in. Maya's breath caught, and her heart fluttered. She had always thought of herself as a woman who would never lose her head over a man, yet being with Gage left her so undone.

"I'm Tim Baker, the forensic artist." A young man she hadn't noticed before, long dark hair tied back in a ponytail, offered his hand. "I'll be working with Casey this afternoon."

"Tim has a lot of experience working with children," Gage said.

"I find that most children, even very young ones like Casey, are very intelligent and know a lot more than we give them credit for," Tim said. "The challenge is finding a way to help them communicate the details they know."

"I imagine it's a bigger challenge when the child is deaf," Maya said.

"Yes, but she does have a language," Tim said. "With Darla as my interpreter, I'm sure I'll be able to understand what I need to create an image of her attacker."

"I'm sure I can help, too," Maya said.

Gage touched her arm. "I thought while Darla and Casey are working with Tim, I'd take you to lunch," he said.

"Children are sometimes more forthcoming when

Mom isn't hovering." Tim opened his computer bag and began setting up a laptop. "Since Darla and Casey have already established a relationship, everything should be fine."

Maya started to protest that she wasn't Casey's mother, but Gage interrupted. "Come on," he said. "You could use a break, couldn't you?"

Casey had already turned to greet Darla, who in turn introduced Tim. She barely glanced over when Darla signed that she should say goodbye to Maya, then waved half-heartedly, her attention quickly captured once more by the affable young man. Tim picked up one of the markers the girls had been working with and wrote his name, then drew a cartoon of a penguin that had both girls laughing.

"Rhea, I think your grandmother is ready to take you home," Gage said.

Rhea's eyes said she wanted to protest, but Gage soothed her feelings by putting his hand on her shoulder. "Casey has work to do now," he said. "We'd better leave her to it."

Gage and Maya left Rhea with Adelaide, then walked out to his SUV. "It feels strange to leave her like that," Maya said, looking back toward the sheriff's office.

"She seemed happy when we left," Gage said. "And you can't say she's a timid child."

"No, she isn't," Maya agreed. "She's much more confident than I was at her age—or at any age. How many adults would have the presence of mind to hide from a killer and call 911? Or survive two days and nights alone in the woods? I don't know if I'm cut out to raise a child like that." There—she'd said it—she'd given voice to the fear that had lurked in the back of her mind since news of her sister's death had sunk in. How was she qualified to be a parent? If she had contemplated having children at all, it had been as something that would happen years from now, once she was further along in her career and happily married to the man she wanted to be with for the rest of her life. Even when she had signed the papers agreeing to be Casey's guardian, she had never believed it would happen.

Gage reached over and took her hand. "I'm guessing at some point every parent in the world has thought the same thing," he said. "All parents have to learn as they go. You'll do fine."

"I guess all I can do is try." But his vote of confidence made her feel better. He had a gift for knowing just what to say and do—at least for her.

"What do you feel like eating for lunch?" he asked. "The selection in Eagle Mountain isn't the most varied in the world, but we could run over to Junction if you like."

"I don't want to go to a restaurant," she said.

He went still, though his expression didn't change. "Oh?"

"No. I want to go back to your house." She wet her lips. "To finish what we started last night."

He glanced at her, as if making sure she was serious. Then he keyed the mic on his radio. "This is unit two," he said. "I'm going ten-seven until further notice."

GAGE TOOK HIS cue from Maya and played it cool. He drove to his house, unlocked the door and followed her inside. She deposited her purse on the table by the sofa, then walked back to his bedroom, as if she had done so dozens of times before. When he caught up with her, she was standing just inside the doorway, surveying the king-sized bed with its navy blue comforter, and the simple oak dresser and nightstand. "It's much neater than I expected," she said.

"My mother insisted we make our beds before breakfast every morning," he said. "It's a habit that stuck." He put his hands on her shoulders and gently turned her to face him. "Are you saying you expected me to be a slob?"

"Aren't most people? Trust me, if you had walked into my bedroom unannounced, you would have found the bed unmade and clothes on the floor."

"If I walked into your bedroom unannounced, I wouldn't be thinking about your housekeeping practices." He pulled her close against him. "I'm not thinking about them now."

"So I can tell." She tilted her head up to his in an invitation he wasn't about to refuse. She kissed him back—unhurriedly, with an intensity that stirred him. Her fingers brushed the back of his neck, her nails pressed against his scalp. Her other hand was at his back, fingers splayed across his ribs—or where his ribs were under the tactical vest.

She broke the kiss and pulled back a little. "All this hardware is sexy in its own way," she said. "But I'm looking forward to feeling you out of it."

He unbuckled his utility belt and set it, clanking, on the dresser, then began unbuttoning his shirt, starting at the top. She tugged the shirt from his waistband and undid the bottom button, working her way up until they met in the middle. He captured her hand and kissed it, sucking the fingers into his mouth one at a time, enjoying the way her eyes glazed and her breath grew uneven. Then he released her hand and stripped off the shirt.

While he removed the vest and the rest of his clothes, she also undressed until she stood before him in bra and panties, both pale pink and relatively plain and as erotic as anything he had ever seen. She had a trim waist and rounded hips and small but full breasts that swelled over the top of her bra, and he couldn't resist cupping her in his hands, smiling when she gasped as he dragged his thumbs across her hardened nipples. "Is this the kind of lunch break you had in mind?" he asked.

"Definitely." She arched against him and he reached around and unfastened her bra and slipped it off. Closing his eyes, he savored the feel of her against him—soft heat and firm curves that made him doubly grateful to be a man here with her right now.

As he pulled the bra out of the way, she walked backward to the edge of the bed, dragging him down on top of her. She stared into his eyes, and he glimpsed need and hope. "Make me forget everything else," she said. "Just for a while."

He did his best to fulfill her request, pleasuring her with his hands and his mouth, learning the contours of her body and reveling in her exploration of his. Neither of them hurried, determined to wring every last drop of pleasure from the moment. By the time he slicked on a condom and positioned himself over her, they were both panting and trembling with need. She welcomed him inside of her and they moved together with both the awkwardness of new lovers and the confidence of two souls who knew each other well. When her climax shuddered through her, he gave a cry of triumph and followed after her.

Afterward, they lay beside each other, silent and sated. If he had had the energy left for words, he would have said he had loved her with all of his being, and she had loved him with all of hers. The idea amazed him. Always before, sex had been about pleasure or release, about having fun and making sure his partner was satisfied as well as himself. He hadn't needed or wanted love to be part of the equation.

"That was exactly what I needed." She rested her head in the hollow of his shoulder, her body curled against his. "I feel like myself again."

"Glad I could help." He caressed her shoulder, keeping his voice light. He needed time to process these new feelings before he bared his soul.

A buzzing from somewhere near the floor disturbed their languid silence. "Is that your phone?" she asked.

"Yes." He sat up on the side of the bed and groped for his pants. He was composing a tart reply for whoever had interrupted them when he saw that the call was from Travis. "What do you need?" he asked.

"The artist has finished working with Casey," his brother said. "You need to get over here and see this."

Chapter Sixteen

The drawing tacked to the conference room whiteboard showed a burly man with a prominent nose, high cheekbones, sharp chin and lips curled in a sneer. A black knit cap pulled low over his forehead hid his hair, and dark sunglasses obscured his eyes. Maya wrapped her arms around herself and suppressed a shudder. This was the person who had killed her sister and brother-in-law and attacked her? No wonder Casey was terrified of him.

"I did the best I could," Tim said. "But from a child's perspective, this is what a bad guy looks like—larger than life, you might say." He began packing up his supplies. "Casey didn't want to talk about him at first, but we played some games and I got her to loosen up and confide in me. She's a very intelligent child—very aware."

Darla had taken Casey to another part of the station for a snack so the other adults could consult in private. "I hope talking about this man didn't upset her too much," Maya said.

"In my experience, talking about someone they're afraid of this way—actively participating in efforts to stop him—is very comforting for children," Tim said. "It reminds them the person is human, with a particular kind of nose and a chin and lips and all the little details every other person shares. It demystifies them somewhat."

Gage studied the image, frowning. "It's like a cartoon villain, isn't it—exaggerated features."

"Like I said—larger than life." Tim nodded to the drawing. "He was always wearing the cap and sunglasses when she saw him, which makes it impossible to know details like his hair and eyes. I used my computer program to tone down the features a little and make some guesses on the hair and eyes, but they're just speculation." He picked up a stack of papers from the table and handed them to Gage. Maya moved to look over his shoulder as he paged through half a dozen drawings of men who were similar to, but not exactly like, the drawing on the whiteboard.

"Do any of those look familiar to you?" she asked Gage.

"Yes and no." He set the stack of drawings aside. "There's something familiar about him, but maybe more as a type than as a specific person. We'll distribute the main drawing and see if anyone comes up with anything. Maybe we'll get lucky."

"Even when I have an adult witness who got a good look at a suspect, the drawing doesn't always produce results," Tim said. "People don't always pay much attention to other people, and context matters a lot."

"If you don't think of your brother or your neighbor as a bad person, it's hard to see them in a drawing of a criminal," Gage said. "Thanks for trying, anyway."

"Yes, thank you," Maya said. "It sounds like you've helped Casey, and that means a lot."

"I was happy to help," Tim said. "Good luck to you."

He left and Gage unpinned the drawing from the board. "We'll get some copies of these made to send out," he said.

"I want to see Casey," Maya said. "I need to make sure she really is all right."

"The two of you will need to hang out here for another few hours," Gage said. "Then we can head back to my place."

Another night at Gage's place, where they would be safe but still so unsettled. As much as she loved being with him, her life wasn't here in this small town. Her life—her job, her home, her friends and everything Casey had ever known—was back in Denver. They needed to get back there, to establish a routine that would help them both to heal.

But as long as a killer pursued them, she didn't see a way for that to happen. They were stuck in limbo and the longer they stayed, the more appealing Eagle Mountain seemed.

Running footsteps heralded Casey's approach. She burst into the room and ran to throw her arms around Maya in a hug. Then she turned and embraced Gage, as well. He looked both surprised and pleased as he patted her back, then awkwardly signed "Hello."

"She certainly has taken to Deputy Walker." Darla spoke from the doorway. "She told me she's been teaching him sign language."

"She's always been an outgoing little girl," Maya said.

"I think this is more than her natural friendliness," Darla said. "I think she trusts that Gage is going to help her and keep her safe. That kind of security is especially important to her right now."

"I think she'll feel even more secure when she's back home in Denver," Maya said.

"That's when the loss of her parents will hit the hardest, I think," Darla said. "You'll both have to work through your grief. I hope you have friends you can lean on."

Angie had been her closest friend. Maya had never had to go through any difficulty in life without her. She would have to build a new support system for her and for Casey. Why had Angela and Greg ever thought they had needed to buy those old mining claims? If they had stayed home, they never would have run into their killer. They would be alive and their family intact right now.

Casey tugged on her hand. "Come play this game Tim showed me," she signed.

Maya forced a cheerful expression to her face. "Sure," she signed. "That will be fun."

For the next hour, she and Casey played a variation of hangman, in which the object was to guess the word the other player had come up with before a complete face was drawn. Maya could see that this was a clever way to get the little girl to think about the different shapes people's noses, eyes and lips took.

"Did it upset you to talk to Tim about the man who tried to take you?" Maya asked.

"At first I was scared, remembering," Casey signed. "But after a bit it was easier, somehow. And Tim said I could help them stop him from hurting anyone again, and that made me feel good."

"You're the best, bravest girl I know," Maya signed and hugged her close.

"I miss Mommy and Daddy." Casey buried her face in Maya's side.

"I miss them, too," Maya whispered and rubbed Casey's back, trying to comfort both herself and her niece.

Casey fell asleep and Maya sat with her, her mind replaying the events of the past few days, marveling at how much her life had changed in such a short span of time. Later in the afternoon, after Casey had awakened from her nap and resumed scribbling on the drawing pad, Gage leaned into the conference room. "Are you two ready to head back to my place?" he asked. He did a pretty good job of making the signs for "going home," and Casey nodded enthusiastically, her ponytail bobbing.

"I thought I'd grill burgers for supper, if that's okay," he said when they were in his SUV, headed to his house.

"I'll help," Maya said. When he started to protest, she said, "Casey should eat some vegetables, so I'll put together a salad or something."

So they ended up working side by side in the kitchen, while Casey set the table and arranged and rearranged the silverware. It was all so easy and companionable—and Maya told herself not to get too comfortable. This was all temporary, never meant to last.

After supper, they did dishes, then Casey and Gage practiced more sign language. "You've been practicing," Maya said when he successfully ran through the finger-spelled alphabet.

"It's interesting," he said. "And I found a bunch of videos online last night after you went to bed that show a lot of signs."

"He's a fast learner," Casey signed.

Yes, and he had very quickly made a place for himself in their lives. She stood. "Time for you to get ready for bed," she told Casey.

"Can't I stay up a little longer? I want to look at more of Gage's pictures."

Maya translated this for Gage and he held up both hands, a clear sign that he was having no part in this argument. "Come on," Maya signed. "You can have another bubble bath."

This bribe worked, and Casey had her bath and was already yawning by the time Maya helped her into her pajamas. Maya kissed her good-night, then returned to the living room.

"You look like you could use this," Gage said, handing her a glass of wine.

She started to say something flirtatious, about how he was trying to get her tipsy to take advantage of her, or about how he was what she really could use. But she couldn't afford to give in to that temptation. Like pulling a bandage off a wound, she needed to do this quickly, before she lost her nerve. "I've decided tomorrow we need to go back to Denver," she said.

He set his own glass on the table beside the sofa. "I don't like that idea," he said.

"Casey has given you all the information she can, and we need to get back sooner rather than later," she said. "The longer we delay, the harder it's going to be to face starting over without Angela and Greg. And I have so many arrangements to make—for their memorial services, for Casey to move in with me and the legal paperwork for her guardianship." Merely listing it all made her feel overwhelmed.

"I could help you with all of that if you stayed," he said.

"I think I need to handle it myself."

He was silent for so long she wondered if he was angry. Did he think because they had made love she owed him something? Or that because he was a law enforcement officer she should give his judgment more weight than her own?

"If you need anything—anything at all—I'll be there for you," he said.

Some of her resolve melted at the tenderness of his

words, but she forced herself to stay strong. "Knowing that you mean that helps more than you could know," she said.

He leaned in to kiss her, but she put up a hand to hold him back. "This afternoon was wonderful," she said. "But I think we had better leave it at that."

He drew back. "All right."

She stood. "It's been a long day and tomorrow will be even longer. Good night."

"Good night."

She lay awake for a long time, listening to Casey's even breathing beside her. She believed she was making the right decision, but why did she feel so awful? Was it because doing the right thing—the adult thing—was all about hard choices and sacrifices? Now that she was a parent, was she facing a life of doing what she should instead of what she wanted?

She wasn't sure when she drifted to sleep, but she woke with a start when Gage shook her shoulder. "Shhh," he whispered before she could cry out. He motioned her to follow him and moved to the door.

Careful not to wake Casey, she sat up on the side of the bed, then stood, still groggy, and trailed him into the living room.

"I'm sorry to wake you," he said. "But I have to go out. There's been another break-in at the school, and one at the outdoor store."

"The same people?" she asked.

"Maybe. A reserve officer will be here any minute and he'll stay with you while I'm gone."

"Do you think that's necessary?" she asked.

"I don't want to take any chances."

A light knock on the door signaled the arrival of the officer. Gage let him in and introduced him, though

Maya, still half-asleep, forgot the name as soon as Gage said it. "Don't worry about anything, ma'am," the young man said. "I'll be right out front."

"Thank you," she said.

"I'd better go." Gage leaned in, as if to kiss her, but instead only patted her shoulder. "Don't wait up," he said. "Everything will be fine."

But sleep was the last thing on her mind now. She stood at the window and watched Gage get into his SUV, then located the reserve officer, seated in his patrol car parked at the curb in front of the house. Reassured, she went into the kitchen to make tea. She remembered seeing a chamomile blend in the cabinet when she had helped Gage make supper, and she brewed a cup now. As she stirred honey into the tea, she mused that for a supposedly safe small town, Eagle Mountain was certainly experiencing a rash of crime lately. And people thought cities were dangerous.

The minty, hot beverage soothed her and she began to feel sleepy again. The sight of the patrol car still parked at the curb reassured her, and she headed back to the bedroom and made her way in the darkness to her side of the bed.

But she sensed something was wrong before she had even pulled the covers to her chin. She rolled over and felt the space beside her—a Casey-shaped indentation that was still warm from the child's body.

She sat up and glanced toward the bathroom, thinking Casey had awakened while Maya was in the other room. But the bathroom door was open and the light off. More unsettling, a breeze billowed the curtain of the window on the wall to her right—a window she was certain had been closed before.

Chapter Seventeen

"I can't believe this happened." Wade Tomlinson raked one hand over his shaved scalp. He had met Gage and Deputy Dwight Prentice at Eagle Mountain Outdoors, dressed in camouflage cargo pants, a University of Northern Colorado sweatshirt and sheepskin slippers. "We've been here, what, almost three years, and we've never had any problems."

"Did you have anyone suspicious in the shop in the last day or two?" Gage asked. "Someone who might have been overly interested in one of the items that was stolen, or someone who questioned you about your habits, where you lived, et cetera?"

"No. Nobody like that." Wade shook his head. "I didn't see anybody who might have been casing the place or anything like that."

"What about Brock?" Dwight asked. "Did he mention anyone acting strange?"

"No."

"Where is Brock?" Gage asked. "Does he know about the break-in?"

"I called and left a message on his cell," Wade said. "But he isn't answering."

"Does that surprise you?" Dwight asked.

"Not really. He's been sort of seeing this woman over

in Junction. I figure he's at her place, with his phone switched off."

"What is her name?" Dwight asked.

"I don't know. I'm not sure he ever told me." Wade raked his hand over his scalp again and stared at the shattered front window. A large chunk of granite rested in the middle of a display of climbing shoes and technical pants and jackets, pebbles of safety glass like corn snow glinting in the folds of the clothing and along the laces of the shoes. "What am I going to do about my window? Anybody could walk in and take what they want right now."

"Call Tommy Milaski over at the hardware store and he'll open up and sell you some plywood to nail over the window until you can get an insurance appraiser and the glass company out to make repairs," Gage said. He looked up at the camera in the back corner of the store. "That camera should have footage from the area around the cash register, right? We'll need to see that."

Wade's expression grew more pained. "That camera isn't actually connected to anything," he said. "Brock installed it when we opened the store, but he never got around to hooking it up to the computer. He needed to order some component and then we got busy and..." He shrugged. "We've never had problems before."

Gage had heard similar stories from other businesses in town. Either they didn't want to spend the money on a security system or they didn't see the pressing need for one. It made his job more difficult, but as the business owners pointed out, the need for such evidence rarely came up. He consulted the notebook in his hand. "You're pretty sure the only things missing are a pair of climbing shoes and the money that was in the cash register?"

"I'm sure," Wade said. "They couldn't get into the safe, and I didn't see anything out of place. The shoes were right there." He pointed to a gap in the display. "Intense Gravity Escalon, $67.99."

"What size?" Dwight asked.

Wade scratched his head. "Size?"

"If the thief took them to wear himself, it might help us pin down what size man we're dealing with."

Wade nodded. "They were eights. Kind of small for a man, which is why we used them for a display."

Dwight made a note of this. "We got a couple of shoe impressions from the high school," he said. "Maybe this will match."

"The high school?" Wade asked. "Do you think the same person who took the climbing ropes from the high school hit my store? Maybe it's those two guys I told you about. Did you talk to them?"

"We haven't been able to find them," Gage said. "Have you seen them since the day you and Brock met up with them while climbing?"

"No," Wade said. "And I've been keeping my eyes open for them. Talk about suspicious characters—so you think they hit the high school the other day?"

"Someone broke into the high school again tonight," Dwight said, before Gage could signal him to keep quiet.

"No kidding?" Wade said. "What did they take this time?"

"We're not sure yet," Gage said before Dwight could answer. Al Dawson had showed up for work and found broken windows and called the sheriff's office. Inside, someone had emptied the contents of three fire extinguishers around the gym. They had made a mess, but so far it didn't appear that anything was missing. As Dwight had said, the perpetrators had left a couple of shoe impressions on the edge of the gym floor, but Gage wasn't hopeful they would prove very useful.

"I'll ask Brock if he remembers anything else about those guys," Wade said. "He's better with details than I am. I just—"

Gage's phone rang. Checking the display, his heart sped up when he saw Maya's name. He put a hand up to silence Wade and answered. "Hello? Are you all right?"

"Casey's gone. Someone's taken her." He hardly recognized Maya's voice, ragged with terror.

"Are you all right?" He gripped the phone tighter. "Is the reserve officer there?"

"Yes. He's parked out front. Someone came in the bedroom window while I was in the kitchen." Her voice broke. "Gage, I'm so scared."

"I'll be right there." He ended the call and shoved the phone back in its holster. "We have to go," he told Dwight. "Someone's kidnapped Casey Hood."

MAYA PULLED A jacket and jeans over her pajamas and went to the front door to summon the reserve officer. Maybe she should have contacted him first, but all her instincts had told her to call Gage. He was the one who had helped her before, the one who cared about Casey almost as much as she did. The officer met her at the door. "Gage called and told me what happened," he said, his eyes dark against a pale face. "I don't know how. I was out front, watching the house and the street, the whole time."

"He came in the back," she said. "Through the bedroom window." She started past him, but he took her arm, holding her back. "I just want to see where he came in," she protested, trying to pull free.

"You might destroy evidence," the officer said. "We need to wait for Gage."

They didn't have to wait long. Gage's SUV screeched

to a halt behind the patrol car, followed by another sheriff's department vehicle. Gage jogged up the walk and took the steps two at a time to reach them. "Gage, I swear I was watching the house the whole time and I never saw a thing," the reserve officer said.

"Not now, Carl." Gage took Maya by the shoulders and looked her in the eyes. "Are you sure you're okay? Did the kidnapper try to hurt you?"

"I never even saw him," she said. "I was in the kitchen making tea, and when I came back to the bedroom, Casey was gone and the window was open. I know it was locked when I went to bed. I always check and—"

"It's all right." He squeezed her shoulders—more of a caress. "You didn't do anything wrong." The steadiness of his voice and the tenderness in his eyes calmed her.

"I started to go around back to check, but your officer stopped me. He said I might destroy evidence."

"He was right." Gage gave the young officer a nod. "Carl, you stay here with Maya while Dwight and I check out the scene. The crime scene techs are already on the way."

Maya hugged her arms across her stomach and watched as Gage and Dwight made their way around the side of the house. Carl, looking miserable, stood beside her, shoulders slumped, staring at the porch floor. The lights in the houses across the street came on—the neighbors were probably watching out the window, curious as to why three cop cars were parked in front of the house.

Gage opened the front door and stepped out onto the porch. "I left Dwight guarding the scene until CSI gets here," he said. "It looks like the kidnapper cut out a pane of glass, reached in and unlocked the window, then came in and out that way. It probably only took a few minutes."

Some of the shock was wearing off and Maya focused

on picturing the scene Gage had described. "Did they plan to knock me out again and take her?" she asked. "Or was he watching the house, waiting for me to leave the room?"

"I think he was probably watching the house," Gage said. "I think the break-ins at the high school and Eagle Mountain Outdoors may have been designed to draw me away from the house so the kidnappers could make their move."

"So we could be talking about an organized group," Carl said. "Not just the person who took Casey."

"That's the way it looked to me," Gage said. "Carl, I need you to take over for Dwight guarding the scene. I need him to follow up on some other things for me."

When they were alone, Gage opened his arms. "Come here," he said.

She went to him, sighing when he wrapped his arms around her and drew her close. She closed her eyes and tried to draw on his strength. As tempting as it was to collapse and weep into his arms, she needed to stay strong for Casey. "I can't believe this is happening," she said. "I feel so helpless. What can I do?"

"Don't give up hope." He pulled back enough to look her in the eye. "I'm sorry they took Casey, but I'm glad you weren't in the room when the kidnapper came through the window. He might have done more than just knock you out."

The impact of his words shook her. "You think he might have killed me to get to Casey?"

"If this is the same person who murdered your sister and her husband, he's already proven he's capable of murder."

"But they didn't kill Casey. Why not?"

"I don't know. But every indication so far is that they wanted to take her alive."

Maya covered her face with her hands. "I can't bear to think what they might do to her."

"Don't." Gage gently tugged her hands away. "Come with me into the bedroom and tell me everything that happened after I left the house tonight."

She walked with him to the bedroom. The window was still open, curtains rising and falling in the breeze like ghostly dancers. The covers on Casey's side of the bed were pushed back, the faint indentation made by the small body still visible. Gage went to stand beside the bed. "I don't see any sign of a struggle," he said. "She may not have awakened when they snatched her. Or they might have sedated her."

"Drugs?" Maya shuddered.

"It would keep her quiet and make her easier to transport," Gage said. "She isn't a very big child, so a man, or even a strong woman, could carry her back out through the window and across the yard fairly easily. If they had a car waiting on the street behind this one, they could get away unnoticed. We'll canvas the houses on both streets. Maybe a night-shift worker or someone with insomnia saw something unusual."

He moved to the window. "Was it exactly like this when you first saw it?" he asked. "You didn't open it wider or push back the curtains or anything?"

"No. As soon as I realized Casey was gone, I called you."

"We'll get the crime scene techs in here to take pictures and look for trace evidence." He turned away from the window. "Is anything else in the room out of place? Anything missing?"

She looked around, trying to remember how the room

had looked when she went to bed. She had folded her clothes and put them on the chair by the door, and Casey's clothes were on top of the dresser. "Casey's jacket. It was hanging on the bedpost and now it's gone." Hope rose in her chest. "If the kidnapper took the time to get her jacket, that must mean he doesn't intend to harm her, right?"

"I don't know what it means," Gage said. He took out his notebook. "So she was wearing pink-and-white pajamas with some kind of design on them." He frowned. "Princesses or something?"

"Disney princesses. And her jacket is pink, with white trim. It zips up the front and has pockets."

He scribbled in the notebook. "We'll make sure this is part of the Amber Alert." He slipped the notebook back into his pocket and put his arm around her. "I could use some coffee. Could you make me some?"

She recognized the attempt to keep her busy and out of the way, but didn't argue. "Sure. Anything else?"

"Just some coffee would be great." She started to turn away, but he grabbed her hand. When she turned toward him again, his gaze met hers. "We're going to get whoever did this," he said. "We're going to find Casey."

She nodded. "I believe you." Gage would do whatever it took to find Casey. Maya only hoped he found her alive and well, before it was too late.

Chapter Eighteen

The more Gage reviewed the events of that night, the more convinced he became that the break-ins at the high school and Eagle Mountain Outdoors had been designed to get him away from his house, leaving Maya and Casey vulnerable. That pointed to a perpetrator who knew him, and who knew enough about the Eagle Mountain Sheriff's Department to know they didn't have the staff to handle multiple break-ins without calling in Gage. That meant the person would also know that the only officers left to guard Maya and Casey would be less-experienced reserve deputies—officers who were less likely to take the initiative to patrol the property on foot. Gage cursed his own carelessness in not recognizing an attacker might approach from the rear, and that locked windows were no barrier to a really determined criminal.

"Both of the break-ins that night were a lot of flash and noise, but no real substance," he reported the next morning, when every available officer gathered at the sheriff's department for a briefing. "Nothing was taken from the high school, and less than fifty dollars and a pair of climbing shoes from Eagle Mountain Outdoors. There was nothing sneaky about either crime. The thief didn't care if he set off alarms—in fact, he wanted to."

"None of the neighbors around Gage's house saw or

heard anything suspicious that night," Dwight reported. "That's not surprising, considering it was three in the morning."

"Not an insomniac or newborn who needed feeding in the bunch," Travis said. "What did CSI come up with?"

"No prints." Gage read from the report he had pulled up on his tablet. "The perp wore gloves—another indication that this was a well-planned hit and not a random grab. Right now, we're operating on the theory that whoever kidnapped Casey Hood is connected with the two men who murdered Angela and Greg Hood."

"That had earmarks of a professional hit, also," Travis said.

"Have we had any results from the drawing Tim Baker did using Casey's description of her attacker?" Gage asked.

"Nothing useful," Travis said. "We've had a few calls from people saying they thought the person shown in the drawing looked familiar—like someone they had seen around town—but nothing concrete that even leads to anyone we could question."

"If these guys thought they needed to silence the kid because she could identify them, why not just kill her, too?" Dwight asked. "Why take the risks involved in kidnapping her?"

"We don't know," Gage said. "But if they believe they have a reason to keep her alive, that buys us more time to find her." He didn't say what he knew every person in the room was thinking—they were working against the clock to find Casey alive. Time could make the kidnappers change their minds, if they hadn't already.

"So we think the break-ins at the high school and Eagle Mountain Outdoors are related to the kidnapping,"

Dwight said. "Carried out by accomplices of the kidnappers in order to draw you away from the scene."

"That's the way it looks to me," Gage said. Beside him, Travis nodded.

"What about the earlier break-ins at the high school?" Dwight said. "When the climbing rope and mats, and the lab equipment were taken."

"Hard to say," Travis said. "My instinct is no—those break-ins were to steal specific things. The one last night was fast and loud, with general vandalism and nothing stolen. I think someone knew about the other crimes and figured doing something similar was a good way to get every available officer on scene and away from the vicinity of Gage's house."

"What about the skinheads Wade Tomlinson reported as suspicious characters?" Gage asked. "Do we have anything else on them?"

"We searched the camping area Wade said they were in and talked to other climbers in the area," Travis said. "No one remembers seeing anyone like them around."

"Those types would stand out around here," Dwight said.

"Exactly," Travis said. "I'm beginning to think Wade made them up."

Gage stared at his brother. "You mean he deliberately lied to us? Why?"

"I don't know. Maybe to grab some attention for himself or his business—you know it happens."

Gage nodded, letting the idea sink in. Plenty of people got an adrenaline charge from being involved, even peripherally, in a police investigation. But Wade Tomlinson had always struck him as much more grounded than that. Still, how well did he know the man? They weren't close friends who spent time together. "It's something to consider. Do you think he made up the story about the break-in at his store, too?"

Travis frowned. "Throwing a rock through your own front window is pretty drastic, but we'll be giving him a closer look. I put a call in to the police chief in Butte, where Wade and Brock supposedly worked for an outfitter before they came here to open up shop. We'll see what he has to say."

"What about Henry Hake's disappearance?" Dwight asked.

"What about it?" Gage asked.

"Do you think it's related?"

Gage and Travis exchanged glances. "Why do you think it would be?"

"Timing and proximity, mainly," Dwight said. "The resort Hake wanted to develop was adjacent to the land the Hoods had purchased."

"That might be just coincidence," Gage said. "Hake disappeared weeks ago, and we haven't found anything to connect him with the Hoods or their property."

"Right now, we're treating Hake's disappearance as a separate crime," Travis said. "And we can't forget about it while we're dealing with Casey's kidnapping and the Hoods' murders. We're still trying to figure out what happened to the files that were in Hake's home office and if they're related to his disappearance."

"Still, it wouldn't hurt to look for more connections between Hake and the Hoods," Gage said. The hairs on the back of his neck had stood up when Dwight had suggested a connection between Greg and Angela Hood and Henry Hake. "I'd like to get Maya back in to take another look at her sister's belongings. Maybe now that she's had more time to think, she'll see something significant that she didn't notice before."

"Do it," Travis said. "Meanwhile, the rest of us are going to be combing every possible camping site and climbing area, just in case those skinheads Wade described show up."

CASEY OPENED HER eyes to darkness. Her stomach hurt and she felt dizzy, but gradually she realized she was in the back seat of a car, which was driving over a rough road. As her eyes adjusted to the darkness, she realized the two people in the front seat weren't her parents, but two men—she had only glimpsed one of them for a few seconds, but had recognized him as the man who had tried to grab her at the inn where she and Aunt Maya had spent the night. One of the men who had killed her parents. Her heart pounded so hard she thought it might burst out of her chest, and she had to bite her bottom lip to keep from crying out from fear. But she must not let them know she was awake. As long as they thought she was still out, maybe they would leave her alone.

She tried to think what to do. She had been sleeping so good in the bed she shared with Aunt Maya in Deputy Gage's house when the man had grabbed her. He had put his hand over her mouth so she couldn't scream, then pressed a handkerchief that smelled sweet over her face and everything went black again.

She couldn't see the other man—the driver—very good, but he was shorter and wider than the first man. He was probably the man who had helped to kill her parents. Were they taking her somewhere to kill her? The thought made her feel cold all over, and she started to shake. She tried very hard to keep still. *Think*, she told herself. She had to get away. Aunt Maya and Deputy Gage would find out she was missing and they would come looking for her. She had to stay alive long enough for them to find her.

She closed her eyes again, afraid one of the men in the front seat would look back and notice her staring at them and realize she was awake. Her hands were tied in front of her with some kind of rope. There were several big knots, but the rope wasn't too tight. She could move her hands a little apart. She had small hands and strong fingers, from using them so much to make words, instead of using her voice. She wiggled her hands and moved her wrists. The rope rubbed against her skin and hurt some, but the pain didn't matter, did it? Not if she could get free.

The car made a sharp turn and she had to brace herself to keep from falling off the back seat. It bumped over a very rough road, then came to a stop. Casey risked opening her eyes just a little bit. She watched the two men in the front seat through her lashes. They looked like they were arguing, their faces screwed up in anger, arms waving and fingers pointing.

The tall man in the passenger seat suddenly unsnapped his seat belt, got out of the car and came around to open the back door. He reached in and pulled her out. She forced herself to keep her eyes closed—to let her body go limp and pretend that she was asleep. But the man pinched her—hard—and her eyes flew open. His mouth moved—he had his face close to hers and was saying something, but she couldn't read his lips or understand what he wanted from her.

He picked her up and carried her, long strides moving swiftly across the ground, the second man running alongside them. She tried to see where they were, but had only a glimpse of shadowy trees and a few buildings. Then they were inside one of the buildings—a chilly space that smelled of damp dirt and rusty metal. The man who had been carrying Casey set her on the ground, then shoved her so that she fell over. She hit the ground hard and rolled, her bottom throbbing where she had landed on it. When she looked up, the man had switched on a flashlight and was shining the light all around the room. But she only caught glimpses of a ribbed metal roof and rock walls. Then the man shone the light in her eyes, making her raise her bound hands to try to shield herself from the painful glare.

The light went out, though the ghost of it still blinded her. Casey lay frozen for a long moment, waiting for her vision to clear. When it did, she could make out two shoebox-sized squares of pale light on the dirt floor. As her eyes adjusted more, she saw that the two light squares came from a pair of vents in the ceiling, which was curved and made out of a heavily ribbed metal. Concrete block walls—not stone, as she had first thought— rose up to meet the roof. The floor was dirt, damp in places, a thin trickle of water running down a channel in the center of the space.

The door was a thick slab of metal set at one end of the room. It fit tightly in its frame, not even a splinter of light showing around it. Casey ran to the door and threw herself against it, but it didn't budge. She stood a moment, scanning every corner of the building, which was about the size of the living room at home. She didn't see any place for the two men to hide, so they must have left her here and gone away.

She leaned against the door and worked on freeing her hands from the rope the men had used to bind them. She strained and grunted, ignoring the pain when the rough cord scraped the skin from her thumb. She flexed and bent and tugged until first the thumb, then the rest of the fingers on her right hand, were free. After that, she was able to free her other hand from the binding. She tucked the rope in the pocket of her coat, then went to the far corner of the room and peed in a rusty metal can she found there. Feeling better, she began searching for a way out of the room.

The only openings besides the door were the two air vents, high up in the curved roof, in the center of the room. Casey tried jumping, but she couldn't come close to reaching those openings. The room didn't contain any furniture or any boxes she could stack to climb onto, and there was no ladder. Frustrated, she sat on the floor and stared at the door. She hoped Aunt Maya and Deputy Gage would find her soon—before those two men came back.

"I NEED YOU to look at your sister's things again and see if there's anything, however small, that you don't recognize or that seems out of character or unusual." Gage studied Maya's exhausted face, wondering if he was wasting time with this avenue of investigation. Was he grasping at straws that didn't exist while a killer did away with an innocent little girl?

"I'll try." Maya rubbed her temples. "I've been going over and over the conversations I had with Angie and Greg about this new venture of theirs, trying to remember any details that might help. But everything was very general—they had bought the property, had plans for it as the start of a new business venture and might move to Eagle Mountain because it was a quiet, beautiful place that would be good for Casey."

"Take a look at their belongings again," Gage said. "Now that a few days have passed, maybe something will stand out for you."

She nodded, and he led her down the hall to the conference room. He watched her while she walked slowly past the tables and the items laid out like the remnants of someone's yard sale, yellow evidence labels standing out against the blues and greens of the camping equipment and clothing. She stopped in front of one of the plastic storage containers and the miscellaneous canned and packaged food arrayed beside it, each item carefully inventoried, including a trio of glass jars with lids. "Angie liked to keep everything in these glass canning jars," she said, picking up one that was filled with shriveling red berries. She squinted at the jar. "What are these?"

Gage leaned over her shoulder to get a closer look at the contents of the jar. "I think the tech said they're rose hips. Wait a minute." He consulted the evidence sheet on a clipboard by the door. "Here it is—approximately one pint of fresh rose hips. Well, not so fresh anymore."

Maya set the jar down. "I'm sure she read somewhere that rose hips are good for something. She was always experimenting with new recipes and jellies and things." She glanced at Gage. "What are rose hips, anyway?"

He pulled out his phone and did a search on the term. "'Rose hips are the fruit of wild roses, valued as a source of vitamins A and C and other vitamins and minerals.'" He looked up from the phone. "She must have found some wild roses on their place and picked these." Except he had tramped over pretty much every square inch of the Hoods' land searching for Casey and didn't remember any roses. He did, however, have a clear memory of the rose hedges alongside Henry Hake's property— hedges heavy with blooming roses, thorns…and fat, red rose hips.

Chapter Nineteen

Maya felt the change in Gage, a sudden tightening along his jaw and straightening of his shoulders, almost like a dog that has alerted on a scent. "What is it?" She gripped his arm. "You've thought of something, haven't you?"

"I'm not sure. Just an idea where your sister might have gotten these. And a connection to another case. I'm wondering if while picking these rose hips, your sister and her husband saw something they shouldn't have."

"Tell me," Maya said. "Could the kidnappers have taken Casey there? Where is it?"

"I can't tell you, but I promise we're going to check it out. Right now. You can stay here and wait, or I'll take you to Paige's place and you can wait with her."

"I'm done with waiting," she said, not suppressing the anger that rose at his suggestion. "If you find Casey, she's going to need me—not a bunch of officers who will mean well but who won't know how to communicate with her. When you find her—and I'm refusing to accept that you won't—you'll need to know what she knows right away. It could make the difference between catching these men and not."

He frowned, but she knew he couldn't deny the strength of her argument. "You'd have to follow orders and stay out of the way."

"I could do that. You know me enough now to know that I won't go all hysterical or try to interfere. But I need to be there for Casey."

"Let me talk to Travis," he said.

"Talk to me about what?" The sheriff, shadows under his eyes and in need of a shave, joined them in the evidence room.

Gage glanced at Maya, clearly debating whether to say anything in front of her. "There's no sense keeping anything a secret from me," she said. "Don't waste any more time."

Gage turned to his brother. "Angela Hood was picking rose hips some time not long before she was killed." He picked up the canning jar and showed it to Travis. "I'm thinking she was around that big rose hedge on Henry Hake's property. Maybe she and her husband saw something they shouldn't have."

Travis arched one eyebrow. "Such as?"

"I don't know. But if Henry Hake's kidnappers took him there to hide him—or to kill him—maybe the Hoods were witnesses and that's why they were killed."

"And maybe the killers took Casey there," Maya said. "There are all kinds of buildings on that property, aren't there? What if they took her to one of them?"

"Can we get a warrant for a search based on a jar of rose hips?" Gage asked.

"With Hake and Casey missing, and the Hoods' murders right next door?" Travis nodded. "Judge Wilson would probably be sympathetic." He clapped Gage on the shoulder. "Grab Dwight and anyone else on duty and head up there. I'll get the request for the warrant to Judge Wilson and let you know as soon as it's a go."

Travis headed for his office. Gage locked up the room, then radioed Dwight. "Get as many officers as you can round up and meet me at Eagle Mountain Resort. As soon as we get the go-ahead from Travis, we're going in."

She followed him down a long hallway to a room with a heavy steel door. He unlocked it and she found herself in a small space filled with weapons, ammunition and even a battering ram. Gage scanned the array of items, then pulled a black vest from a box. "Put this on," he ordered.

Putting on the vest brought home the seriousness of the situation. It was hard and heavy and the fact that he felt she needed to wear it frightened her more than the rifle and ammunition he took from the room. But she pushed down the fear and followed him back out of the room to his SUV.

"You stay in the vehicle," he said as he started the engine. "If I tell you to get down, you get down."

"I will."

The grim expression on his face tore at her. "Gage, you know I don't blame you for anything that's happened."

His jaw tightened. "I should have realized an attacker could approach from the rear of the house," he said. "I should have stationed another officer there."

"You can't anticipate everything—" she began.

"It's my job to anticipate. To protect the people I care about."

The words rocked her back in her seat. Of course, she knew Gage cared. His every action had said as much. But to hear the sentiment spoken out loud touched her deep inside. She reached over and took his hand. "That means everything to me," she said.

He didn't look at her, but he squeezed her hand and held on to it as they drove out of town. Whatever happened next, they would face it together.

THE SUN WAS sending a pink stain over the ash-gray sky as the officers assembled before the gates of Eagle Mountain Resort. The feathery branches of lodgepole pines and white fir looked black in the smoky light, and the air smelled of evergreen. Gage parked his SUV with the bumper up against the gates. Travis had worked quickly, and Judge Wilson had okayed the warrant before Gage was out of cell phone range.

"Unbuckle your seat belt in case you need to get down quickly," he told Maya.

She did as he asked and looked at him, her face very pale, the blue ends of her hair bright in the dim light. Ridiculous hair, but he loved it. He loved pretty much everything about her, yet he had to lock all of that emotion away for now. If he didn't, he would be too afraid for her to do his job.

"Be careful," she said. "Maybe I'm not supposed to say that, but I will, anyway."

"You can say it. And I'll be careful." He thought about kissing her, but settled for giving her a long look he hoped told her everything he couldn't say, then he got out of the SUV and went to meet the rest of the team.

"We've got a warrant to search this place," he said. "Every building." He indicated the pair of bolt cutters Dwight had pulled from his cruiser. "If it's padlocked, cut off the lock. We're looking for a little girl, Casey Hood, who was taken from her bed this evening while she was sleeping. If you come across any sign of her, or anything else suspicious, notify me."

They spread out and for the next hour, they combed over the property, peering into storage sheds full of gardening and construction tools, an empty concrete bunker whose purpose Gage couldn't determine and what had once served as the sales office for the proposed resort, the office furniture and filing cabinets it contained coated with a thick layer of dust. The backhoe and tractor parked in a shed at the back of the property was not dust covered, and judging from the tracks leading to it, had been recently used. Elsewhere on the property tire tracks, shoe impressions, freshly cut trees and newly poured concrete attested to recent activity. But they found nothing suspicious, and no sign that either Henry Hake or Casey had ever been there.

The officers reassembled at the gates to the development, most of them looking as discouraged as Gage felt. "This didn't pan out, so go back and start working our other leads," he said. "Circulate that artist's sketch. Canvas the neighborhoods around my house and around the B and B again. Look for anything we've missed."

As they left, Gage returned to his SUV. He inserted the key in the ignition, but instead of starting the engine, he stared at the tall iron gates and the abandoned buildings and crumbling streets beyond. Something wasn't right here. He couldn't shake that feeling.

"We've missed something," he said. "I can feel it." He opened the driver's-side door again. "I want to take another look around."

"Let me come with you," Maya said. "Please."

He hesitated. But in addition to not finding Casey, his men hadn't found any signs of danger. "Okay," he said. "Maybe you'll see something we've missed."

He led the way around the gates and up what would have been the main street. An eerie silence had settled over the scene, not even the birds calling to each other. Their boots crunched on gravel as they turned down a side street, past the air vents, which had turned out to belong to an air tunnel that led into an abandoned mine, the entrance into the main adit blocked by a heavy iron gate, the hinges so rusted it was obvious it hadn't been opened in the last decade.

"We searched every building on the place," Gage said, sweeping his arm to indicate the half-dozen structures along the deserted remains of streets. "But I can't shake the feeling we're missing something. Call it cop instinct or a hunch or whatever you like."

"I believe you," Maya said. "I feel it, too. The place looks so harmless, but something isn't right." She turned slowly in a circle, then pointed to the end of the street, where a narrow path led into the underbrush. "What's back there?"

"I walked back there until the path gave out," Gage said. "There's nothing." But he fell into step behind her as she held back the low limb of a tree and pushed into the underbrush.

A breeze stirred the still air, bringing with it the scent of blooming roses. A glance to his right showed Gage the pale pink blossoms on the rose hedge along the edge of the property. The vines climbed eight feet up the fence in a thick tangle of blooms and thorns, impenetrable. In between the blossoms glowed bright red rose hips, like beads scattered from a broken necklace.

Maya had seen the roses, too, and left the path to get a closer look. "Careful," Gage said. "Don't let them stick you."

"Angie must have really wanted those hips to risk picking them out of all these thorns." Maya started to retreat and stumbled, and Gage lunged forward to catch her before she fell. He steadied her, and she stared at the ground at her feet. "I tripped over something metal," she said. "Some kind of grate."

He released her and knelt to feel what was definitely a pair of metal grates. They showed no signs of rust. He unclipped the Maglite from his belt and played the beam across the grating. "Maybe these are for drainage," he said. He tugged at the metal, but it refused to budge. "I've got some tools in the truck—let me get them. I want to see where this leads."

"I'll wait here." Maya looked around them. "Otherwise, we might have a hard time finding this again. It's pretty well hidden back in here."

He hurried back toward his SUV, excitement spurring him into a trot. They'd found something significant, he was sure, though what and whether it would lead to Casey—or to Henry Hake—he had no idea. He retrieved a pry bar and a toolbox from his SUV and hurried back down the path. Despite Maya's fears, the place where they had turned off the path was easy enough to find, the brush bent down and crushed by their footsteps. But he didn't see Maya. Had something else caught her attention and she had wandered away to investigate? "Maya?" he called.

Silence was his only answer. Maya had disappeared.

MAYA'S HEAD HURT—a throbbing pain as if someone was using the inside of her skull as a drum. She moaned and tried to roll over, away from the pain, but a sharp ache in her right arm made her gasp and open her eyes. She looked up into Casey's concerned green eyes. Casey, so sweet and seemingly unharmed. Maya closed her eyes again, tears leaking out of the corners. She must be dreaming. Or maybe she was dead and this was heaven— but then why would her head throb and her arm ache?

Casey shook her, and Maya opened her eyes again and sat up. She hugged the girl close and Casey put her arms around Maya's neck and hugged back. If this was a dream, she didn't want it to stop.

"Are you okay?" Casey signed.

"I'm okay." She was alive and that was all that mattered. But on the heels of this thought, panic rose to choke her. Gage? Where was Gage? She looked around her at the dimly lit concrete block–walled room. "Where's Gage?" she asked Casey.

Casey shook her head. "He isn't here. The bad men only brought you."

The bad men. Maya massaged her throbbing temples, a memory more painful than the ache in her skull taking shape. Two men grabbing her roughly as she waited for Gage. One of them, the larger of the two, had pulled her arms behind her back and held her while the other one slapped her when she tried to scream. Then everything went black.

"Who are the bad men?" she signed to Casey. "Where are we?"

But the little girl didn't know the answer to either of those questions. "I think they're the same men who killed Mommy and Daddy and tried to hurt us that day at Paige's house. One of them came in the window at Gage's house and brought me here."

The child must have been terrified, left in this concrete bunker alone. Maya pulled her close. "Gage will come for us," she said, then signed the same message to Casey.

After a while some of the panic subsided and she sat back, rubbing her arm where it still ached. "You must have hurt your arm when they threw you in here," Casey signed. "You hit the floor really hard. I hid when they came back, over in the corner." She pointed to a shadowy corner farthest from the door. "But they didn't even look at me—they just threw you down here."

Maya stood and went to the door. There was no knob or latch on this side, and it fit so tightly in its frame that she doubted she could wedge even a knife into the gap—if she was the kind of person who carried a knife around, which she wasn't. "You can't open the door from this side," Casey signed. "The only way out is up there, but it's too high."

Maya looked where her niece pointed and started at the sight of two metal grates. She was sure these were the same grates she and Gage had been standing over. He would have returned to them by now. What would he do when he discovered she wasn't there?

He would do everything in his power to find them. The certainty with which this thought came to her should have surprised her, but when she thought of Gage, she thought of him going without sleep and walking miles through the woods and doing everything he could to find Casey—and then, once she was found, taking the two of them into his own home to protect them.

"Gage will be looking for us," she told Casey. She pulled the girl close again. "We just have to wait for him. As soon as he can, he'll be here."

MAYA HADN'T WANDERED AWAY, Gage knew. She wasn't like that. She wasn't the type to be distracted by a pretty flower, or to strike out on her own. He examined the ground around the grates and the crushed weeds and broken branches testified to a struggle. A strand of blue thread caught on a thorn attracted his attention and he pulled it free. Not thread, but Maya's hair. She had fought with someone here and been overcome.

Gage followed the path of the struggle, moving as quickly as he dared through the undergrowth. The trail led back to the development, but disappeared when he reached the crumbling asphalt of the street. He scanned the deserted landscape. No sign of Maya. No sign of anyone. He pulled out his cell phone, already knowing he wouldn't find a signal, but needing to be sure. He would have to go back to his SUV and drive down the mountain until he was within range, then call everyone back up here to search. That would take at least twenty minutes—twenty minutes in which whoever had taken Maya could get farther away, or in which they might decide to kill her.

She might already be dead. But he rebelled against that thought. If whoever had taken her wanted her dead, he would have shot her on the spot, the way he had killed Angela and Greg Hood.

He started down the street at a run, but he didn't get very far. A man stepped out of the empty concrete bunker and turned toward him. Gage stopped and stared. "Wade? What are you doing here?"

Wade Tomlinson's eyes were flat, his mouth set in a hard line. "I was really hoping I wouldn't have to do this," he said. Then, before Gage could react, Wade pulled a gun from his jacket and fired.

Chapter Twenty

The impact of the bullet sent Gage staggering back, pain radiating from the center of his chest. Wade fired again, striking lower and Gage fell, grappling for his sidearm. He freed the weapon from its holster and fired, the shot soaring wide. He struggled onto his knees and aimed at Wade's fleeing figure, but before he could squeeze off a shot, someone tackled him from behind. An arm like an iron bar pressed against his windpipe, and a big hand wrenched the pistol from his grip.

"I shot him twice. Why isn't he dead?" Wade came running up, panting.

"He's wearing a vest, you moron." Brock Ryan's clipped voice sounded loud in Gage's ear. Gage fought to free himself, but it was like trying to wrestle with a gorilla. Then he went still as the barrel of a gun—maybe his own weapon—pressed against his temple.

"Don't! Someone's coming!" Wade looked over his shoulder. Gage, fighting to remain conscious as Brock choked off his windpipe, heard nothing, but Wade grew frantic. "They must have heard the gunshots. We have to get out of here."

"Open the door to the bunker," Brock ordered. Still gripping Gage in a choke hold, he dragged him backward toward the bunker. "We'll leave him with the kid."

"The woman is in there, too," Wade said as he fumbled with the lock.

Brock swore. "What is she doing here?"

"I saw her while I was waiting for you—she was over by the air vents. I had to get rid of her, so I stuck her in the bunker with the kid."

"Why didn't you just kill her?"

Wade shook his head. "I told you before, I didn't sign on to kill women and kids. That business next door with the kids' parents was wrong—it wasn't part of this deal at all."

"You didn't have any trouble taking the money, though, did you?" Brock sneered. He took the cuffs from Gage's belt and clamped them around his wrists, then shoved him into the bunker. When the door had closed behind them, he forced Gage against the wall. Gage gasped for breath, the cool of the concrete against his cheek helping to revive him.

"What did you do with Casey?" Gage asked.

"We didn't kill her," Wade said. "I've done a lot of bad things and never blinked, but I draw the line at shooting a kid."

"Shut up," Brock said, though whether he was addressing Gage or his partner was unclear.

"Why did you kill the Hoods?" Gage asked.

"They were like you—poking their noses where they shouldn't," Brock said. "Search him," he ordered Wade.

Wade patted him down and removed the gun Gage wore in an ankle holster, his pocketknife and baton. When he had stepped back, Brock pressed the gun to Gage's head once more. "Walk!"

Gage walked to the back of the hut, where Brock reached high over his head and pressed something on the wall. A panel slid back to reveal another locked door, which Wade opened. They passed through this door into a rock-lined tunnel so narrow Gage and his captors had to hunch over and shuffle along single file. This opened into another concrete-walled room, lit by bright fluorescent bulbs and filled with what seemed to be laboratory equipment. An astringent smell that reminded Gage of high school chemistry class stung his nose.

He turned his head to try to see more, and Brock jabbed him with the gun. "No sightseeing."

They halted in front of a steel door fitted with a heavy lock. "The boss isn't going to like this," Wade said as he fit a key into the lock.

"By the time he finds out, we're going to be long gone." Brock nudged Gage. "And you'll be dead." Wade eased open the door and Brock shoved Gage hard, almost throwing him into the chamber on the other side. Then the heavy portal closed and locked behind him with a heavy *thunk* that chilled Gage through.

"GAGE!" MAYA RAN forward to embrace him. She had never been so glad to see anyone in her life—to know that he was safe and alive, and that the man who had brought her and Casey here hadn't killed him. At the same time, the knowledge that he was trapped with them filled her with dread. If Gage couldn't save them, who would?

She ran her palms up his chest, the solid feel of him reassuring her, but her fingers snagged on a hole in his uniform shirt. She drew back, horrified to realize he had been shot—not once, but twice. "You're hurt!"

"Just bruised. The vest did its job and saved me." He turned his back to her and extended his bound wrists. "The key to these are in my right front pocket."

She retrieved the keys and unlocked the restraints. Casey bounced up and down in front of Gage, fingers moving rapidly as she signed. "Tell her she's talking too fast for me to understand," he said.

"Slow down," Maya signed.

With an exasperated expression worthy of a sixteen-year-old, Casey slowed her movements. "She wants to know if you're all right and what happened," Maya translated. She handed Gage the key and the cuffs. "I want to know the same things."

He flexed his fingers and rubbed his wrists. "Wade Tomlinson and Brock Ryan got the jump on me," he said. "They're the ones who took Casey, and they murdered her parents."

Maya tried to place the names. "Wade is the man who runs the outdoor store, isn't he?" she asked, picturing the muscular man who had come to the police department to report on some suspicious characters he thought might be responsible for the thefts at the high school.

"Yes. And Brock is his partner. The drawing the forensic artist made from Casey's description resembles Brock. He's a big, imposing guy. And strong as an ox."

Maya stared at the bullet holes in his uniform shirt. "They shot you twice but when that didn't kill you, he brought you here? I'm more than grateful, but why would he do something like that?"

"Brock was going to kill me, but they heard someone approaching and wanted to get me out of sight before they were discovered."

"Are you sure you're not hurt?" she asked.

"I feel like I was kicked by a bull and I'll probably have a couple of major bruises, but considering the shape I'd be in if it wasn't for my vest, I'm doing great." He pulled her close. "Better now that I know you and Casey are okay."

She kissed him, his lips firm and warm against her

own, and so alive. She wanted to keep kissing him like this for at least the next several hours, but that was time they didn't have. Reluctantly, she eased back from him.

Casey tugged at his sleeve and signed a question, her movements emphatic, her expression grave.

"She wants to know how we're going to get out of here," Maya said. "The door is sealed tight and the only other opening is up there." She indicated the grates overhead. "I think those are the same ones we were looking at when you left to get tools and someone—I never saw who—overpowered me."

Gage studied the grating, then walked to the back wall of the bunker and started feeling all around. "What are you doing?" Maya asked as she and Casey followed him.

"This bunker is behind the one that's visible at the development," Gage said. "When we searched it earlier, we thought it was just an empty storage space, but it had a hidden door. Brock and Wade opened it and led me through a tunnel to another chamber that was set up like a laboratory. At the back of that chamber was the door to this one." He ran his hands up and down the wall, frowning. "But I think this is the last in the line of structures. Those grates were only a few yards from the fence line, and a few feet beyond the fence is a rock shelf—there's no room for another chamber."

"But what are they doing with all these underground chambers?" Maya asked.

"How much did you see on the way in?" he asked her.

"Nothing. I was unconscious."

"I'm pretty sure that middle space was a laboratory."

"Do you think it's a meth lab or something like that?"

Gage shook his head. "Remember, I told you most of the meth these days comes from Mexico. If Wade and Brock are making drugs here, they'd have to have a way of distributing them. We haven't noticed an increase in traffic on this road, and Eagle Mountain Outdoors is right around the corner from the sheriff's department. We would have noticed any suspicious activity there."

Maya looked at Casey. Even though the little girl was deaf, her lipreading was improving, and Maya didn't want her upset by their conversation. But Casey was over by the door, tracing her finger along the faint crack between the door and its frame. Maya turned back to Gage. "Is that why they killed Angie and Greg? Because they found out about the lab?"

"I'm not sure," Gage said. "Brock said they were killed because they had been nosing around where they didn't belong. That makes me believe they saw something they shouldn't."

"We have to get out of here, or we'll die here, too," Maya said. "Maybe we can wait by the door and when they come back, we can overpower them."

"I don't think they're coming back," Gage said. "At least, Brock said they were leaving."

Panic clawed at her throat as she absorbed these words, but she fought against it. "We have to get out of here," she said again, her voice shaking only a little.

Casey hurried to them. She pointed overhead and began signing. Almost immediately, Maya began shaking her head. "No," she signed in reply. "I won't let you."

"What is she saying?" Gage asked.

"She says we should lift her up and she can crawl out of the grate and go for help. It's a ridiculous idea. Much too dangerous."

Gage tilted his head back to study the opening. "She's the only one of us who could fit through that opening," he said. "If we could get one of the grates out of the way. But we couldn't budge them from the outside." He looked around. "There's nothing we could use for a ladder, but if I boosted you onto my shoulders, you could lift her up."

"Gage, no! It's too dangerous." She took a step back from him.

His eyes met hers. "It's dangerous, but it's not impossible. And it may be our best chance."

"She's only five. How is she going to get all the way into town by herself? And what if she runs into Wade or Brock on the way?"

"She's the smartest, toughest five-year-old I ever met," Gage said. "And she doesn't have to get all the way to town. She just has to get to Jim Trotter's place at the end of the road."

Maya hugged her arms over her stomach, aware that Casey was watching this debate—and aware that everything Gage said made sense. "None of this matters if we can't get the grate loose," she said. "And how are we going to do that?"

"If you stand on my shoulders you can see if you can get it loose from this side."

"Oh, well, if it's that easy, why didn't I think of it?"

"Come on," he said. "Take off your shoes and get on my back. From there, you can climb up onto my shoulders. I promise I won't let you fall."

Skeptical and yes, a little afraid, she nevertheless did as he asked, aware that they were out of other options. She owed it to them all to at least try. She kicked off her shoes and removed her socks as well. Then Gage bent over. "Hop onto my back," he said. "Then you can crouch on my shoulders. I'll straighten up, then you straighten up."

He made the moves sound easy, but they were anything but. "What am I supposed to hold on to?" she asked as she straddled his back, debating her next move.

"I don't know. Maybe—try clasping your hands on my forehead...ouch! My forehead, not over my eyes!"

She moved her hands up, aware that Casey was giggling at the two of them. She managed to plant her feet on his shoulders and crouched there, straddling his head and feeling ridiculous. She was also sure he was risking a back injury and a possible hernia trying to lift her. After all, those gymnasts and ice-skaters being lifted into the air by their partners were usually several inches shorter and many pounds lighter than her.

"I'm going to stand up now," he said.

"Okay." Her voice only quavered a little. She tightened her grip on his head and added a headache to the list of pains she was inflicting on him. He straightened, breathing a little hard with the effort. She crouched on his shoulders, trying to work up the courage to stand.

"You have to stand up now," he said.

"I know. But that means letting go of your head."

"I won't let you fall," he said. "You have to trust me."

Hadn't she been trusting him all this time—to find Casey, to find Angie and Greg's killers, to protect her? Surely she could trust him now to hold her up—or at least, to catch her if she fell. Slowly, she straightened her legs, letting go of him at the last minute, extending her arms for balance. He reached up and gripped her shins, steadying her. When she was standing straight, she let out the breath she had been holding and grinned. "Okay, what do I do now?"

"Can you reach the grate?" he asked. "See if you can move it."

The bottom of the grate was about ten inches over her head. She reached up and grabbed it. It moved a little from side to side, but wouldn't budge up or down.

"There are some metal clip-type things holding the grate in place," she said.

"If you wedged something in them, could you break them?" he asked.

"I don't know. Maybe. But we don't have anything to use as a wedge."

"Come down now." Did she imagine the strain in his voice?

She clambered down, jumping the last three feet to the ground. Gage straightened and rubbed one shoulder. "There must be something we can use to break those clips," he said. He patted his pockets and pulled out the handcuffs, a set of keys and his wallet.

"What about a key?" she asked.

He considered his car keys. "I think the metal is too brittle. I've tried to use keys to pry things before and they snapped off." He replaced the keys in his pocket. "But I think you're on the right track. We need something metal and sturdy." He began unbuckling his belt.

She stepped back. "Gage, what are you doing?"

He slipped the belt from the loops of his khaki trousers and handed it to her, buckle first. The oval silver-and-gold buckle with its decoration of a cowboy riding a bucking bronc was heavier than she had expected, the edges tapered. "That buckle is silver with gold overlay," he said. "It should be strong enough for what we need if you can wedge it under the clips."

She turned the buckle over and read the engraving inside. *Gage Walker, Colorado State Junior Champion Bronc Rider, 2006.* "What if I break this?" she asked. "This obviously means a lot to you."

"It's just a belt buckle," he said. He held out his hand. "Ready to try again?"

Now that she had done it once, getting to an upright

position on his shoulders wasn't so difficult the second time. She managed to wedge one side of the buckle under the metal clip easily enough, but the clip refused to budge. "Pull down hard," Gage said. "Hang all your weight off of it if you have to. I won't let you fall."

She grasped the buckle with both hands and forced it down against the clip and prayed the sound she heard wasn't the buckle shattering. Something hit her cheek and she instinctively closed her eyes. She almost lost her balance and had to open her eyes, and saw that the bottom half of the clip was gone. "It broke!" she shouted.

"Great! Try the next one."

She managed to break three of the four clips, then was able to reach up and slide the grate to one side, out onto the forest floor. She gripped the opening, debating chinning herself up and trying to wiggle out, but she would be lucky to get more than her head through that small space, much less the rest of her. "I'm ready to come down," she said.

Gage lowered her, and Casey ran up to them. "Lift me up so I can go for help," she signed.

Gage knelt in front of Casey and took her by the shoulders. "You don't have to do this," he said.

Maya translated, but before she had finished, Casey was already replying. "I want to do it," she signed. "I can do it. If I don't, we'll die."

Gage nodded. "All right. I'm going to tell you where to go for help. It's a man named Mr. Trotter. He lives at the end of this road. When you climb out, head for the roses along the fence. Follow that fence to the road and the gate. Make sure no one sees you. When you get to the gate, go left. Do you know left?"

Casey looked from Gage to Maya as he spoke and she translated. She nodded, her expression so solemn that she looked older than five. Maya's heart squeezed, and she swallowed a knot of tears.

"Are you ready?" Gage asked.

Casey nodded. He hugged her close. "That's my girl."

This time, Maya sat on Gage's shoulders and he boosted Casey up to her. The little girl scrambled onto Maya's shoulders, fearless, and was up out of the opening before Maya was really ready. She looked back down at them and waved, then was gone. Maya fought the urge to call after her to be careful. Of course, she wouldn't hear, but it seemed Maya should have done something more than simply let her run into danger that way.

She slid off Gage's shoulders and sagged against him. "I hope we made the right decision," she said.

"We gave her a chance." He cradled her head against his chest. "We gave ourselves a chance. We wouldn't have that without her."

We wouldn't have had anything without her, Maya thought. She closed her eyes and gave herself up to the feel of his arms around her, holding her so close. The search for Casey had initially brought them together, and the shared goal of keeping her safe had forced them to become a team. But what had developed between them— this closeness she had never felt with anyone else—that was something so unexpected, so precious. Out of such great tragedy had come this gift that she didn't know what to do with.

He kissed the top of her head. "Let's sit down," he said. "All we can do now is wait."

Yes, they would wait—for rescue, for a resolution to this whole series of awful events and to see if the love she felt for this man could survive outside of the sadness and need, and become something even stronger.

Chapter Twenty-One

Casey pretended she was a little animal—a squirrel or a bunny running through the woods, hiding from the bigger, dangerous animals. She didn't see anyone else around, but she wouldn't take any chances. She scurried to the rose hedge at the fence, the pink petals scattered on the ground like confetti, and followed it to the road. The big black gate that had been closed before was open now, and a black truck sat in the drive, little puffs of smoke coming out of its tailpipe. But no one was inside the truck. Still, she stayed as far from it as she could, then turned and started down the road.

She passed the place where she and Mommy and Daddy had camped. It was empty now. Someone—maybe Deputy Gage—had taken down the tent and driven the car away. She didn't know where Mommy and Daddy were now. What happened to you when you died? Would she ever see Mommy and Daddy again?

She brushed the tears out of her eyes and kept moving, following the road but staying in the woods at the edge of it. She wasn't a sad little girl; she was a little wild rabbit, hurrying along with an important mission. Maybe she even had a little cape, with an *S* on it for Super Rabbit. The idea made her smile.

A flash of color on the road caught her attention and

she ducked deeper into the woods. She hid behind a big tree trunk and trembled as a truck drove past. The man driving was the big man who had grabbed her from the bedroom at Gage's house and taken her out the window. He was the man who had shot her parents. Her heart pounded so hard it hurt, but he never looked her way.

He was headed back the way she had come. Was he going back to kill Aunt Maya and Deputy Gage? She had to hurry to save them. She started running, ignoring the branches that slapped at her and the prickly vines that reached out to grab her. She ran until she could hardly breathe and her side hurt. But she couldn't stop. She had to get help.

She tried to remember what Deputy Gage had told her. She had to go to a man for help. What was his name? She couldn't remember, but that didn't matter. She didn't need his name to go to him for help. He lived at the end of the road.

The road went up a hill and curved, and at the end of the curve, a driveway cut off to the right. She ran faster, arms pumping, legs pistoning, heart pounding. When she reached the end of the driveway, she saw a little house and a man wearing baggy brown pants and a flannel shirt standing outside of it. He had a big white beard, like Santa Claus. This must be the man Deputy Gage had told her to ask for help.

Waving her arms, she ran toward him. The man's eyes widened. They were very pale blue eyes, in a face that was deeply wrinkled. He dropped the shovel he had been holding and opened his mouth and waved his arms, too. She thought maybe he was shouting. Then he picked up a rock and threw it at her.

Casey stopped and stared. Why was he so angry?

She was close enough now to read his lips. "Go away!" he said.

She crossed her arms and shook her head. No. She wasn't going to go away. She needed him to help her. They stood like this for a long while, staring at each other. The man made shooing motions and turned his back to her. Casey moved closer, making the signs for *Help* and *Please*.

He said a lot of things she couldn't understand. She kept moving toward him, one step at a time, the way you were supposed to approach a shy animal. He looked toward the door to his house. Was he thinking about going inside? She mimed making a phone call—everyone could understand that, couldn't they?

He shook his head. No, he didn't understand, or no, she couldn't use his phone. Or maybe he didn't have a phone. Daddy had said something about phones not working up here.

The man was still talking, too fast for her to understand. She looked around and spotted a stick and picked it up and wrote in the dirt. *HELP.*

He stared at the word for a long moment, then moved closer and shrugged, his hands out. She understood that. What did she want from him? How to make him understand?

She grabbed his hand and tugged. To her relief, he followed. She led him down the driveway. At the road, he stopped, but she pulled harder. She was crying now. She hadn't meant to, but she couldn't help it. The man shook his head, but when she tugged at him, he followed.

After a few feet, she began to run. They might not have much time. The man jogged along after her, until they were both out of breath. She slowed down to a walk and he slowed, too. Alternately running and walking, they made their way back to the big black gate, which was still open, though the truck was no longer sitting in the drive.

Casey put a finger to her lips, signaling the old man to be quiet. He nodded that he understood. She took his hand again and led him along the roses, intending to take him to the opening where the grate had been. Deputy Gage could talk to him then, and tell him what to do.

But they hadn't gone far when the old man put out a hand to stop her. When she looked at him, he put his finger to his lips and pointed to the side. She looked and saw the man who had taken her and the other man who had been with him when he shot her parents. They were talking to a man in a black suit. Not talking—arguing, their mouths open wide and their arms waving around.

The old man took her hand and led her deeper into the woods, then up a slope, helping her over the bigger rocks as they climbed. He moved carefully and she thought probably quietly. Instead of boots, he wore soft moccasins, with beading on the toes. They climbed and climbed, until they reached the top of the ridge and could look down on the three men still arguing.

The old man was talking again, though his head was turned away from her. She thought maybe he was talking to himself. He stared hard at the arguing men, then nodded, as if he had come to a decision. He indicated that she should stay where she was while he moved away. She didn't really want him to leave her, but Deputy Gage had told her he would help her, so she nodded and sat.

He moved over the rocks, crouched low and glancing down at the arguing men every few seconds. Then Casey couldn't see him anymore. She hugged her knees to her chest and wished she knew what those men were arguing about. She didn't see any sign of Aunt Maya or Deputy

Gage, so she thought they must still be in the concrete room underground.

The ground shook and she jumped up, startled. The rocks under her feet weren't moving, but she could feel vibrations through her feet, like when she was standing on the sidewalk and a car playing loud music went by. She couldn't hear the music, but she could feel it. She turned to see the old man running toward her, hopping over the rocks, while more rocks—a whole river of rocks— slid down onto the men below. One big rock hit the man who had killed her parents and he fell. The man in the black suit ran away and the other man tried to run, but he tripped, and then he was buried under rocks.

The old man scooped up Casey and scrambled with her to the road, where he finally put her down and stopped. He bent over, hands on his knees, breathing hard, but grinning. Casey waited until he straightened, then she took his hand and tugged him toward the grates in the woods.

A questioning expression on his face, he followed her. When she knelt beside the grate and looked down, he did the same, and then he was talking to someone down below—Deputy Gage and Aunt Maya. Casey lay back on the ground and looked up through the lacy leaves to the patch of blue sky above. Darla had told her she believed Mommy and Daddy were in heaven, where they could watch over her. Casey hoped that was true. She hoped they had seen how she had been brave and had gone for help—how she had saved them all.

"CASEY MUST HAVE turned right out of the driveway instead of left," Gage said as he and Maya and Casey stood with Travis by the gate to Eagle Mountain Resort, watching a rescue crew work to remove the ton of rock that had come down off the ridge when Ed Roberts set off the rock slide.

"They were arguing about killing you two, and the little girl, too," Ed said. When Travis and the rescue crew showed up, he had tried to leave, but Travis had persuaded him to stay and give an official statement. "I was just trying to stop them, though I ain't sorry they're dead, after what they did to that young couple and tried to do to the little girl."

"We're not pressing charges," Travis said. "We're grateful for your help."

"You saved our lives," Gage said, and offered his hand.

Ed hesitated, then took it. "I need to be getting back to my place now," Ed said. "I've had enough of all these people and commotion."

"You can go," Travis said. "And thanks again."

Ed left, and Travis went to consult with the rescue team, who had uncovered Wade and Brock's bodies.

"It's over," Maya said.

"Almost," Gage said. "We'll need to get a formal statement from Casey, verifying that Brock and Wade were the men who killed her parents and kidnapped her. I wish I knew what they saw that led to them being murdered— maybe it was something to do with that laboratory."

"Will you be able to tell what the laboratory was for?" Maya asked.

"We'll call in the DEA for that. And we'll be looking for the man Casey and Ed saw with Wade and Brock. He had something to do with all this." He turned to face her. "What will you do now?" he asked.

"I need to go back to Denver and settle Angie and Greg's estate, arrange for their memorial service and all the legal paperwork for me to become Casey's guardian."

"And then?" he asked.

"And then, I don't know."

He caressed her shoulders. "Stay. I know you think Eagle Mountain is a small place that will limit your opportunities, but there's a lot here for you."

"I know that now. You're here."

He kissed her, a gentle caress of his lips against hers that managed to say more than words.

When he lifted his head, she stared up into his eyes—the kindest eyes she had ever known, burning now with passion for her. "Do you think I can do it?" she asked. "Find a job and a place to live and…"

He touched a finger to her lips. "You'll find a job. If not teaching, something else. As for where you'll live… how about with me?"

"Oh, Gage, I don't know. Casey…"

"Casey can live with us, too. I'm asking you to marry me."

"Marry you?" Her eyes widened.

"I know it's sudden, and if you insist, we can have a long engagement. But I love you and I know it's real, and I want to be with you for always—and to be a father to Casey."

"What happened to the man who didn't make commitments? Who thought relationships and being a cop don't go together?"

"I had to find a commitment worth making, and the relationship that was the right fit. I've found both with you."

She looked into his eyes and saw her future there, building a life together with this man who filled in the pieces of her life she hadn't even known were missing. "Yes," she said. "Yes, I'll stay in Eagle Mountain and yes, I'll marry you and yes, we'll be a family. Together."

* * * * *

ARMED RESPONSE

JANIE CROUCH

This book is dedicated to my sister-in-law, Kimberly. Thank you for always being such a source of joy and encouragement, not just to me, but to everyone around you. And for making Mark read my books. I love you.

Chapter One

The way some women felt about that perfect little black-dress-and-heels ensemble—ready for anything, able to handle themselves, *bring it on*—Lillian Muir felt about her SWAT cargo pants, combat boots and tactical vest.

The heavy clothing and gear she wore might have felt burdensome at one time on her five-two, one-hundred-pound frame, but she had long since adjusted. Now she almost felt more comfortable with the extra thirty pounds weighing on her than she did with it off. The weight was a comfort. A friend.

Her HK MP5 9mm submachine gun rested against her shoulder, just grazing her chin. Her fingers curled gently around it as she moved through the silent winter air of this Colorado night. A shotgun strapped around her back and a Glock pistol low on one hip provided further assurance she could handle what was ahead.

More than a pair of high heels ever would.

And what was ahead was pissing her the hell off. A man—a *father*—holding his ex-wife and their two children hostage at gunpoint.

"Bulldog One, status."

Lillian tapped the button that allowed her to speak into

the communication system attached to her ear under her helmet. "Approaching back door, TC."

"Roger that. Hold for entry." One of the team's newest—and temporary—members, Philip Carnell, was acting as Tactical Command. Carnell wasn't the team's usual TC and his presence added to Lillian's unease about the mission. Not that Carnell wasn't brilliant when it came to planning and calling the shots. He was. Had an IQ of about a million and was able to process tactical information and advantages faster than anyone Lillian had ever seen. His mind was like a damn computer.

But he wasn't part of the usual team. And moreover, he was pretty bitter about that.

They were shorthanded from recent attacks by criminal mastermind Damien Freihof over the past few months. Team members had been hurt and even killed as they battled one assault after another. Explosions. Bullets through windows. Sliced throats. Even assailants at weddings. Freihof had made it his mission in life to wage war on Omega Sector.

Lillian herself had been injured in a mission just two weeks ago, shrapnel from an explosion catching her in the shoulder. She ignored the slight discomfort now. She had bigger things to worry about.

"Bulldog Two, report status," Carnell said.

"I have a visual on the suspect. Single tango. He's pacing. Three hostages. Mom and two kids. All in the kitchen." Bulldog Two's voice was a little too high, too excited. Another person that damn sure wasn't part of the normal elite Omega Sector SWAT team. Damn Damien Freihof and his mole inside Omega.

Lillian ignored that discomfort for now, too.

"I have a shot. Repeat, I have a shot," Bulldog Two said.

Lillian held her tongue. New Kid wasn't her problem.

"Negative, Bulldog Two. Hold your position," Carnell told him.

"I want to take this bastard out," the trainee guy said again. What was his name? Paul?

"Hold, Bulldog Two." This time it was team leader Derek Waterman on the comm unit. He was also out in the darkness surrounding the house.

Lillian's lips pursed. "Derek, request channel change."

"Roger that. Go to channel three, Bulldog One."

Lillian clicked the dial that turned the comm device to a channel so she and the team leader could talk without anyone else listening.

"Go, Lillian," Derek said.

"We going to have a problem with Newbie?"

"His name is Saul. Saul Poniard."

Generally Saul was a good guy. Friendly, surfer-boy looks with a ready smile. He was also pretty excitable, which might have been the reason he was turned down for final SWAT training multiple times. The only reason he was here now was the injuries on the team.

Lillian sighed. "I just don't want him shooting those kids' dad in front of them."

"Roger that," Derek said. "No deadly force unless we have no other options. TC knows that. Carnell won't make that call unless there are no other options and things are escalating."

"I know that. You know that. Just want to make sure New Kid knows that."

Derek grimaced. "Don't worry. I've got him under thumb. I'll pull him out if I need to. Switch channels."

Lillian did so. She'd said her piece, and really didn't have a problem with Saul Poniard except for his excit-

ability, and lack of experience. Derek would handle it.
Which was good because she didn't want to have to go
take out baby-SWAT wannabe before taking down that
scumbag dad on the inside.

Who she could now hear screaming at his wife.

"Tactical Command, this is Bulldog One. I am at the
back door. I have visual on the mom and kids but not
the tango."

She could see them in the kitchen, the woman and
children sitting at a small round wooden table. The mom
had both hands reached out toward her children, a boy
around nine and a girl around seven, and they sat on either side of her, but not near enough to be touching her.

The tango paced into view, gun in hand, but at least
pointing down, and he smacked the mom in the head
with his bare hand as he stormed past and out of sight
from where Lillian crouched at the window. Guy was
still shouting.

"I still have a shot. Repeat, Bulldog Two has a shot,"
Saul said. He was in a tree on the east side of the house,
so Lillian had no doubt the angle gave him a tactical advantage. And yes, if Psycho Dad's actions escalated, then
Saul would need to take him out.

But otherwise Lillian would do everything she could
to make sure these kids didn't see a parent—no matter
how terrible he was—die right in front of them.

Not here. Not today.

"Negative, Bulldog Two," Philip said. "Bulldog One,
can you infiltrate without exposure?"

"Affirmative," Lillian responded. "Especially with all
the noise this guy is making."

"Everyone is in position. Go at your discretion," Philip

told her. The rest of the team—as well as the new kid—was ready to back her up and take out the tango if needed.

Lillian waited until the guy went on another tirade, screaming right in the mother's ear, both kids sobbing, as an opportunity to slip inside a small crack when she opened the door. The Omega SWAT team regularly used Lillian's small stature to their advantage. This was no different.

She kept to the shadows as she made her way closer to the kitchen.

"Tango is starting to wave the gun again." Saul's voice had reached an excited pitch again. "He's got it to the wife's head."

"Roger that, Bulldog Two. Your shot?"

"Still clear, TC. Just give me the word." Saul was damn near panting with excitement.

Damn it. She'd rather the team take out the father than have the mother die.

"Bulldog One?"

"I have no visual," she muttered.

"Okay, Bulldog Two, you are cleared to—"

Lillian saw movement again in the kitchen. "Hold," she said. "Tango is on the move again. Back to pacing."

"I've still got the shot, TC."

The frustration was evident in Poniard's tone, and Lillian couldn't blame him. Preparing to fire, and being cleared to fire, but then having the order rescinded at the last second, was irritating. But exercising control was also an important part of being a SWAT team member.

"Bulldog One, can you beanbag him?" Carnell asked.

"Roger that, TC. Moving into position." Lillian grinned, replacing her HK MP5 with the shotgun strapped behind her back. The beanbag round was only accurate up to about six meters, but she was within range. Its blow was designed to cause minimal permanent damage while rendering the subject immobile.

The fact that it would hurt Screaming Dad like hell didn't bother Lillian a bit. She crawled forward. She was going to have to pull some sort of Tom Cruise roll-and-shoot nonsense in order to get into position in the quickest way possible. She usually went for much less drama. But not today.

Guy started screaming again. Lillian had had enough. *You want to dance, buddy? We'll dance. Together.*

"On my mark," she whispered to the team. "Three, two, one."

Lillian pushed herself from her crouched position in the shadows, twisting her body into a roll as she cleared the wall and came into the opening of the kitchen, landing in a kneel.

She saw surprise light the tango's face. He was swinging his gun around toward her when her finger gently squeezed the trigger on the shotgun, her aim perfect.

The beanbag round hit him square in the chest, propelling him back through the air and away from the table and hostages. The gun fell out of his hand.

Less than two seconds later Lillian was on the tango and the rest of the team was filing through the door, grabbing the children and wife and leading them to safety.

Screaming Dad groaned as Lillian grabbed his hands to cuff them. "Tango is secure."

"You're a woman!" The man's outrage couldn't be more clear.

Lillian arched a single eyebrow. "Yeah? Well, you're an idiot. Turn over."

"I think you done broke my ribs."

Lillian didn't give a rat's ass whether this jerk had a couple of cracked ribs. He was lucky Philip hadn't turned the trigger-happy new kid loose on him. "Shut up. I'll break more than your ribs."

Within a few more minutes the perp was loaded into the back of a squad car and the wife and kids were handed over to the paramedics.

"Nice work, everyone," Derek said over their comm unit. "Let's get packed up and back to HQ to debrief."

Lillian bumped fists with everyone as they made it back to the car. Even Saul, who was smiling like an idiot. Everybody was walking away today. No one seriously injured, even the tango.

That made today a good day.

"Beers on me," Derek said.

That made it an even better day.

LATER THAT NIGHT after the debriefing and the beers, Damien Freihof sat in an abandoned warehouse across town, staring at "Mr. Fawkes." Damien had made it his mission over the last six months to destroy Omega Sector, piece by piece, in payment for taking the life of his beloved wife.

Fawkes, as he so cleverly liked to be called, had proven very useful over the last few months in that endeavor. Fawkes's inside information on Omega had been quite helpful indeed.

Fawkes still wouldn't give Damien his real name. Damien wondered how upsetting it would be to the younger man to know that Damien had figured it out weeks ago. The man might be brilliant, but Damien didn't work with people he didn't know.

Damien's and Fawkes's ideologies were different.

Fawkes looked to destroy and rebuild all of law enforcement. Damien just wanted Omega to suffer the way he did when he'd lost his Natalie. Wanted them to know what it meant to experience unbearable loss.

But if Damien could bring chaos across the country by destroying the foundation of all law enforcement, as was Fawkes's plan, then hell, he was up for that, too.

"It's time," Fawkes said as he paced back and forth hardly visible beside a window, even in the full moon. "You'll be ready, right? We only have eight days."

Damien sat perched against a desk. "Yes, I'll be ready to do my part in your master plan."

"We've gotten rid of two of their team members completely. Another is injured and not fully up to speed." Fawkes continued his pacing.

"It's a mistake to underestimate the Critical Response Division, even when they're weakened." Damien had learned that the hard way.

"They brought in a new guy on the SWAT team. That was unexpected." Fawkes stopped and studied Damien as he said it, as if gauging his response.

Damien knew all about the new guy. "Is that a problem?"

"No." Fawkes resumed his pacing. "The team thinks they're so smart, but they're not. I've left a trail. It's going to lead right to the very heart of the SWAT team. The sweetheart."

"Lillian Muir?" Damien raised an eyebrow.

"I've got special plans for her. Have already left clues in the system that lead back to her as the mole I know they're searching for."

Damien had to admit Fawkes's computer skills were impressive. He'd provided information that had helped

Damien a great deal. Most particularly two weeks ago, when Omega had almost captured him at his own house. Without a warning from Fawkes, Damien would never have made it out.

Nor taken one of the SWAT team out of action in the process.

Fawkes might not be the easiest person to work with, but he definitely knew how to manipulate a computer system. And how to manipulate people, for that matter. People didn't take him seriously enough, including those at Omega Sector.

Which was probably why he was trying to blow up— *literally*—all of law enforcement.

Or maybe he just had mommy issues. Whatever. Damien didn't care why Fawkes was doing it, he just wanted to see Omega Sector destroyed. If Lillian Muir was going to take the fall for that, even better. Damien would do a little checking up on her himself.

Fawkes wasn't the only one with computer skills and digging-up-info skills.

"Is there even going to be anyone left to search for the villain after you get through next week?" Damien asked.

Fawkes stilled. "I'll be left. I will be one of the few tactically trained agents left in the whole agency. Hell, in the whole country. And all the destruction will lead right to Lillian Muir's door. She'll be dead and unable to open the door, but the destruction and blame will still lead right to her."

Damien grinned. One thing Fawkes had was exuberance. "Sounds like a perfect plan to me."

Chapter Two

Jace Eakin stretched his long legs out in front of him in an office chair that probably hadn't been comfortable even when it was new. Now that it was ratty and at least a dozen years past that, it was even less so. His knee was stiff from too many hours cramped in a plane, his shoulder vaguely ached from a bullet he'd taken years ago in Afghanistan. Thirty-two was too young to feel this old.

He was in an office that looked like it was out of some old gumshoe movie, complete with dirty windows and low ceilings. The man sitting behind a desk looked almost as rumpled as the office itself.

Jace knew Ren McClement was anything but.

Jace had first met him ten years ago when they served together in the US Army Rangers in the Middle East. Working side by side with someone in daily life-or-death situations showed that person's true colors. Ren McClement was one of the few people in the world Jace trusted without restriction. He knew the feeling was mutual. Which was why he was here now in this godforsaken seat in some out-of-the-way office in Washington, DC, rather than putting the finishing touches on his ranch in Colorado.

"Ren, seriously, dude, you've got to get some chairs not built for midgets."

Both Ren and the other man in the room, Steve Drackett, chuckled. Ren had gotten out of the army not long after the time he spent in Afghanistan with Jace. Because of his skills and security clearance, Ren had immediately been brought into Omega Sector, a joint task force made up of the best agents the United States had to offer.

Jace knew Ren was one of the highest-ranking members of Omega, and that he worked mostly in covert missions.

Nothing surprising about that. Ren had had the ability to blend in with almost any situation even back in his Ranger days. That the government was smart enough to use him for clandestine work wasn't surprising to Jace.

What was a mystery to him was why Ren had asked *him* here to begin with. Although always happy to see his old friend, Jace was not an Omega Sector agent. He wasn't an agent at all.

"Yeah, budget for this place wasn't very big," Ren said. "Not that I'm in here enough to worry about that anyway."

Ren could probably have a very high-end government office with a million-dollar view of DC, but chose not to. Jace knew for a fact that Ren never entered a government building unless he had to, and even then it wasn't through the front door. The undercover nature of his job prohibited it.

"I can see why you wouldn't want to be here often. And speaking of, why am *I* here? I'm assuming there's a reason other than reliving old times."

Ren nodded. "We have a situation in the Omega Critical Response Division out in Colorado Springs. A mole who is leaking information to a terrorist named Damien Freihof. We know the mole is someone inside the SWAT team. Steve—" he gestured to the other man, who was leaning with one shoulder against the wall "—has requested that I send in someone I trust to help find the mole."

Steve pushed himself away from the wall and handed Jace a thin file with some papers inside. "We found this Manifesto of Change document hidden in one of our Omega computer servers."

On my honor, I will never betray my badge, my integrity, my character or the public trust.

I will always have the courage to hold myself and others accountable for our actions.

I will always uphold the constitution, my community and the agency I serve.

Jace looked over at Ren, then Steve. "This looks like some sort of law-enforcement creed."

Steve nodded. "It's the oath of honor that law enforcement officers take at their swearing-in ceremony. But keep reading."

We all took an oath to uphold the law, but instead we have allowed the public to make a mockery of it. Where is the honor, the integrity, the character in not using the privilege and power given to us by our training and station to wipe clean those who would infect our society? We were meant to rise up, to be an example to the people, to control them when needed in order to make a more perfect civilization.

But we are weak. Afraid of popular opinion whenever force must be used. So now we have changed the configuration of law enforcement forever.

And now, only now, will you truly understand what it means to hold yourselves accountable for your actions. Only with death is life truly appreciated. Only with violence can true change be propagated. As we build anew, let us not make the same mistakes. Let the badge mean something again.

Let the badge rule as it was meant to do.

Jace shifted slightly in his chair. "Okay, I'll admit, this is scary. And I sympathize, I really do, that this has come from within your own organization, but I'm not an agent. There's got to be other people you trust who could do a better job than I could."

Ren glanced over at Steve and then back at Jace. "We're not looking for someone long-term. This is a time-sensitive op."

Steve nodded. "I would've bet my life that the traitor was not one of my SWAT team members. I've known most of those people for years. But intel has suggested that not only is the mole a member of SWAT, but also has a plan that will involve a massive loss of life."

"Do you have details about how? When?" Jace asked.

Steve nodded. "Within the next two weeks. Our strong suspicions are that it has to do with a law-enforcement summit scheduled in Denver next week. It will have police chiefs and politicians in attendance from all over the country."

"That would definitely make a good target." Jace looked back at Ren. "And if you need an extra hand with a rifle, I'm more than willing to help out, especially since I'm headed out to Colorado anyway."

"Still planning on breeding and raising dogs?" Ren asked. "Horses? Opening your ranch?"

"Hey, don't mock my dream." Jace had always wanted to own a small parcel of land where he could raise animals, particularly dogs, that could be trained for service members and veterans who suffered from PTSD. Maybe even make it into a place where vets could come and enjoy space and quiet for a temporary stay when they needed it.

Jace had made some savvy financial investments in his twenties that had given him the means to make this dream a reality now. He'd be able to cover himself financially until he was able to make a living from his business. He was looking forward to working outside, with the land and animals. He also looked forward to not having to be constantly worried about being in danger.

Although risk cognizance had been a part of his life for so long it was second nature to him now.

"I wouldn't dream of mocking it." Ren smiled. "Hell, I may be joining you before this is all over. But I was hoping you would help me out before you got out of the game for good."

"We don't need an agent," Steve said. "We just need someone who can come in and pass for a SWAT team member. Somebody who has the qualifications and physical prowess to join the team. Because of attacks by Damien Freihof, we're down a couple of members, so bringing in someone from the outside wouldn't be unheard of."

"And then once I'm in there?"

"Then there's one person particularly under suspicion

who we need you to get close to." Ren leaned forward on his desk, watching Jace closely. "Lillian Muir."

The name had Jace actually rising from his seat before he even knew it.

"Lillian Muir?" He looked from Ren to Steve. "Lillian Muir is a member of the Omega Sector SWAT team?"

"Not only a member, one of the *best* members. One of the most gifted SWAT personnel I've ever known," Steve said.

Jace began pacing back and forth behind the chair he'd just vacated.

Lillian Muir.

He'd be lying if he said he hadn't wondered what had happened to her over the years. He hadn't seen her in twelve years, since he was twenty and she was eighteen. The day they were supposed to leave to join the army together, to get out of a pretty rotten living situation in Tulsa. To figure out their future together, which for Jace had always meant marriage as soon as he could talk her into it.

He hadn't seen her since the day he'd found her in his brother's arms.

Jace looked at Ren. "You know, of course, that Lillian and I have a history."

Ren nodded. "You and I talked about a woman you cared about a great deal back when we served together. And you'd mentioned her name was Lillian. When I found out the Omega Lillian was the same as your Lillian, I thought we could kill two birds with one trusted stone."

Jace shook his head. "You also know things didn't end well between the two of us. I'm probably not the most neutral person. She decided she'd rather have my brother than me."

Daryl had died in a fire not long after Jace joined the army, but that didn't change the fact that Lillian had chosen Daryl, not him.

"I just want to say officially and on the record that I do not think Lillian is the mole," Steve said, conviction clear in his voice. "As a matter of fact, I'm hoping you'll be able to come in and clear her."

"Clear her? Why me? There's got to be someone better."

"It's a perfect storm of problems," Ren said. "We need someone we can trust. We need someone who has the skills to infiltrate a SWAT team. And we need someone Lillian may be willing to get close to."

Jace shrugged. "The first two I might fit. But Lillian won't get close to me. There's got to be someone else. Friend. Boyfriend. Somebody."

"I recruited Lillian basically off the streets nine years ago." Steve shook his head. "She's got a tactical awareness and physical control of her body that has only improved over the years with training and education. But, despite being an excellent team member, Lillian has never gotten close to anyone since I've known her."

Jace scrubbed a hand over his face. "Even more reason why she's not going to get close to me. Some people are just lone wolves."

Jace knew enough about Lillian's upbringing to not be surprised that she kept to herself. She wasn't ever going to be the life of the party. But never having gotten close to *anyone*? The two of them had been plenty close at one time. Or so he'd thought.

"Our division psychiatrist was killed by Freihof two

weeks ago," Steve continued. "Her case files are confidential, even with her death. But I do know for a fact that Lillian was seeing Dr. Parker regularly. And Dr. Parker believed there was a sexual trauma of some kind in Lillian's history."

Ren leaned back in his chair. "Honestly, we were hoping maybe you knew something about that and could use it to foster a closeness between the two of you."

"I don't. If that happened, it happened after she and I... separated." Jace grimaced, tension creeping through his body. Despite her leaving him for his brother, Jace would never have wished something like that on her. Couldn't stand the thought of someone hurting her that way.

"Like I said, I don't have any details. And it may not even be accurate. But I know Dr. Parker had suggested that finding someone from her past, someone she knew before the trauma, might be the key to helping her overcome it." Steve gestured toward Jace. "Maybe you could be that person. Help us find the real mole. Help her work through whatever is in her history."

"What if she is the real mole?" Jace asked. He didn't want to believe it. He *didn't* believe it. But it could still be the truth. He'd known her twelve years ago and she cheated on him. Had that developed into even darker tendencies as she'd gotten older?

Steve took a step forward. "She's not."

Ren held his hands out in front of him in a soothing gesture. "Steve, you're too close to this. You know you are."

Jace jerked his chin at Steve. "You involved with Lillian?"

"No, happily married and a new father." Steve's eyes narrowed. "Plus, did you not just hear what I said about

her not getting close to people? That particularly goes
for men."

Jace shrugged, studying Steve with hooded eyes.
"Thought maybe you might be the exception to that."

"Steve cares about the entire team," Ren insisted. "He
wants to catch Freihof and the mole more than anyone
else, especially given the people they've lost. And the
mole doesn't know that we're on to him. Or her, as it
may be. So we want to use that to our advantage. Steve
poking around will draw attention. Not to mention he's
not neutral."

Jace sat back down in the uncomfortable chair. "And
you think I am?"

Ren stared him down. "I think I would trust you with
my life—and have—multiple times over. I think you have
an innate situational awareness that was only honed in
your years as a Ranger. I think you will be fresh eyes
and able to pinpoint specifics others may have missed."

Ren leaned back in his chair but didn't lose eye contact
as he continued. "And I think this is a chance for you to
finally put your history with Lillian to rest and move on.
She's not the only one who hasn't gotten close to anyone
else in the last twelve years."

Jace was also a loner. Lillian hadn't had anything to
do with his choice not to settle down with anyone. But
that was irrelevant to the situation at hand.

Ren was right—it was time to leave Lillian Muir behind for good.

"Fine. I'll do it. Another couple of weeks isn't going
to change my plans for the ranch. I just hope I'm able to
do what you guys think I can."

Ren nodded. "Your best has never once not been
good enough."

Jace just shrugged. That wasn't true. They'd lost men in the line of duty whom Jace wished he could bring back. "I appreciate the sentiment."

Steve stepped up and shook his hand. "Welcome to the team."

fixing the trigger...

Chapter Three

Lillian had been quick and wiry her whole life. Not just
fast with running, although she could average a six-min-
ute mile for ten miles in a row, but swift with everything. Her hand movements, her body movements, how
she processed info.

A lot of it probably came from early in her life, when
if she wanted to eat, she'd had to steal food from the grocery store or local market. And if she wanted to sleep
safely, away from her mother's drunken wrath or boyfriends' wandering hands, she'd learned how to move
quickly and silently out the window.

Those lessons might have been hard to come by, but
each of them had made her into the woman—the *warrior*—she was today.

Whatever didn't kill her had better start running.

The SWAT team was sparring and doing some general
workouts in the training area until the new guy got there.
Another new guy. Evidently this one had a little more experience than Saul, the friendly yet trigger-happy newbie who had been filling in for the last couple of weeks.
Or anybody was better than Philip Carnell, the computer
whiz who had been working with them as an analyst in
hostile situations for the last two months.

Carnell had a mind like a steel trap, but the personality of a horse's ass. Which was probably an insult to the hind end of a horse. Nobody liked Philip and he had a bone to pick with everybody about seemingly every damn thing. Lillian avoided him whenever possible. Hell, everybody avoided him whenever possible, unless he was acting as Tactical Command, as he had been a couple of days ago. Carnell was great at finding fast solutions in dangerous tactical situations, but he wasn't physically adept enough to be a part of the tactical team.

He'd only sulked about that fact and gave his opinion about "the unfairness of elitist practices" of the SWAT team about once every hour. Lillian was glad to not have to deal with him in training or in the field.

Saul wasn't so bad. He tried to get a little too friendly, and grinned a little too much for her taste. But at least Surfer Boy didn't make her want to lock him in a trunk, like she did with Carnell.

Right now she brought her leg around in a vicious roundhouse kick and hit the punching bag. Roman Weber, her teammate holding the bag for her, took a quick step back.

"Trying to take out all your aggression on one poor defenseless piece of canvas?" He chuckled as he grabbed the bag more firmly.

"Too many new people, Roman. I don't like change."

"Oh, yeah? Try finding out you're about to be a dad. Now, *that's* change."

Lillian grinned at him. "Yeah, every time that happens to me I swear it's not gonna happen again."

Despite his wounds from an explosion two months ago, she knew Roman couldn't be happier about Keira being back in his life and the baby they had on the way.

Hell, it seemed like just about everybody on the SWAT team had found romance-novel-type true love within the last year.

Lillian was thrilled for them, she really was. She liked each and every one of the women her teammates had fallen for. But love and marriage weren't in the cards for her. She'd long since accepted that. Emotional attachment just wasn't her thing.

But she had a career she savored and kicked ass at. That was enough.

"I hear this new guy is actually qualified to be on the team. An Army Ranger. Steve Drackett vouches for him personally," Roman said.

Lillian punched the bag again. "I just wish Liam was back in action." Their teammate had almost been killed by a biological weapon three weeks ago.

"He's alive and going to recover. That's what matters."

Omega Sector's casualty list at Damien Freihof's hand was getting too damn long.

Liam Goetz, SWAT team member: seriously injured via chemical inhalation. Hospitalized two weeks.

Roman Weber, SWAT team member: seriously injured via explosion. In a coma for more than a week.

Tyrone Marcus, SWAT team member-in-training: killed in action via explosion.

Grace Parker, Omega psychiatrist: murdered in cold blood.

And those were just the worst of the worst.

Especially Grace. *Damn it.* Lillian forced herself to push away the grief that threatened to suck her under at the thought of losing the other woman and the close friend she had become.

She switched with Roman and held the bag as he went

through a series of kicks and punches, at a slower speed and with less force because of his recent injuries. As soon as the new guy came in, they'd be doing some training with him. Running the SWAT obstacle course, some sparring, throwing him immediately into the mix.

"Hopefully this new guy won't crush on you like Saul," Roman said between punches.

She rolled her eyes. "Yeah. I don't think Saul understands that I don't date work people."

"You don't date anyone."

This was an old argument. "I do date. I just don't announce it around here like all you lovesick fools. There's enough swooning going on around here without adding me to the mix."

"I'd like to meet a boyfriend of yours just once."

Lillian took her turn at the bag. "Fine. I'll bring the next one around for approval, okay?"

She wouldn't. Roman was right, she didn't have boyfriends. She had sex with random guys, probably too often, but she tended to check out mentally in the middle of the act itself. Then immediately left afterward. Not being able to remember any part of the sexual act did not lend itself toward building a relationship.

She and Grace Parker had been working on some of Lillian's issues before Grace had died. Lillian's triggers. The fact that she'd *never* been able to have sex and remember it clearly afterward.

Disassociation due to acute sexual trauma. That was what Grace had told Lillian was the clinical term for it. And that it was treatable. That they would continue to work together so that Lillian's mind didn't try to escape every time she became intimate with someone. They'd made progress over the last year.

And now Grace was dead.

Lillian attacked the punching bag with renewed vigor. "I just want SWAT to be ready for when we get the call to go take out Freihof. I'll even date the new guy if he can help us be ready for that."

Roman chuckled. "Hell, *I'll* date the new guy if he can help with that."

"I'm sure Keira won't mind, considering Freihof nearly got her killed."

"If Steve vouches for this guy, then that's all I need to know," Roman said.

Lillian trusted Steve completely also. "Yeah, me, too. What's the guy's name? I promise I'll make an effort at learning it."

"Jace Eakin."

Lillian's head snapped up and she glared at Roman, about to make him repeat the name.

Roman gestured to the door. "Here he is."

It could not possibly be. There was no way. She turned, slowly. No. Way.

Yes way.

"Jace. Jace Eakin," she whispered.

"You know him?"

"I did. A long, long time ago."

She felt like her heart had completely stopped beating. *Jace* was the new guy? Part of her wasn't surprised that he was qualified. He'd been strong, fast and smart when she knew him twelve years ago. Evidently the army had turned him into someone even more dangerous.

And he was particularly dangerous for her. He knew every secret she'd gone to such lengths to keep hidden from the team. He knew how she used to steal and run illegal items all over town for the gang they'd both been in. She'd been fast, trustworthy and had looked innocent. She'd never once gotten caught.

Jace Eakin knew every secret she'd made sure no one else at Omega Sector knew.

Except one. And he would never know that one.

She kept him in her peripheral vision as she returned to her assault on the punching bag.

"If you know him, don't you want to go talk to him?" Roman asked, grabbing the bag.

She shook her head. It was all she could do to not run from the room. And Lillian was known for not running from anything.

She saw Jace put his bag on the floor and talk to Derek. A few minutes later he was headed toward the locker room.

Fifteen minutes after that Derek was calling the entire team together, including Jace.

"Everybody, this is Jace Eakin. Eakin, the team." Derek looked around at everyone. "They'll all introduce themselves individually."

So far Jace had avoided looking at her directly, but Lillian had no doubt he was aware of her presence. She could almost feel his awareness of her.

The same way she was aware of him.

"Jace is coming in to help us with the Law Enforcement Systems and Services Summit next week in Denver," Derek continued. "The LESS Summit, as everyone knows, is going to bring in the bigwigs from all over the country. Our job is to provide internal protection for that event."

Ashton Fitzgerald, team sharpshooter and general smart-ass, spoke up. "LESS is more."

Everybody echoed Ashton's statement, the slogan for

LESS, as they always did. LESS was a system that would link together law-enforcement-agency computers all over the country, providing valuable instant connectivity and the ability to share data.

"Denver is also expecting a number of demonstrators and protesters, so if needed, we'll help out with that. Everybody knows we're a little undermanned right now. Roman and Lillian are both coming off injuries. Jace is joining us as temporary replacement for Liam. Saul is also going to be joining us as a full member for the LESS Summit."

Everyone was quiet at those words. Building the cohesion needed for the team to run smoothly in just a week wasn't going to be easy. Lillian shifted restlessly. She wasn't the only one.

Derek looked at each one of them. "You're angry at Damien Freihof. All of us are angry after what happened to Grace Parker, not to mention our team. We all want to get our hands on Freihof and make him pay. And that time is coming. But our focus right now is on the LESS Summit. It's about keeping those attending safe. So I want everyone to stay frosty and focused. We have a job to do."

Lillian raised her hand halfway. "What about the rumor that there's a mole inside Omega providing Freihof intel?"

She wanted to nail that traitor bastard just as much as she wanted to nail Freihof.

"I know a mole is suspected," Derek responded. "But to date, no official evidence has been found to support that rumor. We all know Freihof loves to play head games. Getting us to turn on each other, go on witch hunts, is exactly what he wants. So we're not going to do that. If you see anything suspicious, you report it to me, but we don't go around accusing each other of anything."

Lillian nodded. She glanced over and found Jace openly studying her. Their eyes met and she was determined not to look away first. Jace, damn his still gorgeous blue eyes, seemed to have the same determination.

Derek saved them both from their battle of wills.

"We're going to get into training immediately to get us working as a team. And this week we're going to put in long, team-building hours." Derek turned to Jace, who had changed into workout clothes from the khakis and collared shirt he'd arrived in. "Eakin, although you come recommended from a man we all highly respect, if you don't mind, we'd like to see what you're capable of."

Jace nodded. "You'd be a fool not to."

Lillian froze at the sound of Jace's voice. The deep timbre still did something to her. Nudged at parts of her that had been sleeping so long she'd thought they were dead. The most feminine parts of her. For a moment she couldn't breathe as her mind attempted to figure out what she was feeling.

Desire.

It had been so long—twelve years, in fact—since she'd felt clear, untainted desire for a man.

And she was feeling it for the man who, with just a sentence or two about her past, could destroy the rapport she'd taken years to build with her team and probably cost her her job.

Omega Sector generally frowned upon employing people who were once part of an unofficial gang in the streets of Tulsa. While their gang hadn't had turf wars and drive-bys, she'd definitely broken the law multiple times throughout her teenage years.

"We'll hit the team obstacle course this afternoon," Derek continued. "But I thought we'd begin with some sparring."

"Sounds good to me." That deep voice again.

"Who would you like to start with?"

Jace's full lips were turned up at one corner as if he knew some private joke. "Why don't you just pair me with your best close-quarters fighter and I'll go from there."

Everybody chuckled at the new guy's guts.

Even Derek smiled. "Even better, why don't you tell me who *you* think our best close-quarters fighter is?"

Surely Jace would pick Roman or Derek. Both of them were big—over six feet tall with biceps the size of tree trunks.

Lillian could take down both of them. Had done so, in fact. She was pretty damn fast, stronger than she looked, and had spent the last twelve years making sure no man—no matter what his size—would be able to force her to do something she didn't want to do.

Never again.

"Sure." Jace looked at everyone around the circle, as people started stretching and warming up while listening. "There's a number of people who I think could give me a run for my money. But if I had to guess who's most capable of kicking someone's ass, I think it would be this one."

He pointed straight at Lillian.

She could hear the soft chuckles of her teammates, and felt Roman pat her on the shoulder. They didn't know why Jace had chosen her. Because he really thought she was the best close-quarters fighter? Because he thought she'd be easy to take down? She wasn't.

Damn it, she didn't want this. Didn't want to touch

Jace Eakin in any way. But she'd never been one to back down from a fight.

She wasn't going to start now.

Stretching her shoulders, she put on the sparring mask and gloves and met Jace in the sparring ring. They gave each other a brief nod and then began.

They spent the first couple of minutes dancing around each other, throwing a jab here and a few kicks there. Lillian felt herself loosening up. She excelled at close-quarters combat. Her body knew what to do from muscle memory.

Jace got a little more serious, sending a spinning back kick in the direction of her head. She dropped low and hooked the back of her leg behind his, bringing him to the mat with a thud.

For just a moment they were face-to-face near the floor.

"I taught you that move," he whispered.

She leaped up to her feet and he followed, pushing off from his shoulder and straight onto his feet.

Lillian didn't let him get resituated. She used her greatest advantage—her speed—and flew at him with a series of punches and kicks. Jace was forced to go on the defensive, and did a damn good job of it.

She stepped back as he nearly backed out of bounds, ending her attack. "You didn't teach me that."

He grinned. "I sure as hell didn't. Impressive." Without warning he came at her, forcing her to go on the defensive this time.

All in all, they were pretty evenly matched. Derek eventually called the match to a halt when it became apparent neither of them was going to win easily. "Let's save some energy for the rest of today's training. There's a lot of hours still left."

Jace took off his gloves and held his hand out to shake hers. "Nice job, Tiger Lily. Although I'm not surprised."

You could've heard a grasshopper karate-chop a fly. *Tiger Lily.* Nobody ever called her Lily, not if they expected to live to see the next sunrise. And no one had ever called her Tiger Lily—the beautiful and exotic flower—but Jace. Hearing the words did something to her she couldn't explain and didn't want to delve into too closely.

So she kept her cool.

"Welcome to the team, Jace. And it's Lillian. Just Lillian, nothing else."

Chapter Four

"Lily, hold up."

He smiled as he saw her shoulders stiffen at the name. Her curt instructions on the sparring mat not to call her anything but Lillian had just spurred his desire to call her by her old nickname.

But it was her whispered words as they had left the sparring area that had really caught his attention.

Don't say anything about who we were.

Jace wasn't sure if that meant their personal history or the gang-related activities they'd participated in during their youth. She might not have ever told anyone about that, especially the latter. Since she had never been arrested, nor had he, it wasn't in either of their permanent records. She didn't have to worry about him spilling her secret. Not that one anyway.

Working with her today, fighting with her, seeing how everyone else interacted with her... Jace couldn't help being impressed. She had taken all the natural physical skills she'd had as a teenager—speed, flexibility, sheer grit—and had formed herself into nothing short of a warrior.

He'd known it from the first punch she'd thrown in

the sparring ring. She'd always been feisty, but now she was deadly. Small but fierce.

She'd been the only woman in the room or on the field, and that hadn't seemed to bother her at all. The men hadn't treated her any differently than they treated each other. Even with their limitations because of injuries, the team members had relied on and functioned around each other's strengths.

No point in Lillian being the one on the bottom hoisting her teammates up the fifteen-foot wall that was part of the obstacle course. Could she have done it if she needed to? Jace had no doubt. But it wasn't her specialty, so instead the team had sent her up and over first. Nobody in this close-knit group played politics: you weren't given an assignment just because you were a man or a woman, you were given an assignment because of your strengths and talents.

Part of the course had also involved an underground tube, which there was no way in hell Jace was ever going to fit through. Neither were most of the men on the team. But Lillian had no problem. So she was sent.

Again, nothing to do with gender, everything to do with what was best for the team.

The men respected her, she respected them. Even the outsiders, the couple of guys besides Jace who obviously weren't regular members of the team, respected her.

And Jace would bet his next paycheck that everything Steve Drackett had said was true. Lillian had not been intimate with any of these men. There was no flash of recognition, no secret smiles...

No nicknames that had been only for them twelve years before. Like Jace had just said to her again.

"I told you, it's Lillian now. Not Lily. Nobody ever called me that but you anyway. And definitely not Tiger Lily."

He jogged the rest of the way to catch up with her. "Old habits. You know how it is."

"It's not like you've been saying my name very often in the past twelve years, so it shouldn't be too difficult for you to make the change."

"I'll do my best." He held his hand up with his fingers open in Mr. Spock's Vulcan *V* symbol. "Scout's honor."

She thawed minutely. "Jackass." She shook her head. "You were never a Boy Scout *or* a Vulcan."

And he wasn't going to stop calling her Lily, either.

They reached her car, a gray Honda Civic. About as unflashy a vehicle that was made. She opened the trunk and set her duffel bag inside. Then turned to him.

"Why are you here, Jace?"

Giving her as much truth as he could was probably his best option. "Ren McClement asked me. He and I served in the army together for a few years. You know him?"

She shrugged. "Not personally. But everyone knows *of* him. He's pretty much an Omega Sector legend."

"Steve Drackett and Ren said the team needed someone with experience who could jump right in. To help with this LESS Summit thing." Jace looked over to where some of the others were coming out of the building. "No offense, but your team is a little shaky right now. And the two new guys are not exactly anything to write home about."

Lillian rubbed her fingers against her forehead. "That's for damn sure."

"Carnell doesn't play well with anyone. And that guy Saul Poniard is a little too flippant for my taste. That could be disastrous in a lot of situations."

"I agree. Steve recognizes it, too, but right now we don't have a lot of options."

He took a slight step closer to her, unable to stop himself. "Exactly. Ren knows me and knows he can trust me. And you guys needed someone with my skill set."

Talking coming from the parking lot caught their attention and Jace took a step back. They both waved to the other members of the team as they got in their vehicles one by one.

"And did you know I would be here when you said yes to Ren?" Lillian finally asked as her teammates drove away.

This was a much trickier question to answer. He knew he shouldn't have any qualms about lying to her. After all, she had been the completely dishonest one all those years ago. But he found the thought of telling her lies to be more difficult than he expected.

"Ren mentioned there was someone else here from Tulsa. A Lillian. But I couldn't be one-hundred-percent sure that it was you. You were impressive out there today, Tiger Lily."

She glared at him but didn't press the nickname issue. "Thanks."

"Seriously. You can handle yourself. I mean, you've always been able to handle yourself, but this was so much more than that."

Lillian leaned back against her car but didn't meet his eyes. "Thanks. You, too. Of course, I'm not surprised or anything. You were always built like a military man. Physically and mentally. I guess you just honed that over the years. So you got out?"

He nodded. "Yeah. For almost a year now. I loved the army, but it was time."

"Moving back to Tulsa?"

"No. Nothing for me there anymore. I actually bought some land here in Colorado. I'm opening a ranch of sorts."

Her brown eyes got big. "A ranch? I didn't know you had any interest in animals."

"I didn't, really, not when you knew me before. Not that there was much space for animals in downtown Tulsa anyway. But we had bomb dogs when I served over in the Middle East. Really found I had a love for them. So I'll be raising them and some other animals. Working with vets, too."

Hopefully providing people with PTSD a place to come and heal for a little while when things got to be too much.

"That sounds amazing. I'm glad your experience in the military was a good one."

"You would've done well in the military, too." The words were out of his mouth before he could stop them. Lillian should've gone into the military with him. That had been their plan. The military had catered to both of their strengths.

Now she *really* wouldn't look at him. "Yeah. I always thought so."

He had to decide right now whether to battle this out— what had happened between her and his brother—or leave it alone. He didn't want to fight with her the entire time he was here—that would be counterproductive to his ultimate mission of getting closer to her—but he didn't want to leave Daryl as the elephant constantly in the room between them.

He leaned in just slightly closer to her. "Twelve years was a long time ago. I think it's safe to let bygones be bygones, right?"

Now her brown eyes peered up at him. "Yeah, I'm sure that's true."

"And if it means anything, I'm sorry Daryl passed away so soon after the two of you got together. I don't know if it would've lasted or whatever, but I'm sorry you didn't get the chance to find out."

Jace had never seen the blood drain from someone's face so quickly. Lillian's slight weight fell back more heavily against her car. Jace couldn't help himself. He reached toward her. "Are you okay?"

Did the thought of Daryl's death still hit her so hard?

"Daryl and I would never have made it as a couple." Her laugh was bitter. "If there's one thing I'm sure about, that's it."

She pushed herself away from the car and he could almost see her withdraw into herself. Part of him wanted to press, but on the other hand, he *really* did not want to know intimate details about her relationship with his brother.

She turned and reached for the car door, opening it. Jace took a step closer, boxing her in.

They both felt it. The attraction between them. Daryl or not, it was still there. It had been buzzing around them all day, and now it was pooling in the air between them.

It didn't matter about twelve years, it didn't matter about Daryl, it didn't matter that they didn't know enough about each other now to be sure if they even liked each other.

The heat was still there, just like it had always been.

"You need to talk to Ren," she finally said, her back to him.

With his hand on the frame of her door and the other on the roof of her car, she was, in essence, trapped in his arms. If she turned around, it would almost be like in an embrace.

But she didn't turn as she continued. "Tell Ren this won't work. Help him find someone else."

"Why do I make you so uncomfortable, Tiger Lily? You're the one who gave me up, remember? And like we said, it was over a decade ago. It shouldn't matter now."

She shook her head with a little jerk. "It'll be easier for both of us if you're not here."

"Since when have you or I ever done anything the easy way? We are a good team. You had to have seen that out there today."

She nodded stiffly. Jace took a step forward, which caused Lillian to turn around. Suddenly all he could see was her mouth.

Cursing himself, he brought his lips down to hers. He couldn't help himself, it was like being caught in some tractor beam from a science fiction movie.

Her lips were as soft as he remembered. As sweet. Sweeter, if possible.

She held herself stiffly for the first few seconds, as he teased her lips slowly, nibbling at them, but then he felt her give in. She sighed as if she couldn't fight it, either.

Her fingers slid into his hair, pulling him closer, and a sound of hunger left him, his mouth moving more hungrily on hers, their tongues twining. The attraction and heat pushed at them in waves.

When Jace finally stepped back, they both just stared at each other. Then, without another word, Lily got in her car and started it, pulling away so quickly that if he hadn't stepped back she might've run over his toes. All he could do was watch her drive away.

He muttered a curse under his breath. He'd been sent

here to do a job, get more info, find out if Lillian had anything to do with this mole. Not kiss her senseless within the first few hours of his being back in the same general vicinity as her.

He'd counted on his sense of betrayal to help him keep his distance from her. To be able to remain objective and even cold.

Jace should've known better. He'd been many things around Lillian Muir, but cold was never one of them.

Seven hours into this mission and already things had become a hell of a lot more complicated.

Chapter Five

Showing up at Omega HQ the next day knowing Jace would be part of the team, part of her inner circle after twelve years of not having seen him at all, was pretty much inconceivable to Lillian.

And the fact that they'd made out yesterday? She couldn't even wrap her head around that. She didn't make out with people. Making out was for teenagers.

And she especially didn't make out in the Damn. Parking. Lot. Sure, the entire team had left by then, but still. What would people say if someone had seen her lip-locked with the new guy just a few hours after meeting him?

After the Tiger Lily comment, plus the fact that she'd mentioned it to Roman, everyone had heard or figured out she and Jace had a history. But that still didn't account for her sucking face with him.

And hell if heat didn't course through her at that thought. Again. Like it had done all night long.

Lillian had a lot of sleepless nights. But never had they involved being so caught up thinking about a kiss that she couldn't get to sleep. It was like something out of a Sweet Valley High novel.

She wished she could call Grace about it. Get her opinion as both psychiatrist and woman. Although she knew what Grace would tell her.

To take a chance. To be willing to leave herself unguarded for once.

But Lillian couldn't call Grace. Because Freihof had killed her.

That was enough to wipe all thoughts of teen-romance-books-style kisses out of her mind. Jace was here for a purpose. That purpose had nothing to do with Lillian and everything to do with keeping the LESS Summit safe, especially if Freihof decided to make some sort of play.

She would do well to remember that.

Jace Eakin was now, at least temporarily, taking up residence in her home—Omega HQ was much more home than the one-bedroom apartment that basically just housed her stuff. She would work with him. Get him up to speed. Keep it strictly professional. Definitely no more kissing.

In the locker room she changed out of her civilian clothes and into her training fatigues. She arrived in the SWAT station house living room thirty minutes before she was scheduled to be there. Derek was already there sitting at the conference table that took up a good section of the room, looking over paperwork for the team.

Jace was there, too, on the opposite side of the room.

Ignoring Jace, she walked over to Derek and sat down next to him. Derek slid a file over to her.

"Today's schedule."

Nothing out of the ordinary. Some PT, time to go over the building plans of the LESS Summit and one of Lillian's favorite drills.

"The Gauntlet. Haven't done that one in a while. Pretty brutal."

Derek grinned. "I thought it would be a good team-builder. Trial by fire." He glanced over his shoulder. "I'm going to have you pair up with Eakin."

"For the Gauntlet?"

"That and for the summit."

"Seriously?"

Lilian glanced over at Jace, who was leaning against the wall messing with his phone. The slight smirk lifting the corner of his mouth let her know he could hear everything being said.

She made a show of looking over the schedule again. "Maybe you should assign Jace to someone else. Team me with Saul. Or even Carnell." She swallowed her grimace at both offers. She didn't want to be assigned to either of them. It would limit her effectiveness at the summit.

"No. Carnell will be tactical command and computers only. He's not ready for active missions. Saul is better, but he's still not top-tier. Unless I see something over the next few days that makes me think Eakin doesn't have the skills I think he has, you two will be the Alpha team."

Everybody was important on a mission like protecting the LESS Summit, but the Alpha team was second in command to Derek, able to make judgment calls and decisions without approval when needed.

"Is that going to be a problem?" Derek asked when Lillian didn't respond. "There's obviously history between you two."

Yes, there was history, but she wasn't going to let that stop her from being as effective as possible. From making the entire team be as effective as possible. They'd need to be as strong as they could for whatever Damien

Freihof had planned. Putting ancient history aside would be no problem.

Lillian glanced at Jace again, his blue eyes now piercing hers. She didn't look away. "No—no problem," she told Derek. "Our past was a long time ago. It's over. It was over before it even started."

IT WAS OVER *before it even started.*

Lillian's quiet words stung even hours later. They shouldn't; after all, they were only the truth. Their relationship—at least the sexual side of it—had ended almost as soon as it began.

Trying to stick to the letting-bygones-be-bygones promise he made yesterday was proving a little more difficult than he had expected.

Jace pushed the entire conversation from his mind. There was no room for worrying about the distant past out here on the Gauntlet, which was a glorified obstacle course full of real-life dangers—fire, barbed wire and paintball-type ammunition that wouldn't seriously wound someone, but would hurt like hell if you got hit.

Harsh words were the least of his problems right now.

Evidently there was some sort of multimillion-dollar training simulator nearby, but the way everyone had started crossing themselves and balking when it was mentioned made him think it wasn't very popular.

So here they were, out in a wooded area, having just crawled 500 yards under barbed wire. He and Lillian were a team, moving together. There were four other two-person teams made up of the various SWAT members he'd met yesterday. This exercise was part race, part team-building.

It wasn't unlike some of the obstacles and exercises

he'd been a part of as an Army Ranger. He understood the importance of pushing the body and the mind, and doing it with the person who was going to have your back when you went into battle. It looked like he and Lillian would be that person for each other.

And she wasn't too happy about it.

Unhappy because she was being forced to work with an ex? Or unhappy because that ex was a new person on the team who might recognize some suspicious behavior on her part that her other colleagues could miss?

Either way, she was pushing those feelings aside now. She seemed vaguely surprised that he was able to keep up with her rapid crab-crawl pace under the barbed wire, roughly eighteen inches over the ground. Her small stature gave her a decided advantage for an obstacle of this type, and Lily knew how to use it.

But Jace knew how to make his body move quickly also. Even though the wire was sometimes only an inch or two over his shoulders and back, he used his abdominal muscles to keep himself straight and low, speed from his long reach making up for the caution he had to use because of his size.

As they reached the last of the wire and rolled out, they took cover behind some trees.

"You're fast," she said.

"Not my first rodeo."

The rest of the teams were making their way along the ground, Philip Carnell having the most difficult time.

"Do we need to go back in and help Carnell?" he said.

Lillian gave a brief shake of her head. "No. Normally Derek doesn't even allow him to do this sort of training even though Carnell insists he should be given the chance. But he may be needed to do something besides provide tactical assistance next week in Denver, so today he's in."

"Is he going to make it?" Carnell's partner was Saul Poniard, who might also be new, but was light-years ahead of Carnell when it came to physical abilities.

"Saul will get him through hopefully. And we'll get Philip out as a team if he needs it. Not that he'll thank us for it." Lillian shook her head. "As Alpha team, we're going to have our own problems. We'll need to take out the sniper before he picks everyone off."

"Sniper?"

Lillian grinned. "You didn't think Derek was going to miss the fun, did you? That man loves his paintball gun. You and I will have to take him out before everyone else gets there. That's Alpha team's primary challenge."

"Then let's get moving."

They navigated a series of obstacles, including a fifty-foot rope climb, before coming to a pile of five large, heavy logs.

"Each of these has to be maneuvered through this next section." Lillian referred to the logs. "Every two-person team is responsible for one log. We choose to make it either hard on us or hard on the other teams coming behind us."

Jace raised an eyebrow. "So…heaviest?"

Lillian's smile was huge and he had to fight to keep it from taking his breath away. "I was hoping you'd agree. But it's not going to be easy."

"Then I guess you better stop grinning like an idiot and get to it."

Jace couldn't stop the grin on his own face, either. Lily wanted to push herself. That was something he understood. He had known it about her even back in the day, and it was one of the reasons he had thought the army would be such a good fit for her also.

He tamped down the spring of bitterness over the way things had turned out. Bygones. Much more important to focus on the problems at hand.

The log was damn heavy. The exercise required them to lift the log over some obstacles, under others, and even carry it over their heads as they crossed a small creek.

Lillian never complained, never slipped in supporting her part of the awkward piece of wood. By the time they threw it down half a mile later, they were both pushing the edges of exhaustion. They slumped together against the back of a tree, shoulder to shoulder, so they could each catch their breath.

"Now we have to take out Derek and his evil paintball gun." Her eyes were closed as she allowed her body to attempt to recapture some of its strength just as he did.

"How do we do that with no gun of our own?"

"Technically for this exercise, all we have to do to defeat him is for one of us to make it over the finish line without getting hit." She didn't sound very enthused about the idea.

"Easier said than done?"

Those brown eyes opened. "Derek is a mastermind at this. Plus, he knows all our strengths. We have about a five-percent success rate when it comes to getting past him."

"What about splitting up and running from two different directions?"

She shook her head. "We've tried. It's such a narrow strip of land, he can cover it and almost always get both people before they get across. We don't have very much cover."

"What are the rules about just one person getting across? If that's all we need, we should wait for everyone else, protect one person and everyone else can take the hits."

"First, the hits aren't gentle. They hurt like hell." She obviously had firsthand knowledge. "Second, to keep us from always grouping, the rule is, whoever makes it across the finish line unhit has two minutes to get the wounded the fifteen yards across no-man's-land. Almost impossible if it's one person trying to get multiple people across. And particularly impossible with the group coming up behind us."

Jace leaned his head back against the tree. He could hear the frustration in her voice. The Omega SWAT team was not up to the level it usually was. Too many new people. Too many wounded.

"I have a plan," he said.

Now he had her full attention.

"We'll use Derek's assumptions against him, with a little bit of trickery thrown in. But I'll warn you, this won't be easy. Particularly on you. We won't be playing to your strengths. But we will be using your strength."

She sat up. "Okay. I'm game. What's your plan?"

"Derek expects you and me to make a break before the rest of the team gets here. To try to overcompensate for their limitations. To use your speed and my strength to get everyone else through."

"And we're not going to do that?"

Jace just smiled.

Ten minutes later the other members of the team began catching up with them. Jace explained his plan. Everyone stared at Lillian once Jace told them what she would need to do.

Even Lillian looked a little skeptical.

"You can do it," he said.

"You're going to take a lot of hits," she responded. "Derek won't like it and won't show any mercy."

Jace grinned. "I can handle a few bruises."

"Are you sure you don't want me to make a dash for it?" Saul asked, enthusiasm fairly radiating from him. "I'm fast."

Jace shook his head. "No, that's exactly what he's expecting. For you or Lily to run, to try to use your speed. And you're too big for me to use in this plan."

Saul grimaced. "Are you sure she can handle her end of this?"

Jace shook his head at the same time Lillian's eyes narrowed. Saul might be new, but he would learn fast not to underestimate Lillian if he wanted to stay part of this team. "Don't worry. I'll do my part."

It was a pretty damn big part.

Jace turned to Philip. "You've got to sell it, to get us more time. Derek will come after you just to teach you a lesson."

Philip didn't look thrilled, but then again, Jace wasn't sure he ever did.

"I can handle a few bruises," Philip echoed.

Jace nodded at the other team members. They weren't excited about being left out of most of the action, but they understood the advantage of his plan. Of keeping Derek off balance as long as possible.

"Remember." Lillian turned to him. "Rules are that you can only take five more steps after you're hit. Make them count."

They all stood and made their way closer to the twenty-yard square area Derek was guarding. There was some cover of trees and boulders, but not a lot. Derek definitely had the tactical advantage.

Jace and Lillian separated from the rest of the team. Philip and Saul would be drawing Derek's attention—hopefully—from the other end of the field.

"If Saul gets all gung-ho and takes off, then gets hit, this isn't going to work," Lillian whispered. "I'm not sure it's going to work even if he doesn't."

Jace couldn't help himself—he bent down and kissed her, fast and hard. "If there's anyone I would trust to get me out of a situation when I'm wounded, it's you."

"You're nuts, Eakin." She shook her head. "Let's try this crazy plan."

They waited for the signal. It came just moments later.

"Because we have to stick together, Poniard, don't you dare leave me here to get shot." Philip's words were soft, like they weren't meant to be heard. Jace and Lillian could barely make them out.

But that meant Derek could, too.

Jace didn't wait. He scooped up Lillian—she rolled herself into as tight a ball as possible—and he ran. He only had to make it halfway before he got shot. Far enough that his back would be to Derek, and the team leader wouldn't see the hidden person Jace had curled in his arms. Derek would be expecting Lily to try to run her own route and make it through. Wouldn't expect her to agree to be carried.

"Damn it, Saul, wait!" Philip again, hopefully going from the script, and not saying it because Saul really had taken off.

It bought Jace the few extra seconds he needed. He kept Lillian tucked high against his chest as he felt the first paintball hit his back. Three more followed rapidly.

Damn, those *did* hurt.

This whole plan was relying on the fact that Derek wouldn't stay and watch Jace "fall" onto the boulder in front of him. He had too much else he had to keep track of. Jace got his five more steps in, then set Lillian on the ground. She immediately began sprinting toward the finish line.

Whooshes of air blew as more shots were fired from the paintball gun. But not at Lillian.

Philip squeaked, "Ow, damn it." He took his five steps closer to the finish line, then fell.

Jace turned to watch and saw the exact moment Derek realized he'd been played. He turned and aimed his gun at Lillian, but she was already crossing the line.

Derek smiled and looked down at his watch. "Okay, Muir. You've got two minutes to get them both across if you want to claim your victory."

Lillian sprinted back to Philip first. She sat him up and then swung his arm over her shoulder, dragging him across to the safe area.

She stopped to take a breath, looking Jace in the eye. He weighed significantly more than Philip did.

But Jace had no doubt she could do it—that she would get him over to that safe zone. Especially now, with the entire team looking on.

She jogged back to him and got down to business. The boulder helped, putting Jace more upright. But she would still have to fireman-carry him. There was no way she could drag him like she had done with Philip.

He could hear the cheers of their teammates as she pulled his torso around her shoulders and slipped her hand through his legs and wrapped her arm around his knees. A huge groan came out of her small body as her legs straightened and she took his whole weight, lifting him off the ground.

She couldn't walk straight, and she might not have been able to walk for long—especially after the grueling workout they'd already gone through on the course—but Lillian got them both over the finish line just as the time was running out.

Jace immediately dropped his leg to the ground and took his weight as the rest of the team ran over, hooting and hollering. Even Philip was grinning. Lillian dropped back against a tree to get her breath. Everyone was slapping both of them on the back until Derek came over and told them to complete the rest of the course.

"Good job, you two," he told them as they walked to the next section. "Completely had me fooled. Some partnerships are just meant to be."

Jace didn't say anything. He'd once thought that exact same thing also.

He'd been wrong.

Chapter Six

Everything seemed to take a turn for the better after the Gauntlet in terms of team building. The paintball win had given them all the boost they'd needed and the confidence that they could work together successfully. Lillian was glad to see it.

What she wasn't quite so glad about was that Jace seemed to be within arm's reach every time she turned around for the next five days.

All the damn time.

Admittedly, a lot of it was the training they were doing as a team. More obstacle courses. The shooting range. The different scenarios within the multimillion-dollar simulator on the outskirts of the Omega Sector campus.

It came as no surprise to her that Jace fit right into the team as if he'd been there all along. He'd always been charming and affable even back when they were teenagers. The polar opposite of his bastard brother. Tension coursed through her body at the thought of Daryl, so Lillian pushed him from her mind. She'd had twelve years of practice doing that.

But charm meant nothing to a SWAT team without the skills to back it up. Jace had those in spades, too, and they'd been especially evident when he'd proven himself with the Gauntlet plan. His sharpshooting abilities impressed even Ashton Fitzgerald, the team's sharpshooter. Jace's close-quarters fighting skills she already personally knew about. He also had a specialty in explosive devices.

When Ashton, team clown, asked Jace if he would go steady with him, Lillian knew Jace had won over the team.

Saul and Philip weren't too happy about Jace's instant inclusion into the inner circle, when they'd both been fighting so hard for that same acceptance. But there was just an innate authority with Jace that neither Saul nor Philip had. Nobody said anything about it, but they all knew it.

The parts of Jace that had drawn her when they were both teenagers were even more prevalent now. His strength. His focus. His dedication.

Add that to the fact that he was opening a ranch where he would raise animals that would help soldiers with PTSD? How was she supposed to process that?

She wanted distance from him but couldn't get it. There literally was no time. The LESS Summit was coming up in just days and they would all need to function seamlessly as a team by then.

They trained day and night, since the summit would require them in both daylight and nighttime hours. Sometimes that meant little sleep or crashing on whatever couch or floor was available in the team break room.

Jace definitely wasn't a diva. Just like everyone else, when they had a break in the middle of a twenty-four-hour training session, he found a spot, curled his head back and promptly fell asleep.

But damn it, that had ended up being right next to her every single time.

Just like how every time they were at the practice range he ended up next to her.

And every time they were in the SWAT van traveling somewhere, it was his leg pressed up against hers.

When they ate. When they did their ten-mile runs.

Always there. Always next to her.

He never did anything to make any sort of big deal out of it, hadn't kissed her again or made any moves on her since that brief kiss at the Gauntlet. But he didn't have to. Lillian was aware of him in a way she hadn't been aware of someone…for twelve years.

And it felt good. In the scariest way possible.

Her body and mind trusted Jace in a way she hadn't been able to trust another man in twelve years…actually her whole life. She wasn't well versed in psychology—damn, she missed Grace Parker—but Lillian knew enough about her own mind to know that the passion between the two of them a dozen years ago was the only untainted memory of sex that she had.

Sometimes she still thought about those nights they'd had together. How uninhibited and all-encompassing her feelings had been. They'd had the entire world and forever in their future. No grasp at all of how quickly life could change.

She and Jace had been friends for a long time before they were lovers, since Jace was older than her and refused to sleep with her until she turned eighteen. Then they'd only had about a month after her eighteenth birthday before…

Before he left for the army. Before everything in her world crumbled. Lillian felt her body turn cold even now.

Jace seemed to have forgiven her for *leaving* him—God, the thought still made her want to vomit—for Daryl.

It was good that he'd forgiven her, without even having one iota of understanding about the true circumstances.

Jace was a good man. He'd been a good man then, and he was still a good man now. So she was glad he had gotten over his sense of betrayal at her perceived actions.

And if she had any choice in the matter, Jace would go to his grave being the man who was good enough to forgive an ex-girlfriend for running off with his brother. He would never know the truth.

Because that would just hurt him so much worse.

"What are you thinking about over there?" Jace's voice broke in to her thoughts. "Whatever it is, it can't be good."

This time he was across the table from her in the Omega canteen. It was lunchtime, and while they had been here all night for a dark-based training op, they'd all be leaving to go home for a break soon. The team would be going to Denver tomorrow.

She shrugged, ignoring his question, since there was no way in hell she was going to answer it truthfully anyway.

"You worried about something concerning the summit?" he asked between bites of his sandwich.

This she could answer. "To be honest, I'm concerned about everything to do with this summit. Hitting something this high-profile may not align perfectly with Damien Freihof's MO, but I think it aligns with his mind-set."

"I thought Freihof had been using other people to do his dirty work. Stirring up the pot with people in the past who had an ax to grind with Omega agents and helping him try to get their revenge."

"He has." Lillian's hands balled into fists. "But then he killed Grace Parker, our team psychiatrist, himself. Brutally, and in front of everyone. I think he's escalating. And I think trying to humiliate Omega by attacking the summit would definitely suit his purposes."

"Sounds like he has it in for you guys. What's that about?"

"Evidently we had a hand in his wife's death. She was killed when Omega went in on a bank raid."

"Freihof brought his wife along when he robbed a bank?"

"No. Freihof has been involved with a lot of different criminal activities for the last fifteen years. But in this case, evidently they both just happened to be in the wrong place at the wrong time. Someone was robbing the bank, the wife freaked out and tried to make a run for it when SWAT arrived, and she got shot and killed. By us. And Freihof has decided to make everyone who has ever been a part of Omega Sector pay for that mistake."

Jace seemed to process all that as he ate. "And he maybe has someone helping him? Someone inside Omega?"

Lillian shrugged. "There's been no official word, but a lot of rumors. And some of the stuff Freihof has known, he couldn't possibly have known without help from the inside. I have no doubt there's a traitor within Omega, as much as I hate to say it. But like Derek said, we can't all go around accusing one another of being the mole and expect to work effectively as a team."

Jace nodded, studying her.

It had been a long few days and they were all supposed

to go home and rest. They would all need to be on high alert at the summit.

If Lillian was Freihof, the summit was where she would strike. If he could take down the LESS device, he would be serving a great blow to law enforcement all over the country. Doing that while humiliating Omega Sector seemed to be cut directly out of his playbook.

Not to mention the summit would be crowded with politicians, law-enforcement leaders and ordinary people there to observe or protest. Plenty of people to try to hurt or kill.

"You headed out?" Jace asked as they finished up their food.

She wasn't particularly interested in going back to her empty apartment. She tended to spend as little time there as possible. But no need to advertise that fact. "Absolutely. We all need to get a little R and R before heading to Denver."

The rest of the team had already left. Most of the guys had families now. A lot of times Lillian was invited over to their houses for meals or just to hang out. But not right now. The wound of losing Grace Parker was still too fresh, too open. All the guys just wanted to be with their wives and children and hold them close and thank God for them.

Lillian wasn't going to boo-hoo just because there was nobody thanking God she was alive. If Jace wasn't here, she would probably head out to a bar and find a guy to hook up with for a few hours. It was never fulfilling, and sometimes it was downright scary the way she checked out emotionally during sex, the way she didn't remember any of it even though it had happened just a few minutes before.

But anything was better than sitting at home alone.

Yet something about Jace being nearby made the thought of some random, emotionless hookup seem even more unappealing.

"How about you?" she asked him. "I don't even know where you're staying."

"Hotel a few blocks from here. There didn't seem to be much point in renting a place, since I was only going to be here a couple weeks. And I didn't want to have to drive back and forth every day from my ranch."

That made sense. And they were probably paying him enough to make it worth his while anyway.

"Okay." She nodded. "I guess I'll see you tomorrow."

"Yeah, see you tomorrow."

They dumped their trays and headed off in separate directions for the men's and women's locker rooms.

Lillian was used to being in here by herself. It usually didn't bother her. As a matter of fact, there had been plenty of times when she had to change clothes in front of the guys. She honestly didn't even think they saw her as a woman anymore.

She hardly saw *herself* as a woman anymore. She had all the woman parts but didn't tend to have many of the emotions that were tied to the female gender. She couldn't remember the last time she had cried.

She didn't mind being the only female on the team. She respected her colleagues, they respected her and they trusted her to do her job. She would die before she let down the team. She was part of something bigger and more important than herself, and she loved that.

But right now she just felt pretty damn alone. Not to mention all ramped up to get to the action tomorrow.

So she might as well stay here for a while longer and

look over again the plans of the Denver city hall, officially known as the Denver City and County Building, where the summit would take place.

The LESS device was something that would change the face of law enforcement forever. Would allow a true merging of technology in all branches. The ramifications would be significant. Interstate cooperation would be much easier with the LESS system.

It was her job—the team's job—to make sure that happened. Studying the building plans one more time could only help.

She brought her duffel bag out of the changing room with her and moved to the main computer work space area in their building. SWAT members didn't have their own desks, but they had computers available for the team's use. They were mostly used for training, updating education, or situations like this, where someone wanted more details about the particulars of an op.

The big desk gave her plenty of room to set up a notebook and take some notes, as she brought up the building plans.

The 3-D replication of the building allowed her to take a virtual tour. Extremely helpful. But she knew that whatever she could find on a computer, Damien Freihof could, too.

She studied the plans for nearly an hour, going over each window, doorway, elevator shaft and staircase. She wanted to be able to find her way around the building even if she was blindfolded.

She closed down her browser and drew the plans of the first floor from memory, then compared it back to the actual drawing. Pretty close.

Lillian sat back in her chair, stretching her arms over

her head and her legs out in front of her. That was enough for today. She'd already been up all night with the training. It was time to go home.

She just wished she had someone to go home to.

She shut down the computer and stood up, giving a small gasp when she saw Jace leaning against the wall a few feet behind her.

"You're lucky I didn't have a weapon, Eakin. What the hell are you doing standing there all stalker-like?"

"I didn't want to interrupt your memorization exercise."

"I wanted to make sure I was as familiar with the building as I could be. I thought you had already left."

"Smart. And no, not yet. I had a little bit of work to do here."

She couldn't help noticing how good he looked in jeans and a black long-sleeved shirt rolled up at the wrists. He even had his boots on. He'd owned similar ones back in the day.

His brown hair was cut shorter than it had been then, closer to military regulation, although it had obviously grown out a little bit. The tips of her fingers itched with the need to run her hands through it. Those icy blue eyes stared at her with a touch of friendliness and something she couldn't quite discern.

But one thing she could discern for certain: he was the sexiest-looking thing she had seen in a long time. Whatever she was feeling right now definitely wasn't emotionless. The opposite, in fact.

There would never be anything emotionless when it came to her and Jace Eakin.

The thought of feeling something—something *real*—while a man touched her had Lillian crossing to Jace.

Just once she wished she was more of a high-heels-and-short-skirt sort of girl. A girl who knew how to do something with her hair besides pull it back in a ponytail. A girl who knew how to put on makeup to cause her eyes to look mysterious and sultry.

A girl who knew how to seduce a man like Jace.

But she wasn't that girl. All she could do was make her offer straight up with no pretense.

She stopped when she was directly in front of him. From this close, all she could do was remember that kiss from a few days ago in the parking lot.

"If you're done with your work, why don't you come over to my apartment? We've got eighteen hours before we have to report back here. Seems like we ought to be able to find something to do with that time."

Passion—the same heat she felt—flared in his eyes for just a moment as he eased closer to her. She felt his fingers grip her hips and knew she would feel those lips on hers again any second. There was nothing she wanted more in the world. Those kisses, as much as she'd tried to tamp them down, had never been far from her conscious mind.

But then his fingers clenched on her body for just a second before letting her go. He stepped back. Her eyes flew up to his, but his handsome face was carefully masked.

"I don't think that's such a good idea. For a number of reasons."

Everything that had been burning inside Lillian turned to ice. She took a step back, feeling like he'd slapped her.

"Tiger Lily, it's not that I don't feel the attraction," he continued.

Maybe she'd been wrong, maybe he hadn't truly been

able to forgive her for leaving him. "It's about before. About Daryl. Right?"

He shook his head. "No. It's not even that. It's about now, and us being a team and…"

She waited for him to finish, but he didn't. Whatever he *wasn't* saying was just as important as what he was. But ultimately it came down to one thing, didn't it?

She took another short step back from him. "And we really don't know each other, do we? Not anymore." Something flickered in his eyes and he reached for her again, but Lillian moved smoothly out of his reach. "You're right, Jace, this is probably a bad idea. The team has to come first. And casual hookups probably just aren't your thing."

His dark head tilted to the side. "Are they yours? They weren't at one time."

She knew he was talking about how she had felt about her mother when Lillian was growing up. How she'd disdained her mother's constant revolving door of men. How she swore she would never be that way. That sex would never be a meaningless act.

She laughed softly even as she felt the wounded heart she hid deep inside crack a little further. For a long time, Lillian hadn't thought about that promise she'd made to herself. How she'd utterly broken it. She couldn't even blame it on Daryl. That had been all on her. "I guess we all change. Grow up. Face the real world."

"Lily…"

Lillian knew she had to get out of here. She couldn't continue to face his blue eyes without crumbling. Knew that if he asked her about her secrets now she would tell him.

She closed her eyes and regrouped. When she opened

them a couple seconds later, she was able to put a smirk on her face. She punched Jace good-naturedly on the arm. "Get some rest, Eakin. I'll catch you tomorrow. Big day."

Without another word she turned, grabbed her bag and walked out the door.

Alone. As always.

Chapter Seven

The next morning when the team met at Omega Sector headquarters in preparation to depart to the LESS Summit, Jace wanted to punch a wall.

Still wanted to punch a wall. He'd wanted to do so ever since yesterday afternoon, when Lillian offered… whatever it was she had offered.

He hadn't known how to handle it. On one hand, there was nothing he wanted more than to get Lillian in his bed. His body didn't seem to care what had happened between them twelve years ago, or care that she might be the traitor.

But he found that he couldn't betray her in that way. Couldn't take her to bed just to get close to her to find out more about her activities. Ridiculous that he would take her feelings into consideration when it came to the issue of betrayal.

He'd watched her yesterday on the computer for a long time. She'd been so focused she hadn't even realized he was there. She'd studied the building plans, examining them over and over until she was able to draw them without looking.

Unfortunately, the action didn't necessarily prove her innocence. Maybe she was studying the plans because she wanted to be as prepared as she could possibly be as a member of the SWAT team.

Or maybe she was studying the building plans because she had nefarious reasons of her own.

All Jace could say for sure was that she had not tried to communicate with anyone or leave any sort of cryptic messages while he'd been watching, as the mole had been known to do.

Jace's gut said the same thing about her now that it had said about her back in Ren's office: she was not the traitor. But God knew his gut had been wrong about Lillian before.

He'd basically glued himself to her side for the past week and all he'd found was that she was a damn fine SWAT team member. He hadn't found anything else that would suggest she was the mole. Lillian had secrets, Jace had no doubt whatsoever that she had secrets. But he didn't think those secrets had anything to do with national security.

That look on her face when she'd mentioned casual sex was still haunting him. Hell, Jace hadn't been a saint for the last decade. He'd had plenty of casual relationships with women in that time. He didn't hold a double standard. If Lillian had chosen to have a slew of casual sexual encounters, that was her prerogative.

What gutted him had been the look in her eyes, the completely humorless laugh, when she said that those sexual encounters had been her choice. Obviously somewhere deep inside she wasn't okay with it. She was hurting herself.

Steve Drackett's words of concern about possible sexual assault in her past had been echoing in Jace's mind for the last eighteen hours. Ever since Lillian had offered a casual hookup with eyes that told him she hated herself.

He was back to wanting to punch a wall again.

Not to mention he'd turned her down, which had probably stung also, even though he was doing it—or *not* doing it—for the right reasons.

Regardless, Lillian was now in a different vehicle on the way to Denver this morning. She'd been coldly polite to him as they'd all worked together to pack up equipment. Not unfriendly or rude, just obviously not interested in prolonging any conversations with him. The closeness they'd been building through sheer proximity over the last week was now completely gone.

Jace had no doubt Lillian would be coolly professional to him throughout the mission. That wasn't going to help him get close enough to her to find out if she was the one sabotaging Omega Sector. But he wasn't going to sleep with her to get that info, either.

Especially not after how she had looked at him yesterday, with such shadows in those brown eyes.

Jace was going to have to concentrate on the mission in front of him. At this point, if the mole was going to strike, and Lillian was that mole, all he could do was be close enough to stop it. After that, hell if he knew what he would do if she was the mole.

The LESS Summit started in two days. Already people were gathering in Denver. It was going to be crowded, full of angry and excited people. The situation was already hectic; throw in a potential terrorist attack and the situation became even worse.

They didn't even make it all the way into downtown Denver before they hit trouble.

"Change in plans, everybody," Derek said from the

front seat as the SUV picked up speed. "Just got a call from Denver PD. Evidently, as expected, all the crazies have rolled into town with word of the LESS Summit. There's a jumper on a highway bridge and we're closest. They need our help."

Jace could see the shift come over the team, especially the more experienced ones.

"A jumper? As in someone trying to commit suicide?" Philip asked. "Why the hell is SWAT being called in? Just let the person jump."

Nobody responded. Being part of a SWAT team was not just about hunting bad guys, shooting and securing buildings. Sometimes it was about defusing situations. Helping people who didn't know how to help themselves. It had been the same for the US Army Rangers.

If someone couldn't understand that, they probably shouldn't be on the team at all. This was probably a big part of the reason Carnell was only temporary.

"Shut up, Philip," Saul muttered, rolling his eyes. Everyone else was obviously thinking the same thing.

They pulled up at the bridge crossing the highway. Local police were stopping traffic on either side of the road, where a man was standing on the highest part of the overpass, on the outside of the railing, one arm around a light post.

If he let go, there would be nothing to stop him from flying onto the busy highway below.

As they got out of the vehicle, a uniformed officer came running over to them. Derek showed him credentials and the officer fully admitted to being in over his head.

"He's been out there for about ten minutes. Hasn't said a word."

Lillian and the rest of the team from the second vehicle jogged over to where they were.

"Okay." Derek glanced at the man's chest to get his name. "Officer Milburn, we're going to take over if that's all right with you."

Milburn nodded enthusiastically.

"Everybody on open comms, channel A," Derek continued. "Ashton, Saul, Jace—you need to clear everyone else off this bridge. Everybody wants to be a YouTube sensation, but let's not make it easy. Carnell, get on the laptop. As soon as we can get this guy's name, you find whatever info you can on him. Lillian, you're with me."

Lillian shook her head. "Derek, you know I'm no good with the touchy-feely stuff."

Derek nodded. "Just in case he responds to a woman better than a man. Lillian and I will be on open comms. None of us deal with this sort of situation a lot, so if you've got insight, let us have it."

The open comm channel meant that everyone could hear anytime someone else spoke without them having to press a button. It could be chaotic, but in a situation like this, also useful. Jace jogged over to the other side of the bridge and moved the barrier back farther. They couldn't stop people from recording what was happening, but like Derek had said, they could make it as difficult as possible.

Jace heard Derek ask the man his name. Ask if it was okay if they stood there and talked. Explained that they wouldn't come near him.

Derek did everything right. But the man wasn't interested in talking.

"Hey, guys." It was Saul. "I've got an empty vehicle

over here that doesn't belong to anyone. Registration of the vehicle says it belongs to an Oliver Lewis."

"Start running the name, Philip," Derek said softly. "You try talking to him, Lillian."

Jace watched as Lillian took her turn, easing a little closer to the man. "Hi, sir, my name is Agent... Lillian. My name is Lillian. Can you just tell us your name?"

The man shook his head.

"Is your name Oliver Lewis?" Lillian continued gently. "There's a car registered to someone named Oliver Lewis. Is that you?"

"Don't come any closer," the man said even though they hadn't moved. "You can't stop me."

"No, sir," Derek said immediately, hands out. "We won't come any closer. We just want to know if that's your name."

The man gave the tiniest of nods.

"That was a confirmation on the ID," Jace said so Derek wouldn't have to take a chance on talking and spooking the guy. "Run everything you have on him, Carnell. Hurry."

Derek and Lillian continued to try to get Oliver to talk, but without much success. Finally Philip came back on the comm.

"Oliver Lewis. Twenty-seven years old. Married. Got out of the army six months ago after nine years in."

Lillian turned away from Oliver to look over at him. "Jace, you try."

He met her eyes from across the bridge, but spoke softly into the comm unit. "I don't have any background in this sort of thing."

"But you're military. Maybe he'll respond to you."

"Yes, Jace," Derek whispered. "We're not getting through to him at all. If anything we're doing more harm."

He could at least try. He jogged up, slowing to a walk as he neared.

"Oliver," Derek said, "this is Jace Eakin. Jace isn't a normal part of our team, he just stepped in to help out."

"Yeah," Jace agreed. "I just got out of the service. They needed some help here with all the protests and stuff happening in Denver this week, so I'm assisting."

"You were in the service?"

"Army. Tenth Special Forces group."

"Ranger," Oliver whispered, turning to look at Jace for the first time.

Lillian and Derek were backing away to give Jace and Oliver some semblance of privacy. Jace nodded. "That's right. You army also?"

"How did you know that?"

"Not many people would know that the Tenth Special Forces group are Rangers unless they'd been in the army themselves. How long have you been out?"

"Six months."

Jace took the slightest step closer. "How long were you in?"

"Since I was eighteen. Was the only thing I've ever known. And now…" He trailed off.

Jace nodded. "Adjusting back to civilian life can be really difficult. Especially if you did some hard tours."

"Two back-to-back in Afghanistan."

Jace asked Oliver questions about his tours. Where he'd been located. Tried to get him to talk about friends, other men and women who'd served in his unit. He continually shifted closer under the guise of discussion, or leaned against the railing, or just listened.

Although it really wasn't a guise at all.

Jace would've sat and listened for however long Oliver wanted. People like him were the reason he was opening his ranch in Colorado. For guys like Oliver, who just needed somewhere to go for a while as they sorted out the mess in their head, tried to adjust back into a world that didn't always fit how they'd been trained.

"Oliver," Jace finally said after they'd talked for nearly twenty minutes. "Why don't you step back over the railing? Whatever it is you're feeling? Let's just wait it out, try to find another way. A less permanent solution to whatever's going on with you."

"I hit my wife," Oliver responded, his tone dripping with remorse. "I freaked out during a nap and punched her in the face. She's pregnant, Jace. How can I be trusted to be around her? To be around a baby, for God's sake. I'm toxic."

Jace tensed, prepared to make a dive for Oliver if he let go of the railing right now. He was almost close enough to pull back.

"We've already got the wife on the way, Jace." Derek's voice came through the comm. "She's been frantic looking for him. Definitely doesn't want him to do this."

"That's really hard, man." Jace might not be schooled in talking down a potential suicide victim, but he knew enough not to discount Oliver's feelings. "Have you talked to her since it happened?"

"Why would she ever want to talk to me again?"

"How long have you two been married?"

Oliver glanced at him. "Four years."

"Well, maybe your wife doesn't want to throw out four years' worth of good, just because of one moment of bad."

"She woke me up in the middle of a nightmare and

I hit her. Hard. Before I even knew what was happening. Could've broken her jaw. She was scared of me. I could see it."

Jace nodded. "Yeah, but knowing she might have to give you space and wanting you to end your life are two different things. You can see that, right?"

Oliver shrugged. But at least he was holding on to the railing again.

"Listen," Jace continued, "I know this isn't an answer to all your problems, and you and your wife are going to need to work through a lot, it sounds like. But I have a ranch I'm setting up, just outside Colorado Springs. Horses, dogs, hell, even a few cats. It's a place for vets to come, spend some time."

"You're just making that up. Just trying to get me to come down."

"No, man, I'm not. Like Derek said, I'm just helping out with law enforcement temporarily. The ranch is going to be my full-time work. Soldiers can come, sort stuff out in their head while riding or walking or just hanging out with the animals. People like you, Oliver. Because if you feel this bad about what happened with your wife, that means you want to do what's right. I can't guarantee the ranch will help, but it's at least worth a try before you leave your unborn child with no father at all."

"You're not lying?" For the first time, there was the slightest bit of hope in Oliver's voice. "This place really exists?"

"I give you my word, as one man who served to another, I am not lying. You can be the first person to come visit. Hell, you can come help me get everything set up."

Oliver just stared at him.

"This bridge is always going to be here, Oliver." Jace

knew this might not be the right thing to say, but it was the truth. "There will always be a way to kill yourself if you want to go that route. But today why don't you choose to do something different? To give life a chance and see if there's any way to fix things that maybe a few months from now might not be as broken as you think."

Oliver stared at him for a long time before finally nodding and stepping one leg back on the safe side of the railing. As soon as his other leg was also over, Jace crossed the few feet to the man and pulled him in for a hug.

"I was telling the truth," Jace said. "I don't know what happens now, but I'll make sure you get the information about the ranch."

Jace stepped back when he heard a woman screaming Oliver's name and running toward him. She didn't give him any choice but to catch her as she leaped at him, sobbing.

The size of the bruise covering half her face left no doubt that this was Oliver's wife. But instead of being mad, she pulled back from him and cupped his cheeks in her hands. "Together. Whatever it is, we get through it *together*."

As he walked back to the rest of the team, Jace realized Oliver probably wasn't going to need his ranch. He was one of the lucky ones. Oliver had the support he needed right at home.

Chapter Eight

Lillian punched the lumpy pillow under her head as she lay in the too-soft hotel bed. Damn things were keeping her from getting any sleep.

Who was she kidding? The bed and pillow had nothing to do with her not getting rest. She never slept well outside her own bed. Hell, she didn't sleep all that great in her own.

Too much time, alone, in the dark, to think…to remember? Not her friend.

Daytime and her job at Omega Sector allowed her to stay busy, to stay focused, to push herself to her limits.

To keep the demons at bay.

But nighttime, especially after a day like today, when she hadn't expended a great deal of physical energy? Not as easy. The darkness seemed to press in on her.

How many times had she come back to her senses in a bed sort of like this one with a guy she didn't quite remember, her skin crawling with the knowledge of what she'd done? Again.

Jace had been right to turn her down. She was damaged in ways that would taint every relationship she had. And it might have started with Daryl, but Lillian couldn't deny that her own choices, the patterns she allowed to

take over in her sexual escapades, were what had per-
petuated the problem.

And watching Jace today, talking to that vet, connecting to the man on such an honest, authentic level... Lillian rubbed her chest in the general vicinity of her heart.
He was going to raise dogs, horses. Animals that would
help people who'd been traumatized by war.

She couldn't help wondering if a dog might help her
through the trauma of a different kind of war. Maybe it
could provide the companionship she'd refused to acknowledge she so desperately needed.

Who was she kidding? She couldn't take care of a
puppy. A dog needed attention. Love. A regular schedule. She wasn't capable of any of those.

She glanced at her watch to find it was 3:30 a.m. and
swung her legs around to the floor. She might as well
get up. She knew well enough she wouldn't be able to
get back to sleep.

Knew that it was just a matter of time before the darkness around her—even though she had a light on in the
bathroom—started to eat at her sanity. Lillian *never* slept
in the dark

She would go for a walk. It was what she usually did.
Although sometimes those walks led her to a local bar
and then to the home of some nameless guy for meaningless sex. She always hoped that it might be different.
That she might connect. *Feel* something.

She had no desire to go find some random guy now.
The kisses with Jace had just reminded her how utterly
empty those other encounters were. Attempts to punish
herself, Grace had said. Lillian had scoffed. What did
she have to punish herself for? she'd argued.

But Lillian knew the list was long and never far from her mind. And growing.

For not being able to fight back against Daryl.

For not being strong enough to escape and go to Jace.

For not having the guts to admit to him—then or now—what had happened and why she was so broken.

For not being able to stop Freihof from killing Grace and hurting others.

Lillian was dressed in her cargo pants and T-shirt in under a minute. She grabbed her jacket from the closet and left the voices behind.

The chill of the February air helped chase away the voices. There weren't many people around this area of downtown at this hour. The bars had already let out, and most of the buildings were government or offices anyway—no one was burning the midnight oil.

Lillian found herself wandering down toward the Denver City and County Building, the picturesque government building where the LESS Summit would be taking place.

The massive white marble building was iconic in the state of Colorado, beautiful and dignified. Although she knew the plans almost by heart, she wandered around it slowly, getting a feel for it from the outside. It would not be an easy building to secure. Multiple entrances and exit points in the form of doors and windows. The doors would need to be secure, although the windows had alarms and none of them would be open.

Lillian did a double take at one of the windows she was just thinking about on the far side of the building from where she stood.

Someone was easing themselves inside one of the windows lowest to the ground. The same windows that

Omega, with the help of Denver PD, had secured earlier today after they'd finished with the attempted suicide.

Someone had missed a window. On purpose?

Was this Freihof entering the building now? The mole?

Silently, Lillian crouched down to grab her backup sidearm from its ankle holster in her boot and took off in a sprint toward the window. If this was Freihof, she was going to catch him and nail the son of a bitch.

Right. Damn. Now.

The window was still missing part of the grate that should've been covering it to stop this sort of entry into the building. Staying low, she gazed inside. The small basement storage room was dark and she couldn't see anyone. Whoever had entered had proceeded into the hallway.

Lillian holstered her weapon and edged herself through the window, thankful her size made it easier. Once inside, she crouched low again, weapon back in hand, looking and listening. She was fairly certain no one was in the room, but she didn't want to take a chance.

Once she knew the room was secure, she moved quickly to the door, opened it and glanced up and down the darkened hallway. This wasn't an area of the building used for daily government purposes. The hall was littered with unused desks and furniture, cleaning supplies and bookshelves.

Plenty of places for someone to hide. And damn well too many areas where someone could leave an explosive device.

Lillian looked up and down the hall, trying to ascertain which way the suspect had run. This was a virtual maze of connected halls and doors. Was the perp trying to get up to the main section of the building?

She heard a muffled noise farther down one of the hallways and began to move toward it, stepping quickly but silently.

Now would be a good time for backup, but by the time they got here it would be too late. And the three-man private security force who patrolled this building at night wouldn't be much good against Freihof.

Lillian could still remember watching Freihof pull the knife across Grace Parker's throat, helpless to do anything to save her friend. If Freihof was in this building, Lillian wasn't going to lose him calling for backup. She'd take him down herself.

She eased farther down the hallway, coming to an intersecting one. She didn't know which way the perp had gone. She moved quickly down one hallway, only to find it came to a dead end at a locked door. Cursing, she spun around and ran back down to where the halls crossed, hoping the perp hadn't made it out. She wished she'd studied this floor's plans as much as she had the other levels.

She took the corner too quickly and wasn't expecting the assailant to be right there. Mistake. She'd been too desperate to catch him to be as careful as she should have been.

She swallowed a cry as the perp hit her arms with a hardcover law book, knocking her gun to the floor and sending it skidding across the hall. Pain radiated through her right forearm at the force of the blow.

Mistake on his part, too. He should've clocked her with that book and knocked her out while he had the chance. He wouldn't get a second opportunity. Lillian spun back toward him, already perfectly balanced on her feet.

Her opponent was around six feet tall, probably close

to two hundred pounds, and he was wearing a mask. Lillian was determined that would be coming off.

The guy dropped the book—smart, it would slow him down—and Lillian went on the offensive. She kicked him in the midsection, then used her momentum to swing her other leg around in a roundhouse kick to catch him in the head.

He blocked her kick at the last second, bringing his own fist around in a hook that would've knocked her to the floor, if not unconscious, if it had hit her jaw, where he was aiming.

Guy wasn't playing around.

Neither was she.

As always when fighting someone bigger and stronger, Lillian used her speed and agility to her advantage, keeping out of reach of his blows and using her legs and kicks as much as possible. The guy adapted quickly, bringing himself closer to her, so her legs couldn't inflict any damage. Also meant she had to stay focused in order to not get caught by one of his fists.

He had some skills.

She had more.

Lillian spun, her elbow connecting with the perp's jaw as she flung around. Momentum propelled him backward, allowing her to hit him with a right uppercut and then a left hook. He was going down and they both knew it.

Too late Lillian heard the click of a Taser and felt the voltage run through her body. Was there a second person here or had she just missed it?

She fought the blackness but it overcame her.

As soon as she came to, Lillian realized the direness of the situation.

A noose wrapped tightly around a neck had a very distinct feel.

She was sitting on a crate that rested precariously on a step in a stairwell. Her arms were tied behind her back. A few moments later the rope attached to her neck began to move upward as it was hoisted from the other side. Lillian could stand or she could suffocate.

The rope continued to move upward, pulling her up, until she was standing on the crate, then it kept going until she was on her very tiptoes.

The bands restraining her arms behind her back weren't that tight, but weren't so loose that she could get out.

"Someone has to take the fall," a voice whispered from the other side of the stairwell, near the door. Lillian couldn't tell whose it was. Someone she knew?

And that was why the restraints weren't tight on her arms. This needed to look like a suicide.

"This isn't going to work, you know. Whatever you have planned."

Lillian winced as the rope jerked the slightest bit higher as the masked man tied it to the door. The door pulled to the outside, which meant if someone opened it she was a goner.

So much for yelling for help.

She was on the very tops of her toes, the square crate balancing precariously on the rectangle step that was much more narrow.

"No one is going to believe I killed myself with my arms tied behind my back." The words came out in breathy gasps as she focused on holding herself steady.

Masked Man just tilted his head, studying her. But she

knew if he didn't cut her arms loose she had no chance of survival.

The box tipped forward and she felt sweat drip down her forehead as she attempted to get it back straight with what little leverage she had. She wasn't sure she had much chance for survival anyway.

The man moved away from the door and came up the stairs, giving her a wide berth—as if she could kick him and still maintain balance on the crate—and without another word cut the cord from her arms.

Lillian immediately brought her hands up above her head and took her weight from her legs, then swung her legs back down, twisting and using momentum to propel them toward Masked Man, hoping to catch him around the shoulders.

But he was expecting it and had moved up the stairs out of her reach. Her legs fell downward to the crate again, to give her arms supporting her weight a rest.

"Goodbye, Omega Sector."

She heard the whisper from behind her and saw an envelope drop to the floor before the crate was kicked out from under her. Immediately her arms took the weight of her body. She swung her legs up to try to wrap them around the rope, but couldn't, with the length and angle of the noose. She reached her foot out to the side, trying to reach the banister, and cursed when her legs weren't long enough to reach it.

She couldn't see the bastard behind her but knew he was waiting. Waiting to watch her die as her strength gave out and she couldn't support herself anymore.

She tried to yell—even if someone came rushing into the room, it wasn't going to do much more damage than her swaying here until her strength gave out—but the sound was cut off by the rope over her vocal chords. If she wanted to yell, she was going to have to use one hand to pull the rope away from the front of her throat. That meant supporting all her weight with one arm.

Her muscles were already straining from the constant state of pulling up. Supporting her weight with one arm wasn't going to work.

But she'd be damned if she was just going to die in front of this bastard.

She swung her legs up, trying to catch the upper part of the rope, but failed again. Even if she could get her legs hooked up there, she wasn't going to be able to get herself released.

She heard a low chuckle to her side. Bastard. He was enjoying this.

And then the alarm started blaring.

Masked Man muttered a curse and took off up the stairs. Lillian felt her arms begin to shake as the exhaustion from holding her own weight began to take its toll. If it wasn't for the rigorous SWAT training, she'd already be dead.

But even training wouldn't be enough. Physics would win. Her arms began to tremble more and she was forced to let go of the rope to give them a break.

Immediately the rope cut off all oxygen.

When everything began to go black, she reached up and grabbed the rope again. It wasn't long before the tremors took over.

She didn't want to go out like this. Wished she hadn't squandered this second chance she'd had with Jace in her life.

But even thinking of Jace, with his gorgeous blue eyes

and cocky grin that still did things to her heart after all these years, couldn't give her any more strength.

She reached back up with her arms and found them collapsing before she even took her weight. Then the noose tightened and jerked around her neck, pulling her body forward, all air gone.

Blackness.

Chapter Nine

The door to the stairway was heavy as Jace opened it. Abnormally heavy, like someone was slumped against it. Fear coated his throat. Was it Lillian against the other side of the door, unconscious?

What he found when he pushed it open was much worse.

Jace immediately took in the situation, cursing violently as he flew up the steps toward Lillian's swinging form. "Lily!"

He dove to get himself under her legs and lift her, taking the weight off her throat and airway.

"Lillian? Lily? Come on, baby, talk to me."

His heart was a hammer in his chest as he wrapped his arms around her thighs and hoisted her up.

God, he couldn't be too late.

"Lily!" he yelled, shaking her and tapping her leg, trying to get her to wake up. The only thing he could hear was silence and the desperate beating of his own heart.

"Come on, Tiger Lily, damn it. Fight." Lillian Muir was nothing if not a fighter.

Jace reached into his pocket for his army knife, trying to position himself where he could hold her weight and saw through the rope above her head. He still couldn't tell if she was breathing or not.

Holding all her weight while on the awkward stairs made cutting the rope nearly impossible. But there was no way in hell he was going to let her go.

"Hand me the knife."

Lillian's hoarse whisper sent relief flooding through Jace. He gave her the knife, lifting her body farther to provide her the slack in the rope she needed. A minute later she fell completely into his arms as she finished cutting the binding around her throat.

He set them both on the stairs and pushed her clawing fingers away from the noose, loosening it and lifting it over her head. She slumped back against the wall.

There was already angry red marks and bruising on her neck and throat where the rope had been suffocating her.

"Jesus, Lily." Jace hauled her to him in a fierce hug, swallowing the terror that still scratched at his insides. "What the hell happened?"

He was thankful when she didn't try to pull away. "Masked man." Her voice was painfully hoarse. "Saw someone crawl through a window and I followed him. He must've had a partner. Bastard Tasered me. When I woke up, he had me strung up, standing on a box. Then he tipped it."

"Damn it." Jace's eyes closed again. "You were holding your own weight up?"

She nodded and silence fell between them as Jace realized how close to death she'd really been. The fact that she was sitting here alive right now was a testament to both her physical and mental strength. Strength very few people had.

"Sick bastard. Why didn't he just shoot you?"

She pulled back from him and grabbed a note from behind him on the stairs. He unfolded it.

I CAN'T LIVE WITH WHAT I'VE DONE. WITH BETRAYING MY COLLEAGUES. SO MY FIGHT ENDS HERE.

It was written in block letters, which had been smart. It would've been difficult to prove whether Lillian had written it or not, which was exactly what the killer wanted.

"He wanted to make it look like a suicide," she whispered.

"We need to get you to a hospital and report to Derek. Let him know what's going on."

She pulled away from him, shaking her head. "I don't need a hospital. We go to Derek first. I'll get the team medic to check me out."

Jace grimaced but knew Lillian was probably right. There wasn't much a hospital could do for her except help her manage her pain. "Fine. But if your throat starts feeling any worse, you have to let someone know immediately. Swelling could still be an issue. And swelling could mean airway blockage."

She tilted her head, studying him. "How do you know that?"

"I had a little bit of medical training in the army."

She nodded and he could tell even that small movement caused her discomfort. "Okay, I'll tell you if it gets any worse."

"We need to let the building guards know about that window. It shouldn't have been missed in the security sweep."

He kept a hand at the small of her back as they moved through the door and toward the elevators.

"Maybe they weren't missed." Her voice was low, husky. "Maybe someone deliberately left it unsecured."

"You think the mole is here in Denver?"

"I think it's awfully suspicious that the guy who broke in was wearing a mask. He would've blended in better without it."

"A mask definitely screams *bad guy*."

"Exactly. Why bother with it at all if nobody's going to recognize you anyway?"

Jace nodded as he led Lillian into the main lobby of the building. The guards were surprised to see them, and they had to show their identification quickly to keep the security team from calling backup.

Backup Lillian could've desperately used twenty minutes ago.

Without going into too much detail—particularly until they could talk to Derek and figure out a plan—Jace informed the guards about the unsecured window and that Lillian had followed someone in.

Lillian and Jace waited as the security team followed their protocol and brought in other members of the staff, as well as police. They showed them the window so it could be secured, and the area was swept for possible DNA. Whomever Lily had fought would be long gone by now, but maybe they would get lucky and get some sort of forensic clue to point them in the right direction.

Ultimately, there needed to be a great deal more security in this building, but not just the type that was barely paid more than minimum wage. City hall would need to be reswept. If Derek didn't make the decision to move the LESS Summit to the secondary location.

Jace kept an eye on Lillian as they left the building and walked back toward the hotel, carefully watching for signs that her throat was swelling and closing off. Although she moved stiffly—he couldn't even imagine what sort of trauma her upper body muscles had been through trying to hold her own unsupported weight for that long—she didn't seem to be suffering from shortness of breath.

He hated what she'd been through, what had almost happened, and it had damn well taken twenty years off his life seeing her swinging there unconscious. But tonight had also proven one thing beyond a shadow of a doubt.

Lillian was not the mole.

There was no way she could've faked what had happened tonight. No way she could've known that Jace would come through that door when he did. If he had been another minute later, just *one* minute, she would've been dead.

And if someone was leaving a suicide note on her and trying to kill her, then Lillian Muir was not the mole.

The relief coursing through Jace now was almost as prominent as the relief of knowing she was alive after he'd seen her hanging there in the stairwell.

The proof of her innocence changed damn near everything for him. Every single reason he had for not giving in to the attraction that sparked between the two of them vanished as soon as he'd cut her down from the rope that had almost taken her life.

Jace couldn't stop himself from staring at her. She was alive and she was *innocent*.

"I'm not going to collapse, Eakin, so you can stop ogling me."

She had no idea why he couldn't drag his eyes away from her. She would soon.

If she would still have him.

They went straight to Derek's room. The sun was already coming up and he was awake. One look at Lillian's neck had his eyebrow raised, and he eased his door open farther for them to enter his room.

"You two get a little too excited with the sparring?" Derek asked.

Jace explained what happened, with Lillian filling in details, speaking as little as possible to protect her strained voice.

Jace sat down at the edge of the bed and pulled Lillian down beside him. She was starting to look a little paler. Was probably in a lot of pain.

"We told the building's security team about the break-in and unsecured window, but didn't give them much info about what happened to Lillian. I wasn't sure how you wanted to handle that. They brought in locals to process the scene and woke up every guard who's ever worked there to get them on-site."

Derek rubbed a hand across his face. "It's still not enough. I'll make a call. We're going to need further backup for the summit. We'll also need to move the summit to the secondary location. The bigwigs won't like it because it's not nearly as picturesque as city hall. Plus, we'll need to lock down an entirely new building." He turned to Lillian. "You need a hospital? You've been Tasered and strangled. Maybe you need to sit this event out."

Lillian stood. "I'm going to pretend I didn't even hear that. Bastard got a lucky shot, but it won't happen again. And I'm damn well not going to miss the LESS Summit. We're shorthanded enough as it is."

The tough-person speech would've been much more

convincing if her voice hadn't broken three times during it.

Jace couldn't help himself—his hand moved to her back to rub gentle circles. The fact that she didn't pull away both thrilled and worried him. "She's agreed to let the medic examine her. Then she'll be in my room."

He ignored Lillian's raised eyebrow.

Derek nodded. "I don't want to see either of you before thirteen hundred hours at the secondary location. We'll start the security lockdown and then prep for a run-through of the summit."

Jace and Lillian both stood and headed toward the door. Lillian turned back to Derek.

"You know what the mask means, right?" she croaked.

Derek rubbed the back of his neck. "It means Omega definitely has a mole, and that you would've known his face. We'll be sure to keep an eye on any reactions today when you show up. Because as far as that person knows, you died in that stairwell."

Jace's fists clenched. They'd come so damn close to that being the truth.

"Freihof is making his move, Derek. The summit is too good a target for him to pass up," Lillian whispered, her voice almost gone.

"And we'll be ready for him," Derek responded. "This is going to end. But first, go to the ER or at least go see the medic, get checked out. Then try to get some rest. Because you're right, we do need you. I have a feeling we're going to need all the help we can get."

Chapter Ten

Everybody needed to stop telling her to go to the ER. Jace. Derek. The medic. She was fine.

Lillian was angry as hell, but physically she would be fine. So the medic informing Jace—as if Jace was the boss of her—that she needed to be under constant supervision for the next twenty-four hours didn't do much for Lillian's temper.

"I'm fine," she muttered as they left the medic. "I don't need to stay in your room."

Jace looked at her calmly as he used the card key to open his hotel door. "Less than two hours ago you were unconscious from lack of oxygen. Your body is depleted. Exhausted. I understand you not wanting to go to the hospital, but please humor me on this. Stay with me."

His voice rolled over her like gentle waves, soothing her. Calming her.

But she also knew even soothing, calming water could drown her if she wasn't careful.

Lillian wanted to stay. And wanted to run. Maybe she was more injured than she thought, because she truly couldn't decide.

But finally she admitted to herself that the reason she wanted to run didn't have anything to do with proving her health and everything to do with how sexy Jace looked standing there against the wall in his jeans and shirt, holding the door open for her.

Holding the door open to the room that had one king-size bed as the main piece of furniture.

Lillian wasn't a coward, so she walked through the doorway, feeling Jace's hand at the small of her back as she did. Just like she'd felt it as they'd walked down the hall.

She knew she shouldn't read into it. He'd already made it quite clear he wasn't interested in anything more than a professional relationship. Working together. That was it. Being a friendly colleague was enough for her with everyone else. It would be enough with Jace, too.

Plus, she owed him. If he hadn't gotten there when he had, she'd definitely be dead now.

"Thank you for saving my life." She stood staring at the big bed for a moment before a thought occurred to her and she turned to him. "What were you doing at city hall anyway?"

She expected an immediate quip about insomnia or the problem with having a job that wasn't nine-to-five—with SWAT, probably the same as his time in the army, daytime and nighttime hours could run together.

Instead, Jace stepped closer. Directly into her definitely-more-than-just-professional space. There weren't a whole lot of things that threw Lillian off balance. This was one of them.

"I was looking for you."

Lillian took a slight step back, Jace's proximity a little too much for her system. "Okay. I'm glad you found me or else I'd—" She stopped, realization dawning. "You were following me?"

He nodded, features unreadable.

She tried to process the possible reasons why Jace would be following *her*. "Why?"

Now he stepped out of her space slightly, eyes shuttered. He paused so long she thought maybe he wasn't going to answer.

"I'm not just here to fill in for the SWAT team. I was also sent in by Ren McClement to look for the mole working with Freihof."

The mole. Lillian stepped away from Jace and walked over to the window that didn't provide much of a view. She leaned her forehead against the cool glass, taking in all the ramifications of Jace's statement.

"They sent you in because they think I'm the mole," she finally muttered. Somehow she'd always known there was a deeper purpose for Jace's sudden infiltration into the team.

She could hear him move closer behind her, but she didn't turn around. "They sent me in because Ren trusts me, they needed someone with a particular skill set and because…yes, they know there's a mole."

"And your past with me had nothing to do with them sending you in?"

Jace sighed. "No. They knew we'd known each other before when they asked me to join the team. You were one of the suspects. Although if it helps, your boss, that Steve Drackett guy, was adamant you weren't guilty."

"And you?" She hated the weakness in her voice as she whispered the question. Hated that the answer mattered so much to her. "Did *you* think I was guilty?"

She knew it was unfair. After what had happened between them twelve years ago—or what Jace *thought* had happened—expecting him to trust her carte blanche just wasn't fair. But God, how she wanted to believe he would find it impossible to conceive she was a traitor of that magnitude.

"Never mind," she said before he could answer. Before he could say the words she knew would tear her apart even though they shouldn't. "We don't really know each other, and what you did know about me wasn't complimentary. Of course you thought I was guilty."

She tried to give a lighthearted laugh, but it came out a brittle croak even to her own ears as she continued to stare out the window with no view. When he didn't respond, she continued, moving into a deeper register of her voice so it wouldn't crack. "We should get some rest like Derek said. Obviously we've got a ton of fortification work to do in a few hours now that we're moving to the secondary location."

"Tiger Lily…"

Damn it, he could *not* call her that. Not right now. Not when every part of her felt vulnerable.

She turned from the window but didn't meet his crystal eyes. She couldn't. Not right now. "You know what? I really am fine. I'm just going to head on up to my own room. I promise if I feel even the slightest bit—"

"No," he interrupted before she got any further. "I never thought you were guilty of treason. I didn't think it when Ren recruited me a couple of weeks ago. Hell, Lily, I didn't even think that when I felt the worst about you."

God, she wanted to believe that more than anything. "But yet, you came here, because of me. Followed me because you thought I might be up to something."

He took a step closer and ran a hand through his brown hair, causing short pieces to stick up at crazy angles. "I came here because of you, yes. Because, despite everything, I've never been able to stop thinking about you. Because I wanted to put you—put the *past*—behind me once and for all."

That hurt almost as much as him thinking she was the mole. "Yeah, I can't blame you for that, either. Although I guess I'm glad you don't think I'm trying to kill my friends and betray my country, even if you don't like me personally."

His fingers gripped her upper arms. Not hard enough to hurt, and they both knew she had moves that could get her away from him if she wanted, but a firm enough touch to let her know that he was serious.

"It took me about three and a half minutes after seeing you to figure out that this heat between us was very definitely not in the past."

She couldn't look away from those eyes. "But what about the other day at HQ? You turning down my offer to come over? I thought you weren't interested."

He stepped closer. All Lillian could feel, smell, breathe...was Jace.

His volume dropped to a husky whisper. "I didn't want to be with you that way under false pretenses. I didn't want to have sex with you and then you think I had used it to get close to you to see if you were the mole."

"You *did* want me?" It had to be the near strangulation that made her voice so weak. So thready.

His hands moved up from her arms to cup her face. Her eyes closed and she breathed him in. He smelled of heat and desire and a scent that was pure male. Not just any male. *Jace.*

It had always been Jace. *Only* been Jace.

"Oh, hell yeah." His deep whisper sent chills across her skin. "But not with lies between us. And so while I hate what happened to you tonight, I'm also thankful for it. Because now there's no doubt in my mind you aren't the mole."

He was so close Lillian couldn't think clearly—all she could do was feel. And it felt so different than most interactions Lillian had with men. By this point of closeness she was normally checking out mentally. Fading away to some place in her mind that no one could touch. Even though her encounters with men weren't violent, her brain just wasn't able to process the intimacy.

But not now. She wanted to be here. With Jace. In every way.

She almost felt giddy. The desire coursing through her veins like a fire was heady. She felt almost tipsy on it.

"I'm a little nervous about that smile," he said, lips so close to hers she could feel the hot sweetness of his breath. "You look like the cat that ate the canary."

"I just want to be with you." She couldn't help it, her smile grew wider as she pulled him closer. She wanted to revel in this feeling. "And it sounds like you want the same."

"Oh, you better believe it."

She let out a soft gasp as her body was pushed up against the window while his mouth came crashing down on hers. This kiss wasn't gentle or searching. Wasn't the kiss of the two teenagers they'd been.

It was hot. Forceful. Encompassing.

Everything about Jace demanded that Lillian's mind and focus stay here with him in the room. On him. On *them*.

Not that she wanted to be anywhere else. And hell if it wasn't the most authentic emotion she'd had in years. In twelve years.

Desire.

He kissed her with utter absorption, as if he couldn't get enough of her. Her fingers threaded in his hair as his hands slid down her back to her hips and he jerked her against him.

Lillian couldn't hold back the moan that broke free.

"I want you, Lily," he said against her lips.

Good, because she wanted him, too. In ways she thought had died long ago. She kept herself plastered against him as he picked her up by bending his knees and wrapping his arms around her hips. Then he lifted her and carried her to the bed.

He laid her down gently, without breaking the kiss, bringing his weight down on top of her. Lillian tensed.

She knew a man's form resting on her was one of her triggers—she and Grace had talked about it in depth in therapy—and Lillian waited for numbness to inch through her mind as it always did so she could fight it off.

But it didn't come.

All she could do was feel as Jace's lips moved over her jaw, taking special time to gently kiss down her injured throat. Finally he reached that most sensitive point, where her shoulder and neck met. He bit down gently and a soft cry escaped her.

She was feeling a million things. Numbness definitely was not one of them.

Jace's weight wasn't frightening, wasn't overwhelming her senses in a way that caused her mind to switch off in order to survive. That frightening place she'd barely survived as an eighteen-year-old wasn't looming in the distance.

Instead his weight was comfortable, as if her mind

knew him, her body remembered him. Knew she was safe. And she was. Lillian knew that on every level.

Jace equaled safety.

As his hand ran down her body from her shoulder to her waist, unbuttoning her shirt as he went, she gripped his hair so she could see him face-to-face.

"I want you," she said, staring into those blue eyes that had once meant everything to her.

He gave her a half grin that stopped her heart and seemed to have a direct link to the most feminine parts of her. "You seem a little surprised by that statement."

"I just want to be here with you, all the way with you. Here and now." She knew she was being cryptic, that he couldn't possibly understand what she meant. And she definitely wasn't about to explain, especially not now.

But Jace just nodded. "Then stay with me, Tiger Lily. Here and now, in this bed. Just you and me." He bent down and brought his lips to hers again tenderly.

And she did. For the first time in twelve years she stayed—mentally—in a bed with a man. Not just any man. *Jace*. Experienced every kiss, every touch. Every moan and lick and sigh. Things she'd thought she was long past able to feel.

And found there was nowhere else she would rather be.

Chapter Eleven

"What the hell were you thinking, Freihof? If I hadn't come in and saved your ass, you'd be arrested right now."

Damien stared at "Guy Fawkes," his eyes narrowed to slits. The hell of it was, the younger man wasn't wrong. Damien had made a mistake. Had miscalculated. It didn't happen very often, but it had this morning.

It was the anniversary of his beloved Natalie's death. The day Omega Sector had swept in six years ago and taken her from him. Killed her in their heavy-handedness.

Damien hadn't planned to do anything about it. Moving on a day connected to Natalie would be too obvious. But he hadn't been able to stop himself.

They needed to pay.

He'd been toying with them for months, chasing and killing their loved ones so they could know the pain that he'd known from losing his Natalie.

But it was no longer enough. It was time for them to stop feeling the heartache of death and start feeling death itself. One by one… Groups… Damien didn't care which.

He just wanted them all to die.

Setting a trap in city hall—a bomb that would take out the entire SWAT team—had seemed like the perfect plan. Yes, it would've messed up some of Fawkes's destroy-all-of-law-enforcement plan, but Damien didn't care. He was tired of the game. Tired of Fawkes and his grand scheming. Tired of Omega Sector cheating death every time.

Tired of the same old story, so Damien was planning to turn some pages.

For Natalie. He could still picture her in his mind. Her blond hair and blue eyes. The perfect all-American girl. And she'd been all his. His most prized possession. Until they'd taken her away forever.

"Freihof!" Fawkes slammed his fist down on the table in the small apartment Damien had rented. "Are you listening to anything I'm saying? I took a big risk helping you and then again getting here to talk to you in person. You've probably ruined what I've taken months to set up."

The temptation to end Fawkes's life right now was almost more than Damien could bear. But it would be a mistake and Damien had already made one of those several hours ago. Fawkes was still useful and Damien needed to get his emotions under control.

A time and a place for everything. That was what he'd always told his beloved Natalie, and it was still true now.

"It won't happen again," Damien muttered through tight lips.

"It doesn't matter if it happens again!" Fawkes began pacing back and forth. "Thanks to your stunt, they're moving the summit to the secondary location. This changes everything for my plans. Networks I've painstakingly linked together for months ruined because you had to sneak in through a damn window in the middle of the night."

Damien watched the younger man pull at his own hair.

Damien wouldn't have to kill him. He was going to give himself a stroke. "Fawkes, I will fix this."

"How?" Fawkes glared at him. "How exactly will you do that?"

"You let me worry about it. You concentrate on keeping your team from figuring out your grand scheme. From figuring out who you are."

Fawkes pulled at his hair again. "We have a limited window, Damien. If all my systems are not aligned when LESS goes live in thirty-six hours, my plan fails. And city hall is the center of everything. Ground zero."

Damien nodded. "Like I said, I will make sure the summit is returned to the original location."

It would take work, but Damien already had a plan in mind.

"And Lillian Muir? She didn't die despite me stringing her up. I'm lucky I borrowed your mask because she would definitely be able to identify me, since she didn't die. And now she's even more suspicious."

"Yes, she's suspicious, but she's not suspicious of *you*. That's all that matters right now. She doesn't know who she saw entering that window. She doesn't know who strung her up in that hallway and she doesn't know any of the plans. Besides, I have something very special in store for her. And her boyfriend."

"Damn Eakin. Everybody accepted him into the SWAT team like he was some sort of god. I even saw Lillian making out with him in the parking lot last week."

The words fairly dripped with jealously. In just over a week, Eakin had done what Fawkes had been trying to do for months: make the team, get the girl. And, more importantly, gain respect. But pointing that out to the young Mr. Fawkes wasn't going to do any good.

Damien could see he'd been wrong to get so impatient. To want to jump straight to killing the SWAT team rather than torture them. They would still die, but first they would suffer.

Lillian Muir would especially. He had something special planned for her.

"I was wrong." Damien's voice was full of sincerity that for once he wasn't faking. "I shouldn't have tried to circumvent the plan. I will make sure we get back on track."

Fawkes nodded, somewhat appeased. "Good. What I'm doing is important, Damien. It's going to reshape law enforcement all over the world. The badge will mean something again. The badge will rule as it was meant to do from the beginning."

Ah, quoting the infamous "Manifesto of Change" once more. Fawkes constantly hid behind it, allowing it to mask his jealousy, fear and ineptitude. After all, killing thousands of people because you just couldn't make the SWAT team didn't have the same ring to it. But this manifesto, which he planned to release publicly after his massacre at the LESS Summit, made Fawkes feel more legitimate.

But Damien wasn't about to try to convince Fawkes of his own folly. He just nodded. "Change is necessary. There's a time and a place for everything. Omega Sector's time and place has come and gone. Together, we'll destroy them."

"There are things you don't know, Freihof. Plans I've made beyond what I've told you that even the precious SWAT team won't figure out."

"Are you sure they're not on to you?"

Fawkes just shrugged. "They suspect damn near everyone. But they'll never have proof. And soon they'll all be dead."

"Maybe it's time you let me know all the details of your plan. I'm sure I can help."

Fawkes grinned, but anger laced the expression rather than joy. Anyone who couldn't see that had to be blind. Then Fawkes began to tell Damien his entire plan. Damien just listened.

He realized that *everyone* had underestimated this young man.

And they all would burn.

WHEN JACE WOKE up after a couple hours of sleep, Lillian was gone. He wasn't surprised. The medic had told him to keep an eye on her to make sure she was okay.

Jace had kept a very close eye on her. On *all* of her. For hours.

It was like they were trying to cram twelve years of not making love into a few short hours. *Intense* was an applicable term for the last few hours they'd spent in bed, but would be an understatement.

Mind-blowing, earth-shattering, game-changing—those would be closer to the truth.

Jace wasn't so naive as to think that everything was perfect between him and Lillian just because they'd had some awesome sex. There were still a lot of years and a huge betrayal between them. He'd told himself—and her—that he was going to let the situation with Daryl be left in the past, but he had to admit he wasn't one-hundred-dred-percent sure he was there yet.

Lily had seemed as enraptured in their lovemaking as he had been. She'd actually seemed a little surprised at their connection. At the heat. Had mentioned more than once how she wanted him, as if the notion caught her a little off guard.

A heat that all-encompassing after twelve years *was* a little surprising. Of course they'd had heat at the beginning, too.

That hadn't stopped Jace from finding Lily in his brother's arms a few days later. So there was no reason to think something similar wouldn't happen again. He needed to remember that. Keep his head on straight when it came to her.

Mind-blowing sex? No problem. Jace would partake as often as possible during this mission.

Giving Lily a piece of his heart? Absolutely not. He couldn't allow this to become more than a burn-the-sheets-off-the-bed sexual encounter between two friendly colleagues who would go their separate ways.

He brutally squashed the niggling voice that tried to tell him that Lillian Muir had always held a piece of his heart.

Jace showered and grabbed a bite to eat before dressing in full SWAT gear. He knew Lillian would meet at the secondary location at 1300 hours, like Derek had requested. Knew she would act as if nothing had happened, in both her near-death experience and the passion between the two of them. Lillian was never going to be one to wear her heart—or her weaknesses—on her sleeve.

Jace would be professional, too. Because although he definitely planned to have Lillian back in his bed, they couldn't deny that there was a very real threat here at the LESS Summit. Freihof and his crony might not have succeeded in making it look like Lillian was the mole, and taken her out of the picture, but that didn't mean they would turn their backs on an opportunity to do damage.

By surviving, Lillian had just upped the ante for whatever they had planned.

Omega would need to be ready.

Chapter Twelve

Jace was making his way to the federal building serving as the secondary location when the call came through. The entire team was to stop what they were doing and head to the lobby of the adjoining building. Some sort of elevator emergency.

He met Lillian as she was running from the federal building. Roman Weber and Saul Poniard were just two steps behind.

"Why the hell are we being brought in for a stuck elevator? Why didn't they call the fire department?" Jace asked as they ran, having to dodge picketers holding signs and chanting. The summit didn't start until tomorrow, but the public and news crews were already out in full force.

"Maybe the fire department has more on their plate than they can handle. But you can believe that Derek wouldn't call the entire team from our current assignment if we weren't needed."

Jace already knew that they were needed. It was confirmed a few minutes later as they all met up in the lobby. People were rushing by them, not screaming in panic, but not calm, either.

The presence of a SWAT team wasn't helping. People could tell something was wrong.

Derek spoke fast. "As we knew, the summit is bringing out the crazies. We've got four different bomb threats across the city, all tied to elevators. People are stranded in them all, and the guy is threatening to detonate all the bombs in thirty minutes if he doesn't get his demands met."

Saul cursed next to Jace. The ugly word very neatly summarized how he was feeling also.

"A police negotiator is talking with the bomber, criminal psychiatrist assisting, but they both have already signaled that they think the bomber has every intention of killing people today. Wants the attention, not the three million dollars he's demanding. Local police is spread thin, so we're working this building."

Now muttered curses could be heard all the way around.

"What's the plan, Derek? If he's going to blow it, let's get the people out before he can," Lillian said, her small body already strumming with energy.

"Elevator is caught between the sixteenth and seventeen floors. Eight people inside. We're going to have to jimmy the door open and pull the people out. But our clock is limited, especially if this guy is wanting to kill people solely for the attention. We have twenty-two minutes exactly."

The entire team set their watches. Anybody who was crazy enough to plant a bomb that would kill innocent people wasn't someone who could be trusted to keep his word, but until they had other intel they would move as if they had twenty-two minutes.

"Roman, Ashton, you need to help clear the stairwells and keep people moving without panic. Especially if this thing blows." Both men nodded and moved toward the main stairwell.

"Jace, Lillian, Saul," Derek continued, "you're with me."

The entire team sprinted to the stairwell and up the sixteen flights, the benefits of their daily physical training kicking in. Jace worried for a moment that Lillian might not be able to keep up because of her injuries, but she never faltered.

Less than three minutes later they were in the hall of the sixteenth floor. Derek used the elevator-emergency drop key to release the outer doors and pried them open.

Immediately they found the elevator car was over three quarters of the way up from the building doorway. There was no way anyone would be able to fit through the small space. They would have to go to the next floor.

Jace let out a curse, doing the rough math in his head based on the height of the stairwell.

"What?" Lillian asked.

"That car is too high on this floor to get them out here, but based on the height of the ceilings and stairwell, it's going to be damn tight trying to get them out on the next floor as well."

"We've got to try," Derek said. "We're down to seventeen minutes."

Immediately everyone sprinted to the next floor. The emergency drop key was reapplied on both the outer and inner doors and Jace's theory was unfortunately proven true. There was less than fifteen inches of space for the trapped passengers to fit through.

The passengers inside were talking, but weren't hysterical. They probably thought it was just a malfunction rather than a deliberate act of terror.

"This is the SWAT team," Derek called out. "We're going to pry open the door. Please stand back."

A small cheer went up from inside the car as force was applied to the inner door...until the door was pried open and the passengers could see the small space they'd have to get through.

"Can't you get the elevator up or down farther to give us more room? Some of us aren't going to fit."

Fourteen minutes.

The team looked to Derek. Nobody wanted to cause a panic, but they were going to have to work pretty damn fast to get all eight people out of there in time. And the guy who spoke up was right, it was going to be tough for some of them to fit. Jace himself would have a hard time.

But not everybody. Before they knew it, a petite woman was being hefted by someone in the elevator and was easily sliding through the fifteen-inch opening. One down, seven to go.

"Good!" Derek called out. "Send up as many people as you can."

Two more women and a skinny teenager were sent through next. Jace helped the team pull them out. Lillian, knowing her lack of upper body strength was a hindrance rather than a help, particularly after what she'd been through less than twelve hours ago, scooted out of the way. She eased her head inside the elevator car to get a good look at the remaining four passengers.

When she pulled back out, she was shaking her head, lips pursed. Her eyes met Jace's, but she spoke to Derek. "That last guy isn't going to fit," she said softly so only the team could hear.

"He's going to have to," Derek muttered, pulling passenger number six through.

"He's three hundred pounds, Derek," Lillian replied. "There's no way he's going to make it through that opening, even if we could pull him up."

Before Jace knew what was happening, Lillian gracefully poured herself through the opening and into the elevator car.

"Muir, what are you doing?" Saul yelled.

Jace met Derek's eyes as they hoisted the seventh passenger—a large man who barely fit through the opening—out of the elevator. Jace already knew what Lillian was doing. She knew they weren't going to be able to get the last guy out, so she was looking for other solutions to the problem.

"She's searching for the device," he muttered to Derek.

"What device?" the man they'd just pulled through asked. "A *device*? Like a bomb?"

The other people gasped and the elderly lady grasped her chest. "There's a bomb?"

Derek and Jace ignored them. "Disarming is the only option if we can't get everyone out," Jace said. "I'm going in with her."

Jace glanced at his watch. Eight minutes.

The civilians were now crying. Derek turned to Saul. "Lead them down the stairs."

The older woman gripped her chest again, her breathing ragged. Jace studied her briefly before turning back to Derek. "Saul isn't going to be able to get them all down."

Derek nodded. "I'll help him. You're the explosives expert. I sure as hell hope you can work a miracle."

Jace did, too.

Derek stepped closer. "But if you can't, then you make

sure the body count is as low as possible, you understand? One is bad enough. We don't need to make it three."

"Agreed."

"Lillian won't see it that way."

"Lillian already almost died once in the past twelve hours. I'm not going to let it happen again now."

Derek nodded curtly and moved to help the other civilians. Jace lowered himself into the elevator.

"What the hell is going on here?" the man too big to fit through the opening said loudly, sweat pouring down his face. "Why is SWAT here rather than the fire department?"

Lillian was ignoring him. She was using an electric screwdriver to open panels on the elevator, searching for the bomb.

"Fire department is busy in other parts of the city, sir," Jace responded to the man.

"Well, then get a damn elevator repairman out here. Whatever this girlie is doing can't be helping. A woman with power tools always makes me nervous. One in a broken elevator is downright terrifying."

Now Jace understood why Lily was ignoring the sexist jackass.

She turned to him. "These panels are all clear. Nothing. I didn't think it would be here, but it was worth a shot, since that would've been the easiest access." She pointed to the roof panels. "Hoist me up."

They both ignored the man, who was still spouting off from the corner. Jace linked his fingers by his knees and Lillian immediately stepped into his hands. He lifted her until she could reach the ceiling panels and unscrew them. A few moments later she grasped the sides of the opening and lifted herself through.

Her muttered curse told him the news was not good.

"Tell Derek to let the other locations know there's a primary device on the main cable and a second one on the emergency break," she said down to him.

"Device?" the guy yelled. "What kind of device?"

They ignored him again.

Jace relayed the message to the team leader, then continued, "This is beyond my pay grade, Derek. No way I'm going to be able to defuse this in time."

The big guy went crazy, became livid. "There's a bomb up there? Don't you think you should've told me about that, you bitch?"

What was it with this sexist freak? Jace pointed a finger right in the middle of his chest. "You know what? There's only one person stuck in this elevator without a way out. It's not me and it's definitely not her." He pointed up to where Lillian was on the roof. "So shut the hell up and help us save your life."

The man shut up and nodded, thankfully.

"Lillian, I'm coming up." Jace crouched and jumped, catching the opening in the ceiling and pulling himself the rest of the way through. Lily was shining her flashlight on the small explosive device.

"Four minutes." He shone his own light at the secondary device on the emergency brake.

"Hell, I don't even know what I'm looking at, Jace. The entire team knows that explosives aren't my specialty. I don't have the patience for it. Tell me what I need to do."

Jace studied the bomb in front of him. There wasn't time to inspect both separately. He would have to work on his and walk Lillian through hers at the same time. "Tell me what you see."

What was in front of him was a hot mess. Definitely not something crafted with care. It almost seemed to have been thrown together.

Derek's voice came in through his earpiece. "Report, Jace. You're running out of time."

"This device isn't what I was expecting, especially for someone we would've thought had been planning this since the summit was announced. This device is almost haphazard."

"The other three buildings couldn't find any explosive devices in the elevators. Looks like the bomber was just using those as decoys to spread rescue personnel more thinly."

"It worked," Jace muttered, still studying the messy IED in front of him. "Something about this whole thing is off, Derek."

"That's not going to stop us from being less dead in three minutes if we don't get this figured out," Lillian quipped.

"You focus on the task at hand," Derek's voice said in his ear. "We'll figure out what doesn't fit later."

"Roger that," Jace muttered, clicking off his transmission. "Lil, I need you to figure out the four main parts of your bomb. Main charge, a trigger switch, the ignitor and the power source for the switch."

"Okay."

"We've got to separate the trigger switch from its power source."

Lillian blew out a frustrated breath. "So this is going to be more than just cut the red wire or the blue wire?"

"Actually, believe it or not, it is a case of just cutting a wire. But if your IED is anything like mine, it's a mess.

Bomber didn't take much care with this explosive. But like you said, it will still get us just as dead."

"We're under two minutes, Jace. Which wire am I supposed to cut?"

They both heard the guy in the elevator start crying, promising God he would go to church every day for the rest of his life if he survived this.

"Tell Him you'll stop making sexist remarks, too. Maybe that will help," Lillian called down to him.

Jace grinned. This woman.

He couldn't wait to get her back in his bed. All the thoughts about keeping his distance from her seemed ridiculous now.

The bomb was messy, but still cleverly put together. Not easily disarmed. Jace gently pried the battery—the trigger switch's power source—away from the main charge. He barely saw the tiny aluminum wire attached to the bottom of the red wire—the one that would need to be cut to separate the trigger from its power source.

A fail-safe. If that tiny wire got cut by accident—by someone who didn't see it—the explosive would detonate. The person who built this might have been in a hurry, but he was very smart.

They were in serious trouble.

"Lil, you need to go."

She didn't even look up. "Like hell I will. Especially not without you."

"Negotiator was right. Whoever rigged this didn't plan on anyone surviving here today, no matter what demands he gave."

Guy below them began crying louder.

"Is it possible to defuse it?" she asked. Their eyes met

across the roof of the elevator. Hers were calm, like his. Lillian could handle it.

"Yes, but it's tricky."

She grinned. "Tricky is my middle name, Eakin. What do I do?"

He quickly explained about the aluminum wire, the need to separate it gently from the other wire that had to be cut. It was glued and nearly impossible to do. Just getting the device in front of him defused would take all his time. There was no way he'd be able to help Lillian with hers.

"Okay, I see it." She muttered a curse. "I really don't like whoever put this damn thing together."

"You found the adhesive, I see. Forty-five seconds."

"Yep, damn it. Wanna race?"

Jace couldn't keep from chuckling. Lily. God, if he had to go out, there was no one else he'd rather go with.

Guy inside was wailing now.

Jace carefully eased his blade through the tiny wire, using the utmost caution not to cut the aluminum wire around it. He took in a breath to focus and then made the final cut.

"Clear," he breathed.

He looked over at Lillian. They had less than fifteen seconds. Jace stayed where he was. The best thing he could do now was let her do her job. Trust her to do it. And he did, he realized. She was crouched there, small flashlight now in her mouth pointing down at the device, completely focused on the task at hand.

That was the Lillian he'd always known. Able to handle anything.

C'mon, Tiger Lily. Save our lives.

He'd no more than finished the thought when she looked up, grabbed the flashlight out of her mouth and grinned.

"Clear."

Chapter Thirteen

"Canceling the LESS Summit is not an option," Congresswoman Christina Glasneck said an hour later, since she had decided to attend the SWAT debriefing to provide her own input. Colorado was her state and LESS was her baby.

And she wasn't happy.

"Omega Sector is supposed to be made up of the best agents the country has available for service. So, can you handle this or not?"

Lillian would've told the woman off, but Derek remained unflappable. "Yes, ma'am. We can handle it."

Congresswoman Glasneck tapped a heeled foot as she leaned back against the conference-room chair. "So we had a break-in at city hall last night and a bombing scare today. Are the two incidents related?"

Lillian was glad she'd worn a high-necked dry-fit shirt under her gear. The bruising around her neck was extensive. And although Derek had let the team know she had thwarted some sort of break-in at the City and County Building, he hadn't provided many details.

Although someone—probably someone sitting inside this very room—knew many more details about last night than they were letting on.

"It's too early to ascertain with any certainty," Derek responded to Glasneck. "But as of right now, we have nothing to suggest the two events are related."

Lillian glanced over at Jace. His face was stoic, as were the faces of the entire team. The congresswoman had requested everyone be here for this meeting, which wasn't normal protocol and was a waste of time. There was a crap ton of more useful things the team could be doing than sitting here listening to a lecture from some-one who wanted to feel like she had a finger on the pulse of law enforcement.

It gave Lillian a new respect for Derek, who had to sit through these types of meetings all the time.

"As you know," Congresswoman Glasneck contin-ued, "LESS has been my project from the beginning. I pushed it through Congress to get the necessary fund-ing." She looked over at Philip Carnell. "Mr. Carnell, you've been instrumental in the setup of the system, and I know a number of other members of Omega Sector have worked tirelessly across the country to make sure this system happens. I think you helped, too, didn't you, Mr. Poniard?"

Saul nodded. But Carnell, true to form, barely even acknowledged the congresswoman's words. He sat with his arms crossed over his chest.

Derek nodded. "We all understand the importance of LESS, Congresswoman. And of protecting the summit. None of us want it to be canceled, but we do need to de-cide on a final location. Right now it seems the primary and secondary locations have been compromised."

The congresswoman's lips thinned. "I agree that this federal building is out. After the elevator incident today, I'm sure no one wants to place a large group of VIPs here.

But I disagree about city hall. That's one of the oldest buildings in Denver. Iconic."

Again, Lillian wanted to jump in and argue why the outer appearance of a building should be the last thing they were concerned about. This was why Derek had told the entire team to just keep quiet unless they were asked a direct question.

"It is a beautiful building," Derek conceded. "But the fact is, it was compromised. We had eyes on someone infiltrating the building, but that person got away."

"I'm not trying to tell you how to do your job, Agent Waterman, but isn't it true that we have no credible intel on what the person who slipped into that window was doing? We don't know if the perpetrator had anything to do with today's bomb scare, nor do we have intel suggesting it was someone with nefarious purposes aimed at the LESS Summit. As a matter of fact, a broken cash box in the café on the first floor suggests it might have been a burglary. Perhaps even a juvenile."

Lillian had had enough. "Like hell. That was no kid I fought last night—"

Derek held out a hand and Lillian quieted.

"Agent Muir is one of our top team members, Congresswoman Glasneck. I trust her implicitly. If she says it was an adult she fought, even though the perpetrator was wearing a mask, I believe her."

Glasneck glanced over at Lillian and gave her a slight nod. "I appreciate any woman who works and fights in the midst of what is primarily a man's world. I know a little about that. So I'm honestly not trying to be disrespectful when I say that I'm sorry the perpetrator was able to get the best of you in a fight."

"Guy had the help of a Taser," Jace said.

"That's just about the only way someone would get a jump on Lillian otherwise," Saul insisted. Everyone else nodded.

At least Lillian knew her team felt she was fully capable of taking care of herself in a situation. Derek hadn't provided any details about what had happened after the guy had Tasered her. Lillian didn't know if Congresswoman Glasneck knew, either.

Not that it mattered. The long and short of it was, Lillian had gotten her ass handed to her. And almost died because of it.

"I'm sure that's true," Glasneck said. "But the point is, Agent Muir wasn't in any shape to ascertain the perpetrator's true intent. It quite possibly could've been a burglar she stumbled in on."

"The facts of the situation let us know that it was definitely not a simple break-in," Derek said.

Lillian knew he was trying to keep the details about the "suicide" note confidential.

"Suffice it to say we have definite cause to believe the person who broke in was someone who knew Lillian. Was probably a terrorist named Damien Freihof that has been plaguing Omega Sector for months."

The older woman huffed out a breath. "But you have no proof of that."

Derek remained steady. "No, no proof. But we also know, based on evidence left at the scene, it was someone acquainted with Agent Muir. So although it may not have been Damien Freihof, it also means it wasn't a simple break-in."

Derek definitely wasn't mentioning the mole was probably sitting somewhere inside this room. That would not instill confidence.

"Okay, it wasn't a burglar." The congresswoman held out her hands in front of her. "But you can agree that maybe it was someone with a vendetta against Agent Muir. And that it had nothing to do with the summit itself."

Derek nodded shortly. "Yes. That is possible. But I can tell you that hosting the summit at the Denver City and County Building, no matter how picturesque, is a mistake. Someone wanting to attack the summit has had too much time to prepare. Moving to an unknown secondary location will put any potential attacker back at square one."

"Also puts us back at square one," Carnell muttered. "Finding a suitable replacement, getting all the plans, figuring out the details…that's going to take time we don't have, considering the summit is tomorrow."

A lot of that work would fall on Carnell because of his computer skills, so Lillian couldn't blame him for his frustration. Neither option—sticking with the building they were familiar with, but so was their enemy, or moving to an entirely unknown place—was very good.

"Agent Waterman, we have dozens of important people from all over the country coming to witness the initialization of the LESS system. And that doesn't include the thousands of other government officials and law-enforcement officers who will be watching from their stations as LESS goes live."

"We're all aware of the VIPs, Congresswoman. You're one of them."

"I'm least of them," the woman said, and laughed. "But thank you. I don't want this summit to take place in some back room across town just because of what might be a potential threat, but might not be. The very purpose of LESS is to show terrorists and criminals that law enforcement will not cower. We will face terror and crime head-on, standing together."

It was a rousing speech, one the woman obviously already had planned before this debrief had started. But Lillian could see her point. Looking around, she saw it was obvious the rest of the team could, too.

"Yeah, boss," Saul said. "Let's prove what we can do. What law enforcement can do. We don't cower."

Lillian almost had to roll her eyes again, but she couldn't fault the newbie's enthusiasm. Evidently, neither could Derek.

"All right, Congresswoman, since we don't have conclusive evidence of any upcoming attack, we'll keep the summit at city hall. But you have to understand that if intel changes, so will security plans. I won't put people at undue risk just for some photo ops."

Glasneck nodded. "Agreed. And I wouldn't expect you to. Now, I'm sure your team has better things to do than sit around and talk to me. I'll let you get to your business and I'll handle mine." The woman nodded, then left, her aides and Secret Service agent, on special loan for the summit, following behind.

Derek turned to the team, who was mostly lined up across the wall. "Okay, people, you heard the lady, we're back at the City and County Building. We will be re-sweeping it from top to bottom. I know it's nobody's favorite job, but we'll be doing it anyway. We'll be checking every damn nook and cranny until we know it's secure."

Saul was already nodding enthusiastically, like he couldn't wait to get to it. That would pass. It was something Saul didn't understand and it might be part of the reason why he'd never been chosen for a permanent part of the team. He wanted action all the time. But a lot of SWAT work was boring. Routine. Knowing how to handle the boredom was just as important as knowing how to handle the action. Maybe even more so because there wasn't any outlet for the boredom.

You either figured out how to handle it or got another job.

And now they had a lot of hours of tedious work in front of them. Made even more difficult since they didn't know if the mole was someone on the team. It was the other reason why Derek hadn't pushed harder against Congresswoman Glasneck for a new location for the summit. Because if one of their inner team members was the mole, changing locations wasn't going to protect them against an attack.

Nothing would.

LILLIAN STOOD TO join the rest of the team as they began to exit the conference room. Dizziness assailed her and she grabbed the back of a nearby chair to steady herself.

Jace was immediately next to her. "You okay?" He said it softly enough that no one else could hear and blocked the rest of the room from being able to see her. He was protecting her in the way he knew would mean the most to her.

Just like he'd trusted her to get the bomb defused earlier. If he hadn't, if he'd tried to rush in and take over for her, they'd both be dead. Them and that poor sexist bastard who'd been hyperventilating in the elevator.

Jace was strong enough not to feel threatened by her strength. He also knew her well enough to know she wouldn't want him fawning over her in this moment. That the best way he could help was by being a human shield to keep others from seeing her in a moment of weakness.

How could this man still be so perfect for her after so many years?

Lillian couldn't help it, she breathed in his scent as he stood so close to her. Sweat. Male.

Jace.

They were both still in full tactical gear from the elevator incident, so being too close wasn't even possible. But he was still the sexiest thing she'd ever seen.

"Lil?" he asked again when she didn't answer. "You okay?"

"Yeah." She nodded, clearing her voice when the word came out hoarse from the earlier trauma. "Just stood up too fast. Plus, it's already been a long day and it's about to get longer."

"You need a break?"

She felt his hand on her elbow.

"Maybe we shouldn't have used all your downtime for…other activities this morning."

Lillian smiled. She couldn't help it. She couldn't even pretend that what had happened in the hotel room between them was anything short of spectacular. "I liked the *other activities*."

Jace winked at her and she felt heat zip through her. "Good. Because I'm hoping to show you some variations on those *other activities* later."

More steady now, she turned with Jace and followed the others out of the room. Derek joined them, shooting off assignments as he went. Denver PD would be sending backup to help with the initial securing of the building, but someone from Omega Sector would be double-checking every floor. And then a different person from the Omega team would check it again.

To an outsider it would look like diligence, having two separate team members looking for security leaks. And maybe it was diligence. But it was also to try to protect themselves from the mole.

As they walked back over to the City and County Building from the federal building, the crowds of people were steadily getting bigger. Lillian noticed Philip Carnell was walking alone. Not unusual—most people didn't want to converse with Carnell unless they had to.

But Lillian noticed he was walking stiffly, as if he was in pain. A few moments later he moved the material of his long-sleeve shirt—and she saw a bruise on his forearm.

Right where bruises would've been if he'd blocked some kicks and punches in a fight.

Lillian tried to focus on the details of her fight with the masked man. Could it have been Carnell? She didn't think Carnell was physically capable of the fighting skill level of the man she'd gone up against.

But heaven knew Carnell was brilliant enough to have been faking his weaknesses. The guy had a mind like a computer—he could've figured out long ago that he needed to appear weak physically to the team to throw suspicion off himself.

The masked man she'd fought had been roughly the same height. She'd thought he was more muscular than Carnell, but he tended to wear such loose clothing at Omega Sector that Lillian couldn't say for certain what his actual physique was.

Was this the bastard who had attacked her, Tasered her, then strung her up in the hallway, leaving her to die?

"Carnell, wait up." She marched over to him as they

reached the steps to city hall. He slowed slightly, looking at her with irritation.

"What do you want?"

The guy really was a jerk.

"Where'd you get that bruise on your arm?"

Carnell's eyes narrowed. "None of your damn business."

She grabbed his wrist. "Is it new? It's pretty purple. Hasn't turned green, so it must have happened in the last twenty-four hours."

Carnell snatched his arm back and pushed down his sleeve. "What do you want, Muir? I'm trying to work out the best way to split up the team to be most effective in securing the building. I don't have time for your little power play."

Before he could move farther away, Lillian had his left wrist in her hand. She twisted it, to bring his arm around his back, and pushed him against the metal banister of the stairway, her other hand reaching up and applying pressure at his throat. "Do I look like I'm playing anything, Carnell? Where the hell did you get the bruise on your forearm and why are you walking so stiffly? Do you have other bruises? Maybe take a kick to the ribs? A punch to the sternum?" All had been blows she'd delivered during her fight.

"Are you crazy?" Carnell yelled, eyes wide. "Let go of me!"

"Mind if I get in on the fun?"

Lillian heard Jace's voice just over her shoulder.

"He's got bruises on his forearm, Jace. Looks a lot like defensive wounds. And he's walking funny, like he got in a fight recently. Pretty suspicious, don't you think?"

"What the hell are you talking about?" Carnell spat out.

"Let him go, Lillian." This time it was Derek over her other shoulder.

"Derek—"

"I understand your concerns," Derek continued. "But let him go so he can talk."

Reluctantly Lillian took her hand from Carnell's throat and released his wrist. She didn't lower her guard, ready to move quickly if he went to draw a weapon or run.

Carnell looked over at Derek. "Did you see that? She attacked me for no reason. She's emotionally unstable."

Derek turned to the rest of the team. "Everyone else inside. You know your initial assignments, so get to them."

The rest of the team dispersed, although they looked like they wanted to stay.

"Where are the bruises from, Philip?" Derek asked once everyone was gone.

"I don't have to tell you," Carnell sputtered. "It's none of your damn business."

Lillian felt the heat of Jace's body directly behind her shoulder. "It is when it seems like some of your bruises match some of the hits taken by the guy who attacked Lillian late last night."

"Know anything about that, Carnell?" Lillian asked.

"What? No. I wouldn't attack you, Muir. Why the hell would I want to fight you? Everybody knows you could kick my ass. Everybody on the team could kick my ass, that's why I'm not an official SWAT member, remember?"

She narrowed her eyes at him. "Maybe you've just been acting like you couldn't fight. Throw suspicion off yourself."

"Suspicion of what? Me being the mole?"

"You know anything about that?" Derek asked.

He rolled his eyes. "You said there was no proof, but we all know there's a mole somewhere inside Omega. Somebody's helping Damien Freihof. But it's not me."

"Where'd you get the bruises, Carnell?" Lillian asked again. He certainly had the know-how and the smarts to be the mole. She didn't like to think that he'd beaten her in a fight, but it was possible.

"It's none of your damn business, but if you must know, I got a little roughed up by a couple of guys outside a bar last night."

Derek's eyebrows shot up. "What the hell were you doing at a bar when we're all on duty?"

Carnell snorted loudly. "I wasn't actually at the bar. I don't need a lot of sleep, so I was walking around town. I passed a bar as a couple of guys were coming out and I may have made a disparaging remark about the team on their sports jerseys. They didn't like it and I took a few punches."

Lillian looked over at Jace and then at Derek—they both wore matching bemused looks. None of them had a problem imagining Carnell getting beat on because he ran his mouth to the wrong people.

"I blocked one punch," he continued, "but still took a couple to the midsection. Luckily some other people came out of the bar, and I left while they were distracted."

Was he telling the truth? It seemed like it, but Lillian didn't know the younger man well enough to know. And she had to admit after everything that had happened in the last twelve hours—attacked, almost killed, earth-shattering lovemaking, almost killed again by a bomb this time—she was not at her sharpest.

"Can anybody vouch for you?" Derek asked. "Your whereabouts?"

"I'm sure if I could track down the jerks who jumped me they'd be glad to try to finish the job. But no, other than them I wasn't really socializing. Why the hell do you guys care anyway? I'm sick of being everyone's punching bag. First strangers and now my so-called teammates. Don't we have enough bad guys to concentrate on?"

"Go on in the building and get set up, Philip," Derek said. "We'll be inside in just a minute."

Carnell was still muttering to himself as he left and walked into the building. Lillian wiped a hand across her face as she turned to look at Jace and Derek.

"That very well could be our mole," Jace said, taking a step closer to her. "God knows he's smart enough to be."

"The guy you fought knew what he was doing, right, Lillian?" Derek asked.

"Yes. If it wasn't for Carnell's bruises, I would never have suspected he could've been the guy that got the jump on me."

Jace shook his head. "It could've been a second person. You don't know."

"Following Carnell stealthily, trying to see what he was up to without his knowledge, probably would've been the better plan than a hostile confrontation."

Derek's tone was completely neutral, but Lillian knew she'd made a huge tactical error in what she'd just done. "I'm sorry, Derek. I screwed up."

"You're tired, in pain and your judgment is being affected."

Again neutral. But Lillian still felt like she might vomit. "I—"

Derek held out a hand to stop her. "You'll go back to the hotel and rest for twelve hours before coming back on duty."

What? "You need me here. You need every man you can get."

"I'll need you more over the next two days as the summit swings into full gear. So get the downtime you need so you can come back in top shape." Derek put his hand on her shoulder. "Lillian, if anyone else had been through what you had yesterday and today, you would encourage me to give them the time they needed to regroup. This is not a reflection on your ability. This is about keeping the team running as efficiently as possible."

She knew Derek was right, but it still sucked. She felt like she'd let him down. Let the team down.

"We're going to be on rotating shifts from now until the summit is completed," Derek continued. "You're just taking the first down shift."

"Okay." Damn it.

Derek looked over at Jace. "You two are on my very short list of people I know I can trust. I'm going to need you firing on all cylinders." Derek squeezed her shoulder, then turned and walked into city hall.

She looked at Jace. "I guess I'm grounded and am going to take a nap."

He smiled. "I guess I shouldn't have kept you up this morning."

She rubbed her eyes. "Then we can agree that me acting like a complete moron and losing us the upper hand with the potential mole is all your fault."

"You reacted. It happens."

Lillian rubbed her eyes again. "Derek's right. I'm tired. My judgment is impaired."

He pulled her closer by her tactical vest. "Then do what the man says and get some rest."

She grabbed her extra hotel card key out of a Velcro pocket, held it up to Jace and told him her room number. "Join me later if your downtime happens to coincide with mine?"

She didn't want to think too hard about the butterflies she got inside her chest when he nodded and smiled. He kissed her on the tip of her nose, turned and jogged into the building. She couldn't tear her eyes off him.

She was in so much trouble.

Chapter Fourteen

It had been a long-ass day. Jace had worked with the others, helping to confirm the security of the Denver City and County Building. Derek had used Jace mostly to double-check particularly vulnerable places, since he knew Jace couldn't be the mole. There were definitely no unsecured windows or doors in this building now.

For the moment. Jace and Derek both knew the mole could come back and change that situation.

Jace had left a few markers—invisible to anyone but him—in areas he thought would be potential targets for Freihof or the mole. These markers, generally made of pretty innocuous items like tape and string, would let him know if windows or doors had been opened or tampered with when he went back and checked them. Derek was doing the same, trying to keep the LESS Summit secure and catch the mole at the same time.

They both knew fighting a war on two fronts was the surest way to lose. But right now it was their only option, especially with someone potentially working against them.

Was it Carnell? The bruises were suspicious. Even in the short time Jace had been around he'd noticed the man was always angry. Always talking about elitist problems in Omega Sector and the lack of pedigree in law enforcement in general. Definitely corresponded with some of the "Manifesto of Change" document Ren McClement had shown Jace back in his office in DC.

But Lillian had said the man she'd followed in the window had put up a pretty good fight before she'd been Tasered. Jace had difficulty believing she couldn't drop Carnell in under five seconds flat.

Hell, she could drop Jace in under ten if he didn't use every skill he had.

So neither he nor Derek thought Carnell was the man who'd fought and strung up Lillian last night.

Speaking of, that damn key card had been burning a hole in his pocket for the past seven hours. Jace had purposely forced himself not to think about Lillian, to focus on the task at hand as he worked. The job required his focus, and Lillian needed time to rest.

Seeing how upset she'd been with herself over how she'd handled Carnell had been painful. Derek had been right to give her the first down shift. Everybody had their limits. Lillian's body and mind had evidently reached hers.

Jace damn well hoped she'd spent the last few hours sleeping. Now that Derek had told him to break, Jace planned to wake her up in the most pleasurable way possible, then hopefully talk her back into another nap afterward. In his arms. Both of them naked.

Full-on grin covering his face, Jace found himself all but jogging back to the hotel. It was already dark again. He should be exhausted, but as he peeled away his tactical gear and showered, all he could think about was getting to Lillian.

She'd given him her room key. And while that wasn't

exactly an engagement ring, Jace recognized it for what it was: a statement of trust.

Nothing about Lillian then or now suggested she gave her trust easily.

He used the key to enter her room. It was dark inside except for the light on in the bathroom with the door cracked. Evidently Lillian didn't like the dark.

"Lil, you awake?" he said softly, looking at her small form huddled in the bed. She'd kicked part of the blankets off, showing off one leg. She was dressed in just an oversize T-shirt and her underwear.

It was possibly the sexiest thing Jace had seen in his whole life.

"Lil?" he said again, moving closer.

"Hey," she said sleepily, turning toward him. "What took you so long?"

It was all the invitation Jace needed. He stripped his shirt over his head, pulled off his sweats and climbed into the bed with her. God, he had been purposely *not* thinking about this all day, knowing he'd never be able to focus on the task at hand if he did.

Bracing his elbows on either side of her head, he lowered his weight on her. "Hey, sexy."

He brought his lips to hers, easing them open. She shifted beneath him, a soft sigh escaping her. He grabbed her under one of her knees and hooked her leg up over his hips, bringing their bodies closer together. He couldn't stop the moan that escaped him. Didn't even try.

He ran one hand up and down the outer part of her thigh on the leg wrapped around his hip. His other gripped her hair, tilting her head back so he could kiss her more fully. He felt her fingernails grip into his shoulders and groaned again.

His lips moved down her jaw to her throat, to that place right under her ear that he knew was so sensitive. He nipped at it. "You have no idea how good it feels to be here with you. It was difficult convincing myself that national security mattered when I knew I had that key in my pocket."

He waited for a sarcastic comment, but none came. She hadn't said or done anything since he first climbed on top of her. He hiked her leg up a little higher, rubbing their bodies together more fully. Maybe she just needed a little bit more time to wake up.

He brushed his lips back down her throat, the bruises still noticeable even in the semidarkness. She was hurt, a little fragile, he needed to remember that.

"You okay, sweetheart?" He moved the edge of her shirt aside with his lips, kissing across her collarbone. She still didn't answer.

He leaned up on his elbows so he could look down at her more clearly. Her brown eyes stared directly at him. "This can wait, you know." He smiled and trailed a finger across her cheek. He brushed her lips against his and her mouth seemed to automatically open for him. He kissed her again softly. "We can just sleep if you want. Believe it or not, I can convince certain parts of my body to simmer down when needed."

Again, no smart-aleck remark. He didn't even think Lillian was capable of that.

"You're going pretty easy on me tonight," he said. "Are you sure you didn't get some sort of head injury?" He kissed her again. Her lips opened as soon as his touched hers, but then she didn't respond.

As a matter of fact, her hands were still on his shoulders, and hadn't moved. Her leg was still around his hips, where he'd placed it.

As soon as he removed his lips from hers, her mouth closed. Jace bent down to kiss her again and they opened.

But then did nothing.

What the hell was going on?

"Lillian?" He eased his weight off her farther. Her hands remained on his shoulders, her eyes open and looking right at him.

"Lillian." He shook her a little. "Lily? What's going on? Talk to me, sweetheart."

Did she have some sort of head injury he hadn't been aware of? She'd been fine earlier. Maybe a little off her game, stressed, but she certainly hadn't been blanking out when she handled that bomb scare today.

He rolled his weight completely off her. Her arms dropped to her side on the mattress. Her eyes still had that blank stare. Like the body lying here was just an empty shell of the strong, vibrant woman she usually was.

Jace had seen this sort of blank stare before...a checking out of reality. But it had been men in the army suffering from PTSD.

And always, if the person was in no danger of hurting himself or others, the best thing was to leave his subconscious to work through it in his own way.

"Come back to me, Lil. Whatever it is, whatever you're going through, we can work through it."

Tears streamed out of her open eyes and down the sides of her face, but she didn't move, didn't blink, didn't talk.

She was trapped in some hell in her mind and there was nothing Jace could do.

It was only a little over twenty minutes before Lillian

came back to him, but it was one of the longest passages of time that he'd ever lived through.

He was still sitting next to her on the bed, holding her hand, when she finally started blinking. Tension rolled through her body and she began breathing more heavily.

"Lily? It's Jace. You're safe."

She snatched her hand out of his before scooting over to the far side of the bed, pulling the comforter up to her chin. Her eyes darted around the room like she was looking for danger. Like she couldn't figure out where she was.

"You're safe, Lillian. You're at a hotel in Denver."

She got out of the bed now, back to the wall, obviously ready to fight.

Jace kept his voice even and his body still, not wanting to send her into a full panic. And he sure as hell didn't want her reaching for the sidearm that sat on the bedside table while she was in this condition. "We're on a mission with the SWAT team to protect the LESS Summit. You…fell asleep. You're disoriented."

It took her a few more moments of him repeating the same words before they began sinking in. And while she didn't relax, at least she didn't look like she was about to fight off an entire army.

"Jace?"

Thank God. "Yeah, sweetheart. It's me. You scared me there for a bit. We were in the middle of making out and I lost you."

To his utter dismay, big tears filled her eyes and rolled down her cheeks. Not counting the tears that had seemed to leak out of her eyes of their own accord a little while ago, this was the first time Jace could remember seeing Lillian cry. The sight of them gutted him.

"Lily—"

She took a step back. "I'm sorry, Jace. Please don't look at me like that. It's not you, it just happens sometimes."

His eyes narrowed. "What happens?"

She squeezed her eyes closed, one hand pulling the blanket more tightly around her, the other gesturing toward the bed. "I blank out during sex. But I promise it's not your fault. It's me. Please don't take it personally. It wasn't you."

Jace could feel bile pooling in his stomach as he took in the ramifications of her words.

This wasn't the first time this had happened to her.

The blackouts didn't have anything to do with combat. This was centered around sex. Steve Drackett had been right back in Ren's office.

Lillian was recovering from some sort of sexual assault.

He forced himself to ignore the way his heart seemed to be shattering around him. He had to understand exactly what she was dealing with. "This happens to you a lot?"

She kept her eyes tightly closed. Almost like a child who believed the monsters would go away if she didn't face them. "I don't want to talk about it. I just didn't want you to think it was your fault. That it was something you did."

He eased a little closer on the bed. "Did it happen this morning when we were together?"

Now her eyes opened. "No! No, this morning was... great. I was there. *Completely* there. The whole time. But this morning was the exception, not the norm."

"But...it happens to you a lot?"

Her tiny nod told him everything he needed to know. The thought of this happening to her when she was with someone else. Someone who wouldn't notice, or worse, take advantage. Jace struggled to tamp down the rage. "*How* often?"

"Until this morning? Pretty much always."

"For how long?" Maybe the trauma was recent. That, while still being horrible, was at least understandable.

She shook her head, obviously not wanting to answer the question. Keeping his hands out in front of him, palms up in a gesture of nonaggression, he eased closer again.

"It's behind me," she whispered. "That's all you need to know."

"It's obviously not behind you, based on the fact that thirty minutes ago when we were kissing, your eyes were open and your hands were on my shoulders, but your conscious mind was miles from that bed. It had hidden itself away to protect your psyche."

She opened her mouth to respond, but no words came out. Finally, she just shook her head.

"You were raped." God, he hated to even say that word to her. It was bitter, unbearable in his mouth.

She nodded, her brown eyes not leaving his.

He thought his heart had already been shattered, but he'd been wrong. Watching that small move of her head confirmed everything he'd feared, but hadn't wanted to believe… The pain nearly doubled him over. "How long ago?"

She shook her head adamantly.

Why would she not want to answer that question? Was it so recent that she couldn't bear to think about it at all?

"Lily, I need you to tell me. I want to be careful not to do or say anything that will trigger you in any way."

He got out of the bed and took a step closer, now just a few feet from her, relieved when she didn't flinch away. "What we had this morning was special. It can be again. But I need you to trust me enough to tell me what happened to you so we can navigate this together. Please, baby."

"I can't, Jace," she whispered, those big brown eyes begging him to let it go. "I'm sorry."

He didn't want to push. Didn't want to ask her to give more than she could. But he also couldn't risk doing something that would have her retreating into that shell again.

"Okay, you don't have to talk to me." He pushed down the hurt. This wasn't about him. "But I'm going to go. I don't want to stay here with you and take a chance on triggering you again."

"Jace..."

The pain in her voice tore at him.

"I'm not mad, Tiger Lily." He took a chance and stepped closer. When she didn't move away, he slipped a hand in her hair at the nape of her neck. He pulled her forward until his lips met her forehead. "I understand you don't want to talk about it. But I can't stay here and take a chance on hurting you further. Doing damage because I'm not sure of how to navigate your emotional terrain."

He backed away, giving her the best smile he could. His Lillian was broken, and she didn't trust him enough to try to help her put herself back together. He really wasn't mad about that—she needed to work through this however was best for her. He would be her friend if she wanted it. But he would not take a chance on hurting her further. Of using her the way she'd obviously been used by other men.

"We'll talk more when you're ready. Maybe after this op is over." Pulling away was like a knife ripping him in the gut. But what else could he do? "I just don't want to hurt you more."

He gave her a gentle nod, then turned and walked toward the door. He was almost to it, hand on the knob, when he heard her words. He'd thought nothing she could say would've been worse than the initial knowledge that she'd been raped.

He was so, so wrong.

Her words changed everything he'd always held true.

"Twelve. I was raped twelve years ago."

Chapter Fifteen

What was she doing? Was she really going to tell Jace the truth? The truth about her? About Daryl? About what had really happened?

She'd only ever spoken about it to Grace Parker. And even then she'd left out details. Jace was not going to let her leave out details.

He turned from the door and moved back into the main section of the room. She could see his blue eyes staring out at her. Not in disbelief—she'd never for one second thought he wouldn't believe her—but in full tactical mode.

He was trying to put together the pieces.

"Lil, you have to just tell me. Because I swear nothing you could say would be any worse than what I'm imagining in my mind."

Wanna bet?

She didn't say the words but knew the truth was worse than whatever Jace was thinking. Was almost more than she could bear to think about. She didn't want to hurt him unnecessarily. Daryl was his brother. They'd never gotten along, and Jace had joined the army to get out from Daryl's thumb as soon as possible, but Daryl had been his brother.

No one would want to believe their own flesh and blood was capable of what his brother had done.

"Oh, God, it was Daryl, wasn't it?"

The anguish in Jace's voice made her want to rush to him, to hold him. To erase the agony in his eyes as she nodded.

He seemed to age right before her eyes. "Tell me."

"It was after my eighteenth birthday. The day before we were supposed to leave. After you and I…" She nodded and shrugged.

Jace knew what she meant. After they'd had sex. She'd wanted to have sex with him for months before her birthday, but he'd refused everything but making out. Had said they'd have a lifetime together to make love. They could at least wait until they were both legal.

God, she'd loved him for that. It had made her feel so special, cherished. That she was worth waiting for.

"I got a text from you saying to meet you at the warehouse," she continued. Daryl's warehouse, where a lot of his illegal activities had taken place. "I knew you didn't like me to go there alone, but I thought you'd gotten home from your job for Daryl early. The last job. I can't even remember what it was anymore." Not surprising, given all that had happened afterward.

"I was supposed to deliver an order of pharmaceutical drugs," Jace whispered. "To a place clear on the other side of the state. The dealer I was supposed to deliver them to never even showed up."

They looked at each other, realizing now it had all been a setup.

Lillian moved back over to the window, needing some distance, unable to face the blueness of Jace's eyes for this next part. "I got to the warehouse and Daryl was waiting for me. Said he had found out we were leaving to join the army. Said there was no way he was going to let two of his best and most loyal runners leave at the same time."

God, she'd been so naive. Had thought there was nothing Daryl could do to stop them. Had laughed at Daryl and told him that. Now that she was eighteen she could go wherever she wanted. And Jace had already been twenty. He would've left earlier if it hadn't been for her. If he hadn't wanted to be able to leave with her legally.

She wished they'd just run away from the very beginning.

"I told him he couldn't stop us, we were leaving the next day." She pressed her head against the cold glass. "He hit me in the stomach over and over. Dislocated my shoulder. Kicked me in the legs. It was before I knew how to fight. How to protect myself."

The muscles and bones in question still twinged in horrific memory.

"He didn't hit you in the face."

She could hear the coarse tightness in Jace's voice.

She shook her head against the glass. "No," she whispered.

"Because he didn't want there to be any bruises I could see. He knew that if I thought he'd forced you in any way, I would fight him. Kill him."

She heard Jace pacing.

"Or die trying to get you out."

"He—he raped me. Then locked me in the tiny janitor's closet and left me in there all night. I knew you'd be looking for me. That all I had to do was survive until you found me." That whole day was a blur of pain and trauma, but *that* she could remember. The knowledge that Jace would come for her. Would make her world all right again.

"Lillian…"

The pain in his voice was too much. She continued faster. She wasn't helping either of them by dragging it out like this. She took a second to distance herself from the story mentally. "Daryl came back and got me the next morning. I was in pretty bad shape from the beating. He raped me again, then threw clean clothes at me to put on. Told me to get dressed, that you were coming over."

She heard Jace's strangled sound behind her. She continued. "Daryl told me there was no way both of us were leaving. He told me he had one of the guys in the rafters of the warehouse, with a rifle on you. Told me that if I didn't just sit there and shut up, he would have you shot. And that while you were bleeding out he would rape me again right in front of you before you died."

Jace's curse was vile.

She finally turned from the window. "Looking back on it now, I think he was bluffing. You were his *brother*. I don't think he would've killed you. He might have killed me to keep you from leaving, but he wasn't going to kill you."

"Lily…" He took a step toward her, but she held out a hand to ward him off. He could not touch her right now. Not at this very second.

"Daryl overplayed his hand. I think he thought you would come back. That you would fight him for me or something. I'm not sure. I don't think either of us thought you would just believe his lies so easily. Believe that I just jumped into his bed straight from yours."

Jace shook his head, no color left in his face. "Daryl came to see me a couple hours before I came by there.

Told me you had come to him. That you had said I was moving too fast, that you didn't want to leave. That you didn't know how to tell me you weren't coming with me to join the army. That you wanted his protection and were even willing to sleep with him if that was what it cost."

She hadn't known any of that. "You believed him?"

"No, although I had to admit it was not outside the realm of possibility. I was talking forever and marriage and you were barely eighteen, for crying out loud. Thinking I was pushing too hard was my button. And Daryl didn't just push it, he *stomped* on it."

"It was always his talent."

"When I got to the warehouse and saw you there, saw you clinging to him… I thought for once in his miserable life my brother was telling the truth. That I had pushed you too hard."

She nodded. "He manipulated us both."

"I'm so sorry, Lily. I should've gotten you alone. Talked to you."

She shook her head. "I wouldn't have told you. I really thought he would kill you."

"Why didn't you come find me afterward? Once I was in the army Daryl couldn't hurt me."

She'd told him this much. She had to tell it all. "He kept me locked up. In that closet. He knew I would run, would tell you if I got the chance. He kept me there in the dark and only let me out when he…when he…"

She didn't finish, but she didn't have to. Jace knew what she meant. Daryl let her out when he raped her. Those days, those weeks, were all a blur of agony and darkness to her. When Daryl had gotten tired of her, he'd given her to a couple of his best men as a reward.

By then her brain had learned to check out every time a man touched her. So she didn't remember that at all.

"He had other girls there, Jace. Daryl did. I think it's part of the reason both of us were feeling the itch to get out. It was one thing to run drugs or weapons every once in a while…"

"Quite another to find out human trafficking is involved," he said, finishing for her, and nodding. "I had my suspicions things might be heading that way before I left, but didn't have any proof. And then Daryl died and everything he'd put together disbanded, so there wasn't much point in trying to prove it one way or another."

She had to tell him all of it, Lillian knew that. Would he hate her for it? It didn't matter, because even if he did, she didn't regret her actions. "I killed him, Jace."

He didn't even blink. "Good."

"I'm serious. I was…with him when the fire started. He ran over to see what was happening and I hit him over the head with a bottle of tequila he had lying around. The whole building was going up in flames and I ran."

"Good," Jace said again.

"You don't understand, I could've told someone Daryl was still in there. There probably would've been time to get him out."

"No, you don't understand, Lily. I'm glad you killed him. That saves me the trouble of committing cold-blooded murder now. Because that's exactly what would be happening if my bastard brother was still alive."

Relief coursed through Lillian.

"You look surprised." He shook his head. "Did you really think I would be okay with what Daryl did to you?"

She shrugged. "He was your brother."

"He stopped being my brother twelve years ago, the

second he touched you. Don't have any doubt about that." He scrubbed his hands across his face, looking older. Pained. "I can never make up for what happened to you. But I am so sorry."

"It wasn't your fault."

She flinched as Jace slammed the back of his fist against the wall. "It damn well was my fault. At least part of it. I knew Daryl was edging from risky ventures into downright dangerous ones. Knew he was crossing lines that no one would think was okay."

"That's why you wanted out."

He took a step toward her. "That's why I wanted *both* of us out. Because he was becoming unstable. It was just a matter of time before everything blew up in his face—which it did, literally—and I didn't want us caught in the flames."

They stared at each other for long minutes.

"Why did you believe him, Jace?" Why hadn't he been able to see the truth?

"It's like you said, Daryl was the master manipulator. He'd played on my deepest fear, that I really was rushing you. You were so young. Hadn't had any life experiences. That I was forcing you into a life you didn't really want, taking away your choices."

"I wanted to go," she whispered. More than anything in the world she'd wanted to leave with Jace.

"I was a fool. Blinded to the truth by my own insecurities. That you might want someone like Daryl. More powerful. Stronger. He hinted that it was true and I bought it like a sale at Christmas."

Her heart broke as she watched his eyes fill up with tears.

"I'll never forgive myself, Lily."

"You didn't know."

"I should've reconfirmed. I should've made sure you were okay. Hell, even if you really did want him, I should've barged in and tried to convince you otherwise. The first thing we learn in the army is that you never leave someone behind. I left you behind, Lil. You were tortured, for God's sake."

She wanted to disagree with him but knew words wouldn't pacify him. And he was right. She had been tortured. Physically, mentally, emotionally.

She couldn't take his pain away, but she could help him understand what had come from it. The phoenix that had risen from the ashes. "But I grew stronger, Jace. Yeah, I may still be a bit of a mess when it comes to sex." He flinched, but she continued. "But I'm also a kick-ass warrior because of what Daryl did to me. I became determined never to be a victim again. And have spent my life trying to keep other people from being victims also."

"You *are* a warrior, Lil. A formidable one."

She felt something ease in her heart. "I am. I know that. And because of it—knowing the lives I've saved in the years since I've joined Omega—I can't fully regret what happened to me."

"The blackouts…"

Now it was her turn to rub a hand across her face. "The blackouts are problematic. And part of it was because I refused to get emotionally attached to anyone before having sex with him. I was working with a psychiatrist about that before she…died. But I didn't have a blackout with you this morning, Jace. I was with you. Completely focused on the moment. And it was the best thing that has happened to me in a dozen years. My body remembers you, I think. Or my mind knows that you would never hurt me."

He took a step toward her. "I would never hurt you, Lil. Never."

She smiled. "I know. I've always known. And even with my blackouts... I'm not afraid. I'm confident of my ability to fight my way out of any situation if needed. But it's like my brain doesn't know how to process the old and the new information together. I feel a man's weight on me and my brain just shuts down."

"And when you come back?"

"I have no memory of what has happened. My brain is still trying to protect me from trauma even all these years later. Even though I don't want it to. Grace—my psychiatrist before that bastard Damien Freihof killed her—said it was because those men meant nothing to me. That eventually when I had sex with someone who I truly cared about, my brain wouldn't shut down."

"Like this morning." The ghost of a smile crossed his lips but then disappeared. "How can you ever forgive me? How can you even bear to be in the same room as me? I failed you so completely."

She walked over to him, more confidence filling her with every step. Grace had been right. Her brain had been shutting down because she was making bad choices, not because of fear. Now that she had the chance to be with someone she knew cared about her, she wasn't going to shut down.

"Jace, you would never have left me there if you'd known." She cupped his cheeks. "I always knew that. You would've died trying to get me out. We both made mistakes. We both paid a price. But I refuse to give Daryl any more of my history. He's dead. He can stay dead."

"You blanked on me tonight."

She shrugged. "I'm always going to have triggers. Maybe just make sure I'm always fully awake before starting anything."

"Deal. As long as you promise to tell me if anything I do or say starts to frighten you in any way."

She breathed a silent sigh of relief when he wrapped his arms around her. She listened to the reassuring beat of his heart for long minutes. "I was afraid you wouldn't want me once you knew."

"Not wanting you is never even going to be an option, Tiger Lily."

"Good, because I'd like to give tonight another try. I hate to think I'd missed out on all the fun."

"Are you sure? We can just sleep. We don't have to—"

She kissed him. She knew he was feeling guilty. But if there was one thing her training had taught her, it was that facing problems head-on as soon as they came along meant that they didn't grow into something insurmountable the next day.

Like she said, she refused to give up any more ground to Daryl Eakin. He'd taken too much. Now he could stay in his grave, where he belonged.

The brother she was always supposed to be with was here in her arms. She pressed herself closer to him, deepening the kiss. When she heard him groan, she knew she had him.

And this time she wasn't sure she was ever going to be able to let him go.

Chapter Sixteen

Four hours later, Jace was out for a run, pushing himself much harder than he should have, given the parameters of the mission and what would be required of him over the next two days. Lillian had reported back for her shift about thirty minutes ago.

He turned down Oak, a deserted street, glad the temperature was at least a little over freezing even though it was February, and he didn't have to worry about ice. He knew enough about Denver to know he was on the rougher side of town, but he wished—Jace literally looked up at a star in the night sky and *wished*—some asshole would mess with him right now.

Jace wanted to fight. To feel the bones of some predator breaking under his hands. To throw his head back and howl in agony.

But mostly he wanted to go back in time and change what had happened to Lillian.

Daryl.

Jace wasn't kidding when he said it was a good thing his brother was dead. Otherwise Jace couldn't promise he wouldn't be about to turn his back on everything he'd ever held important and true—law, order, justice—and be on his way to kill his brother right at this second.

He was glad Lillian had left the bastard there in that fire. Had saved herself.

Jace had been in boot camp when Daryl died. The body had already been identified by one of Daryl's friends and put in a closed casket by the time Jace arrived, so Jace didn't know if Daryl had suffered, had burned. He'd hoped not, at the time. But now that had changed.

He took a turn down another deserted street, relishing the feel of the colder wind as it blew between buildings, the ache of his muscles as he pushed them further, the tightness of his lungs as he tried to draw in air.

Jace wasn't sure he was ever going to be able to draw in a full breath again for the rest of his life without it hurting.

He had failed Lillian in the worst way someone could fail another. The thought of her helpless in Daryl's clutches for two weeks burned like acid in his gut. She'd been so young, maybe not exactly helpless, but nowhere near the warrior she was now.

She'd been raped and abused so many times that her mind had shut down almost every time she'd tried to have sex since then.

And Jace...well, he'd just happily lived with his self-proclaimed righteous anger for a dozen years, believing *he'd* been the one who'd been wronged.

It would be downright laughable if it wasn't so pathetic.

The miracle of it all was that Lily didn't hate him. He'd watched her as she'd slept after their lovemaking tonight.

Lovemaking that had taken on an entirely new tenor. Now that Jace knew how close he'd come to losing her—

physically, emotionally, in every way possible—all he could do was cherish her. Worship her with his body.

She hadn't let him treat her like she was fragile. And he did understand that. Lillian wasn't fragile.

But damn if he wouldn't treat her like the treasure she was. The treasure he would've had next to him, healthy and whole, for the past twelve years if he hadn't been so blinded by his own insecurities and tricked by a psychopath's words.

So many mistakes.

Watching Lily as she slept, he'd tried to process everything. Tried to wrap his head around the enormity of it all. He'd refused to let rage consume him at that moment. All he wanted to do was be there for her. Hold her if she needed it. Pull her back if she began to slip away again.

But she hadn't. She'd stayed there with him—with them—the entire time. No scary blank stares and waking up not knowing where she was. He'd counted every single second with her as a treasure.

When she'd gotten up and dressed to head in for her SWAT shift, he'd just watched her. Leaned back in the bed with his arm tucked behind his head, and stared at her as if he didn't have anywhere else in the world he'd rather be.

Which was damn near the truth.

"Pretty sexy, huh?" She'd gestured to her cargo pants and tactical boots.

"Damn right, more sexy on you than me."

She grinned at him, waggling her eyebrows. "I'm not so sure about that."

In that moment, grinning at each other, just enjoying each other's company the way they always had, it was impossible to reconcile that this woman—so in control, capable, strong—had been damaged in such a way.

He'd fought to not let his smile slip. Refused to look at her with concern or sympathy in his eyes. That wasn't what Lillian needed. The phoenix had risen from the ashes on her own. He would not drag her back down as he came to grips.

But now as he was out running, away from her, the rage coursed through him. Jace let it. Let his muscles take the punishment as his mind struggled to comprehend everything. By the time he made it back to the hotel, he was dripping with sweat, despite the cold. He wiped himself down with his sweatshirt before entering the lobby. Even though it wasn't time for his shift, he'd grab breakfast and head back to city hall.

Because sleep was not in the cards for Jace any time soon. It would be a long time before he could close his eyes and not picture an eighteen-year-old Lillian hurt, terrified, hoping he was going to rescue her from the darkness.

A rescue that had never occurred.

Rage pooled through him again.

"Eakin, are we not giving you enough to do that you need to spend your downtime doing extra workouts?" Derek was getting a cup of coffee from the small breakfast section of the hotel.

Jace couldn't even smile at the other man. "Just needed to work off some steam. Trust me, this will help me be more focused."

"You look like you'd like to go ten rounds with someone in the ring. This have anything to do with a petite brunette we both know?"

"She's not the one I want to fight, believe it or not. Although I'm sure she'd give me a run for my money anyway."

Derek offered Jace a glass of water from his table while he continued to sip his coffee. Jace thanked him with a tip of his head while he drank it down. The two of them studied each other in silence for a long moment.

"Is this where you warn me not to hurt her? To keep away from her?" Jace knew his tone was combative. Left over from his own frustrations.

Derek, unflappable as ever, just smiled and shook his head. "Lillian can take care of herself. If you hurt her, she'll be the one to kick your ass. I won't have to do it. To be honest, I'm just glad she's letting someone close enough to even be in the realm of possibility of hurting her."

"Maybe she has her reasons for not letting people close."

"Maybe." Derek held his hands out in a motion of surrender. "I'm not trying to fight with you, Jace. I've been her team leader, and *friend*, long enough to know that Lillian has some scars. And I'm human enough to know that not all scars are visible."

All the frustration just flowed out of Jace, despair taking its place. "Scars I could've prevented."

Derek pushed out the chair across from him with his foot and gestured for Jace to sit in it. "My wife is a forensic scientist. Works part-time for Omega now that we have a baby at home. Molly is quite possibly the most opposite of Lillian possible."

"How so?"

"Molly is shy, quiet, insecure outside the lab. She

couldn't do a pull-up to save her life, and despite my best effort to teach her otherwise, still punches with her thumb resting against the side of her fist."

That caused the slightest of smiles to break out on his face. "Like a girl."

Derek's smile was much bigger. "Exactly."

"Lillian doesn't punch like a girl."

"No, she very definitely does not. Molly is soft. And I mean that in the very best way that word can be used. And we both know that Lillian is not soft. And I mean that also in the very best way."

Jace knew Derek had a point, so he took a sip of water while he waited for him to continue.

"A couple of years ago a psychopath kidnapped my Molly." All hint of a smile was gone from Derek now. "Drugged and tortured her. Got her a second time and began breaking her fingers one by one while he was on the phone with me."

Jace sat up straighter. "Damn."

"What would Lillian do if someone did that to her?"

"I don't know. Probably work out a dozen different moves so that it would never happen again."

"Exactly. That's *exactly* what Lillian would do. Because Lillian needs to know that she can take care of herself physically in whatever situation she finds herself in. That under normal circumstances—Tasers being the exception—no one will ever get the drop on her again. Something she learned the hardest of ways before I ever met her."

Jace could only nod.

"Lillian and Molly are different because I've tried to teach Molly some self-defense moves, and while she'll learn them to humor me, generally after twenty minutes of practice she leans over and whispers that she'll just trust me to come rescue her if she ever gets back in another dangerous situation." Derek grinned. "Then distracts me into activities not having anything to do with self-defense."

"Somehow I can't imagine Lillian ever doing that."

"Of course not. But mostly because Lillian is never going to need you to come rescue her from a dangerous situation."

"Because in almost all situations she can rescue herself." Jace leaned back in his chair. "It's not that I don't appreciate it, but I'm not sure I'm getting the main point of your little pep talk."

"My point is, I never mistake Molly's softness for weakness. And her trust that I will get to her no matter what if she needs me is a vow I take very seriously. I will save her or die trying. But the fact is, Molly also saved me. Her strength—her emotional fortitude—is what dragged me out of the darkness when I couldn't find the way myself."

Jace nodded.

"Now, my wife is brilliant," Derek continued after another sip from his cup of coffee. "So she never asked me if I needed any emotional self-defense lessons. Not that she had to be brilliant to figure out that I'm too stubborn to admit I might need help in that department. But the fact of the matter is this—the same way she trusts that I'll get her out if she's in trouble physically, I know she'll get me out if I'm in trouble emotionally."

"And you think that's what Lillian needs."

"I think she can take care of herself physically, but emotionally is a different story. She won't ever ask for help. Hell, I don't even know if she knows *how* to ask for it. I sure as hell didn't with Molly."

Derek was right. Probably about all of it.

"And believe it or not, helping her in that way—helping her discover and meet her emotional needs—is going to help you just as much as it helps her. I'm going to assume that whatever has you running like the hounds of hell are chasing you in the middle of a February night has to do with Lillian's scars."

"Maybe."

"Well, running or fighting or smashing your fist against a wall may help you feel better temporarily, but ultimately it's going to be helping Lillian heal in the way she needs most that's going to make this rage pass."

"Derek, I'm not sure this rage is ever going to pass."

"Maybe not. But she doesn't need your rage. Lillian's got enough of that herself. She doesn't need you to fight her physical battles for her, but she needs you to stand with her emotionally. Of course, if you're just around temporarily, then maybe you shouldn't even try to get close to her."

"That's not the issue. I've owned a ranch outside Colorado Springs for a number of years now. Have plans to raise animals."

"Like what you were talking about with that bridge jumper?"

"Exactly. Someplace people could go who have PTSD, who just need to get away."

"It's interesting that the two of you lost touch with each other so long ago and then ultimately ended up settling within fifty miles of each other."

That fact had not escaped Jace's attention, either. He nodded. But he also knew that physical proximity wasn't enough. "I just hope she'll give me the chance." Because despite the great sex and friendly banter between them, Jace wasn't sure Lillian would be able to ever truly give herself to a man again.

Especially not him.

Chapter Seventeen

Dawn on the day of the summit found the streets of Denver packed with people of every type: angry, happy, scared.

And they were all loud and carrying signs.

The cold front that had settled over Denver this morning hadn't seemed to deter people. Nobody had expected this many this early, and while the Denver PD were in charge of crowd control, and so far doing a good job of it, Lillian had found she had to fight her way just to get from the hotel back to the City and County Building.

It was going to be a long day. The entire team would be on high alert as the politicians, police chiefs and other high-profile shareholders in the LESS program from all over the country arrived. The official debut and demonstration was scheduled for six hours from now.

Jace was already on-site, the rest of the team either already there or, like Lillian, on their way. She and Jace hadn't had much more time off together, but just having him near, knowing the truth was finally out between them, had eased a heaviness in Lillian that, along with the weight of everything else, she hadn't even known she'd been carrying.

Jace had never stopped looking with anything less

than respect in his eyes. No pity. No sideways glances to make sure she wasn't about to fall apart. Just respect.

And lust. She'd take both.

But not right now. Today there was no room for anything else but the LESS Summit.

Derek was coordinating with the transportation security team of the summit members. Once they were released from the vehicles in the underground parking garage and escorted into the building, the summit members would officially be Omega Sector's responsibility.

As Lillian elbowed her way past another set of protestors, she couldn't shake the feeling in her gut.

Trouble. The air was all but saturated with it.

Lillian wasn't prone to superstition or gut feelings. She liked to make informed decisions based on facts and preparation.

But she couldn't get the hairs on the back of her neck to settle down. Someone was here with death on their mind.

It didn't take a genius to guess that person was Damien Freihof. This was a perfect stage for him to continue his sick play. But they had spent the last day and a half making sure security was as tight as it possibly could be inside city hall.

She ducked as a protestor haphazardly thrust a sign in her direction, her feeling of dread increasing. What if Freihof's plan wasn't to destroy the summit itself, but to attack the people out here? Nobody was guarding them.

Freihof had never gone after innocent people. He'd focused his attacks over the past few months on people attached to Omega Sector. Their loved ones. But that didn't mean he wouldn't change his MO. And ultimately they couldn't protect everyone in the world from him.

But they would damn well make sure city hall and the summit were secure.

Lillian finally forced her way through the crowd and into the building. She identified herself to the security officers. She was about to head to the third floor—to the auditorium where the summit would be held—when she caught sight of someone slipping through the door leading down to the basement. The same one where she'd almost died.

And if she wasn't mistaken, it was Philip Carnell heading down there. Philip, who should be up in the control room right now, finalizing details. Lillian could think of a number of reasons why Carnell might be heading down to the basement level, and none of them were good.

She'd stayed away from Carnell over the last day, since she'd accused him of being the mole. Both Jace and Derek had been watching him and assured her they didn't think Carnell was the traitor. That he hadn't made any suspicious moves.

This was damn well suspicious.

She reached for her comm unit, then cursed when she remembered she hadn't checked in yet, so she didn't have it. She jogged over to the corner door Carnell had disappeared through. She didn't want to go barreling in, accusing him once again of malicious intent—that was probably the surest way to get herself on administrative leave. But she wasn't going to just let him get away with whatever he was doing. If Carnell was moving to assist Freihof in some way, she was going to stop him. And she'd text Jace or Derek once she knew what was going on.

She opened the stairwell door quietly, closing it behind her gently so it didn't make a click. The subbasement was three floors below the lobby level and she could hear Carnell's steps as he moved quickly down the stairs.

Lillian followed silently, listening for the door she knew would lead to the basement. When the sound didn't come she moved more quickly, trying to figure out what was going on. When she got to the door, she stopped, staring at it.

It was closed. Locked with a bolt and padlock Omega had put there to keep this entire basement floor unavailable for the summit. There was no way Carnell just opened this door and went through it without her hearing. She spun around, but Carnell was nowhere to be found and there was nowhere to hide. The only other room was a small closet at the end of the hall. She'd seen it herself yesterday while double-checking the security of this level.

If Carnell was in there, he was hiding, because there was nowhere else to go.

Maybe waiting with his handy Taser? Not this time, rat bastard.

She pulled out her extendable sentry baton from its holder at the back of her belt. With a flick of her wrist it was open to its full length of over eighteen inches. A Taser wasn't going to help Carnell this time.

Deciding the element of surprise was her best bet, Lillian threw open the closet door, then jumped back, expecting to see Carnell pounce toward her. When nothing happened, she grabbed her flashlight and shined it into the closet, baton still raised.

Empty. Cleaning supplies, shelves, but no Carnell.

What the hell?

There was nowhere else he could've gone. She'd come

through the lobby level, and the subbasement level was still locked. So where the hell had Carnell gone?

She was turning to backtrack, to see what she'd missed, when she felt it. Just the slightest of breezes. But it was coming from the closet behind her, not the hallway.

How could a breeze be coming from a closet?

Lillian spun her flashlight back around, looking more carefully at the walls of the closet. One of the shelving units was ajar, not flush against the wall. Putting her baton back in the holder, she stepped closer and aimed her flashlight more fully at the gap between the wall and shelf.

It was an opening of some kind.

Knowing Carnell could already be into the deadly stages of whatever he had planned, Lillian didn't hesitate. She flipped off her light and slid the shelf just the smallest amount needed for her to fit through.

She stayed low and alert, allowing her eyes to adjust to the darkened space, expecting another basement room. It was more. A series of rooms, interconnected with a number of doors.

What was this place? The damp, darkened cinder blocks suggested this had been built decades ago, if not longer. Definitely not recently.

But these rooms should've been in the building plans. Even if the rooms weren't being used, the information about them should've been made available.

She had to call this in. There was no way in hell Carnell could accuse her of acting unreasonably now by following and accusing him of misconduct. City hall was not secure.

Her phone was in her hand when she saw Carnell come running out of one room—a look of frustration and concern clear on his face—before turning and opening another door. What the hell was he doing?

She couldn't lose him now. Lillian slipped her phone back in the pocket of her tactical vest and, keeping to the edge of the wall and shadows as much as possible, moved toward the door Carnell had just entered.

She opened the door and found Carnell with his back to her, kneeling on the floor.

Facing the largest explosive device she'd ever seen. That thing would bring down the entire building and everyone in it.

Lillian pulled her weapon out. "Step away from the device, Carnell. Do it right now. Get your hands up."

"Muir, listen…"

"Right damn now, Carnell." Lillian took another step closer.

Carnell raised his hands. "It's not what you think."

She let out a curse with her laugh. "Really? Because what I think is that I am looking at you messing with a big-ass bomb. Is that not the case?"

Lillian felt the movement behind her just a second too late. A gun was resting at her temple before she could make a move.

"I think what dear Philip is trying to tell you is that it's not *his* big-ass bomb, isn't that right, Phil?"

Saul Poniard.

"What the hell are you doing, Saul? Are you guys working together?"

Saul gave her that friendly smile she now realized had always been completely fake. "Nah. Not working together. Phil must've stumbled onto my contribution to the LESS Summit." He pressed the gun deeper against her temple. "Gun on the floor, Muir."

Lillian gritted her teeth and placed her Glock on the floor. She would be able to take him in a fight, but there was no way she could stop him from shooting her with his gun at point-blank range. He immediately kicked it away.

"Did you position yourself on my weak side on purpose, Saul, or did you just get lucky?"

Saul shot her a grin. "What can I say, Lily? You taught me well."

"I also taught you not to call me Lily."

"Eakin gets to, so why can't I?"

"Maybe because Jace isn't a lying, traitorous psychopath who plans to blow up a bunch of innocent people."

Saul actually chuckled. "Don't be so shortsighted, *Lily*. I plan to do much more than just blow up the people here."

"Oh, my God, those things are real?" Philip, still standing over by the explosive device, sounded like he was going to vomit.

"Shut up, Phil. It's not quite time to reveal the whole plan. Get down on your knees, hands behind your head."

He gave Lillian a shove toward the floor. Reining in her temper, she dropped to her knees. A time to fight was coming, but she needed to wait until she had some sort of a chance. If Jace was here, he'd do something to distract Saul long enough for her to be able to move on him.

Philip Carnell just looked like he might pee his pants. No help was coming from him.

And if she tried anything on her own right now, she'd just get a bullet in the brain for her troubles. But when Saul secured her wrists behind her back with a zip tie, she wished she had tried.

"Saul," she said, "you have to know that Derek's going to notice that we're missing. Maybe you not being around would've been overlooked, but all three of us not being at our proper places? They'll never hold the summit here. They'll cancel it outright."

"That's why you're going to call your boyfriend and tell him you found proof that Phil is the mole, that you've got him in custody and you'll be reporting soon. I'm sure in all the chaos and relief that they finally caught the person giving information to Freihof, they won't even notice I'm missing."

Lillian just shook her head at him. "You know I won't do it, Poniard. You can go to hell."

The friendly surfer facade disappeared from his face. Saul grabbed her by the hair and snatched her head back. He pointed the gun at her temple again. "I think you will."

"You're going to kill me anyway. We both know that. So why would I help you blow up a building full of innocent people? Not to mention all the protestors outside that would also get hurt in the panic."

He gripped her hair harder and jerked her head to the side, pulling out a knife from his own SWAT vest. "I think you will, Muir."

Lillian didn't even try to stop the laugh that bubbled out of her. "You think you can torture me into helping you? You're the one on the clock, Saul. Every second we spend down here is another second the team continues to wonder where we are. Just a matter of time before they empty the building. I daresay I can withstand any torture you want to dish out until they do that."

Damn it, she didn't want to die. Not now…right when she was beginning to find herself again. And Jace. Not when there was the possibility of a wonderful new beginning.

But she would. She would take whatever Saul thought he could do to her to get her to lie to the team.

She saw his fist flying toward her face but couldn't brace herself with her hands tied behind her back. She fell to the floor hard, but forced herself to sit back up immediately.

She spat blood to the side of Saul's feet. "You're going to have to do better than that."

She expected his fist again, or a kick. But instead Saul just laughed. "Actually, you're right. Nobody could ever break you physically in that short amount of time. But I don't have to break you." He turned to Philip. "I'll break *him*."

Saul began walking toward Philip, who had stayed silent during their exchange. Before she could say anything to stop him, Saul did a one-two combination move, punching Philip in the abdomen, followed by a roundhouse kick to the jaw.

Philip fell to the floor, groaning.

Saul turned and actually winked at Lillian. How had she ever found him likable? "You helped me perfect that move. Thanks."

She watched in horror as he turned back to Philip and stabbed him in the shoulder, ripped out the blade, then brought it back down and sliced through Philip's arm. Philip's anguished cry tore at her heart.

"Damn it, Saul…"

"One call, Lillian. Just two sentences."

Philip shook his head back and forth. "No, Lillian, you can't."

Saul sliced at Philip again. Saul was trained in combat. Philip's fighting ability was minimal at best, and without a weapon, he was a sitting duck.

"Enough, Poniard," Lillian yelled. She had to get Saul's attention back on her.

"I don't have time for this. So you either make the call or the next stab is into a vital organ of Phil's. Then, if you still won't do it, I'm going outside, grabbing the first mom and kid I find and bringing them down here. We'll see how long they can withstand torture."

"Lillian…" Philip's words came out between jagged breaths. "He's bluffing. Don't…"

Saul brought the knife back up and she knew he meant what he'd said.

And knew what she had to do.

"Stop!" she yelled. "I'll do it."

Saul snickered at her but at least walked away from Philip, who was still lying on the floor groaning, blood spilling from his wounds.

Saul got right into Lillian's face. The temptation to head-butt him was overwhelming, but she knew it wouldn't accomplish anything.

"You know what your problem is, Lily? Lack of follow-through. You can't stand to see others get hurt, even when it's necessary for change. Surely you can see that we've reached a point where change is necessary in modern law enforcement?"

"The only thing necessary for me is for you to stop monologuing. Give me the damn phone."

He pulled out her phone, along with his Glock, and after punching Jace's contact button, put the gun to one of her ears and the phone to the other. "Talk to the boyfriend and tell him you've got Philip in custody and have proof he's the mole. That you'll be back as soon as you can." He tapped the side of her head with the gun. "You try to tell him what's really going on and I will make sure you see innocent people die right in front of you as horrifically as possible. They'll die screaming."

Lillian pursed her lips. "All right, simmer down there, Hulk-Smash. Give me the goddamn phone."

Saul hit the send button for Jace.

"Hey, you."

Just hearing his deep voice helped settle her. Like it always had.

"Hey." Her own voice came out husky.

"Where are you? Derek was expecting you nearly thirty minutes ago."

Saul narrowed his eyes at her and brought his knife up in Philip's direction.

"Jace, tell Derek it's going to be a while before I make it in. Don't be mad, but I caught Carnell sneaking into the marked-off basement and I followed him. I caught him, Jace. Have him in custody. I'll explain later, but Carnell is definitely the mole."

"You're sure?"

She had to find a way to warn Jace. She hoped this worked. "One-hundred-percent. I swear on my brother's life I'm telling the truth."

Jace laughed. "You don't have a brother."

Lillian gave the most lighthearted chuckle she was capable of. "Fine. Then I swear on your brother's life that I'm telling the truth. You know how much I love your dear brother."

"Yeah, a lot of love." The slightest change in Jace's tone clued her in. He knew there was something up. She had his attention now. "You need help bringing in Philip? There's nothing going on around here until the bigwigs arrive."

Saul shook his head in warning.

"Nah. I can definitely handle Carnell. You stay where you are. He won't get the drop on me down here again."

Would Jace understand? It was all so vague.

"You sure?"

"If Philip keeps running his mouth, he's going to end up just like that perp Daryl. You remember me telling you about what I did to Daryl?" She chuckled again to try to throw Saul off. "Carnell is going to end up just like him if he keeps talking trash to me."

"Hey, you be good," Jace finally said. "And be careful. Don't want you to get in any trouble for roughing up a suspect."

"I'll see you in a bit."

Saul hit the disconnect button as soon as the last word was out of her mouth. She could only pray Jace understood what she was trying to tell him.

"Who the hell is Daryl?" Saul hissed. "Why'd you bring him up?"

"He's just some guy I fought with once. And I brought him up because if I treat Jace like we're nothing more than professional colleagues, he's going to know something's up, okay? You got what you wanted, Saul, you damn coward, so just shut the hell up."

She saw his face turn red with rage, as his arm flew toward her. The world spun to black as he cracked her in the back of the head with the butt of his gun.

Chapter Eighteen

The second Lillian's call disconnected, Jace was running out into the hallway to find Derek.

"We need to evacuate the building right now."

Derek immediately put away the papers he was looking at. "Why? What happened?"

"I just talked to Lillian. She's in trouble. And there's a bomb in the building, probably in the basement."

"She told you that? Why didn't she radio it in? Call the bomb squad?"

"She was talking to me under duress, trying to get me a message. She was talking about my brother, Daryl."

Derek looked confused. "Your brother, Daryl, planted a bomb?"

"No, my brother, Daryl, is dead. But he died in an explosion. Lillian was trying to get that across to me by mentioning him."

Derek shook his head. "No offense, Eakin, but are you sure? Maybe she was just bringing him up as part of a conversation."

Jace stepped farther into Derek's personal space. They didn't have time to waste. "She told me she had proof that Philip Carnell was the mole. That she caught him. That she would swear on her brother's life that it was him."

"I didn't know Lillian had a brother."

"She doesn't. When I brought up that point, she said she would swear on *my* brother's life that Carnell was the mole."

"Okay, weird. But what makes you think she's under duress?"

Without providing details about Daryl that Lillian might not want to share, Jace explained what she had said about Daryl and what she was trying to explain to them.

Jace knew without a shadow of a doubt that Lillian had risked her life to get him that message. He wasn't going to waste what she'd done, regardless of whether Derek agreed or not. He didn't want to have to go over Derek's head, but he would if he had to.

Jace trusted Lillian. Trusted what she was trying to tell him. He couldn't even allow himself to think about the fact that she had now served her purpose for whoever had forced her to make that call and might already be dead. Because that damn well wasn't going to happen.

"Derek, I'm right. You know Lillian would've handled this differently if Carnell really was in custody. She wouldn't just leave us in the middle of an important lockdown when every person on the team is needed. Not to mention, she would've died before calling and leading us astray unless she had a plan to try to warn us. *Mentioning Daryl was that plan.*"

"All right, I trust you. And moreover, I trust Lillian. Let's get this building cleared now. But calmly."

Within seconds Derek was on the comm units with the rest of the Omega team and the added security personnel. Thankfully, because of the LESS Summit, half the people who would normally be working here had been given the day off. Within minutes everyone with security clearance was helping to escort people quickly out of the building.

All Jace wanted to do was find Lillian and make sure she wasn't harmed. But he knew she would want to make sure the building was secure first. That innocent people were safe. And while Jace didn't like that, he would respect her wishes. He had no doubt she'd paid a price to get that info to him. He wouldn't let it be wasted.

As they were escorting the last of the people from the building, he could hear Derek explaining on the phone what was happening to an obviously livid Congresswoman Glasneck.

"Glasneck refuses to cancel, so we're going to the emergency third location." Frustration was etched on Derek's face.

"I didn't even know there was a third location." And to be honest, he didn't care about the LESS Summit anymore. All Jace's attention was focused on getting to Lillian.

"The Clarke Building. An ordinary office building about three blocks away." Derek provided the address. "Small, unimpressive, nondescript. A conference room with no windows on the second floor. Opposite of what Glasneck wanted."

"I'm not coming, Derek. I've got to find Lily. She's in trouble." Jace respected the man but didn't care. What could Derek do, fire him? Even if this was his real job, Jace wouldn't care.

But Derek just nodded. "Find her. LESS is now going to be bare-bones anyway. The ceremony and pomp will have to be done some other way. This is just going to be Congresswoman Glasneck and a couple other key people flipping a switch." He provided a few more details about where they would be.

Jace was already taking off toward the lobby. "I'll report in as soon as I know something about Lillian. And we'll get to you if we can."

He prayed they'd be able to.

The last of the civilians were being led out the main entrance and police were clearing all the protesters in the vicinity of city hall. Jace had already tried calling Lillian's phone a dozen times. Each time the call went straight to voice mail.

"Jace."

He turned to find Saul behind him. "Is your sector clear?"

Saul hesitated a second before nodding. "When last I checked."

"Okay, I think the building's clear, then."

Saul didn't give his usual grin, just nodded. "Good. I'm glad you figured out that there was a threat."

"It was all Lillian, she clued me in, even though I'm almost positive she was under duress. Have you seen her? Or Carnell?"

"Um, yeah, a while ago, before we started the evac. I think she was just getting here. Said something about having proof about Carnell."

"Yeah, that's what she told me, too. I'm sure Derek can use your help securing the new LESS location. The Clarke Building, two blocks east of here. It's bare-bones, most of the VIPs won't be a part of it now, but LESS is still going live."

Saul's lips thinned. "Okay, I'll head over there right now. I've just got one thing to do first."

Jace didn't know what could be more important than

getting directly over to the summit, but he honestly didn't care. Protecting the summit was Derek's concern now. This building was clear and Jace was damn well going to find Lillian.

"Eakin!" Saul called as Jace ran toward the stairs. "When I saw her as she came in, Lillian mentioned something about the roof. I don't know if that's where she is, but maybe."

Jace gave a wave of acknowledgment but didn't slow down. As he turned the corner bringing him to the main stairwell, he had to make a decision. Up or down. If Saul was right and she was on the roof, Jace didn't want to waste time looking in the basement section.

He won't get the drop on me down here again.

Those had been Lillian's words. *Down here.*

Maybe she'd been heading toward the roof when Poniard saw her earlier, but she wasn't there now. Or at least hadn't been when she called him to get the people out of the building. He headed down the stairs, memories of finding Lily's swinging form haunting him from the last time he'd taken these stairs. He prayed he wouldn't find something worse.

A few minutes of storming through rooms—even the ones behind the padlocked door—had Jace worried he'd made the wrong decision. Maybe she was up on the roof. He was about to make his way up there when he heard a sound coming from the supply closet—like a call for help.

But Jace knew before he even opened the door that couldn't be right, the sound was from too far away to be coming from the supply closet.

He reached for the handle and found it locked. That was strange. It hadn't been locked as they were securing the building the past two days.

He heard the sound again—a muffled male yell—and stepped back to kick in the door. The door flew from its hinges when his foot hit it and opened.

Nothing. Nobody bound and gagged, like he expected.

He wiped a hand over his eyes. Wishful thinking. The stress was getting to him. Obviously the sound couldn't be from here. He would check the roof, since he'd already checked every possible room in the basement.

But as he was closing the door he heard it again. Jace's head jerked up. That damn well hadn't been wishful thinking or stress. That had been a yell for help. And it had been coming from right in front of him. Right through the wall. A wall that should lead nowhere, according to the building plans he'd studied extensively.

Jace immediately began knocking against the far wall, more frantically, when he heard the yell again.

"Who's there? Keep yelling," Jace yelled back. When he moved a shelving unit he saw the hole. Doubling his efforts, he threw the shelf to the side and crawled through the hole.

What the hell?

"Help. Please."

The voice was becoming weaker.

"I'm here. Keep yelling."

"Eakin? We're here. Help us. Hurry."

"Carnell?" What the hell was going on? Jace moved farther into the large room. What was this? "Where are you?"

"Here. God, hurry, Eakin. There's a bomb."

Jace ran toward Carnell's voice and found him tied up in an adjoining room. Bleeding heavily.

Lillian was tied up and gagged next to him. Very much alive. She was not only alive, but had also somehow gotten her pocketknife out and, with her own wrists secured behind her back, was attempting to cut through Carnell's tied hands. She'd already gotten his gag out, and would've had them both untied before too long.

Jace glanced at the explosive device. But maybe not fast enough.

"You're hurt," Jace said to Philip before diving down to help Lillian.

"I'll be fine. Thank God you're here," Philip said as Jace cut through Lillian's bonds first then did the same to Philip's. "We've got to get everyone out of here. That bomb is set to go off in less than twenty minutes."

"We've already evacuated the building."

As soon as her hands were free, Lillian reached up and pulled the gag out of her mouth. "You understood. Thank God."

Jace reached over and cupped the back of her neck, pulling her forehead against his. "Mentioning Daryl was smart. Clued me in immediately."

"It was my only option," she whispered. "Poniard was torturing Philip. Threatening to grab a mom and kid—"

"Poniard? Poniard is the mole?" Jace let out a blistering curse. "I just saw him. He was acting a little weird, but everything was already crazy with the evacuation."

"Thank God you stopped the summit," Philip said as Jace got Lillian to her feet and helped him stand. "I didn't even get to the part that sent me down here in the first place. The much worse part."

Phillip looked from Lillian to Jace.

"What?" they both demanded at the same time.

"You know how Saul has been traveling to police stations all over the country for the last eight months to help with the setup of the LESS system? What he conveniently failed to mention was that he also rigged those stations with biological weapons. If LESS had gone live today, Saul had rigged it so the connecting systems all over the country would've released the biological hazard. The death toll would've been in the thousands, maybe tens of thousands. All law enforcement."

Lillian's ugly curse was the exact sentiment Jace was feeling. And she didn't even know the half of it.

"That's a pretty big problem," Jace said. "Because we got this building clear, but the summit is still on at a different location. And I just told Poniard where it's being held."

Chapter Nineteen

Jace was reaching for his cell phone before he finished his sentence. He immediately cursed before putting it away.

"No signal. Poniard had to figure I would eventually end up down here. He probably set up some sort of jammer."

Jace and Lillian both ran over to the bomb. "We've got to get this thing disarmed," she said. "If the building comes down, there's no way there won't be complete panic outside."

"I'll take care of the bomb. You guys have to get over to the summit and stop Poniard." Jace told them where the summit had been moved to, then began studying the explosive device more closely.

Lillian's gut clenched. "Jace, there's no way for you to call for backup. For you to get the bomb squad in here. You'll be completely on your own."

Jace stood, wrapped his hands on either side of her face and brought her in for a hard, quick kiss. "There's no time for them to get here even if I could get a call out. Law enforcement is maxed out outside. We're on our own."

Lillian grabbed his wrists and kissed him again. They both had jobs to do. He was trusting her to do hers, and she had to trust him to do his. "Then I'll see you soon. You damn well better make it out of this."

His grin sent heat to her core. Almost enough to melt the ice of fear surrounding her for him. "Bet on it."

He let her go and turned back to the explosive device. Lillian studied Philip. "We're going to have to move fast. Can you make it?"

"I have to. I'm the only one who can get LESS shut down in time to stop it from killing thousands of people."

They were through the passageway, out of the building and running into the Denver streets as fast as the crowds would let them. Backing people away from the City and County Building had just made the other areas more crowded. The sounds of chants and jeers were nearly deafening.

Lillian cleared a path for Philip, who was looking more and more pale. But he was right, they didn't have any choice: he had to make it. She had a new respect for the determination in his eyes.

They finally made it to the small, almost unnotice-able building between two much taller ones. This was everything Congresswoman Glasneck *hadn't* wanted for the LESS Summit.

Not knowing the building specifics put Lillian at a tactical disadvantage, but Saul hadn't known about this backup location, either, so he couldn't have left them many surprises.

"We've got less than fifteen minutes," Philip said as they made it inside. "And we can't just go barging in. Saul has had this set up for months. He's only waited for the LESS Summit because he wanted to have these law-en-forcement offices and stations around the country to be as crowded as possible. All he has to do is flip the switch to make LESS live, then start the computer program that opens the containers. He's probably already got it saved to a single keystroke. That's what I would do."

Lillian let out a string of curses. "So you're saying if we knock the door down and shoot him, he still might have a chance to put the program in motion and release the biological weapons."

"Exactly. I'll bet you any amount of money he's walking around with either a keyboard or a phone. Either can be used as his trigger. All he needs is a second to end the lives of thousands of people."

"Okay, then I'll knock the phone or keyboard out of his hand."

Philip shook his head. "That buys you time, but not much. He has a timing device as a backup plan. That's how I stumbled onto this whole thing to begin with, the countdown. Once LESS goes live, one minute afterward the canisters will release."

This just kept getting worse. "Can you stop it?"

"Yes. If I can access Poniard's digital trigger, whether it's a phone or a computer, I can stop it. I'll have to work the system backward, but I can do it."

"In under a minute?" Lillian tried to keep the incredulity out of her voice, but failed.

"You have your gifts, Muir. I have mine."

Lillian nodded at him. "I owe you an apology." For more than just accusing him of being the mole. For the way she'd treated him—like he wasn't good enough to truly be on the team. Now he was standing in a puddle of his own blood, ready to fight in the best way he knew how. It was all anyone could ask.

Maybe Philip wasn't such a jackass after all.

"Later, Muir. I don't have time for female hysterics or teary heartfelt hugs."

Or maybe he was.

Lillian notified the extra security guards of the problem and set them up outside the conference room door, ready to breach on her mark. She quickly explained the danger of rushing in too soon.

Since the summit had been downscaled, the only security out here was private sector and Denver local PD. Any Secret Service agents who'd been assigned here were in the closed conference room with Congresswoman Glasneck. Derek was in there, too. All of them could be counted on to take out Saul, but not if they didn't know Saul was the traitor.

And Saul would be waiting for someone to come through this door. Would be ready for that.

"Lillian, we've got less than ten minutes until LESS is scheduled to go live."

"Turn on your comm unit," she told him. "Be ready to burst in with the security team. I'll get the trigger away from Poniard, and then you'll work your magic."

"This is the only door. There's no windows. How are you going to get into the room?"

"You have your gifts, I have mine, Carnell. And right now mine includes my size."

Less than a minute later one of the security guards was giving her a boost up to the industrial-size air-conditioning vent. Lillian belly-crawled as quickly as she could through the small ductwork without making noise.

Arriving at the square grate over the room took longer than she wanted, and then she cursed when she found the situation to be even worse than she'd thought. Things had already escalated.

A Secret Service agent, most probably dead by the amount of blood lost from the bullet wound in his neck, was lying slumped over in the corner. Lillian shifted to be able to see the other side of the room better, and her breath caught in her throat. Derek had been shot also, perhaps multiple times. A man in a suit was holding a balled-up shirt against Derek's thigh, and blood was running unchecked from his shoulder.

Saul Poniard was pacing back and forth. "The current state of law enforcement is a laughingstock. Surely you can see that by resetting the baseline I am doing this country a great favor. Something that is needed."

"By killing innocent people?" Congresswoman Glasneck asked. She was over against the south wall, huddled with half a dozen other people.

"The price of liberty is sometimes death itself. Plus, these people are not innocent, they are part of the problem."

"And us, Saul?" Glasneck asked again. "I've been working with you for months. Are you going to kill everyone in this room also?"

"I will not be deterred from what I am meant to do. It is my destiny. Individual lives are not what matter. Change is what matters."

Lillian looked at her watch. Four minutes. Four minutes until LESS was scheduled to go live and the bomb at the City and County Building was set to detonate. She couldn't even allow herself to think about Jace. She trusted him to be able to do what he needed to do.

"They'll know it's you." An older, heavyset man next to the congresswoman glared at Saul. "Do you think you're going to get away with this? That no one is going to notice a room full of dead people, including a congresswoman?"

"I think there's going to be enough chaos in just a few minutes to leave everyone in utter confusion. The lives of half a dozen will be of very little consequence in the bigger picture. And out of the confusion, I will rise up and lead. Lead law enforcement to the greatness it can be. To reset the path of this country the way it needs to be reset."

Saul's voice was rising with his passion. Lillian used the noise to speak into the comm unit.

"Philip," she whispered. "Poniard's got a phone in his hand, like you said. Gun in the other one. He's ready for an ambush through the door, so make sure everyone stands down."

"Roger that. But we're out of time, Lillian. Less than three minutes."

Saul was still yelling at the people huddled against the wall. "And never again will someone like me—someone with vision, focus and purpose—be denied the chance to serve in whatever capacity they see fit. To be a part of the most elite. Never again will I be rejected. For years, Omega Sector thought I wasn't capable of being on their precious SWAT team. Unfortunately, they'll all be dead, so I won't be able to gloat in their faces that I'm smarter than them."

Spittle flew across the room as he said it. Lillian barely refrained from rolling her eyes. This was all about Saul being jealous because he didn't make the SWAT team?

"Lil, once LESS goes live, the one-minute countdown is on, no matter what," Philip reminded her in her ear. "You've got to take him."

Philip was right. Lillian was treating this like a normal hostage situation, where she could just wait out the perp.

Eventually he'd tire himself out and lower his weapon or become complacent.

They didn't have that kind of time now.

As Saul continued his rant, Lillian silently moved the grate that covered the vent opening, progressing slowly but with purpose.

"Thirty seconds until LESS goes live."

Lillian said a quick prayer that Jace had gotten the bomb disabled. They'd know for sure in just a few seconds. Saul would, too, and once he did, he wouldn't hesitate to immediately release the biological weapons all over the country.

Lillian waited until he crossed under her again, then forgot all about quiet and yanked the grate up and dove out of the opening, headfirst, landing on top of Saul.

Her training said to get the gun out of his right hand, but she pried the phone from his left hand instead. Keeping him from triggering the canisters was most important.

She was able to get the phone out of Saul's hand. She was too close for him to shoot, but she grunted when he hit her with his gun, barely missing her head and grazing her shoulder. Damn it, this bastard had hit her with that gun enough times for one day.

Keeping the phone out of his reach, she used her momentum to roll both of them forward, bringing her elbow up to catch him in the jaw. She jumped to her feet and grabbed Saul by the shirt, pulling his back off the floor. She slammed her fist into his nose, hearing the crack as it broke under her force.

"It just went live, Lillian. LESS just went live!" Philip's voice shouted into her ear.

One minute. That was all the time they had left.

"Breach! I've got Saul's phone." She heard the door burst open behind her and turned to toss Philip the phone. The security force trained their weapons on Saul.

Still held up by her fist on his clothing, Saul began to laugh. "You're too late. That bomb in the City and County Building is nothing compared to what's coming."

Lillian glanced over. "Philip?"

Philip didn't look up as his fingers typed rapidly on Saul's phone. "Working voodoo now. Do not disturb."

She brought Saul closer to her face. "Philip found out about your canisters and knows how to stop them."

Saul's face mottled in fury. "Don't do it, Carnell. Omega Sector is just using you. You know how elitist they are. We can be a part of something new. Better."

"New and better by killing tens of thousands of people?" She brought her fist into his jaw again. "Shut up."

Saul spat blood. "Philip. You know I'm telling the truth. Omega's best-of-the-best crap? According to who? The wrong people are making the decisions. It's time for a change."

Philip walked over to them. "You know what? You're right, Saul, it *is* time for a change."

"Philip." Damn it. Philip couldn't let Saul get into his head now. There were only seconds left. "Don't let him…"

Philip dropped the phone on the floor next to Saul. "But not your way. Law enforcement, Omega Sector included, needs to take a good long look at itself. Make the needed changes. I want to be a part of that. But not your way." Philip turned to Lillian. "I did it. The connection to the canisters has been severed. It's safe."

Saul jerked away from Lillian and made a tackle for

Philip, but Philip was ready. It was his fist that hit Saul this time. Saul fell to the floor, moaning.

Lillian nodded at Philip as the guards handcuffed Saul and led him away. One was already on a radio, calling in an ambulance for Derek. Lillian rushed over to him where he was propped against the wall. Congresswoman Glasneck joined her at his side.

"Derek?" His normally tan skin was devoid of all color. He was so still, Lillian reached up to take his pulse. "Wake up."

"I'm awake," Derek muttered. "You did good, Lily."

"Excuse me, but you're not allowed to call me that." Only Jace was. "Don't think that just because you've successfully gotten yourself shot twice, I'm going to let you call me anything short of my full name."

She said it jokingly as she removed the shirt covering the wound on Derek's thigh to glance at it.

"How bad?" he muttered, eyes closed.

He knew she wouldn't lie. "Not life-threatening." Unless he kept bleeding. "But bad enough that you need to be taken straight to the hospital."

Derek nodded, then leaned farther back against the wall.

"I have to go check on Jace. We had to leave him with the explosive device in city hall. Poniard had set it up so the explosion would happen the same time the canisters were released. Maximum chaos and damage. There hasn't been an explosion, so I'm assuming he took care of it." Thank God.

Congresswoman Glasneck stood when Lillian did. "Thank you. I had no idea Saul Poniard was capable of such treachery."

Lillian gave a half shrug. "He was convinced of the rightness of his own actions. I hope the LESS system can still be utilized."

Glasneck shook her head sadly. "Maybe one day, but not right now. If there's anything I've become convinced of in the last hour, it's that although connecting all law-enforcement systems may help fight crime, it also allows for law enforcement as a whole to be attacked rather easily. You bring down LESS, and it can do countrywide damage."

Lillian gave the congresswoman a nod and then turned to jog out the door. She gave Philip—who was now sitting on the floor looking exhausted—a nod and continued past him when he gave her a small salute. Saul was loudly explaining his intentions and proclaiming his innocence to the guards who had taken him into custody. Lillian ignored him completely. She'd heard more than enough out of him today.

Outside, the local police were still clearing the area, keeping demonstrators back from the buildings. She saw her teammate Ashton Fitzgerald helping with crowd control and made her way over to him. She explained what had happened with Saul and Derek.

"Do I need to get in there to help Derek?" Ashton had to shout to be heard over the roar of the crowd.

"No, just make sure the paramedics can get to him. You're needed out here. Have you seen Jace?"

"No. Cell-phone coverage is still down, and honestly we can't do anything until we clear this crowd out."

Lillian nodded. "I'm going to check on him and then I'll be back." She had to see with her own eyes to make sure Jace was okay.

Ashton nodded. "Okay. Comms aren't worth a damn out here, either, with the noise level. So just find me when you're back."

Lillian sprinted for the City and County Building. They needed as much help with crowd control as they could get. She entered the building and ran down the stairs toward the opening in the supply closet.

"Jace?" Nothing. "Eakin, you okay?"

She scurried through the hole, into the opening. "Jace! I just wanted to make sure you're okay."

She heard some sort of scuffle from farther back in a room, past where the explosive device had been placed. "Jace?"

Something was definitely not right. Had Jace hurt himself somehow after defusing the explosive device? Was someone else down here? Lillian pulled her sidearm, keeping it close to her chest.

The muffled sound came again and Lillian rushed into the far room. At the other end, near some sort of second entrance, stood Damien Freihof, a gagged-and-bound Jace in front of him.

He had a gun pointed directly at Jace's temple.

"Agent Muir," Freihof said, his smile large and wide. "I was wondering how long it would take before you came to look for Mr. Eakin."

Lillian's weapon was immediately pointed directly at Freihof. She didn't have a shot right now with Jace in front of him like a shield, but Jace wouldn't be anyone's human shield for long, particularly not Freihof's. Jace didn't seem to be hurt. When he made his move, Lillian would be ready.

She glanced at Jace's face, ready to read whatever it was he would want her to do.

The sheer agony she saw in his eyes caught her off guard.

"What the hell did you do, Freihof?" she whispered. Had he hurt Jace? There had to be some sort of terrible wound she couldn't see that was putting that look on his face.

"No need to be angry. As a matter of fact, everyone should be thanking me." Freihof's voice rang with childlike excitement. "I haven't done anything bad. As a matter of fact, all I did was stage a reunion between brothers!"

A reunion between bro—

"You remember Jace's brother, Daryl, don't you, Lillian?"

For the first time in her professional career, Lillian's weapon faltered as her own personal nightmare stepped out from the shadows beside her. Her hand began to shake as shock flooded her whole body. The Glock shook so greatly in her hand she could hardly keep hold of it.

"Hi, Lillian, baby. I've been looking for you for a long time." Daryl trailed a finger down her cheek. All she could do was stare at him.

His fist crashed into her face and Lillian let the blessed blackness consume her.

Chapter Twenty

As soon as Daryl's fist flew toward Lillian, Jace dove at them. Freihof was expecting it and just laughed, grabbed Jace and pulled him away. He watched, helpless, as Lillian fell to the floor.

"Brother dearest seems pretty excited to see your girlfriend," Freihof whispered in his ear. "He told me a little about what happened between them. Don't you just love a classic romance?"

Jace dove toward them again as Daryl crouched down to stroke Lily's face. She was already regaining consciousness. Freihof grabbed Jace and threw him to his knees, clocking him against the back of his neck with the gun. Jace ignored the pain, yelling at Daryl through the tape.

"I think your brother wants to talk to you, Daryl." Freihof ripped the tape off Jace's mouth.

"Don't you touch her, Daryl. Keep your damn hands off her."

Lillian was moaning on the floor, still having not quite woken up. It wasn't because Daryl had hit her that hard. Lily could take a punch. It was because her brain didn't want her to wake up. Didn't want to force her into trauma she wasn't ready for.

Daryl now looked as evil on the outside as he was on the inside. Burns covered over half his face and trailed down his neck before they were cut off by his T-shirt.

"I can't believe you would choose her over your own flesh and blood, *brother*," Daryl spat out. "She left me in that warehouse to die."

"We both know why. What you did to her." If Jace could reach his brother right now, he would rip him apart limb by limb.

"I had that warehouse ready to blow up," Daryl scoffed. "I knew the cops were closing in. I had been stupid to move into trafficking. Even had a body that looked sort of like mine. Some dealer from across the border who happened to be the same height and weight as me."

Jace sucked in a breath as Daryl stood. He pushed Lillian with the toe of his boot but didn't do anything further. "Lillian was the one who was supposed to be in that fire, not me. Fortunately one of my guys came in and dragged me out after she clocked me over the head with that bottle. The rest of our scheme went as planned. He identified my 'body' to the police. Then we took off."

Lillian gave a pitiful moan, her head tossing back and forth. She'd be waking up soon. Waking up to a nightmare.

Daryl nudged her again with his foot. "I looked for her. All over Tulsa, then even farther. Never dreamed she'd join law enforcement, as pathetic as she was. But she won't be any good to anyone—especially law enforcement—once I'm through with her."

Lillian's eyes opened at that moment. Bile rose in Jace's throat as a look of terror blanketed her features. Almost immediately she was shaking again, her brown eyes darting all around.

"Lillian, look at me, baby," he whispered, trying to eliminate the desperation from his tone. Her eyes continued to dart from place to place, her rapid, shallow breathing causing her to shake further.

"Tiger Lily." He kept his tone firm. Calm. Banished every bit of fear and panic threatening to bubble up from inside him. "It's Jace. I'm here with you. I'm here with you, and you're going to be okay."

Her eyes finally rested on him. "Jace?"

He would give every cent he owned to never see this look of terror and helplessness cross Lillian's face ever again. "I'm here, sweetheart. With you. I'm here."

"You're here." Her words were weak, but her breathing slowed just enough that he stopped worrying that she would pass out again. He nodded at her, keeping their eyes locked.

A roar erupted from him as Daryl reached down and snatched her up by her hair, yanking her face back. "Guess what, I'm here, too, bitch!" Daryl backhanded her and she fell hard to the floor.

This time, she didn't pass out. This time her small hand tightened into a fist.

That's right, sweetheart. Find your fight.

Daryl was weak, pudgy. Lillian was capable of taking him down in under ten seconds. Her mind just had to believe that she could. She sat back up, her eyes finding Jace's again. They were still laced with fear, but her breathing was more under control. If Daryl kept pushing, he was eventually going to find that Lillian could now push back.

Much, much harder.

"That's right, Tiger Lily. You just take a minute and remember who you are. What you can do."

"Stop talking to her!" Daryl screamed, shoving her again.

Her other hand was clenching into a fist now, too. Jace tensed his muscles, trying to balance himself more fully, ready to throw himself backward at Freihof when Lillian completely woke up and made her move. It wouldn't be long.

But then Daryl stopped yelling. Stopped the violence. He dropped behind Lillian, wrapping his arm around her shoulder, pulling her back up against his chest.

Eyes so much like Jace's own looked back at him as Daryl trailed his fingers up and down Lillian's throat and cheek from behind. "You two were so inseparable when you were kids. Like she was your family instead of me. Like I hadn't raised you and given you everything."

"You raised me in a gang and had me performing illegal activities before I was a teenager."

"You got to go to school. Got to eat three square meals a day. Had clothes and money when you needed it. And then you met Lillian and everything changed. Everything became about her. All I wanted was my brother back."

Lillian was frozen in Daryl's embrace.

"Let her go, Daryl. You can have me back. We can do whatever you want, we'll make it work."

Daryl snuggled in closer to Lillian's neck, breathing in her scent. "Did I ever tell you how sweetly she begged? Begged me to spare your life? Begged me not to put her back in the closet where I kept her. Begged me not to hurt her. She was so good at it."

Daryl nuzzled her neck, then forced her head back and kissed her.

Jace prayed she would come out swinging, that she would use one of the hundreds of ways she knew to break out of Daryl's embrace.

But as soon as Daryl moved away from her, Jace recognized that blank stare. Pain and violence had scared her but kept her present. She would eventually have fought back.

But not from this. Just like the other night, Lillian had completely shut down. Her brain had disassociated, was keeping her conscious mind at a distance.

She wasn't feeling any fear, but this Lillian was helpless. Not able to fight, not able to provide any tactical assistance to help get them out of here. There was no way Jace could fight both Daryl with his knife and Freihof with his gun, especially bound like he was.

"I think I'd like to hear you beg again." Daryl leaned away from her, pushing at her, obviously expecting hysteria and fear like before. But Lillian just looked at him with wide eyes, almost like she was a child.

No fear. No pain. But also no fight.

Daryl didn't have the insight to realize what was going on with Lillian, but Freihof did. "Interesting," he said quietly from behind Jace. "Disassociation."

"What are you looking at?" Daryl finally said when Lillian just continued to stare at him blankly. He slapped her, and her head fell to the side. She blinked but then looked back up at Daryl like she was waiting for him to tell her what to do.

Jace began to struggle more frantically against the duct tape that bound his hands behind his back. Lillian frightened and shaking had been nauseating to watch.

Lillian utterly defenseless was beyond terrifying.

Daryl stood and yanked her up by her tactical vest. At her continued blank stare he pulled her right up to his face. "Not scared anymore?"

His mouth covered hers in what would've technically

been described as a kiss, but was really meant to be a device of pain and dominance. On any other given day, under other circumstances, Lillian would've kicked him on his ass.

Now her hands just came up and weakly rested on Daryl's shoulders. Just like they had on Jace's in bed when she blanked out. She wasn't kissing him, but she wasn't pushing Daryl away, either.

"Lily! Come on, baby. Come back to me," Jace called out.

Daryl stepped back, smirking at Jace, keeping an arm wrapped around her limp shoulders. "I've been waiting a lot of years to find sweet Lillian here. To remind her whom she belongs to. When Damien found me a few days ago and told me he knew where she was—where both of you were—I knew I couldn't miss the chance. To get her back. To make her pay for this." He gestured to the scars that ravaged most of his face.

Jace ignored him. "Lillian, come on, sweetheart…" She just continued to stare blankly ahead.

"I'll admit I thought it would be a little harder. Thought I might have to kill you both outright." Daryl pulled out a knife. "But now it looks like I'll just take Lillian with me. I'll find a nice cage to put her back in and take her out when I want to play with her."

Daryl held the knife right in front of Lillian's face like it was a toy. "That okay with you, little pet? Ready to be my dog?"

Jace lunged for Daryl again as he took the knife and made a shallow cut along the side of Lillian's neck. Freihof grabbed him and pulled him back, but Jace immediately lunged again as Daryl made another small cut and Lillian didn't move.

Freihof's pistol came down on the base of Jace's skull again, making him sink to the floor. Through the haze he heard Freihof chuckling. "I realize this might be the pot calling the kettle black, but your brother is pretty sick. I never knew I'd be getting such entertainment when I brought him here."

Jace looked up, fighting back blackness, to look at Lillian again. "C'mon, baby. Fight for me, Tiger Lily. I love you." Her blank brown eyes stared out at him.

Daryl moved away from her and walked over to stand in front of him. "She'll be coming with me. But you, baby brother, you're just a loose end that needs to be tied up. I guess I'll finally need to finish what I threatened to start twelve years ago."

No emotion crossed Daryl's face as he stabbed the knife through Jace's shoulder. The force threw him back, but Daryl grabbed him by the hair and twisted the knife. Agony flooded through Jace.

"That's for the fact that you would've chosen her over your own flesh and blood all those years ago." He pulled out the knife and brought it to Jace's throat. "And this is for the fact that you would still choose her today. Even as broken as she obviously is."

Chapter Twenty-One

The fog was soft and cloudlike all around her. Gentle, yet permeating. Time moved differently here. More slowly. She didn't have to worry about all the things waiting for her on the outside. She could just stay here, where no one could hurt her. Where there would be nothing left to remember when the fog finally lifted. Just blessed numbness.

But even as she clung to the fog—the only darkness she'd ever known that wouldn't hurt her—something beat against her mind. The knowledge that something was different.

Lily.

The voice penetrated the fog. A good voice. Strong. A voice that would never hurt her. But she pushed it away. That voice didn't belong here. Nothing belonged here but the emptiness. The numbness.

Come back to me.

Lillian tried to melt further into the fog. Why wouldn't this voice leave her alone? There were things outside the fog that would hurt her. If she followed the voice she knew pain waited at the other end.

Agony. Terror.

Fight for me.

She didn't want to go. Didn't want to face what was out there. Knew that the devil waited just beyond the fog. That if she faced him now, the fog would never protect her again.

She couldn't do it.

She felt the prick of pain in her neck at a distance. It didn't really hurt, not much. But she shouldn't feel it at all. The fog had never let anything in before. When the prick at her neck came again, Lillian tried to pull herself back more fully into the blessed darkness.

"Tiger Lily."

Jace. That voice was Jace's.

She didn't move. Didn't blink. Didn't breathe.

But the fog began to sink away in layers.

Jace. Jace was here.

"I love you."

More of the fog slid away and she could see as well as hear.

Oh, God, it was Daryl. Daryl was here. He was alive. Her mind demanded that she go back into the fog. That if she stayed in the light, if she left the fog, she might never be whole again.

She couldn't risk it.

The fog fell back around her as Daryl turned away and walked over to stand in front of Jace. He said something that didn't penetrate her haze and then stabbed Jace in the shoulder.

Jace didn't yell, didn't beg or scream. But she could see the blood pouring from the wound as Daryl twisted the knife and pulled it back out.

And then he put the knife to Jace's throat.

No.

With that one thought, the fog fell completely away.

It couldn't hold her if she wouldn't let it. As it left, terror and pain rolled over her, threatening to drown her in their enormity.

No.

She would not stand here protecting herself in numbness while the man she loved lost his life to the monster who had stolen so much from her.

She would not do nothing. Not now. Not ever again.

She sprang.

With all the rage of the eighteen-year-old who hadn't been able to protect herself, she *attacked*.

Neither Daryl nor Freihof was expecting any resistance from her. She was able to kick the knife out of Daryl's hand and away from Jace's throat, then used her momentum to propel herself around so her other leg swung out over Jace's head and connected with Freihof's gun, sending it flying across the room.

Daryl roared as he tackled her from behind, arms coming around her torso. Lillian didn't hesitate. She brought her head back full force against his face, breaking his nose, then swung her booted heel into his kneecap. Daryl screamed and released her.

Never again.

Freihof ran for his gun, but Jace threw himself at the other man, knocking them both onto the floor. She ran over to help Jace, who would never be able to defeat Freihof while wounded and without the use of his hands. Freihof quickly got back to his feet, about to kick Jace in the head, when Lillian leaped for him, knocking him away.

She wasted no time, striking Freihof with a fierce uppercut, then with a heel to his face broke her third nose of the day.

That's for Grace, you bastard.

As Freihof fell to the floor, Lillian leaped and spun, knowing Daryl would be back on her.

He was, knife in hand.

"Time to die, bitch. I should've done this a long time ago."

Daryl's voice—the voice of her nightmares—sent a sliver of fear through Lillian, but she pushed it away. He jabbed at her with the knife and she quickly stepped to the side to evade. But Daryl was expecting that and caught her with a punch to the jaw. The blow spun her head around.

"Remember my fist, sweetheart?" Daryl sneered. "Don't worry, I'm going to make sure you remember every part of me before you—"

Lillian didn't let him finish. She stepped back so she was out of the reach of the knife and brought her leg around in a flying roundhouse kick that caught him in the head. She followed it with a side kick that barreled into his chest, propelling him backward half a dozen feet.

She realized her mistake as soon as he hit the floor. He landed right where he'd taken her sidearm from her earlier. Daryl was going to have it in his hand before she could get to him.

"Lil…"

She heard the weak call from Jace on the other side of the room, then felt something hit her foot. He'd kicked Freihof's gun over to her.

Daryl swung his arm around with the gun in hand as she dropped and grabbed the weapon Jace had provided. She heard a gun fire, felt the recoil of her own. She waited for pain but felt none.

Daryl groaned as he fell back, his weapon falling from his hand. She'd gotten off the shot. Hit him in the chest.

She ran over, kicking the gun away, but she needn't have bothered.

Daryl was dead. For good this time. Checking his pulse confirmed it.

Lillian brought her weapon back around to train it on Freihof. He was just as deadly. But he was no longer where she'd been fighting him, over by Jace. Instead he was at a back entrance to the room.

"I reset the bomb. Hope that's okay." He gave her a small salute. "Another time, Agent Muir. Give my regards to your colleagues."

He slipped out the door.

There was nothing Lillian wanted to do more than go after Freihof, but she couldn't.

Lillian ran over to Jace. He had lost a lot of blood from his shoulder wound. She grabbed the knife and cut through the tape binding his hands. "You're bleeding bad, Jace."

He nodded. "I know. But we've got to stop that bomb. Get me over there. I stopped it once, I can do it again."

Jace was shaky on his feet. She put his good arm around her shoulder and, taking as much of his weight as she could, led him back over to the explosive device. She held him upright, and with shaky hands he once again dismantled the bomb, with just seconds to spare.

"There," he said to the bomb when he was finished. "Stay dead this time."

"Exactly my feelings about Daryl." She kissed his shoulder as they both slid to the floor. "You got that gun to me just in time."

Jace gave her a smile, bringing his hand to her cheek. "You came back from where you were just in time."

"Because you called me back. It was you who got through the fog."

"I'll always call you back, Tiger Lily. Just like you do for me."

Lillian reached up to kiss him, but before she could, he collapsed to the floor.

Chapter Twenty-Two

It was touch-and-go for three days. The shoulder wound was bad enough, but it was the internal hemorrhaging from being clocked on the head that actually put Jace's life in danger. The surgeon had to drill an emergency hole in his skull to allow release of the pressure. Then he had to be kept in a medically induced coma to give his brain every opportunity to heal.

The time between Jace collapsing in her arms and when those blue eyes opened to look at her again were the longest three days of Lillian's life.

She hadn't left his side. Teammates had brought her clean clothes and food and necessities. Lillian wasn't leaving Jace alone.

Because she knew if the roles were reversed, he wouldn't leave her alone, either. She trusted that—trusted *Jace*—with every fiber of her being.

On the third day of Jace's coma, the day they began waking him up, she sat holding his hand, staring at his face. Willing him with every bit of energy she had to open those blue eyes. The doctor had explained that it took each person a different amount of time to wake up. To find his or her way back to consciousness.

But, the doctor also had to warn, on rare occasions they never found their way back.

Jace would. He would find his way out of the fog. She would lead him, the way he'd led her.

She reached over and planted a kiss on his unmoving lips. "I'm here, Eakin. Find your way back to me."

A few hours later Jace still wasn't awake. The doctor had come by twice outside his usual rounds, and although she hadn't said anything negative, Lillian knew she was concerned.

Jace would find his way back to her. He had to.

Molly Humphries-Waterman wheeled her husband through the door in a wheelchair an hour later. Derek was still recovering from his gunshot wounds, but the prognosis was good. It was going to take physical therapy, but Derek would eventually be back to full speed.

But it was yet another member of the Omega Sector team down, thanks to Damien Freihof.

"How's he doing?" Derek asked as Molly went to get them coffee.

"Nothing yet." Lillian had Jace's hand in hers. "The doc says it takes different people different amounts of time to wake up."

"It won't be long. Eakin is strong. And even more, he has someone here waiting who is the most important thing in the world to him."

She reached over and brushed a small lock of hair off Jace's forehead, willing him to open his eyes.

"So you heard Saul Poniard made a full confession?"

She looked over at Derek. "No. I've pretty much just been here. I don't know what's going on."

"I'm sure Steve Drackett will be providing an update to you soon. But yeah, Poniard gave up his whole Manifesto of Change, parts of which had been discovered within the Omega system a couple of weeks ago. Saul had nicknamed himself Guy Fawkes."

"As in the guy who tried to blow up the British parliament?"

"The very same."

Lillian rolled her eyes. "I have to admit, I never saw it. Never really looked past his surfer-boy grin."

"Poniard was setting you up for the fall, Lillian. Making it look like you set up both the explosive device in the City and County Building and the biological weapon canisters that would've gone live with LESS."

"I never dreamed Poniard hated me that much."

Derek shrugged. "Honestly, I don't think he did. I think you were an easy target. No family, no close friends. A loner."

"Someone easy to set up."

Derek smiled. "Not as easy as he and Freihof thought."

"Freihof got away." Frustration still ate at her. She'd been so close to taking him down.

"But with Saul out of the picture we've crippled Freihof in a lot of ways, including the broken nose you gave him. Plus, Ren McClement says there's been some new developments. We'll be hearing more about that soon, I'm sure."

"Good."

"And Daryl Eakin is dead. I know you know that."

Lillian hadn't told Derek many specifics about what had happened in the past with Daryl, but Derek knew it hadn't been good.

She nodded. "I got a second chance to fight my own personal monster, and this time I won. Not everybody gets that sort of second chance."

Derek pointed at Jace. "That man loves you. He would fight your monsters for you."

"I know, but—"

She stopped her sentence as Jace's voice interrupted her from the bed, husky and low. "No. I wouldn't fight your monsters. You can do that yourself. But I'll stand with you as you fight them. Every single time."

Lillian leaped over to him, cupping his cheeks. "That's even better." She smiled, kissing him as she stared into those blue eyes. "Hi. You found your way back to me."

"I always will. No matter how long it takes, I always will."

They would always find their way back to each other.

LILLIAN SLEPT IN the hospital bed with Jace that night.

Maybe he'd been slow to initially come out of the coma, but once he started Jace made much faster progress than was expected. Within a few hours he was sitting up with no dizziness and not long afterward was even taking steps by himself.

Different members of Omega Sector had come by all day to check on them and Derek. To shake Jace's hand and hug Lillian tight. To thank them for a job well done. Even Philip came by, finally stitched up from the wounds Saul had given him. He even smiled and spoke without making anyone mad.

The traitor who had resided inside their family was now gone. Freihof would fall next.

The last visitor was someone Lillian hadn't ever talked to directly in person, but knew about. Ren McClement. Omega's most revered and somewhat notorious agent. In his midforties with brown hair and dark eyes that looked like they never missed a thing.

Rumors were that McClement's specialty was under-cover ops. Long-term assignments. The ones no one with family or friends would take. McClement answered to very few people and always got his man, no matter what the cost.

The only thing that people agreed on about Ren Mc-Clement was that no one really knew him.

Except Jace. Evidently Jace knew him, given how the two embraced with a strong hug before Ren ruffled Jace's hair.

"Nearly dead wasn't what I was expecting when I brought you on for this mission, Eakin," Ren said as he sat down in the chair on the other side of Jace's bed from Lillian and nodded at her. "Agent Muir."

"Lillian, please."

She enjoyed watching the two men banter with each other for the next couple of hours. Despite insults thrown on both sides, the respect the men had for each other all but permeated the air. Both of them made a point to draw her into the conversation as much as possible.

"I'm glad you two are okay," Ren said. "Your dead brother showing up was…unexpected."

Jace's eyes met hers. "Yeah, for all of us." He turned to Ren. "I'm sorry Freihof got away."

"Well, speaking of dead people being alive, we've had a pretty big development when it comes to Freihof."

"How so?" Lillian asked. She wanted Freihof behind bars so badly she could taste it.

"Evidently Natalie Freihof, Damien's beloved wife whose death is the very reason he's been taking his re-venge on Omega Sector, is actually alive."

"What?" Jace and Lillian both said it at the same time.

"Yep. We're not sure if she's working with Freihof or

not, but we're going to find out. I *personally* am going to find out."

Ren's dark eyes were so cold Lillian felt a little sympathy for the woman she'd never met.

"Whether she's working with him or not, his obsession with her is the key to drawing him out and trapping him. One way or another she'll help us bring Freihof down. I'll see to it."

Collateral damage sometimes happened in battles like this. But Freihof had to be stopped. If this dead wife could help, Lillian wouldn't argue against it.

"But this is all on me now," Ren said. "You two are just supposed to heal. Jace, I'm sure Steve Drackett's going to be in here any minute now asking you to join the Omega team permanently."

Jace smiled. "Nope, not for me. All I want is to get to my ranch and get it started. I'm out of this game for good."

Ren smiled. "Since your ranch just happens to be forty miles from Omega HQ, I'm sure Steve may still call on your services from time to time."

"I'm thankful for many reasons that my ranch is only forty miles from Omega." Jace turned to Lillian, heat clear in his eyes. "But none of them have a damn thing to do with Steve Drackett."

In the evening after everyone was gone, Lillian settled down in the uncomfortable lounge chair next to Jace, ready to try to get some rest.

She heard the bed shift and the next minute Jace's arms were scooping under her and tucking her in beside him. He lifted her as if he hadn't been stabbed and in a medically induced coma just a few hours earlier.

"Pretty sure heavy lifting isn't a good plan, Eakin," she said, but snuggled into his chest.

"First, not even under the most absurd of circumstance could you be considered heavy lifting. Second, you sleep next to me. Every night from here on out."

She didn't try to move away. There wasn't anywhere she wanted to be besides right next to him. But she couldn't just let his words slide. She had to make sure he knew what he was in for.

"I'm still broken," she whispered. "I know I made it back from the darkness and fought Daryl, but that doesn't end the nightmare for me. There are parts of me that... might never work correctly again. I'm permanently broken, Jace."

She felt his hand slide over her hair. "I've worked with the most elite soldiers in the world and can say that you are stronger and more capable than anybody I've ever known."

"Daryl almost won. I didn't even fight. If you hadn't found a way to call me back..."

His lips rested against her temple. "But you did fight. You fought your way out of the darkness and then you fought Daryl and won. You kept Freihof from killing me and thousands of innocent people."

"My PTSD can get pretty bad. I just want to make sure you know what you're getting into. Before you start saying things like *forever*."

"Then I'm glad I'm about to have a ranch full of animals specifically for people like you."

"I thought you were supposed to be helping soldiers."

"It's for people who need time to put themselves back together. That includes you."

She wrapped her arm around his waist and threw a

leg over his hips. "I can't promise I'm ever going to be normal. That I'll ever be like other women."

His thumb reached down and tilted her chin up so he could kiss her. "Thank God. I wouldn't want you any other way than what you are."

"Then you better hurry up and heal so I can get you home and back into a real bed."

"I don't care what bed we're in as long as every day that I wake up, you're in it with me. We have twelve years to make up for. And everything else we'll work through."

"I can't leave my job with Omega."

He laughed. "I wouldn't dare even try to suggest it. It's more than just your job. They're your family."

"You are, too. You always have been."

"And I always will be."

* * * * *